ALL EYES ON ME

ANNA COLE

Emma Bloor

This novel is written in UK English.

www.emmabloor.co.uk

ISBN - 9781838492809

Cover design by: Hefjay Concept
Printed in the United Kingdom

Also by Emma Bloor: **ALL EYES ON ME** series

Anna Cole
Arla Stevens

For more information, please visit www.emmabloor.co.uk

Contents

Characters List: ANNA COLE

Non Conformers (NCs)
Anna Cole (researcher at Little Hampton police station)
Mark Cole (Headsman at Thurstworthy Manor Estate)
Richard 'Chie' Cole (UK patronage leader of the NCs)
Teela Franklin (Anna's boss)
Jonah Francis (orphan)
Lily Francis (orphan)
Tom Strauss (IT specialist-come-genius)
Chaperone Shelley
Reticent Rusty
Logistic Lionel

The Asiders:
Not-Pervy Pete

The International Neighbourhood Baruun (I.N.):
The Imperial Kiengir Ciel Tisak (world leader)
HS Paul Fraser (House Security agent)
Esta Darab (palace servant)
Sul Darab (Tisak's private guard)

The I.N. agents GBR Island:
Greg Prentice (Anna's Colleague)
Simon Pothrall (Commanding Chief—Teela's boss)
Alex Saunders (employee at Sudeley Castle)

Civilians:
Melly Saunders (Christian)
Minu Darab (rescued victim)
Harvard Jones (assistant security at Thurstworthy Manor Estate)
Javad Shirvani (Braithwaite's employee)
Dan Hawkins (Pastor)
Claire Hawkins (Pastor's wife)
Ian Stymer (Entrepreneur)
Robert Forbes-Hamilton Junior (heir to Thurstworthy Manor)

Glossary

Asiders
Factions of resistance among civilians
Fred
Male NC
GBR
Grand British Republic
Honer
Nanotech implant that LeyLucient detects to move mass
I.N.
Abbreviation for International Neighbourhood
Island
UK as the GBR 'capital'
ISNA
International Small Neighbours Association (Social Services)
Ley
The essence collected at Leyline points
LeyLucient
Material that can manipulate mass particles
Lifeday
Replaces birthday as part of gender-neutral language changes
Mouglar
Global cryptocurrency
NC
Non Conformer and political resistance
Portals
Pass-through places created by LeyLucient
Rapture
The Christian belief that Almighty God will come and rescue His children before He brings His wrath
Shan
Female NC

1 Emotional Adultery

Peeking through the silver blinds of my Irish boss' office was the easy part. Getting her to notice me tapping my watch without knocking on the door and disturbing the on-speaker conference meeting was harder. No matter what I tried, Teela didn't look up, so I took out my phone and messaged her.

We're ten minutes late already.

Teela glanced at her phone, then slyly pulled it onto her lap to reply:

I can feel your impatience through the wall, Anna. It's only to organise a birthday party! What are you stressing about?

Rachel Cole is who I'm stressing about. Mark's mother and timekeeping are like…married.

She'll understand.

I know she will because you're getting the blame.

The conference meeting voices were getting heated, and when Teela slumped in her chair, the topic suddenly became interesting to me.

"We need to start implementing procedures now, in case these things come up, or if mass protest starts again," the man through the speaker defended. "We don't want to be where we were a year ago. We need to be ready, and we envisage the process to take around six months."

"And the criminals we look for now are criminals because they counter government legislation?" a woman asked. "Who arrests the rapists and murderers?"

Teela rolled her eyes and replied, "Not us, evidently."

"I am not here to debate it with you. You have your orders the same as me. Do them."

I backed away from the door as Teela scooped up her bag and was glad that I did when she flew through it with a face like thunder. The Teela Franklin Team Leader sign rattled in its frame when it slammed shut.

"Please, don't ask because I can't tell you. And frankly, I want to forget about it."

We raced down the corridor and onto the high street. Running wasn't usually such a catastrophe for me if I wore the right shoes and had tied my hair back. Doing it in black kitten heels with strands of dark hair whipping at my face made me look more like Mr Bean than an athlete. Coincidentally, Teela didn't find the sprint difficult in her Caterpillar boots and had reached McCaffrey's bar before me.

With a cheeky grin, she asked, "Who's making us late now?"

"You're still getting the blame."

Teela laughed. "Grand. I can take it!"

I opened the door to cheers and clapping from the planning committee, and I was instantly embarrassed. My chest reddened. I tightened my scarf, thankful that the blush wasn't showing on my cheeks.

Celebrating our arrival were Mark's colleague and close friend, Harvard Jones, Mark's silver-haired mother, Rachel Cole, and our mutual friends, the McCaffreys. On his way to the bar, West-Indies born Harvard hugged me and the tight plaits in his hair dug into my neck. Over his shoulder, Rachel caught my eye and patted the seat beside her with a smile. She had lost more weight since my wedding six months ago. Her shoulders were bony in my arms. She pushed a pile of photos toward me.

"I thought you could put these up at the party on the oojamywhatsit for the wall."

She meant a projector.

I scanned through the photos of my husband, Mark, growing up with his younger brother, Richard.

"I can't believe he's thirty next month! Sixty-two definitely feels old now!"

"Age is just a number," Teela replied mysteriously. She hung her jacket over the chair and sat down, glancing at the pictures. "Oh, look at the two of you. It's embarrassing."

"Gimme a break! That was not long after we met."

"Time doesn't matter to you two. You're just as soppy now."

Coyly, I replied, "So what? I love him."

Teela smirked. "Crikey, pass me the gush bucket!"

"My eldest has never been happier since he met Anna, so you can leave her alone!" Rachel defended warmly, then leaned across the table and whispered, "Although you'd think they would've calmed down a bit after six years."

Teela laughed and replied, "Tell me about it. We've worked together for three years, and they're always calling each other. She misses him when she's at the station."

I couldn't deny it. Mark had delivered a fake court summons to me at work once, announcing, 'You've been served'. I nearly died of shame because I knew a private weekend was coming, and so did the rest of my team. I had to wait three hours for my shift to end, and despite the teasing, it was anticipation at its best. When I met him outside the police station later, he was waiting in his car with the passenger door open, inviting me in. There was plenty to miss while I was at the station.

To Teela's dismay, Harvard sat down without bringing the drinks.

"Mark is the same. I think it's cute."

"It's sad. Where's my gin?"

"Coming! Where is your patience?"

"Waning, listening to this lot."

The planning committee erupted with laughter, and my chest blushed again.

"I am here, you know," I replied, smiling at their teasing.

Teela blew me a kiss. "We know. We can feel your pining."

"Aw, are you jealous?"

"Crikey, no! I'm too busy to have feelings."

Harvard coughed. "I'm busy too. I should be at work with the much-loved Mark, so can we get on?"

Rachel kissed my cheek and whispered, "I'm glad we're doing this. Pray that his brother comes."

While Teela fidgeted, keen for her drink, goosebumps rose on her arms and the back of my neck prickled. The temperature in the bar had dropped significantly. Rachel exclaimed. I jumped at the sound of smashing glass and turned. Strewn across the wooden floor were fragments of glass in puddles of alcohol, and a plastic tray had flipped upside down, juddering to a stop like a spun coin coming to rest. Next to it were the barman's clothes in a neat pile on his shoes. And his were not the only ones.

A punter jumped from his table, yelling that his wife had disappeared, and an older lady wore a confused frown as she threaded the brim of a cap through her fingers. My shocked friends sprang up from the table. They were more proactive than I was. I was fixated on the barman's empty clothes until Teela's shout of "don't touch anything; it's a crime scene" filtered through to me.

"I don't think they'll find any fingerprints!" someone said with a nervous laugh.

It was a moment before I focussed and heard Rachel's fast breaths. I sat her down, peering into her confused and misty blue eyes, saying calming words that I tried to believe myself while screams drifted in from the street. Apprehensively, Teela and I neared the floor to ceiling window and saw people running out of the shops.

The bus coming towards us didn't register at first, and although I accused my eyes of playing tricks on me, I stepped back: one step, two, three, four.

It bounced over the curb and through the window with a deafening crash. Glass sprayed everywhere. The best I could do was turn my back on what was coming toward me. A strong, dark hand grabbed at my arm, pulling me out of the way as the bus scraped the wooden tables across the floor. It crunched them into the bar, splitting the wood in two, then halted with the engine still running. A small fire burst out from the grill and licked the broken furniture.

People ran screaming, and panic spread while I stared open-mouthed at the wires from the now non-existent window lights. They swung in the breeze, firing out dangerous sparks. Shards of jumbled glass with the McCaffrey's logo scattered across the floor like jigsaw pieces, and scratch marks from the table and chairs drew a route that disappeared under the bus's wheels.

The few passengers inside were banging on the windows and tugging pointlessly at the emergency door handle. Harvard went to help lever it open while one brave passenger limped down the aisle to the driver's seat and switched off the ignition. The seat wasn't entirely empty. The driver's trousers hung down to his empty shoes.

Teela pulled me off the floor, and from my shock.

"Anna, are you okay?"

I nodded blankly.

"What's happening? Where did those people go?"

Slowly, I moved around the rear tyre of the cooling bus, looking for Rachel. She sat alone, staring at her lap. Our table lay on its side with a broken leg while the other chairs were gone.

"Mum?"

Calling her mum still felt strange to me. The last time I called anyone that was eight years ago, when I was sixteen, before my parents were killed in an accident on their way home from an anniversary dinner.

"Mum?" I repeated when she didn't respond.

Harvard came up behind me and put his fingers to her neck. Without him confirming it, I knew. Rachel hadn't looked well before and it wasn't like she had fallen asleep. The fright had killed her.

The distant sirens eventually got louder as I held Rachel's hand, waiting for her sons to arrive. The emergency services had just started conducting witness statements when, hours later, Mark turned up, ashen at the damage and making a beeline for his mother and me. His six-foot-nine giant frame crossing the floor forced the paramedic to move away from the stretcher. Mark drew me into his arms, grateful I wasn't hurt, before he pulled the sheet from his mother's face and wept.

Mark's brother, Richard 'Chie' Cole, pulled up just as Rachel was being loaded into a coroner's van. His wary eyes swept over the scene, concentrating on the number of officials in uniform before he came towards us full of questions. He was two years younger than Mark and shorter with lighter hair and a medium build. Even so, Chie looked just like him.

I answered what I could, but there were no answers to where the people had gone. Nobody knew, and everyone was just as stunned as we were.

"It is the work of the Christian God!"

I pulled a face, and the woman stopped walking.

"Mock as much as you like; I didn't believe it either. Now, I'm left behind, and my husband and kids have gone."

She sniffed, turned, and walked on.

If that were true, and there was a God, why would He leave Mark and me without parents? Why would He have tormented the world with one pandemic that bankrupted it, just to follow it up with another two years after? Why would He allow so much suffering?

The green in Mark's eyes deepened, and his mouth twitched. It was rare to see, but his temper was about to explode. I took his hand and made him look at me, and Chie thrust keys into his other, afraid that an outburst would draw attention to us.

"You can drive."

"To where?"

"The hospital."

"What's the point? She's dead."

"Let's go home," I suggested, "they have my statement."

Mark looked at his brother.

"Are you coming, or are you going to disappear again?"

Sighing, Chie replied, "I have my reasons for that. But yes, I'm coming."

Mark tossed him back his keys. "I'll take my own car and see you at home if you can remember where it is."

Head low, Chie walked away.

"I know you're angry and grieving, but it isn't Chie's fault."

Mark got in the car and slammed the door shut. I got in beside him with a deep breath, scooting close enough to cuddle him. His body rocked with tears.

"You're angry and grieving, but so is Chie. Can we go and comfort him as well?"

Mark nodded and kissed me.

"Thanks, Anna. Love you."

~

Present Day - Six Years On

All night, the bed felt lonely, and because of the wave of anxiety thrashing inside me, I had barely slept. The dawn rising behind the curtains drew me to the window, but I did not welcome the prospect of another new day. I breathed, hoping I would not be put out onto the street with nothing but my clothes. Legally, Mark could serve me with divorce papers and kick me out of our home, leaving me destitute. I breathed fearfully and made my way down the stairs to face what I had left behind last night.

Filling the doorway to our kitchen with a curling lip was a hateful Mark. I inched past him and into the lounge, unable to look at the angry eyes that usually glistened with love.

Whispers of disgrace dripped with venom, and him calling me disgusting stabbed my heart.

"After everything that's happened and the trouble it caused, I can't believe you're in love with *him*!"

The forceful smack on the lounge door startled me. It flew open, banging against the wall, and I cringed when he approached me.

"He killed my mother!"

"Apparently, he didn't, as you well know!"

Mark rounded the coffee table, and I moved closer to the window, trying not to think about the forty-six ways he was trained to kill a person using just his hands. I had found it attractive once, and knowing he could take care of me had made me secure. I hadn't doubted that until yesterday when I had confessed. Melly had warned me it would be difficult, and from the moment I'd opened my mouth, I knew trouble would brew, but I couldn't keep it secret anymore. So, for a fortnight, I had hidden it. A long two weeks that had caused a mixture of emotions in me, primarily fear. The most unacceptable and disgusting thing in the world had happened to me.

"And what now then? You want me to what…share you?"

Despite my angst, I couldn't help the slight smile and shake of my head. Mark had an odd way of looking at things. Share me was hysterical; there was no competition, and Mark didn't have the right to be so upset. I wasn't running off into the sunset with a new beau on my arm, was I? Nor was I planning on setting up a ménage-à-trois home.

At the thought of that, I let a giggle escape.

Insulted, Mark threaded his fingers through his floppy, black hair.

"It isn't funny! How can you f…" He neared me with a red face and a raised fist. I took a few steps back and shut my eyes to my husband's intent on hurting me. My recoil was enough to stop him. He walked away, but at the lounge door, he looked back.

"I can't do this with you, Anna, because it ain't just a once-a-week thing. Is it?"

I shook my head. It was already a constant access to a well of love so deep that I had not reached the bottom.

The torturous spasm on his face made me take in a ragged breath. I'd confirmed a truth he wasn't completely sure of until now. He was unyielding.

"I won't do it. I don't want to live with it."

A tear rolled down my cheek. "I don't know what to say."

"You choose," he said quickly. "Him or me."

My mouth fell open, and by the time I could respond to the demand that said our marriage was over, Mark had left the house.

There would be no competition; I'd met someone who had changed everything. He had etched his way into my every waking thought, dream, and decision. The letter he had given me was read repeatedly, and each time, the words revealed something new about him.

My new friends were such a contrast to those I had known, whose lives centred around themselves and their cosy community. That comfortable, cosy bubble of our lives mattered in these times of uncertainty and change—their job, pub, and lives. I felt like a hypocrite when I realised I had been just the same. However, not long ago, my eyes opened to a world beyond that little bubble, and I could not go back. It would be like emerging from a zipped-up canvas tent to view snow-capped mountains and silken waterfalls, only to be told to return to my claustrophobic hideout. Mark wanted me to go back and be the Anna he knew, but no amount of emotional blackmail could pull my eyes away from the awesome scenery that lay before me.

It did not stop him from trying. Every time I saw him, he asked if I had made my decision. I avoided a simple yes or no answer by challenging his right to ask me. His last words to me were, "make it, or I will make it for you," and he still hadn't.

An uneasiness crept into my stomach when I heard the key scraping the front door lock. Mark was home. The conflict I saw inside him kept me silent. I hadn't seen anyone look stubborn and sheepish at the same time. I tried to smile in a way that said I was sorry he was hurting and I still loved him, but he turned his stocky frame and walked away. I almost went after him, but it was as though I was rooted to the spot. So instead, I stared at the empty lounge doorway with unsaid words disintegrating into thought dust.

I tried to focus on the positive. Mark had come home, and it was not to pack his things, but I couldn't escape the neon flashing and the trunk-waving elephant in the room. He would ask me for my answer. I sighed as my mind swarmed with unfamiliar insecurity.

Mark didn't speak at dinner, but I caught the swift side-eyed glances in my direction. I didn't look up to acknowledge them. I couldn't bear the agony written on his face. His white-gold wedding band glistened as he toyed with his fork, and the latest

World on your Wrist, WS wristwatch, flashed a notification. It was read and dismissed, just like me. Usually, we would talk about our day and share funny stories about Teela or Harvard, but there were none as we ate that night. No attack of the swans, no fall from tree branches, or my personal favourite—no sinking through a rotting boat in the middle of Thurstworthy Manor Estate's lake. Instead, the centrepiece was the mocking form of the elephant, growing uglier and becoming more of a gargoyle with each passing second. The angst was more than I could take, and I flew upstairs to hide without clearing the dishes.

~

I woke from a fitful sleep and felt just as agitated. My grandad used to say, 'Never go to bed on an argument,' and my mum would add, 'It slices through the psyche like razors.' Well, I didn't need to remain asleep for it to feel like a thousand razors slashing away at me. I had to end it and look for Mark, but he wasn't in front of the muted sports channel covered in toast crumbs like he was most Saturday mornings. I peeked through the patio doors and sighed at an empty garden, but the early spring sun pushing through wispy clouds lifted my spirit.

In the kitchen, I touched the glass of the coffee pot sitting on the breakfast bar. It was still hot, so he was here somewhere. I grabbed my clip, pulled my thick hair into a messy ponytail, and noticed the blurred colour of his salmon t-shirt through the frosted glass of the back door. He was sitting on the top step. I didn't need plain glass to recall the thickness of his neck showing faint creases or the massive contours of his muscular shoulders and back. Every detail was kept in my perfect, crisp memories, like the first time we met twelve years ago.

I had never instantly fallen for a person before. I'd had crushes and fancies like every other girl, but the day I met Mark was indescribable. We had dated every day from then; 'dating' had only lasted a week, then Mark had practically moved into my digs, and I had to work extra hard to get my dissertations in on time. He was worth it, though, and his spontaneity thrilled me.

The back door creaked as it swung open, and I was brought back to the present. A present I was no longer content in. A present that had become too cold over the last three days. The edge and unpredictability that usually excited me were harrowing now. I yearned to be back in my memories and see anything other than the flat look in his eyes. Mark guessed how apprehensive I was when he caught me rubbing my palms together in half circles and was torn between what he wanted and how much it would wound me.

"Morning," he said and walked to the coffee machine.

"Let me," I suggested, coming up behind him and taking his used cup to refill. It gave me an excuse to lay my hand on the small of his back.

The thing about muscle memory was that it sometimes betrayed you. Mark lifted his hand to the back of my neck and playfully squeezed, then remembered. He withdrew quickly to sit back on the step, still hating me.

With the drinks ready, I took a deep breath and opened the back door. Mark leaned on his elbows with his hands clasped together and head bowed. He stiffened when he heard me and did not look up. The sun peeked around the oak tree and lit his left side with a yellow glow, and a sob caught in my throat.

I sat down, offering him a cup. He took it without speaking, and I fingered a strand of cotton on my jumper.

Eventually, he looked up, and my heart stuttered at his pleading green eyes.

"I don't want to hurt you, Anna, and I don't know what else to say."

"I don't want to hurt you either; I love you. But I can't help what's been awakened in me–"

He sighed angrily. "Spare me the preach! You made your feelings quite clear. I can't compete with…*him*."

"You know how crazy you sound?" I accused, even though no one could compete with the extraordinary man I had recently met.

Mark opened his arms out and shrugged. "It's emotional adultery!"

I raised an eyebrow; I was seen as a cheater now. I wanted to argue, but my emotionally battered husband looked just as miserable as me.

"Seriously? That again."

He jumped up, glaring at me. "You confessed to being 'in love' with…with…"

"You can say his name, you know. It won't smite you! It's not new. You've said it every day for years."

"That's different," he spat, frowning at me, "it meant something else then. Now, it's poison on my tongue."

I shut my eyes, hoping it would stop me from hearing his words. But instead, they churned in the acid at the pit of my stomach.

"This Jesus is coming between us."

It was so matter-of-fact that it brought me up short. Irritation flushed, and the warmth spread across my chest. I resisted the urge to tell him that Jesus only brought people together, and we were all one in Christ. Then I remembered Jesus did talk about division. He'd said: "Father against son and son against father, mother against daughter and daughter against mother…" So, thanks to the Gospel of Luke, I was left with nothing to say.

"Explain it to me," Mark demanded, "tell me how you can love me, no, be in love with me still and be in love with him?"

I was about to answer when he continued.

"How is it different? I'm dispensable now…redundant."

Surprised, I blurted, "You are not redundant; don't say that because it isn't true! My attraction to you hasn't changed. My need to be with you will never change. You are funny, kind, and sexy. I love you with the kind of love that would break me if it wasn't returned. I won't give an answer to your demand. You make the choice."

My lip trembled when Mark looked at me, and his glare softened.

"It will always be returned," he whispered sincerely.

Admitting it was a start, I sighed, relieved and hopeful of a compromise. Then I wiped away my tears.

"My feelings for Jesus are different because they don't come from my heart or head. It comes from my spirit; He woke something in me. This love isn't like the love between us. This spirit of love is overwhelming. It is encompassing, irresistible, and unfathomable. It's something that I can't rationalise or explain." I smiled wistfully. "I think back to the times you've made my heart skip and when I could barely breathe in the excitement of seeing you. To think this is more than that is incomprehensible."

Mark sighed heavily and said, "That's why it feels like adultery. You're the nucleus of my world, and I'm not yours anymore."

I laughed. "I think that's a bit over the top."

"You weren't just a pretty girl in a pretty dress to me! It seemed like I'd known you my whole life. I wouldn't have thought it possible, but you are more radiant these days than ever, not because of your love for me. Is it?"

"No," I answered, "it's because of His love for me!"

We both fell silent, listening to the sparrows calling. I was hurting him and sickened by it. I said a prayer as I fiddled with my wedding ring.

My husband breathed heavily beside me. I stood up, collected the empty cups and turned to open the door. Before I stepped through, I turned to him and said,

"Can we just try?"

He swivelled to look at me.

"I won't choose, and I will not let you or this government tell me how I should feel about a God you don't even know. So, can we just try?"

Mark looked away without answering. I let the door slam behind me.

2 Collective Thought

Melly Saunders was one of my new friends, and she was already at the coffee shop by the time I arrived. It was raining, and the silver tables and chairs lined five down and five across like a regiment were filled. She was seated along the right-hand side, impatiently bouncing up and down on her chair, her blonde curls springing about her shoulders. I was a few minutes late, true, but not that late. I was surprised she had allowed me time to order at the counter because her words flooded out before sitting down.

"How did it go? Tell me he hasn't hurt you, has he?"

Her eyes quickly scanned any skin not covered by my t-shirt.

Although I laughed nervously, wondering why she would come to that conclusion, the memory of Mark lifting his fist trailed in my mind.

"He gave me an ultimatum, which was unexpected."

Amused, she countered, "Not that unexpected, surely?"

I smiled, ashamed. I had expected Mark to understand and gracefully accept my faith in my naïve little world, but being so honest about my new feelings had not been wise. Who could understand emotions that were not my own, burning in, through, and out of me in a constant flow? No one could unless they had felt God's love; such strength mingled with tender compassion that it wrapped me securely, welcoming me to reciprocate.

"It didn't help trying to get him to understand. On the contrary, it made it worse."

"Jealousy does that," Melly retorted, "some new fathers can be the same. When someone's had your undivided attention and suddenly—poof—there's someone else. They can't bear it. Little babies themselves, most of them! As if they expect you to just be there, ready to respond to their every whim, not expecting you to have any independent thought or life of your own."

Melly frowned, staring through the window, absentmindedly tapping a sugar packet through her fingers. I knew little about her life. She rarely talked about her past. Like me, she was a closed person, but where she didn't let anything out, I didn't let anything in. She was twenty-eight, two years younger than me, and worked at the supermarket. She divorced last year, and the father had no contact with their six-year-old daughter, Arla.

"Melly, is everything all right?"

"Hmm?" She looked back, her eyes becoming less misty, but the smile she gave didn't reflect in them.

"Yes, I'm okay, just thinking, don't mind me. What are you going to do?"

I was reluctant to answer but didn't want to push her until she was ready to share.

"If I choose, I will have to leave him, so I haven't given him my answer and will keep going home. What else can I do? The only right thing is to let him choose to stay with me."

"Or not."

"Yes," I said with a frustrated sigh, "or not."

Whether Mark could live with it could only be decided by him, and the thought of him leaving caused a fissure to crack across the surface of my heart. It tore me, but it did not compare to the cost of losing Jesus.

Melly fell quiet and more distracted. When I asked what was wrong, she swerved it by asking about Mark and me. The more I revealed, the further withdrawn she became. I tried to ease it out of her and even tried a hint of manipulation, but her mouth was buttoned up tighter than a virgin's cardi!

Eventually, I went with the direct approach.

"Why did you ask if Mark had hurt me? Is that what happened to you?"

"Yes," Melly replied quickly, as though she might change her mind if she took too long to answer. She glanced up and met my eyes. "He thought he could beat the Jesus out of me."

I gasped, "Oh!"

"The last time, I was so badly hurt, Pastor Dan took me to hospital." She paused, remembering the trauma with tears.

"When I came home, my ex was gone. He'd left Arla with Dan and Claire, and as you know, I haven't heard from him since. But I have my suspicions."

I narrowed my eyes, and she shifted in her seat.

"Don't get me wrong; I'm happy he's gone, though it's not fair on Arla. But selfishly, I'm chuffed he isn't coming back. He wasn't a violent man before, but when he found out, he absolutely flipped. That was my life for a few months. I tried to hide the bruises, but Claire was not naïve. One week, I didn't go to the house, so Dan came to me. I don't understand how Arla ended up with Dan and Claire. My ex didn't know them. He wasn't even there when Dan came over, and Arla was playing next door. As I said, I have my suspicions."

"Go on," I urged.

"I think Dan had a word and sent him away and then took Arla home with him." She shrugged decidedly. "It's the only thing I can think of."

"Then you got divorced?"

Melly rolled her eyes. "He divorced me. It was over in weeks. The court loved it. 'She's trailing after some fictional hero coming to save the world. Too busy in La La Land'. He actually wrote them as grounds for divorce." She sighed. "He could've just written Christian. It would've been enough."

It was sad, and I understood her resentment. I felt a wave of anger against the united Collective Thought that allowed people like Melly's husband to 'correct' people like me. Those laws said that any citizen wishing to divorce on the grounds of religious transformation was the innocent party. If a spouse chose to believe in gods, rapid divorces could be obtained often without much evidence. A Bible in a drawer, for example, was enough to convince society that their share in property and assets might be used to fund religious institutions and were confiscated into the ownership of the plaintiff. Along with any children the marriage produced, if that was what the petitioner wanted.

Mark might still do that or send me to one of the rehabilitation centres. They helped unfortunate souls like me who had been "sucked into a cultish lie that distorted reality."

"Since Collective Thought came into play three years ago, people like you and me walk a dangerous road. We can't even have church in a public building, only in homes, and now we're invisible.

Guilt riddled me. I had helped to impose those laws, and I'd have laughed if someone had said to me, "One day, Anna Cole, you're going to become a Christian." No one was more surprised at that than me, especially after what was now commonly known as the mock rapture. But things had started to change long before that.

The tracks leading into the future were laid during the first virus that saw us hiding in our homes for a year until a vaccine was available. There were 158,000 deaths alone in Great Britain. The second pandemic had spread fast, with cases reported across the globe within a day. The earth closed again, and every nation's survival concerns forced them to stop helping others. We had barely recovered from the first virus. The hint of new muscle on the bone then fought to protect itself from another. Currency had died, the stock market crumbled, and trade had collapsed.

The UN's upcoming and newly appointed secretary general tweaked cryptocurrency trading schemes to create a real-time, global network of systemised currency trading in mouglar. It saved us, and the single currency had united most of the world, setting the stage for a new normal.

As if the nations hadn't gone through enough already, we had to experience the vanishings. It had been chiefly Christians and some, but not all children, who left everything but their bodies behind. Major cities became blocked with rows of cars that looked like streamers dangling from fatal crash sites, and for six months, the consensus was that it must have been the biblical rapture. The idea had gained momentum, the biblical theory was respected, and multitudes turned away from the religion of their cultures and looked to the Bible. Mark and I hadn't. I had questioned God's existence, for if there was one, why would He allow millions to die while He took His own?

"Looking back on it," I mused, "the mock rapture was the turning point for that."

Melly pursed her lips. "I reckon it was more the returning."

I breathed in surprise. She was right. Six months after the people vanished, they returned, and just as quickly. Each one was naked, without medical things like stents and fillings, and all were completely oblivious to where they had been. Months had gone by, but it had only been seconds for those raptured. The catastrophic results of millions of people disappearing at once had the same effect when they returned to the exact same place they had left.

"I remember," I replied and sighed heavily.

The barman at McCaffrey's had reappeared confused when he took in newly decorated surroundings. The punter's wife returned to sit on the lap of a man who was not her husband, and the bus driver was sitting in the middle of the road, wondering where his bus had gone. If anyone had been driving on the M4 at the time of their disappearance, then on the M4 they reappeared.

"The rapture theory burned real quick after that, and everyone's patience thinned. God and His Bible lost all respect. Even elite Christians fell away from the truth."

"And those who turned from their original beliefs didn't return to them."

Nothing but conjecture and conspiracy had filled the void. No one knew why or how, and nothing could be proved.

Less than a year later, civil war broke out in every country. Even in a quiet town like Little Hampton, Wiltshire, differing opinions triggered the fighting. Every viewpoint was labelled, every rebuke distorted, and anger boiled among the citizens. Britain had been among the first to disestablish the government. Our Royals became a laughingstock. We had lost many lives over that time: police workers, councillors, and religious leaders. Those in authority were fair game, and that included me. That conflict saw the unveiling of the UN collaborative army. Swarms of navy-uniformed troops flooded Britain and all the countries of the world. Martial law was enforced, and only those with valid reasons to be out of their homes were allowed on the streets. I could return to work in relative safety, but I kept my ID hidden in my pocket, just in case a protester lingered to take my 'authority bound' life.

Melly threw the sugar packet across the table.

"I blame him!"

"I am beginning to see the threads, yes," I agreed and sipped my lukewarm coffee.

Hatred, war and a huge drain on the human spirit resulted from all that tragedy. Then the internet had developed a mind of its own. Every online bank account across the world was devalued, and every device connected to Wi-Fi played Axel F's 'Crazy Frog' on repeat. It had meant no radio, no TV, and no computer access. It meant a silent and disconnected world. During that disconnection, the UN revealed the answer to our troubles: Ciel Tisak, the hugely popular French secretary general, was appointed as our leader. Not just Britain's leader, but the entire globe and the International Neighbourhood (I.N.) was born.

"You should listen to Pastor Dan. Ciel Tisak holds the world in his hands. His first act of leadership was implementing the new internet system. But promising to restore all banking funds if we would join with him kinda gave him away."

Melly grabbed her phone and scrolled.

"I saw this quote of Tisak's the other day; listen. 'I speak to those enslaved under dictatorship and self-appointed leaders, secular and religious, to throw off your oppressive yokes, be free of lies, fear and terror, and become part of one great, peaceful family united in thought and deed'. I mean, come on."

Tisak's enduring, persistent character brought about the way of the world as it was today. However, his over-friendly nature left the world panting for more, with each nation desperate to do anything he asked—and they did everything he asked.

After all, he was our saviour.

We finished our coffees in companionable silence. I hugged Melly tightly as I said goodbye, reminding her I was always there for her if she needed to talk to someone about her ex-husband.

~

Mark was late. He was usually home from securing Thurstworthy Manor Estate by now, starving and picking food off his plate before I'd finished serving it. It was ten to seven, and I kept a casserole warm in the oven while my stomach rumbled in protest. The nausea at its pit objected, though, as I drew the plates from the cupboard and laid them ready on the counter. Was it from hunger or apprehension?

I caught myself in the hallway mirror and tucked the loose hair strands away from my pale oval face. I smoothed the hugging fabric of my black dress over my tiny hips, hoping that Mark would not conclude I'd worn it for his sake. A longshot, I admitted to myself, but these last few weeks had been lonely. I missed the affection flooding from Mark's captivating emerald eyes. Even after twelve years, I missed his fleeting kisses that left me breathless and in love as much as the first time. Lately, he flickered between betrayal and consternation. The safe and secure way he could take care of me held a different connotation today, and I considered him using his training to beat the Jesus out of me.

When Mark came home, he brought a whiff of stale alcohol on his breath and suffered from a headache.

"Let me get you some painkillers."

I reached for the cupboard with a racing heart and could feel his eyes raking over me in my dress.

"Before you do, wait a minute."

When I spun around, we collided, and one of his strong arms rested across the back of my shoulders. He nestled me into his chest while stroking my hair with his fingertips. I was only 5'3, and Mark needed to duck in doorways, so he bent to kiss the top of my head, and at the same time, swept me from the floor to bring my face closer to his.

"I thought you had a headache?" I reminded him while wrapping my legs around his waist, not that they were long enough to go all the way around to comfortably clasp together my ankles.

"I do," he replied, fighting the conflict that looking deep into my chocolate-brown eyes had brought him.

Then he kissed me. Urgently. He parted my lips with one push of his tongue and pressed them hard to mine while sitting me down on the worktop so he could pull me closer still. My heart raced for all the right reasons. I quietly thanked God, and the headache was quickly forgotten.

~

I woke abruptly during the early morning hours, feeling stiff across my shoulders. I shuffled over to lay my arm across Mark, but the sheets were cold. It reminded me of when we got the final demand to complete the time-consuming Collective Thought survey, and Mark had gone a little grey. So, every day for a month, I woke alone because when that demand came, it was to submit it or face prison.

The thousands of questions and scenarios were presented to people over thirty to complete. I was too young then but went through his as a team, choosing our answers that collectively were thoughts coming into law. No, there was no god. We did not need religion or spiritual assistance. Yes, the call to prayer and church bells often disturbed the peace. Trade was important, money was vital, and sex shouldn't be so frowned upon. If girls liked other girls or men liked men, let them be. To each their own. Freedom.

We agreed with this, but not with that. We supported marriage and divorce. We acknowledged divorce could be validated for any reason if that was what one party wanted. Who were we to judge their motives? We agreed the best way to be unified was to teach the law to children from an early age, so it became normal for them to understand this…fluidity. Abortion had been a difficult topic, and we left the section blank, but the right to die was a fair point, and we'd both agreed to that.

The global survey results led to laws renamed Collective Thought. It became accepted: defining what we thought, what we said, and what we did. Together, as one. Most people adjusted to the popular beliefs (or what they were told was popular) and let go of their true choices. Mark and I had done the same so that we could be 'included'. However, people's need for acceptance never changed, and we worked hard to be in unity with what Collective Thought had established as collaborative.

My position had been secure until I read what the scripture already said about the world I live in today.

The bedroom door was ajar, and a soft glow from downstairs filtered in. I crept cautiously down to the hall. Quiet sobs came through the lounge door. I reached out and wrapped my fingers hesitantly around the door handle.

Mark sat on one of the sofas crying into his hands. I curled up beside him and stroked his shoulders and down his back.

"I'm sorry, Anna, I'm so sorry. I don't know what that was. I don't know what came over me, I..."

His words morphed into more sobs.

"I didn't plan it; I didn't mean to do it. I only wanted to talk."

I didn't want Mark to think what happened had distressed me. I frowned, and it prompted him to go on.

"I marked you, look."

He pulled down the shoulders of my robe, but the lamp was too dim to see anything.

"I never meant to–"

"I didn't notice at the time," I half-lied.

"I was disgusting. Self-gratifying."

There had been an edge to him last night. I had perceived the anger and frustration fused with a fevered hunger, and I'd noticed how roughly he had gripped me. Mark was a strong man and often forgot his own strength. Last night was more than passion, though, and I had been completely under his control. I had felt almost used, and had I not known how much he loved me, my opinion might have been just that.

It was what I had found intimidating. Be careful what you wish for, I thought, remembering how I'd yearned to be closer to him, for him to show me love again. But, instead, he had pushed, pulled, twisted and turned my body to answer his every whim. The detachment of affection was agonising.

"You were angry and frustrated," I reasoned, squeezing his hand.

"That's no excuse!" He lifted his liquid eyes. "I'm sorry I just left you there afterwards, but I had to go. I'm sorry, I'm so, so sorry."

It broke my heart to watch him suffer. I fought back my tears as I empathised.

"Please, stop apologising."

"I can't!" he thundered, aggravated. "You have no idea what ran through my mind!"

"Tell me," I pleaded.

"No."

"Why?"

"Because it isn't how I feel now."

I didn't know, but I guessed the issue was about ego and testosterone competing with Jesus for my affections. Of course, he wouldn't want to admit that, and I didn't push it. Instead, I lifted his arm and bent underneath to snuggle in. He tucked my tiny frame protectively closer and kissed me.

"I love you so much," he whispered. "I'm sorry."

"It's okay, Mark," I replied charitably, "as I said, I didn't notice–"

"Don't be a martyr, Anna. You must have noticed. I don't usually treat you so badly!"

I couldn't outright lie, so I said nothing. I wasn't mad. I wasn't hurt—at that moment.

"I forgive you," I whispered.

It started a new bout of weeping, the healing cry that followed tears of guilt and shame. Mark brought his other arm around me and cried it out.

~

The message from Harvard Jones inviting me to lunch came while I was on the high street, starving, after my shift at the station. It was odd that he should ask to meet me. I made my way to McCaffrey's Bar anyway—narrowly avoiding two children who nearly ran into me—and entered the pub through the double doors.

The redesign put the wooden bar curving away towards the back of the premises. Gold light fixtures hung symmetrically from the bar shelves, reflecting a line of yellow dots and polished wood. Similar lights were attached to the walls, separated by prints from a famous local artist.

Harvard sat in a bay window seat with a sausage roll and a latte ready for me. He smiled as I approached, but with a hint of a struggle inside him.

He came right out with it.

"So…Mark spilt at work this morning. He says you're having a romance with, um, a ghost?"

I huffed a laugh and defensively asked, "Are you going say I'm stupid as well? Dumb enough to believe in a fairy tale god that doesn't see, hear, or answer?"

Harvard looked around nervously, but nobody paid attention to us.

"Actually, I know it all too well. You forget where I'm from. My pops could pray the devil outta Lucifer if he'd a mind."

Surprised, I replied, "Really? I never knew that."

"It's hardly acceptable conversation nowadays, is it? And I am particularly concerned that Mark didn't know the extent of the danger."

I was quick to defend myself. "Like it's an easy thing to discuss with him right now. If he knew that on top of everything else…I don't think we'd survive it."

Harvard froze, face displaying guilt, and I knew then; Mark was so very aware of the circumstances now.

"Harvard!" It came out as a whisper and not like the scream in my head.

Months ago, I remembered a news report stipulating the new International Neighbourhood (I.N.) religious restrictions.

Mark and I had switched it off, uninterested. At the time, it wasn't news. Most non-churchgoers didn't see an issue with the restricted worship law. We weren't being strung up or burnt at stake, so what was our problem? Christians that read the Book, however, understood the undercurrent these laws brought and the spiritual effect they carried.

The I.N. stood for just what it said, an International Neighbourhood, a worldwide community. If only that were true. A cruder way of putting it was the New World Order, the One World Government, or my favourite: nobody else left powerful enough to hold the world leader accountable in this peaceful neighbourhood.

Harvard sat forward, itching his head.

"He's pretty sure you're gonna get arrested or killed."

I rolled my eyes, but the thought of a stint in a rehabilitation centre was not far from my mind. I was always careful not to break any laws. It wasn't illegal yet to worship a god; we were just stupid. My thoughts turned back to Mark.

"How was he when you left?"

I was prepared for the answer, but I didn't receive the one I expected.

"Tolerant, I think, after my parting question," Harvard said, getting out of his seat. He lowered to a whisper, "which was, 'if I loved Jesus, would that make me a suicidal homosexual?'

"Do you?" I asked.

Harvard laughed while slipping on his jacket. "Took Mark the same amount of time to ask the same thing."

I waited for an answer to my question that never came. Instead, he winked and slipped out of the door.

I fingered the logo of my ID badge as I walked home. The Collective Thought stamp and its 'All Eyes On Me' mantra had always unnerved me. Circles that stood for the intelligence of the I.N. headquarters buildings sat at each corner of an isosceles triangle. The symbol represented everything legal and was stamped onto anything sold. But it also stood for the three-fold attitude of the I.N. All eyes on me: as in ourselves, Collective Thought, and our leader, Ciel Tisak.

The I.N. aimed to bring us all under one world, one rule, one mind, and connect us all. But what it actually did was make Mark and my one world smaller and more restricted instead of more inclusive. As a result, people could not always be trusted.

I would never have believed them if a friend had told me, 'One day, Anna Cole, you will be a Christian.'

3 Ciel Tisak

My Irish boss and best friend, Teela Franklin, was a sassy, short-haired brunette with startling blue eyes. She was single, thirty-eight, and fit. She was promoted to her senior role when I was hired as an administrator of the newly formed team.

Our, or rather, their job was investigating cases that lurked on the darker web and black market and were limited to specific kinds of lawbreaking. Our team investigated the instigators of the resistance—famous and infamous, and sometimes, rich and dangerous folks that could have you assassinated with an old-fashioned text message. A lead could take us anywhere in the world, online, so it was my job to make sure every tiny detail was recorded electronically in any format: video, audio, graphics, or word. If the case was viable, it was sent to the nearest team, and they made the arrest.

In Little Hampton, a small town of West Wiltshire in the Grand British Republic (GBR), we had only so far made two arrests. One was within our jurisdiction and had originated from one of Teela's secret sources. That was easy to prove because we had worked the leads, and the threads of evidence were fresh and familiar in our minds.

The second case had come from a team in London. The evidence details were meagre and so disjointed that we had spent long days, often late into the night, piecing the evidence together.

Teela now held the same familiar expression as she poured over a new file. Then finally, she handed it to me.

"It's a joke, Anna. Look at the state of it."

"Missing girls…but there are only five pages!"

She pointed to her desk, where a white, USB drive rested on the top of a small envelope. "That came with it."

"Great! I'll start preparing a complete file for you. Who's responsible this time?"

"Manchester. The NC's in a posh house down Marston way."

Posh house? Rich then. Corrupt undoubtedly. I was about to ask who the Non Conformer was when Teela bent to answer a ping on her monitor.

"It's an e-chat from Manchester."

She touched the screen, and a young man's face filled the space, and his Mancunian drawl was strong.

"Teela Franklin?"

"Yep, that's me. Hi."

"We...I wanted to talk to you about the file I sent."

"That is not a file," I scoffed, peering at him over Teela's shoulder.

"I know, sorry, but I got what I could," he whispered nervously. "I haven't got long, so listen up. There isn't much because they destroyed it all. I recorded the significant things I could remember, but the evidence to prove it has gone. I wish I'd known, had some idea of what was going on, but I didn't expect it." He combed his fingers through his short blond hair and quietly added, "Ciel Tisak had it shut down as soon as I set up the live case. I sent it to you because, well, it's your doorstep, and I'm supposed to be the good guy."

Voices permeated from behind him, and he disconnected instantly. I stared speechless at the now black screen. Marston was only twenty minutes away from here.

"Right." Teela sucked in a breath. "This is going to be fun."

I looked up, surprised Teela would go against regulations.

"Are we investigating then?"

"No harm in having a peek now, is there?" she asked curiously. "It might just be one we get to arrest ourselves!" She salivated at the thought.

At my raised brows, she whined, "Crikey, it's been three years, Anna."

"And nobody needs a quiet life, do they, T?" I replied sarcastically.

"You carry on; let me identify what he sent us. I'll let you know. Take this off my hands, would you?"

She handed me a stack of papers and files and shoved me through the door, closing it behind me.

"Rude!" I called teasingly through her office window and heard a low chuckle behind the closed blinds.

Teela was cheeky, but I loved her, and there wasn't much that I wouldn't do for her. She always looked out for me. Teela had discovered my knack for research during the London case. Piecing that together took tremendous work, research, and patience, which I had shown in abundance. Since then, she had given me assignments exceeding my pay grade. I sought evidence now and didn't just analyse and organise it.

Although she was the police, and most coppers would have said something, she took my becoming a Christian quite well, angelically compared to Mark. She didn't really care. 'Keep it quiet', was what she'd said, 'it's embarrassing to people since the mock rapture.'

Ministry pastor, Dan Hawkins, once said the mock rapture was a scam of Ciel Tisak's making, and the intention had always been to undermine the truth.

"I'm telling you, Anna. It's got his devious little signature written all over it. The true rapture will happen one day, and God will collect those that have come to Him. It is written, so it shall be. We just don't know when. It's been debated for a century. Will it be before judgement, during, or after? Well, I'll tell you, we'll soon find out because we'll either be in heaven waiting or coming down to the Mount of Olives with Jesus at the last trumpet sound. He will split that God-made mountain in two just by stepping on it! Praise the Lord. Come soon, precious Jesus."

Ciel Tisak had deluded us into thinking inside the box. The I.N.'s very particular box. Apparently, we were all on the same page about what was acceptable in society and divisive. The government said God was divisive, and believers were troublemakers. It unsettled me to be reminded of their agenda; it hinted at a destination to complete control and total power. I worried it would elevate our leader to a god-like status. It was why our little bubble was just a few close friends we could trust. It was simpler. We wouldn't turn each other in if we accidentally broke the law. Trust was vital when councils ushered in last-minute laws and amendments, changes that often left us wondering what was and wasn't legal anymore.

~

Once I reached my desk, which was the farthest from the door, I placed the armful of files down and checked my messages. Mark had called, asking if I wanted to join him for an early dinner date. McCaffrey's wasn't too far from the station, and I enjoyed the walk. It gave me time to process and pray about the Manchester e-chat. Discovering that the I.N. could suppress cases was worrying, bizarre even, considering we focussed more on the NCs (Non Conformers) of Collective Thought than on the criminals that committed standard crimes. Since the I.N. installation six years ago, there have been pockets of these insurgents worldwide, and our search algorithms have sought them out.

Which reminded me, and not for the first time, of the conference meeting Teela had in her office and the order to clamp down on protesters with new measures. Had that been the plan from the start and why the team began? If true, Ciel Tisak's obstruction of the Manchester case proved my suspicion. If all our cases involved catching NCs, why would Tisak feel the need to squash one that recovered missing girls and caught an NC?

My attention was drawn to an alleyway where I saw two small heads peer around the corner and back again. I turned to look as I walked past and stopped. Standing halfway down in front of some steps was a young, shaven-haired boy with a smaller girl beside him. Their clothes were shabby, and they looked thin.

"Everything all right?" I asked as they warily eyed me.

The girl tucked herself behind the boy, and he protectively circled his arm around her. He answered confidently, puffing out his chest.

"Yes, we're waiting for someone."

"Okay."

I walked on and spied Mark leaning against the wall of the bar, kicking it with the heel of his trainer. I moved stealthily as I approached.

"BOO!" My clawed fingers attacked his sides while I stretched up on tiptoes, waiting for him to close the distance with a kiss.

"Y'alright?" he asked, not even slightly tickled.

He opened the door and followed me in with his hand at the small of my back. We chose a table at the rear, close to a warm radiator, and a muted TV mounted to the wall in the corner. The headline banner told me we were waiting for the I.N. leader to come and speak. The Imperial Kiengir Ciel Tisak. That was his full title.

Kiengir: KI, as in kite, EN, GIR - gear.

What latest changes were coming was anybody's guess. I looked away and turned to the menu. Mark was already doing that; I rolled my eyes. Men and food!

Mark was talking curries while he browsed, which started an indignant monologue about our old government. Although my feelings towards the world leader wavered, Mark's amusing comparisons of the two leaders had us both in fits. Our laughter drew the attention of other patrons. We ignored them but quietened anyway.

"Kinda glad we're not the country that bends the knee to every stupid thing people want anymore, Christ." He looked from the TV to me. "Oops, sorry."

The stranger seated at a table nearby looked away as my eyes met his. He had been listening.

I refrained from saying that we still did bend the knee, just to the whims of the one person these days.

Instead, I scolded, "You know you shouldn't say that! It's not slang anymore; it's an unwelcome reminder of what happened."

To Mark, the mock rapture was an unpleasant reminder of the day his mother died. He peered at me quizzically and then shrugged as he spotted our food approaching.

We were halfway through our meal when the unmistakable roar of his crowd suddenly burst out from the TV. It was typical for the handsome Ciel Tisak to cause the adoring masses to hang on his every word.

The camera swept across the hordes of people outside the I.N. HQ and palace complex in Baruun, Iran. They waved Collective Thought flags and banners. Some sounded with horns and drums. It sounded more like a sports match than a political speech.

"Greetings, fellow Neighbours, and welcome."

Tisak stood confidently on the podium in front of his crystal lectern. He wore an ash-coloured, buttoned-up suit over a silky black shirt open at the neck. No tie. He smiled, flashing perfect teeth against olive-toned skin, and ran his hand through his caramel-coloured hair. His cobalt eyes glistened with pride, and his smooth, honey tone echoed across the masses.

"Thank you, thank you."

Feigning embarrassment while the crowd continued to cheer, he stretched out his arms, palms down, and bounced them slowly to quieten the people.

"I am delighted to be here and able to speak to all my Neighbours across the world as your elected principal. I once again serve you and yearn to see our world thrive under the common objective of peace and Collective Thought."

More clapping and cheering filled the air.

"Today, I am pleased to confirm that your voices have been heard. Therefore, today, I can announce, we have considered your requests for the fairy tale, man-made holidays to be abolished."

As he said this, a large whiteboard was set up behind him. On it was a chart. The left side listed months going down, and across the top were religious and other unfamiliar symbols. Columns of colour filled in many grid squares representing the various festivals and sacred days belonging to those beliefs. That included Wicca, Druidry, and other pagan beliefs. All religious and quasi-religious denominations and beliefs were frowned upon, including devil-worship and witchcraft.

The strangely old-fashioned way of displaying information bemused me while Tisak continued to stimulate the crowd with his charismatic speech.

"You asked why we commemorate these counterfeit holidays belonging to an obsolete culture. The name Easter, for example, represents something that has not happened; Christmas, an unreal birth, and to think–" his expression was incredulous, "to think each of us was tricked into believing a book of fiction! The rapture of the so-called Saints. Well, look how it turned out!"

At the crowd's roaring laughter, Tisak turned to the whiteboard, revelling in the results of his wit, and picked up a cloth.

"We should have known; we should have realised this was not the act of a god. They say a God of love, but what god would leave so many children behind?"

A God of love wouldn't. Jesus doesn't.

Expressions of pain flooded Tisak's face: his jaw clenched, he frowned, and his lips trembled. It seemed like a performance; he would make an excellent salesman. I guessed he already was. He sold his fresh concepts with a quick tongue, reigning with confidence, courage, and expertise. I mean, who wouldn't want someone so qualified?

"Watch."

Tisak wiped the column of green representing Christianity from the whiteboard and grinned.

"No more of this fake Christ, the imposter Messiah!"

Further cheering swelled from the crowd. I swallowed dryly because the end of lawful religion was on the horizon. Chocolate eggs would be relabelled as spring eggs, and there would still be hen decorations instead of a cross depicting the truth of the seasonal holiday. Christmas was not much of a loss to me. I had worked out that Jesus was not born in December. The Bible indicated that John The Baptist was born in March, six months before Jesus. Maths was not my strong point, but even I could see the fault in it.

Tisak continued, emphasising his words slowly and pronouncing every letter in perfect English.

"Vesak too. Buddha represented love, peace, and unity. Is this not what we already aspire to within the International Neighbourhood? These very things are the basis of our Collective Thoughts, are they not?"

He exuded an aura of energy and convincing sincerity that I could have believed him myself had I not known who he truly was. Physically, Ciel Tisak was the saviour of the world. He had buried our dead, rebuilt our economies, and reintegrated those 'returned' back into the community. Spiritually, he was an evil puppet for the prince in control of this earth. Satan had power, and I would've expected him to have welcomed all kinds of idolatry and witchcraft activity. The rituals, spells, the chants, and candles surrounding spooky symbols weren't things that appealed to him, it seemed. We, humans, were the gods now. It was what we wanted. Everything was about me.

Oozing vigour and passion, Tisak spoke on.

"Ramadan, and the giving of alms to the poor. As close Neighbours, should we not be doing this every day, for everyone? Need we also honour Hajj? A birth of a man that referred his own to another false book?"

More clapping followed as he turned back to the board and wiped away another colour column.

"Just like Mother's Day, Father's Day, Independence Day, and all the other meaningless festivals…gone, gone, gone."

He wiped away another and another from the whiteboard.

"We do not need days and traditions to nurture each other. Look around you; already, we are here for one another. That is what the Neighbourhood is all about."

The people's cheering rang for some time. Tisak stood tall, with his arms behind his back, feet slightly apart with the toes turned in and chin up. Patiently, he waited for the crowd to exhaust their exhortation. In fact, he enjoyed it, even basked in it.

The last whiteboard column was marked Judaism. This had been the most colourful of all, and I briefly saw a smug smile appear on Tisak's face. Now, there was complete silence as he dampened his cloth in preparation and the heightened vibe was tangible.

"The Jew, the Jew. What can I extend to the delightful Israeli?" Tisak appeared dejected. "They have adhered to their Torah throughout the ages. Through captivity, through the age of the Church, many Jews were lost to Christianity through the mock rapture. Now too ashamed to return to their own faith. Oh, the Jew…I say to you, there is no Zion, there is no Messiah, but there is a Neighbour at every corner for you. Come home to us."

He turned to the board and wiped the last of the colours with such vivacity that the board wobbled precariously. Tisak honestly believed somehow his actions had erased Passover.

My teeth clenched together as my throat tightened.

Tisak recovered himself. "I have worked tirelessly to ensure fair trade for these…holidays, and I am excited to reveal four festivals towards the end of March, June, September, and December to coincide with school term breaks. Another special celebration I have prepared for you all is to be held every year from August 14th to the 18th."

His tone darkened with a sinister edge.

"Every business will shut down, by law, and every employee will be free to enjoy time together as an International Neighbour. We will be expecting bonfires, street parties, music and dancing, plenty to eat and drink and be merry!"

He was rejoicing now and brimming with excitement.

Though the TV crowd chanted his name to the rhythm of drums that occasionally were masked beneath the din of horns, the bar patrons were louder. Nearly everyone had jumped to their feet, cheering him and whistling.

Another pleased at the news was Mark, finally able to benefit from bank holidays. His employer needed a security Headsman every day, but this new legislation would change that for him. I didn't blame Mark for not understanding. Why would he have reason to doubt our leader? The application of Collective Thought hadn't changed things for most people. We had noticed changes in logos to incorporate the new alliance—which was 'company name' plus INc (I.N. incorporated) and changes to the names of newspapers and TV channels. None of these had an impact on our everyday lives. Nobody had worried. Nobody needed to doubt him, except for helicopter parents' intent on pushing their kids to learn more than the others and the God-botherers being stripped of their churches.

Tisak spoke briefly to emergency worker bosses and explained how they could use their own judgement with staff levels by suggesting they implement a rota system so that everyone could benefit. Everyone else must celebrate.

"You may keep your war memorial days if you wish." His voice was thick with solemnity.

I noticed his first mistake. Tisak was usually careful to portray togetherness, but suddenly, it was 'your wars' and not our wars.

"I do not advocate war, though," he said, looking down sorrowfully. "Personally, I would rather forget how savage we once were and concentrate on how far we have evolved into a peaceful Neighbourhood. Which brings me to the delivery of some frightful news."

He sighed sadly, pausing dramatically. "It seems some are not adhering to our commitment."

Low murmurs, grumbles, and hisses swept through the crowd.

"I know, I know. How bizarre!" he agreed, astonished by the thought. "But unfortunately, there are. We are doing our utmost to apprehend these Non Conformers. We have task forces in place, and we will succeed in consummating peace for our Neighbourhood!"

The crowd cheered.

A deep unease came over me. I tuned out the voice on the telly that made me want to vomit, but the buzzing vibe within the bar was just as daunting.

"Are you ready to leave?" I asked without taking my eyes off the screen. I did not want Mark to see the defeat in my eyes.

"If you want. You haven't finished your food."

The rest of my pasta had thickened and turned rubbery.

"I've had enough."

Besides, I wanted to add, I think I might throw up! But I resisted the urge as the stranger's eyes surveyed us again.

I was glad to be free of his penetrating stare, and we were quickly inside Mark's Range Rover, heading out into the road.

4 Richard Cole

"How about a walk?" Mark asked, taking my hand and holding it on his lap while he drove.

"Sounds nice," I replied, smiling.

"I found a stream the other week. I've had to include the wilder parts of the land on my rounds since the gardener stripped away all the foliage up at the back of the estate. He's lowered the hedges for the first time ever that I know of. So I thought we could take a wander in the woods behind there?"

"Perfect." I smiled.

I was happy just to be with him like this again. My heart fluttered like a schoolgirl's, delighted that he still liked me after all.

As the view of the countryside flitted by, blurry with green hedges and trees, I tried to find things to talk about and mentioned the weather—a poor excuse for a conversation topic that caused Mark to glance across at me.

Silences between us were usually comfortable and natural. But recently, they hid the unknown thoughts of my husband as I constantly worried about what might be going on behind his eyes. Was I becoming unhinged?

I commanded the radio to shut out the quiet. The news covered a debate between the education authority and parents questioning the validity of certain history stories, among other things. They were future NCs in the making if they weren't already because schools centred around destabilising any sense of permanence, commitment, and obligation. Everything from values, gender, emotions and family were fluid. Myth and legend had made a comeback, and science delved to new depths in genome splicing. The kids nowadays mix varied species of embryos and don't grow watercress. In the I.N.'s opinion, and therefore, the education authority, any parent opposing the education changes were intolerant and not of the same mind as the rest of the 'Neighbourhood'.

The main curriculum subjects were Maths, the Sciences, English (the common language accepted as law across the world), Geography (amended twice when the kingdoms of the world were reduced to ten), and we became closer-international-neighbours, and History—altered to the viewpoint of the Collective Thought. (An extract from the latest textbook edition, History Now, can be read on page 287).

Those parents fought to stop the line blurring between truth and lies and right and wrong. So, what kind of person might the schools raise?

I shivered. Time would tell.

Mark gently rubbed his thumb across the back of my hand.

"Are you cold?" He reached for the heat button.

"No," I answered, "Just a bad rush. What did you make of the speech then?"

I realised it was as good a choice of topic as the weather when his jaw tightened.

"Do you think you will get the four days off in August?"

"Yeah, sounds like it. I'm hardly an emergency worker."

"That would be nice. Just us together for a few days."

Mark's lips made a thin line.

"I really don't want to keep upsetting things, but you still don't seem to understand, Anna. It won't ever be just us again. We'll never have our short breaks together in the same way again."

My stomach knotted as I recalled our holidays.

"You're right; I don't understand. Are you saying the I.N.'s new holiday legislation will stop us from going away together?"

"No, Anna, your choices do. Unintentionally, I realise that. But, all the same," he shrugged, "it's true. I know what you're doing when I find you sitting on the bed or staring out the window. How can I steal you away for the weekend again without Him in the middle of it? Could you just be mine again, sometimes? No book, no praying, no God?"

Mark and I had a happy and playful relationship. However, I hadn't considered the effect my faith would have on him.

I stared at my lap.

My efforts to hide my private prayer hadn't worked. The attentive smile that appeared whenever Mark interrupted hadn't concealed anything! Rightly or wrongly, I hadn't uttered the name of Jesus anywhere near him. I didn't want to keep adding fuel to the fire, so I kept that part of me separate. When Mark would be in bed feigning sleep after my church ministry group, I just smiled and carried on, biting back the impulse to defend my new faith. Perhaps he was jealous of how happy my Christian faith made me, and I had realised that nothing material could match it. One day, I hoped Mark would discover it all himself.

I was careful not to voice these thoughts; I didn't want to alienate Mark even more. I would still read my Bible every day and pray. I would thank God I woke up—that the day was new and better than yesterday because I'd slept on it, and things always seemed clearer in the morning. Then I would apologise to God for overreacting.

I also thanked Him for the things I had: the blessings, the love, the finance, job, house, and husband. I thanked Him also for the things I had lost—the dream of children.

Dream? Wasn't it funny how something becomes so important suddenly when it doesn't happen? I had never thought seriously about having children. Hadn't even thought about whether I wanted them or not. It was assumed when you got married, wasn't it? Until it wasn't, so many years later without a hint of a missed period. I tried not to remember the many tests and negative results that had crushed the dream I didn't know I would value so highly.

So, I thanked God for my loss because it strengthened my relationship with Mark. We decided that what we never had couldn't be missed and make us empty. We turned to each other for fulfilment. That was usually when I would thank God for revealing Himself to me. I would need nothing else again to fulfil me. Even if I had nothing else but Jesus and God's love, I was complete. I couldn't touch Him, yet I could feel Him. I couldn't see Him, yet I saw Him in every little thing. The things I thanked God for changed daily. Every yesterday brought different situations and emotions to pray through, and every morning saw a resolve in my spirit about something I had been praying for. I often talked about Mark, sometimes pleading for God to save him too.

It was a blessing that Mark's question was a rhetorical one. He wasn't waiting for a reply. It was just as well because he would not have appreciated my answer. As a compromise, I could leave my Bible, perhaps, but not my prayers. Jesus was a part of my thoughts now, my very existence, and yes, my morning focus would be on Him, as well as cuddling my husband.

~

The 17th-century wall surrounding Thurstworthy Manor Estate was too high to see the property behind. The other side had lofty trees until the end, where a high hedge fought against mature, wild blackberry bushes. The owners of the Manor, the Forbes-Hamiltons, were Mark's employers, and he was the security Headsman there.

Mark turned onto a dirt track and continued another mile before pulling over, parking with the bumper virtually kissing the trunk of a Sycamore tree. He pointed towards the driver's window.

"It's just through there. It looks different on this side of the boundary, but I think I'm about right."

Besides natural greens and browns, I couldn't see anything. Ferns, thorn bushes, and branches covered the ground.

Mark led the way through the trees, our joined hands swinging. I could hear the gentle trickle of the stream as it meandered, growing louder as we neared. There were scuttling sounds beneath the undergrowth and a flurry of leaves when the breeze picked up.

"What are you thinking about?" Mark asked, letting go of my hand and placing an arm across my shoulders.

"Actually, I was listening. Nature is musical when you stop and listen."

"Exactly why I could never sit inside the gatehouse every day. I love walking the grounds. Sun on my back, fresh air in my lungs."

When I met Mark, he had held the seasonal security position at Thurstworthy Manor for eight years. In the months between May and September, he'd worked. The rest of the year, he trained. He learned to sharpshoot from miles away in all kinds of humidity and weathers; defend himself against an attacker carrying weapons; incapacitate the said attacker with or without his own weapons, and a range of other skills taught by the Armed Forces. He'd described it as claustrophobic and exhausting because the intense training took place inside an undisclosed complex without enough rest, breaks, and sleep.

Mark removed his arm from across my shoulders and took my hand again.

"There's a secret gate just up there." He pointed up and slightly east, following the hedgerow. "Not secret really, just...previously undiscovered. It was overgrown and so well hidden that nobody on the staff even knew it was there. Moss covers it on both sides, so it blends in with the hedges."

"Why is it being exposed now?"

"Search me."

"And as head of grounds security, nobody thought to let you know?" I laughed.

~

After a few more minutes of picking my way through the uneven ground, the stream came into view. We approached it at the base of a curve. One side crept up and slightly east, the other north-west. The rocky base was uneven beneath the flow of the clear water. It looked black in the shadows with streaks of silver weaving where the rays of sunlight filtered through the trees. Moss covered the stepping-stones strategically placed for crossing. Deeper into the woods, the ground was a blanket of king cups and bulrushes.

"Sorry, Anna, I should've thought about you in your office gear. They're hardly the right shoes."

I wore black trousers, a blue shirt, and black heeled boots. Avoiding stones, twigs, and thick tufts of grass was a challenge. My arms were held out to balance, but the ground was relatively firm, so my heels didn't sink into the mud too much.

"It's not so bad; it's kinda funny," I remarked, snaking past him and taking the lead.

The conversation from in the car resurfaced, and although I didn't want to bring it up again, I did want to ask a question. It was better to be upfront about issues or conversations that gnawed inside me before they became dangerous obsessions.

"Mark, I have to ask you because it's bugged me since the car."

The recollection of the conversation was obvious in his eyes. Swallowing, I plucked up the courage to go on.

"Are you really worried about losing out on dirty weekends? I mean…"

With a puckered forehead and a curled top lip, he huffed and shook his head.

"This is not about sex, Anna; it's about togetherness. This is about love; this is about trust, surrender, and passion. Those together times build on our foundations of all that. I was your focus; you were mine—no outside distractions. Nothing could interfere because we didn't want it to. We learned to trust each other and surrender to each other…to love each other."

He pulled on my arm to stop me from walking on.

"I do not demean our relationship to just sex, and I know my behaviour that night was wrong, but…that's not the point anyway. The point is that your trust, surrender, and passion belong to your God now. It is given to Him and for Him, and they will be His even in those intimate moments with me. You were my bride; now you'll be His."

I barely had the theological knowledge to catch up with what Mark said. 'Bride' was ringing some massive alarm bells; he knew more about this than he had ever let on. I thought back to our arguments and how he had given insight into what I was feeling or how I might relate personally to Jesus. The sharing of me. Silly as it sounded, the more I pondered it, the more it became an obvious truth. Mark understood how my focus would be on heavenly and not worldly things.

The jealous Mark hadn't come right out and said it, but he hated my affection for something more extraordinary than the love we shared. He understood my feelings for Jesus before I did. I didn't know I felt the way he'd described until he started to get jealous of a Saviour I was just beginning to know. How could Mark know?

The words were out of my mouth before I had the chance to silence them.

"You know something about all this, don't you?"

I didn't have much experience when it came to the Holy Spirit's promptings, but I prayed this was one of those.

"I, uh, I think it's getting dark fast," replied Mark. "We should head back. Let's not risk picking our way through the trees; I don't have my phone with me. We'll follow the stream back to the Manor border."

Agreeing, I spun around and walked, keeping the stream to my left. Although curious for an answer from Mark, I didn't push it. The light faded to grey, suffused with orange from the setting sun, though light enough to see where I was going. I continued to follow the curves of the stream, breathing through my various balancing stances with oohs, ahs, and ffffs that I wouldn't let develop into swear words. It punctured some of the awkwardness between us.

"Wanna get on my back? Hate to offer, really. I'm rather enjoying myself listening to you," he said, chuckling.

I grinned sarcastically. "Oh, funny! Although I can't see where I'm stepping anymore."

He offered me the crook of his arm, which I gratefully accepted, keen to discover what he was hiding. I shot surreptitious glances his way but was not intrusive. I would wait for him to be ready, hoping and praying it was in a minute.

When I peeked at him again, I lost my footing, and Mark swore as he steadied me.

"You're waiting for an answer, aren't you?" he asked. "And I'd better start talking before you do yourself an injury by staring at me."

"Sorry. I thought I was being sneaky."

Mark laughed. "You're not good at it. Stick to your computer, trust me. You're too short for sneaky looks at me."

He laughed again when I poked out my tongue like a child, then sighed gently, kicking the ground as we walked.

"It, erm, it was a long time ago; the church can be a scary place for kids, especially if it's filled with people who are a bit full on. I was taught the stories and harassed into knowing about my sins and the things I kept doing wrong. I despaired of the dedication people must have to serve their God. I grasped the concept of 'Jesus in me', but I never really got it, if I'm honest. I understood the words, but I had no passion for them. They didn't speak to me—the stories never meant anything to me."

Firstly, I had to deal with my surprise. "You went to church? When? How come you haven't told me before?"

"It wasn't relevant. My dad became a Christian, much to my mum's amusement. She pushed me into going to church with him when I was about fourteen and becoming a bit of a handful. I hadn't thought about it until recently, and I wasn't going to tell you anything. As I said, it meant nothing to me. Even less now, I know it not to be true."

I flinched. "The Bible is just words without the Spirit of God and can't be truly valued. Anyone reading it without Him would not understand and just mock it."

He sniggered darkly. "Well, you would say that. That's how I know. Taught to know what it's like. The centre of all things is God, etcetera."

Anyone truly saved by Jesus did not need to be taught or told what it was like. I was instantly and permanently changed the moment I sat on the kerb to hear that prayer. I met God spiritually before I knew anything mentally, like repenting of my sins. I wouldn't have even known what that meant. My search for Him hadn't been conscious either. I was walking and enjoying the crisp frost of a February morning, happy with my life. What reason was there to look for or need Him? Five minutes later, the music playing through the window had all at once moved me, opened me, and filled me with warmth inside. I felt…complete, whole, and so struck by love I could not move, bent to the will of something that felt so wonderful. Peaceful. Powerful. Without knowing it, I sat down at the roadside—too drawn into the prayer being spoken—and cried. That was salvation. Whatever it was I didn't know I was looking for was found at that moment. The missing piece. The God-shaped piece.

"I can hear the cogs whirring, Anna. You're thinking about what you can preach at me." His words trickled through the sensations of the Holy Spirit's presence.

I laughed and sarcastically declared, "Oh yes, because I'm totally qualified for that! You know more than I do, it seems, except for maybe the power of the Lord. You haven't actually met Him yet."

The uncomfortable silence was thankfully broken when Mark's phone rang on the way home. What unnerved me was that it only rang when usually, the car's AI gender-neutral voice informed us of who the caller was. 'Mark calling', 'unknown number calling' or 'unregistered', for those burner phones now traced with impressive technology updates. The caller's tech was too sophisticated for even the updates to read. It just rang.

"Answer," Mark ordered sharply to the onboard system.

"Mark!"

My mouth popped open in surprise.

"Chie, man, where've you been?" Mark asked, in a mixture of alarm, anger, and relief.

The relief was to hear from him and know he was still alive; anger for leaving it for so long (but Mark and I understood that less contact was safest for all); and then alarm.

Why was he calling?

With a voice quiet and cracked, Chie complained, "Hiding mostly."

The confident man who had joined the Non Conformers last year was melting.

"Where are you?" Mark probed.

"Manchester for now, but listen, I need you to know. It's not us; we're not responsible. Before all the lies start coming out, I had to tell you we wouldn't, couldn't do that!"

Bewildered, Mark asked, "Do what?"

"We found a planted, digital trail in the I.N. network with evidence leading right to us. Evidence that isn't because we haven't committed it."

A pause.

"Is Anna there?"

I had a sinking feeling he was about to ask me a favour.

"I'm here; hi, Chie."

"Anna, can you see what you can find out?"

Boom. There it was. I looked at Mark, who was staring incredulously at the phone now that we were parked on our driveway. He didn't look at me while the glow of the security light created shadows on his face.

"Anna, please will you look into it? I don't want you to pass the information back. I wouldn't ask you to do that, but please, I am begging you. Prove it's all lies. I know you can." He lowered his voice to a whisper, "You have to, or I'm dead."

"DO WHAT?" Mark asked again, irritated.

In the same whisper, he replied, "There's going to be a bombing in London...and we haven't planned any of it. No NC I know has given orders. I swear to you, but someone has made it look like it's come directly from us. Well, me."

I was numbed. What had Chie done? What had London? This act would start another war.

Mark was instantly suspicious. "What do you mean, me? Why your name?"

Crackles on the line were Chie's immediate reply, then he reluctantly confessed, "I'm not exactly unknown to the task force in Portsmouth."

I sucked in a breath.

"You can't think we...they...would..."

Say it, Anna. Set you up?

Silence.

Despite my reservations on who might be responsible, Mark declared his leanings.

"We believe you, Chie."

Chie was waiting for an agreement to his request. "Anna?"

"I'll see," I faltered, wanting to help, but it was dangerous. "No promises."

Chie sighed, relieved.

"Thank you. Love you, both of you. Got to go."

The line was dead before either of us could utter a farewell, and there was a lull in the air while we tried to understand what had just developed and what I had just carelessly agreed to.

~

Overall, the day had been filled with revelation. The video call in Teela's office had revealed some underhanded tactics inside Tisak's regime, the first that I had come across since being in my role. It was disconcerting. The thought of a capital city being destroyed and blamed on Chie sickened me, and Tisak's carefree arrogance in erasing the holy days had stirred up hate for the despicable man. Then, the shock of finding out that Mark's teenage years had a link to Jesus through his father, George, who'd died in the second pandemic. In as much as we had grieved for George, we were also grateful he no longer suffered a debilitating disease that ate away at him. Mark's mother remained healthy, as did Mark and I, but the 300,000 that did not, died within the first two weeks. People had queued up outside surgeries, hospitals, and mobile vaccine stations, eager to be inoculated and back to work.

With all of that whirling around in my head, the memory of getting from the car to sitting at the table with an unwanted sandwich was phantasmagorical. I couldn't recall what was real and what wasn't. Had Mark spoken to me? I had a vague recollection of his mouth moving, but I'd heard no sound. Instead, he was staring at me.

"Sorry, I was miles away. What did you say?" I asked.

"I said, it looks like neither of us is very hungry."

"Well, it's been a bit of a day, hasn't it?"

More so for me than him. More so for Chie, too.

Mark sighed in frustration.

"It would be nice if more of the family remained under the radar of the I.N. instead of hanging signs around their necks saying 'I AIN'T LOYAL.'"

"A lot of people aren't loyal. They won't admit it; they'll never do anything about it, but Collective Thought or not, you can't push someone into thinking something they don't. There is some tolerance for those things, but underneath, in the heart, we continue to think the way we always do."

Until the next generation of robots came up out of I.N. schools. The younger they were, the more vulnerable and open to change they were.

"I hate this," Mark growled, "I can't deny the world out there is off its rocker, and I accepted Chie would fight it all the way, but I didn't expect it to be so…radical. I mean, he did say that Portsmouth basically set him up, yeah?"

"The I.N. generally, but yes, he implied that."

"And then, there's you and what the world sees as your immoral choice to serve a god. If we're losing our Christian holidays to new ones, how long do you think it will be before what you're doing is illegal?"

I looked at him with an 'oh; the penny's finally dropped' expression.

"It's only a matter of time now." I paused to nibble at my sandwich. "Chie will be okay. I'm on it tomorrow; I'll work it out with Teela, I promise."

"I know, thanks, but it's more dangerous for us. Sticking your oar in puts you in the limelight. If they know Chie, they will know me, and they will know you."

I hadn't considered that.

I put down the bread and brushed the crumbs from my fingers. I was family to a wanted NC.

5 Manchester's Girls

Every time I drifted off to sleep that night, I jerked awake, unsettled, after dreaming of a man walking in the dark. His fears and thoughts put a strange feeling in my gut, and it was not the first time I'd experienced it.

Somehow, I dragged myself from the bed into work. I sat at my desk yawning, waiting for a very late Teela. She had not reported in. I left her a message to call as soon as she could, so I could stop fretting. In the meantime, I busied myself with leftover tasks from yesterday and tried to concentrate on them rather than Tisak's speech or Chie's bombshell (pardon the pun). Now, Teela's disappearance. I needed the distraction before I cracked from stress.

My phone pinged, and I snatched it up. It was a message from an unknown number asking for a meeting at Korner's bridge, eleven on the dot. It was signed 'the rude one'. Teela.

"Thank you, God," I muttered, reassured she was okay.

I replied cryptically about my travelling concerns. The bus I would catch would never make it in twenty minutes.

Unable to explain my absence to the rest of the team, I grabbed my things quietly and crept out. They would notice soon enough, but I hoped Teela would smooth things out when we returned.

~

The mid-March sun was bright yet cool. The new spring season was starting, and proprietors were getting their businesses ready for sightseers. Some were repainting outside walls, others cleaning windows. Tables were coming out of storage to sit once again under the canopies of shopfronts. As I waited for the bus, I connected my wireless earphones and listened to music. I was grateful Melly had shared some of her collection with me. There wasn't worship music online. One of my favourite songs started to play, and the lyrics captured me. How it lifted, blessed, and strengthened me.

Thank you for the life you led.
Thank you for every word you said,
I thank you for the Spirit you gave,
that lifts me up right out of the grave,
I thank you for your mercy, Lord.
I thank you for every blessing poured,
I thank you for the gift of grace,
that lifts me up right out of the grave.

Bless you for your miracles.
I bless you when the Spirit falls.
I bless you for the home you've built,
it welcomes me and evicts my guilt,
I bless you for robes unearned.
I bless you, my destiny's confirmed,
I bless you for the house you've built,
it welcomes me and evicts my guilt.

The two children walked quickly towards me, wearing the same tatty clothes as before. They shared a bread roll: the boy giving the fair-headed girl the larger piece. He warily eyed my ID badge as they rushed past and disappeared into the alleyway behind me. I walked on.

The bus journey took longer than expected, and it was nearer twenty past eleven by the time I arrived at the bridge. I stepped onto the footpath and started walking, high above the carpet of green beneath me. I spotted Teela leaning on the railings looking down into the valley, dressed in jeans and a red-patterned tunic. I called out as soon as she was within hearing distance.

"Why have you got me traipsing all this way to meet you?"

Teela glanced over but did not reply. I quickened my pace and peered over to see what she was so captivated by.

"What'cha staring at?" I asked indifferently when she still hadn't turned to greet me.

Tapping her temple with her fingertip, she mumbled, "The thoughts in my head, mostly. I see nothing but trouble ahead."

I didn't want to ask what was wrong. Could I really deal with another situation?

Resigned, Teela continued without prompting.

"I listened to an audio file."

Resisting the urge to add 'and?', I pulled my lips into a tight line and waited for her to go on.

"The sheets in the file were about girls, did you notice?" she asked, without taking her eyes away from the view.

I nodded and replied, "They're missing."

"Right."

Although in agreement, there was something else in her tone, as if she believed they might not just be missing anymore. She didn't continue, and my patience wore thin.

"Teela, spit it out!"

"Okay, okay. I'm trying." She frowned, a painful, deep expression of anguish.

I waited, full of curiosity but not convinced that I wanted to know at all.

Teela gripped the railings bar and looked up, taking a deep breath.

"Those girls are probably long gone now. Manchester, that's what I'm calling him, by the way. You know, the guy from the e-chat. Anyway, he said he'd followed a trail originating from a dark website that had a thin connection to these mis-per reports. The website is used to draw in potential victims." She shuffled uncomfortably. "Through that website, Manchester found a well-disguised link to…another really perverted, evil site which actually, I couldn't spend any time investigating. You get the gist, don't you?"

Yes, I didn't need an explanation of the disgusting things people could do to each other.

"Manchester couldn't do anything with it. There wasn't an NC to investigate from their task force's point of view. Although still a crime, it had nothing to do with the people we investigated, but Manchester couldn't let it lie."

Teela looked over and smiled.

"I think he's like you; he's their version of you, and good—just as good as you are. The copies of the missing girls' reports were kept separately, unseen by the rest of his team. It wasn't done in secret; Manchester just liked to keep summary information on hand, and as that wasn't protocol, no one thought to look. It said on the recording he didn't have the chance to collect and duplicate anything else before the records were removed electronically and physically. Still, he gave us a rundown of the facts. He eventually found a thread leading to NCs. Someone, well, a group, known to the I.N. as the instigators of the riots in Swindon. You remember that?"

I remembered a gang of NCs speaking out against what, in their view, was the totalitarianism of Tisak's rule. They had rallied the city into a frenzy two years ago and attacked Council buildings, the I.N. army base and libraries because the only books remaining now were obtuse and lacked any freedom of thought. Anything that slightly disagreed or differed with the Neighbourhood's worldview had been destroyed. It didn't leave much space for literature or philosophy.

"Manchester took the evidence to his superior, and the team began to investigate. He mentioned Stymer Holdings INc. You know, Ian Stymer, the philanthropist? One of his stock companies is Braithwaites. They formulate and supply high-end equipment. Very technical equipment."

I had seen their logo on expensive medical equipment many times.

"According to Manchester, they discovered a way to harness and convert energy from, now don't laugh, ley-lines of all things, into some sort of reaction with CERN INc…but I don't understand the science."

"The nuclear research facility?" I asked, astounded.

"It's all a bit beyond me, to be honest. But from what I could follow, they found a way to convert this energy by infusing it with the discovered mass particle everybody went on about for months, the Fritzman. Together, it creates a new substance. A new element of some kind."

"What's any of that got to do with the missing girls?" I enquired.

"Nothing directly and nothing provable, of course. Stymer's name just kept popping up as a supplier of funding here and there and transporting equipment. Basically, the more they dug, the more connections they found via money trails between I.N. supporter Stymer, those websites and the missing girls, and the NC group. There's also a connection," she chuckled darkly, "was a connection until the I.N. hid it, between Braithwaites and the NC group."

Indicating each point with my fingers, I recapped. "So, five missing girls are linked to a dark website, which is linked to a pornographic website: funded and protected by Stymer, who has affiliations with a tech company who has supplied equipment to the NCs responsible for the Swindon riots. Is that about right?"

Teela laughed. "Yeah, wow, write that down for me, would you? You just about put it in order for me."

I was still a little confused. "Why the clandestine meeting?"

"It's what Manchester told me to do; keep it quiet. His video call said he recorded everything he could remember, right? But he sent us an audio file of artificial intelligence reading aloud while Manchester recorded it. The whole thing has been erased from his system and can't be traced back. He revealed he was being watched. I just thought it best to start as I mean to go on, and I want you on board with me. Just us. No one else at work can know about this."

I didn't want to get involved. I had enough on, but I wasn't about to let her embark alone.

"Okay," I reluctantly agreed, "there's something I wanted to talk to you about, too."

I quickly explained the call from Chie yesterday.

"Crikey, Anna. Are you sure he's not lying? And since when have you been harbouring NCs?" She scolded me now as my boss.

"We're not harbouring," I argued defensively, "we hadn't heard from him in ages, and no, he's not lying. Burning down a few libraries is one thing, but–"

"What did you say?" she asked abruptly.

I realised instantly what I had said. I hadn't put the two together until now. Last year, when we discovered Chie had participated in the Swindon riots, he confessed to being part of the insurgents. I didn't know how long he had been with them, but he had to be the NC Manchester was looking for.

"It's Chie, isn't it? The connection Manchester found is to his group, and I'll bet the connection is this fake evidence Chie told us about."

"They didn't get an opportunity to find out more," Teela said sadly, "the moment they linked the NCs and Braithwaites, the case went from live to dead in less than six hours."

Wow. That would have taken some doing.

"Why, though? Why would the I.N. do that?"

"It makes you wonder. I've been up all night trying to make sense of it. I've surmised this, assumed that, and as we've no actual evidence for any of it, there's nothing left to piece together but conjecture."

"But this is a bomb, Teela. In London. Connected to a tech company that has created a new…how did you phrase it? Material? Could it be weaponised, maybe?"

"Maybe." She groaned. "What are we going to do?"

"Luckily for me, you're my boss, so you get to decide!"

"Are you sure your brother-in-law is not responsible?" she asked accusingly.

"Absolutely. No doubt at all. If Chie were guilty, which would be so uncharacteristic, he wouldn't have called Mark at all. He'd be proud and his actions justifiable to him. But Chie was mortified. He couldn't allow Mark to believe he was to blame, or capable of bombing an entire city! So no, Chie's not lying."

Teela laughed uncertainly. "Are you sure I needn't worry about your loyalty to the I.N.?"

Yes, you should. I'm not loyal. The guy is a villain to me now, and he gives me the creeps.

I tried not to let the truth show by covering it with a fake expression of insolence and flashed her a look. It was enough. I didn't have to lie.

I remembered another piece of information from yesterday that Teela hadn't mentioned. Didn't she say something about a posh house?

"How does Marston fit into this?"

"Oh yes!" she exclaimed. "I'd forgotten that. Let's talk on the way to my car."

Ian Stymer and Braithwaites had dealings with the owners of a posh house, as Teela kept calling it, in nearby Marston. Manchester had found orders, delivery notes, and invoices between the three but couldn't see what was bought. The descriptions were letters and numbers rather than words. With the evidence gone, there was no chance of us finding out what the items were. There had also been a witness, killed, naturally, who had corroborated that the girls were taken there.

"Taken to the posh house?" I murmured in disbelief.

Silence lingered for the rest of the journey to the station. Teela was likely trying to make sense of everything just as I was. I reviewed the information in my head: five girls, two unsavoury websites, Stymer, Marston, Braithwaites, Chie, fake bomb threat—no, fake evidence about a bomb that hadn't gone off yet.

"We have to warn London!" I blurted out as I realised London might actually be blown up.

"We can't, though. Can we, Anna?"

"Well, I can't stay idle. Couldn't we try to find a way to warn them or find out something ourselves about the plot? We could be nonchalant about it, you know, 'hey, we don't know how serious the rumour is, but you might want to be prepared for an attack' type of conversation with someone there, at least?"

"But they would find out you looked for the information rather than the system highlighting it. So, how would you explain that? Firstly, to me and to get it passed by me, then for me to get it passed by my boss?"

Teela made a fair point. I gripped my head with my hands.

"What can we do then?"

"Absolutely nothing." She sighed and got out of the car.

I walked away; I walked straight from the station car park to the high street. I walked fast. I was seething; with Teela for being right, with myself for even thinking about allowing a city to burn, accepting it for the sake of my career and life. I was angry with Tisak because wasn't he the one who was supposed to be looking after us all? And instead, it looked like he had intervened so that the plan could go ahead.

This wasn't an insurgent plot. Embedded evidence will say it was. So, why had Tisak burned and buried it?

Over and over, I pondered it as I aimlessly walked. I even considered the possibility that Tisak planned to bomb London himself but couldn't think of a reasonable motive. I knew his end game, true, but we, as a neighbouring nation, hadn't done anything capable of triggering a reprisal like that.

6 Somebody's Watching

The following morning, I stepped off the bus carrying an empty basket. I strode to the bakery and bought two sticky bars filled with oats and fruit. I placed them in the basket with two apple pastries and kept walking.

I had a dream about the man walking in the dark again last night, but it had differed from before. The frightened children were waiting for him at the gate this time, and I had woken with a start. They had been on my mind ever since.

I approached the entrance of the narrow alleyway and stepped in carefully. I couldn't see the children, so I put the basket to the side of the concrete steps leading to the flat above the charity shop and left. If it were me, the smell alone would be enough to rouse me from my pit to investigate.

Nearing the station filled me with dread. I hadn't been to work since yesterday morning and was anxious about the reception I would receive from the team. From Teela even. I stepped out of the revolving door, unpinning my waistband ID badge and holding it up to the desk sergeant.

"Morning, Anna."

I nodded and moved towards the security door that would take me through to the 'authorised personnel' area. I raised my badge to the scanner and the door opened to a corridor that offered three choices: the interview rooms on my left, the bustle of squads solving crimes on my right, and the lifts and stairs in the centre. I took the stairs up to two flights, crossed the Perspex double doors, passed Teela's empty office, and went into the large room where my team worked. Greg Prentice was seated at his desk and smiled in greeting.

"Hey, Anna, I trust you're feeling better?"

Sickness must've been Teela's reason for my absence yesterday. I forced a smile: the looming bombing was making me unwell.

"Not exactly, Greg," I groaned, "but I'm here, willing to serve the Neighbourhood."

"Good, good," he replied, distracted, "you should have said something, one of us would have driven you home. But listen, I want you to check something out. Are you up to it?"

I hoped to find reasons to search for the data I wanted to look up for Chie. Portsmouth cases being one of them.

"Yes."

"Excellent."

Greg scratched his greying hair and handed me a notepad. The top page was covered in illegible scrawl. I squinted as I tried to read it.

"Yeah," he said with an apologetic smile, "sorry, you might want your own notes."

He explained his failure in chasing down an underground network of websites that ran parallel to the main internet. Unless we had certain software, even running with the complexities of the I.N. internet codebreakers, we could not gain access to the pages nor trace their origins. When we or the standard internet opened the webpage, the 'page cannot be displayed' flashed up.

"Find out what they're using, will you?" Greg asked. "The site addresses are all there. But unfortunately, I don't have the time to keep resetting the search module, and frankly, Anna, I'm sick of seeing 'no results' flash up every few freaking hours of this crappy job. I've been on it for two weeks, and nothing. Thought you might have some luck."

"I'll give it a go."

"Brilliant, and hey, use every source you can. Search it for every fact, name, and task force you've ever heard of. Find me something."

I raised my eyebrows. "It's that important?"

"I'm being nagged. Teela will be off for a few days on personal leave, and I don't need the bigwigs on my back."

I tore the page from his notebook, only needing the search information, and I could read that scrawl easily enough. The jubilation swelling up inside me was hidden.

"I'll start straight away," I promised.

Triumphed at the prospect of having total freedom in what I searched for, I hurried to my desk. I could search Portsmouth's case listings and delve as far back as possible. I could even risk checking into Chie without reprisal because my orders were to uncover every stone and hint. If something led me there, I would have every reason to look right at him. While I accessed the search modules, my thoughts wandered to the children. Had they seen me leaving them breakfast? Were they trusting enough to eat it? I hoped they knew they were allowed to.

The searches I set up had inconspicuous keywords that fitted with my orders but leaned towards Portsmouth, London, Manchester, bombings, and pornography. I added religious and spiritual keywords, trying to drag something up that might help mine and Chie's dilemma more than Greg's. I was careful not to search too obviously for Stymer and Braithwaites.

I left the search running and went for a morning coffee. I felt like a fish in a bowl. Colleagues I hardly knew were watching me through the glass partition. I pretended not to notice. What were they staring at? What did they know? I breathed slowly, wishing Teela were here. I felt alone. And vulnerable. And paranoid. It was not unusual for men to watch me, as Mark would often say: I was an attractive woman. They probably knew nothing of my undercover operation and might be admiring my legs inside the clingy jeggings I wore. I decided I'd rather that than the alternative.

The system had produced a list of fifteen results when I returned and was still whirring noisily as it surreptitiously searched. I scanned the list, looking for something to help London or Chie. Portsmouth was mentioned three times. I started there, and after checking every tangent, and every tangent extending from those, I decided not to update the system with the details I found. I neither wanted to draw attention to myself and my findings nor give the other task forces ammunition to use against the Christian groups I had uncovered.

Some of the websites Greg had written down were Christian, others were NC related, and now, I understood the urgency to reveal them. The NCs had found ways to communicate under the radar of the I.N., and as much as I understood their reasons for revolting, I did not agree with the innocents being drawn into a deadly war. Whether NCs were responsible for the planned bombing or not, innocent people would die.

Before my shift finished, I refreshed the settings, having deliberately changed my password to a series of random letters, characters, and numbers: something that could never be guessed, and then logged out. I had left the search running, knowing it might not be finished in the morning.

The warm sun cast my shadow ahead, and it reached the high street alleyway before I did. I stopped and looked in. My basket had been moved nearer to the entrance: empty and decorated with a thin, red-ribboned bow tied to its weaved edge. I smiled as I swooped it up and ran the smooth fabric gently through my fingers. My heart swelled. The ribbon was an emblem of thanks. I craned my head to look for the children but saw no one in the shadows. I walked home.

The four hours I had before Mark would return left me plenty of time to prepare food for our evening meal. So, I put together a care package for the children, adding a sharing bag of cheese puffs (I didn't mind volunteering my favourite snack to the cause) and left room for the pastries I'd buy again in the morning. I was scouting through the cupboards for more inspiration when Mark came through the door and peered nosily into my basket.

"Who are you feeding?" he asked, playfully suspicious. "Or are you planning on getting super hungry tomorrow?"

"Just helping someone out." I planted a kiss on his lips while wiping my hands on the tea towel. "Oh, I've already started our little undercover operation. Hopefully, I'll have something soon."

Knowing I was talking about Chie, Mark nodded and went to get changed while I served dinner.

Later, as I put on my shoes to attend a ministry meeting, Mark made it clear he would be asleep when I returned.

"I'll see you tomorrow."

Eager to reach ministry, I quickened my step. I needed guidance and prayer. I needed His protection. I would always try to do the right thing, even if it was the wrong thing in the eyes of Collective Thought. As I knew very well from my job, the truth could easily be manipulated. I was concerned about what was coming next after hearing Tisak's speech on Tuesday. I wondered whether we should be more vigilant now that religion was the centre of attention again on the I.N. stage. I wanted to know if the dates Tisak had revealed as our global celebrations were pertinent to anything historic or occultic. I had my suspicions that the quarterly holidays coincided with the solstices and equinoxes of pagan beliefs. I also needed to confide about Chie and the planned bomb attack. Maybe they had connections in London and might be able to get a message to someone there. I wanted to warn them.

I had offloaded my worries in prayer, but the burden hadn't left me; it had increased, if anything. Sleep had evaded me, and what rest I did get was plagued with the dreams of the man walking in the dark.

~

The first thing I revealed to my Nigerian hosts, the scarred Dan Hawkins and his wife, Claire, was that Mark had had some Christian teachings. I wanted to start on something positive before I mentioned the challenging subjects.

They gave me good advice, but the group said not to push things. Show, don't tell. Live by my faith. An old adage said, 'Don't tell me you're a Christian, let me guess,' and it was the best testimony to give.

I didn't need to voice my questions about Ciel Tisak. Claire was already seething. She said two roman goddesses, Pomona and Diana, had feast celebrations in August but couldn't recall the exact dates. With no record of the ancient lore remaining, it was impossible to check. She also thought the other celebration days were in line with the solstices and equinoxes.

Sharing the London bombing plans was difficult when watching the expressions on the faces in the room. Their quizzical expressions turned into wide-eyed horror as I revealed the details of Chie's telephone conversation and the facts of the burned case we had taken on illegally. They caught their breaths in shock.

The room fell silent until Dan leapt from his chair, and we launched into prayer. We pleaded for London, my brother-in-law, and the intervention of the Almighty. We prayed for strength, peace, and blessing for the church and the innocent. We exalted our God as the Sovereign Lord who reigns and asked for His will to be done.

~

It was gone ten when I slipped on my shoes, exhausted, and quivering from the anointed presence of God. The stars in the cloudless sky decorated an ominous moon over the shops on the main road.

There, something moved in the shadows. I kept peeping over my shoulder but didn't see anything lurking. Nevertheless, it was a worry to walk alone at night. Sex crime was at an all-new high, and the GBR (Grand British Republic) had the worst record compared with anywhere else. I reminded myself not to think about such things, and the hairs on my arms pricked. I ran, then laughed at myself as I closed my front door. Little Hampton was quite safe; it was my police force that kept the peace.

~

The bakery was heaving the next day. Something about Fridays, perhaps folk liked to treat themselves. After adding the pastries, a pack of wet wipes and some water, I left the heavy basket in the same place as yesterday, noting there was still no sign of the children. Or Teela when I got into work.

So much for us being a team when I had not seen or heard from her since lunchtime on Wednesday. I had given her time to decide on our approach, happy to follow her instructions, but she had not replied to my messages to give me any. So, at the end of another fruitless shift, I was worried, and frustrated when the only search result delivered since yesterday was not useful to either Chie or Greg.

I was eager to collect my basket and hoped to see it empty. Instead, it brought a lump to my throat to find a light-blue ribbon tied next to yesterday's red one in a neat bow. The red ribbon had been re-tied too.

The next day gave me a second red ribbon but brought me no breakthrough in either case I investigated. I didn't usually work Saturdays but wanted to leave a basket for the children and see if the lengthy, yet non-productive, search process had thrown out anything new overnight—it hadn't—and I had still not heard from Teela. So, I decided to go to her house and called Mark. He didn't keep me waiting long, and within fifteen minutes, we were on our way across town.

There was no escaping the questions once he saw how agitated I was, pale-faced, twisting my fingers in my lap and breathing heavily. I answered honestly, revealing Manchester's video call and the secret case file sent over. I briefly outlined the outcome of Teela's summons to meet at the bridge and how it had been the last time I saw or heard from her, adding Manchester had confided he was being watched.

Mark pressed his lips together while I talked, his expression widening in concern as I revealed my concerns. Teela had used an unknown number to contact me instead of her usual phone and forced me to meet her miles away because Manchester had told her to be careful. Although she'd asked me to investigate with her, she had not been in contact, and I was worried for her safety.

We pulled up outside her two-storey house. Her car was not on the drive, and the curtains in the lounge window were drawn. It was the middle of the afternoon.

Mark handed me the key. "Wait in the car."

I was about to protest when he put his hands up.

"I mean it, Anna. Wait in the car. Lock it when I get out; I'll be back in a sec."

Mark made his way down the drive and to the porch. He didn't knock, but pressed his ear to the door and listened, then crossed the lawn to peer in the lounge window, shielding light from his eyes with cupped hands. I wondered if there was a crack in the curtains and whether he could see anything. He glanced back at me briefly, then walked to the side gate and peeked over. He unbolted it and disappeared.

My eyes lingered there before they drifted to the neighbours' houses and the street in front. A little way up the road was a parked car. A black, sleek, fast-looking car. I was sure a figure moved in it. I lifted my phone and selected the camera, zooming in as much as possible to capture a clear image, then shook my head at my paranoia.

This isn't an action movie.

Mark tapped on the window, making me jump.

"Teela isn't here, but the back door is open. Do you want to have a look around? I couldn't see anything obvious. No mess, no broken glass, no…blood."

He didn't need to add 'blood'. The image of her dead body with a bullet hole between her eyes had already been there for two days, along with my own. I clambered out of my seat, shaking the thoughts away, and followed Mark into the lawned rear garden and through the back door.

There was nothing unusual, except for the bright afternoon sunlight trying to penetrate her closed lounge curtains. Everything was tidy, clean, and organised; nothing looked out of place. There was no writing on the pad I found on the kitchen table, no notes attached to the fridge, and no coded memos for me to solve as I walked around the other rooms of her small two-bed semi. It was as though she had left for work.

The light on the answering machine near the front door blinked incessantly. The message was not from me. Landlines were obsolete now, and I didn't know she could even have one. It tempted me. Just as I reached out to play it, I noticed her mobile resting next to the lamp. It was switched off and retina access secured, so I put it back and listened to the message left on Thursday evening.

"Shan, it's Fred. Amber alert on the meet tonight. Watch your step. Ditch the burner; it's compromised, and whatever you do, don't call me back. I'll find you. Be where we said if I don't catch up with you."

After recording the message into a voice file on my phone and deleting the original, I felt better.

Mark came into the hall just then, startling me again.

"Will you please stop creeping up on me?"

"Anna, look at the size of me; I couldn't creep anywhere in this jacket." His wax jacket sleeve scraped against the doorframe. "I had a scout outside. There's nothing in the garden or over the fences. I checked the garage and had a good look up and down the street. No cars, nothing."

No cars.

"Oh, you missed the sleek, sexy black sports car then?" I said as we started to head out. "Shame, you would've liked it. I thought I saw someone moving inside; they must have been just going out."

I felt embarrassed I had almost taken photographs of it.

"What do you make of this?"

I played him the message from 'Fred.' I assumed Shan was Teela, and they'd had a pre-arranged meeting last Thursday. Unfortunately, I couldn't be sure of when she was last home.

Mark was just pulling away from the kerb when one of Teela's neighbours emerged from their house.

"Wait, stop!"

I jumped out and approached the man to ask when he had last seen her or her car.

"Ooh, er, let me think, Wednesday I reckon it was. Yeah. I was puttin' the bins out, real late like. She was goin' in as I was comin' out. Didn't speak, mind."

I ignored the judgemental way his eyebrows rose and raced back to the car ahead of his shout of, "You're welcome."

"Not seen since Wednesday, same as me," I told Mark as we pulled away.

"This is looking serious, Anna. Shouldn't you report it or something? It sounds like she might be in trouble."

"I can't; then Teela really will be in trouble if they find out what she's investigating. Besides, that's why I called you. You're the help."

"What can I do?"

"More than Greg and the rest, I'm sure. They're trained in combat, but after seven years of sitting in front of a screen, they would be as much use as me."

Unconvinced, Mark tried to persuade me there must be someone at the station I could confide in, but his sentence trailed off.

"What?" I asked, glancing over my shoulder to see what he was looking at in his mirrors.

"Black sports car, you said?"

"Yes," I confirmed ominously.

"It's behind us, two cars back. I thought I saw it pull out and follow us, but I wanted to be sure. It's following, so we're not going home. Scenic route?"

I nodded and prayed quietly, feeling peaceful considering. When I had a husband who could protect me physically and a Father spiritually, what did I have to fear?

Twenty minutes later, Mark pulled onto a farm lane, then into the field and tucked the car abut to the thick bushes, switching everything off. We were entirely concealed from both roads. We waited nervously while the whooshing of the main road traffic continued. A car crawled past us on the farm track without stopping, and another a little while later.

It was approaching 4 o'clock, and we had sat silently in the car for thirty minutes, listening and watching.

"Do you think Teela got the message?"

"Let's hope so," Mark answered, taking my shaking hand and squeezing it gently, "because we've no way of finding her or where they met, and we don't know who Fred is. Did you try the burner number she messaged you on?"

I nodded. "There's no response."

"Well, let's hope it's ditched and not traced and captured, eh?"

That comment didn't help, and the longer we waited for the cover of dark to come, the more uneasy I became about the days ahead.

7 Jonah and Lily

While preparing food for the care basket, Mark came into the kitchen and saw me putting sandwiches into bags. He picked up the shop bought cake I had just put in and eyed it greedily.

"Who are you feeding? They get better goodies than I do!"

Taking the cake back, I replied, "Just a couple of kids. They don't break the bed when they sit down, so I don't need fruit as a dietary alternative!"

I laughed, remembering Mark upstairs watching the motor racing. I'd taken him a sausage and bacon baguette. As he perched on the edge of the bed to take the plate from me, the side panel snapped, and Mark dropped to the floor. I had pulled the plate back, suggesting I go and fetch him fruit instead.

Mark smiled. "Haha, very funny. Don't get sucked in, though, eh? There're lazy buggers out there who shove grubby kids on the streets for begging, so they don't have to go to work."

"It's just food. I haven't given them money. I don't think they're hustling; you've not seen them."

I picked up the full basket, kissed Mark, and walked to the high street, ensuring I allowed plenty of time to reach Dan and Claire's for ministry. I left the food in the usual place and returned later that afternoon.

I noticed the peeking boy hiding behind the wall of the alleyway entrance but didn't see him again until I turned the corner. He held out my basket with the little girl beside him and not hiding like last time. Instead, she clutched a doll tightly to her chest, wearing a stained yellow dress and staring with large, blue eyes that gazed from my face to my ID badge, back and forth as I came closer. It wasn't the first time they had eyed my badge, and it was always with fear.

The girl pointed at it and whispered, "Devil workers."

I stopped in surprise.

"Shush, Lily."

The boy stepped forward, pressing the empty basket against my unresponsive hand.

"Thanks for the food."

Taking it, I looked at him fully for the first time. He was pale-skinned with a round, freckled face, full strong cheekbones beneath wise yet hollow eyes. His hair was shaved, though longer now than when I first saw him. He seemed lively and about twelve years old, although he didn't seem tall enough to be twelve. He was too thin for the khaki shorts and white t-shirt he wore, but there was the strength of young muscles in his arms and legs.

I looked at the basket and the four pretty ribbons tied in neat bows, two red and two blue. Then, next to them, I saw something glisten and swing against the edge. I peered closer and lifted the earring carefully. It had a small navy ball near the clasp at the top, and from there came long, thin wires adorned with hopefully fake jewels that then bent back into another navy ball at the bottom to create a three-dimensional diamond.

"It was our mother's," the boy whispered. "Lily wanted you to have it. She was sorry she'd used all the wet wipes washing her dollies, and as she'd run out of ribbons–"

"Coz we nearly got caught pinchin' more from the shop," she interrupted.

"Lily!" The boy gave her a nudge with his elbow, causing her to squeal and rub her shoulder. "I'm sure the nice lady don't wanna hear that."

"Well, we did, though, Jonah, didn't we? And we had nothing else to give her."

"You're right, little sister," Jonah conceded, "we almost got caught." He smiled a cheeky grin, and she grinned back.

"You don't need to give me anything, especially not something as important as your mother's earring. Please, take it back."

I was looking at the clasp to see if I could remove it when a sad, quiet little voice stilled my fingers.

"You…you don't…like it?"

I quickly crouched down and looked into her watery eyes.

"Yes, Lily. It's beautiful. Absolutely beautiful. I can see that you love it so much. I'd like you to keep it."

"I do," she said sadly, "but I have another I love just as much, and you can keep that one."

Lily beamed, and I smiled back.

"Thank you."

Before I could find my way to ask about their parents and where the children were sleeping, Jonah stepped forward.

"You should know somebody's watching you. He's always hanging around, hiding, waiting, following you. He's not here today, though. Only fair to warn you. Thanks again for the food."

My brain froze at the words 'somebody's watching you'. I heard them, but they didn't compute. My chest tightened, and the children had slipped away by the time I was ready to ask for clarification.

I turned and ran the whole way home. If anyone wanted to follow me, they could go right ahead—if they could keep up. I was fast. I was a county-cross-country-high-school-trophy-winner, and as it was Sunday, I was in trainers and jeans, which meant I could properly run.

My lungs were screaming when I burst into the kitchen. Mark was perched at the breakfast bar, scrolling on his phone while munching on a roll and was surprised to see me coming through the back door rather than the front. Strands of damp hair stuck to my neck, and my t-shirt was sopping wet.

"Look at the state of you!"

I let the basket fall at my feet and leaned on the worktop, hyperventilating.

"Anna, what's happened?"

Mark swore and fetched me a glass of water. I was not sure if it was shock or fear, but I didn't want to tell him and for him to get angry.

"Is it Teela?"

"No," I said, shaking my head, "those children…they told me a man's been following me. I've just run home through the park."

Mark was off the stool and straight out of the front door. By the time I reached him, he had gone up and down the street, checking every stationary car for lurking spies. We were okay; Mark hadn't needed to drag anyone out of their motors and risk committing a crime.

Back inside, I locked the door and inhaled to speak. Mark put his finger to his lips, checked all doors and windows, drew the curtains and blinds as he went, then checked the smoke alarms and changed the batteries. I hoped there wouldn't be a reason for those to go off.

In the lounge, Mark hiked up the volume on the TV, and the kitchen radio the same, then drew me into a slow dance to the tune on the radio. He brought his lips close to my ear and spoke low.

"I'm taking precautions, that's all. I'll fetch a sweeper from work and check for bugs and cameras. I'll go in a minute."

"Not without me, you're not," I whispered back. "I'm not staying here on my own."

"It's too suspicious. I'd rather they stay here watching you than follow me. The sweeper at Thurstworthy is the best there is. It's only two months old and automatically updates itself. Lock up, watch a film, and I'll be back before it's finished. We have to know if there's anything in here, and we have to know now."

Mark was right, so I didn't argue. He took my hands and looked intently into my eyes, love glistening through his anxious expression, then he pressed his lips to mine. Neither of us breathed as we held each other. I was afraid; he was leaving me. I was in danger and felt vulnerable as I sat alone in the lounge, staring at a movie I wasn't watching. Forty-five minutes, I reasoned. I could allow the twenty minutes each way, and perhaps five minutes wasn't generous enough for him to fetch and load the equipment he needed, but it was all I was prepared to give him. Forty-five minutes.

Thirty-seven.

Twenty-eight.

The strong, northerly wind bashed the long branches of the rose bush against the lounge window. I started. Although I was used to the scratching sounds, my senses were on high alert.

Breathe. Lord, please shut my nerves up.

Twenty-one minutes.

Sixteen.

My knuckles were sore; I uncurled my fingers, stretching them long and wide. Finally, my mobile buzzed to life—I sprang off the settee, but it was only Mark.

"Hey."

"Just on my way back."

Twenty minutes. Again.

"How's the film?"

"Edgy," I replied, not referring to the movie. I peered through the window at the quiet street.

"Get a bottle of wine on the chill. Relax, not long now. I'm speeding, so I need to get off the phone."

Hunting out a bottle of wine from the garage and reorganising the fridge so I could safely fit it in took my waiting time down to nine minutes. It was approaching a quarter to four when I heard a car turn into the street. I heard it slowing, tyres hitting a low ridge and the slight squeak of the brakes. A car door opened and closed, then another opened and closed. A bleep, orange lights.

I ran to the door and opened it just as Mark appeared on the front step holding a black carry case. I locked up and followed him into the kitchen. The worktop was already littered with sleek tech that he had unpacked and was now organising. He assembled the pieces with a push and a slide, and a click into place.

The handheld unit was switched on a few minutes later, emitting a high-frequency hum. We moved through the house together. It whirred and whined, beeped, and buzzed, flashing symbols and lights which meant nothing to me. Mark didn't show concern as we shifted from room to room, with me right up behind him. I was so close to him that I got in the way frequently, and Mark had to keep minding his step.

We finished up back in the kitchen, where the handheld squeaked and made a high-toned purr. It didn't like being near the back door or the breakfast bar. Mark put down the scanner and checked underneath, first with his eyes, then with his fingers, pushing them into the edges and corners, checking for holes and bumps that shouldn't be there. Then he slid his hands quickly around and down the leg supports before picking up the monitor and moving towards the back door. He held the scanner near the light switch and sockets, but it was lower down the wall that it really started screaming. The wall beneath the breakfast bar, the area Mark had already checked.

"What is it?" I wondered aloud.

Puzzled, Mark shook his head, shifting his shoulders up and down. He paused to think, then ventured into the garden, returning with a small, opened box.

"Someone's left a phone," he said with a grin, "I bet Teela's left you a phone."

I sighed in relief. The note he handed me was written in Teela's handwriting. *I will call you.* I took out the mobile and slipped it into my back pocket, grateful she was safe and hadn't forgotten to contact me. Grateful too that we hadn't been bugged. My home had not been invaded, and although I couldn't be sure no one had been in the house, Mark was certain they had left nothing behind.

Free of devices, we were able to speak openly. I fretted, pulling the phone out of my back pocket and checking it was switched on and still working.

"I wish she'd call."

Mark took me into his arms and hugged me close. I could feel his warm breath on my head.

"At least you know she's all right. She'll call when she can."

I pulled away and grabbed two wine glasses, and then we sat down in the living room, each taking a sofa for ourselves.

"How do the I.N. even know? And me. Why are they watching me?"

"Can't say for Teela, but you are Chie's sister-in-law. They're bound to be watching, waiting to arrest him if he comes here."

"Here, yes, but he's not likely to pop up on the high street and walk me home, is he? Jonah said the man was hanging around and following me."

I thought back to the pub where Mark and I had lunch, to the stranger who kept staring, and then the night when I walked home from ministry with the sense that something lurked in the shadows.

"Jonah?"

Mark's question pierced through my thoughts.

"The children, Jonah and Lily," I answered automatically as a small part of my brain registered I hadn't referred to the children by name before. I was still working through my memories, coming now to the sleek, black sports car I'd seen following us out of Teela's road yesterday.

I shifted in my seat. "This is something more, I reckon, Mark. This is connected to the Manchester thing as well. I am convinced the two things are linked. The I.N. must have figured out Manchester had contacted us and worked it out quickly if Teela's been hiding since Wednesday, the day after we received the file." It seemed incredibly suspicious to me. "Then mix that with Chie being family–"

"And you end up with us paranoid as heck and me wondering if we should have a jammer up and running!" interrupted Mark. "I have all my training going on in here at once–" Mark tapped his skull, "and I'm constantly double-checking for things I might've missed. Am I overreacting? This is harder work than the Manor!"

"At least you know what to look for. At least you'd notice the signs."

I was overcome with dread suddenly, and I stiffened. It was Monday tomorrow, my day off.

"Don't leave me tomorrow! Can you call in sick? Please? Stay with me. Will you?"

"I'm going to do more than that," he answered firmly, "we will get you a car."

Mark looked surprised that I didn't protest, even if I did look a bit shocked.

"You aren't arguing, so I assume you feel the same as me about you walking to and from work, etc." (etc., meaning 'church' stuff) "and until you're on the road, no more buses, no more walking, all right?"

I had always argued about the necessity of having my own car. I lived fifteen minutes away from anywhere I needed to be. Mark and I shopped together in his car; I hadn't needed to drive. I could drive; I had a license, but I hadn't a need until now.

~

At eight o'clock, Mark and I were cuddled up together on the settee, enjoying our second glass of wine, when it seemed like the air was sucked out of the room, and my ears began to ring. The ground vibrated beneath us, and I jumped up. The buzz came up through my socked feet all the way to my head, like a ripple. Then I heard the deep, distant rumble.

"Earthquake?" I asked Mark in surprise. They were rare in the GBR.

"I don't know."

The noise grumbled on.

"Where are your keys?" I asked, running into the kitchen.

He followed me, bemused. "Why?"

I found them and snatched them up, replying, "I'm going to get Jonah and Lily and don't argue with me about it."

"I flaming will argue," he cried, grabbing my wrist and prising the keys from my clenched fist. "You are not driving my car. You've not driven for six years, and you ain't getting familiar in my Range Rover!"

Good job he wasn't bothered about my plans to bring Jonah and Lily home. I was already standing at the passenger door, drumming my fingers on the car roof impatiently, waiting for him to unlock it and drive me. People milled in the street, grouped together, debating what the rumbling was. Finally, the vibrations began to subside, and I had all but forgotten the threat of the mysterious watchman as I stood there, alone, stubbornly waiting for Mark. I understood the fear that others felt, but my concern at the time was for those two surely, terrified kids.

Towards the open front door, I yelled, "Are you taking me or what?"

"I'm getting my shoes on."

Shoes! I looked down at my socked feet. Ah, trainers would be good. Mark appeared in the doorway and threw them at me. I slipped them on, and we drove to the high street without seeing any damage to the town along the way.

"Pull up here," I instructed and got out near the charity shop.

I ran into the dark alleyway.

"Jonah!" I called quietly. I listened, but no sound came. "Jonah!" a little louder.

The door above my head squeaked open, and the loose letterbox flapped. I looked up. Jonah was peering down from the top of the steps.

"Miss?"

Lord, had I not told them my name?

"Are either of you hurt?" I asked, going up the steps. I stopped halfway because he flinched in fear with his palms raised and backed away towards his door.

"It's Anna."

"We're all right." He puffed out his chest again, clearly trying to hide the fear in his eyes. "I'm not scared."

"I'm sure you aren't, but I am, and I won't settle not knowing if you're both safe."

"Nothing even fell off the wall. Seen scarier things in one of Lily's films," he crowed with false bravado, then craned his neck to look behind me.

I turned. Mark was in the alleyway.

"Jonah, this is my husband, Mark. I told him how you helped me by telling me about that man. He's grateful and wanted to come and thank you."

Jonah looked wary as Mark moved up behind me. He studied him carefully, then seemed to relax.

"Hullo."

Mark leaned over my shoulder, offering his fist, and Jonah tread cautiously forward to bump it.

"Cheers for what you did, buddy," Mark said awkwardly, stepping back and allowing me some room.

Jonah shrugged but said nothing.

"Jonah, I'd really like it if you and Lily came to our house for a bit. You're here alone, aren't you? I don't think I can leave without you two coming with me, not with the threat of an earthquake."

Jonah frowned. "Miss?"

I could feel a vibe rolling off Mark as he reached out and touched my arm for my attention. I didn't move my gaze from Jonah, my eyes pleading with him.

"Will you come?"

The question hung in the air. Then I saw tiny fingers pushing through the letterbox, and a quiet voice whispered,

"Let's."

Lily was keen, at least.

"One sec."

Opening the door carefully and minding his sister, Jonah stepped inside. I heard mumbled voices and Lily whining, "I want to go," and Jonah shushed her. Then it went quiet.

"Anna, are you sure about this?"

"Never been surer."

"Other than the fact you're inviting two strangers into our home–"

"Children," I said over him.

"–that you know nothing about; we have the other little problem remember? With the I.N. in case you've forgotten."

"I haven't forgotten."

Lily came through the door first with a little bag in one hand and an armful of dolls in the other. She wore pink pyjamas and red slippers, her corn-coloured hair flowing freely without the ribbons tied to my basket. She beamed at me, scrunching her shoulders excitedly and whispered,

"I'm not dressed!"

I laughed and playfully said, "Well, aren't you naughty!"

Lily joined us at the bottom of the steps, giggling. She let go of her bag and grabbed my hand.

While we waited for Jonah, I stole a look at Mark. He was obviously touched by the sight of Lily standing beside me with what appeared to be all her worldly goods.

I crouched down to Lily, pointed, and said, "That's Mark."

"Is he your boyfriend?" she whispered shyly.

"Better," I replied, "husband!"

She drew in a breath. "I'm going to have one, one day."

"I'm sure you will," I agreed, looking up the steps to the door left ajar. "What is your brother up to?"

"He's securing the room," she said casually, then dropped to a whisper, "there's a lot to do!"

Jonah rushed through the door just then, pulling it shut and locking it. He came down the steps carrying his own bag and waving a toothbrush.

"Forget something, Lily?"

He shoved it into the pocket of her bag and then swung it up onto his free shoulder.

Mark led us out to the car, first checking up and down the street before letting us through. He popped the boot, and Jonah placed the bags while I put Lily in the back seat and strapped her in. We didn't own any car seats: there was no need.

Lily's face lit up when we pulled into the drive. She climbed from her seat and took in our house. The navy curtains were still drawn in the large front window that overlooked the front lawn. The driveway ended at the white garage door, down the side of the house, where Mark was opening the front door.

After locking up. I took off my shoes. Immediately, Lily and Jonah did the same.

"You don't need to," Mark said, bending down to Lily's feet and putting hers back on, "you're wearing slippers."

I showed them where the downstairs bathroom was right beside the front door, and as I led them into the living room, I pointed the way into the kitchen.

"Would you like something to drink? We have orange squash or milk if you prefer?"

Lily was arranging her dolls into a row on the sofa, making sure each had some cushion behind their backs.

"Milk, please," she answered as she smoothed the fabrics of their dress skirts and fussed with their feet.

Jonah sat on the floor next to Lily's knees. "Me too, thanks."

The worried Mark looked up from taking the handheld apart as I entered the kitchen.

"It can't be safe for them here under the circumstances. You're not thinking properly," he reprimanded.

"I'd rather here than there, alone in the middle of an earthquake, which, um, appears to have stopped now." I paused in pouring the milk. "If that's even what it was. I wouldn't have slept without checking, and I couldn't just leave them. I didn't want to leave them."

Mark pointed to their bags abandoned at the foot of the stairs. "Is this all they have?"

"It's all they brought," I replied, picking up the glasses. I took them to the lounge and placed them on the small table.

"How are we doing?" I asked, peering at the dolls. "Well, they seem happy enough."

Lily flushed and introduced them from left to right.

"This is Megan, Sally, Sunshine, Millie, Banana Split… 'cause look."

She lifted the yellow fabric doll and pulled its legs open to reveal fluff pushing through a split in the seam.

"See? Banana Split. And this one," she said lovingly as she scooped it up into her arms and hugged it tightly, "is Melanie."

"Is she your favourite?"

She nodded.

"I know a girl called Melanie, but do you know what she asked me to call her?"

Lily shook her head.

"Melly!"

Lily started giggling. "Melly, Melly, Melly. I think I like it!" She beamed.

"She has a little girl your age too. Her name is Arla."

"Is she six too? I'm six, ain't I, Melanie?"

She started to hum a tune.

I turned to see Jonah scanning our films, itching to pull one out to look at. Hard disc copies had grown popular again since the internet had to be shut down. Glory to Tisak for building another to save us. I gave Jonah the go-ahead to put a film on if he wanted and shuffled out of the door.

Mark was emptying Lily's bag onto the kitchen table. He handed me a pair of knickers full of holes and her stained dress—the smallest of night bags. I raised my eyebrows. Where were their parents?

Neither of us felt right about looking through Jonah's bag. So instead, I quietly asked him to come into the kitchen.

"Is there anything you need that you don't have?" I held up Lily's pants.

"Always!" He grinned, then shrugged.

"Where are your parents?"

Mark didn't mean to be intimidating but leaning against the cooker like that and with his tone aggravated, he was, and Jonah recoiled.

"Sorry," Mark whispered quietly. "I'm angry you've been left alone."

"It isn't their fault," cried Jonah, quick to defend his parents, "they didn't leave us, they…"

Dread came over me. Oh Jesus, please, not dead. Not dead.

It was too quiet. Lily had stopped humming. I turned to see her standing in the doorway with tears falling down her cheeks, leaving clean streaks on her skin.

"Devil workers took them."

Mark frowned at me.

"You said that once before; what do you mean by devil workers?" I asked, dabbing at her eyes and cheeks with kitchen roll.

She pushed by me, picked up my ID badge and pointed to the logo.

"Devil workers," she muttered.

Mark looked at Jonah.

"The I.N. took them?"

Jonah nodded.

"When?"

"September last year."

I gasped. "You've been living alone for seven months?"

"Do you know why, Jonah?" Mark asked now.

"A little bit. He said mum and dad were NCs, so they were arrested."

"Who said?"

"Our landlord. He was there when they took them away. He hid us in the shop downstairs and said we could stay in the flat until he rented it."

Lily was getting upset again. I scooped her up in my arms.

"Did you finish your milk?"

She nodded.

"How about a lovely, warm bubble bath?"

Her face lit up with delight.

"C'mon then. Jonah, there's a shower in our room you can use. Let me run the water for Lily, and it's all yours."

"Thank you, Miss."

"Anna, please," I said, laughing. "I'm not a schoolteacher."

I left Mark and Jonah talking while I swept Lily upstairs to run the bath. She splashed and popped bubbles and sent me downstairs three times to fetch a doll she wanted, and I kept returning deliberately with the wrong one.

"Not that one," she'd said with a tut. "That one will get all wet. The one in the blue dress."

To her amusement, I went again and deliberately picked up the one in the green dress.

"Oh, Anna, you're so funny."

I realised Mark had gone out. I peeked out of the landing window to see the empty drive, but by the time Lily was washed, dried and wrapped up in her towel, Mark appeared in the doorway of the spare bedroom.

"I hope you don't mind," he said to Lily, "but I got you a few things."

He handed her a large bag, and she emptied it over the bed. Lots of clothes: cute little dresses, some jeans, tops, and underwear, printed with designs of the latest Risney INc princess cartoon character. I picked up the black and yellow striped pyjamas and laughed.

"What are they?" Lily asked, turning the top around and trying to decide.

"Pyjamas."

"Really?" she asked, surprised, "not dress up?"

Mark laughed half-heartedly—he was hiding something.

"Bees are the new thing this spring," he told her. "There are not many of them left, you know."

Lily dropped her towel to get dressed into the bee pyjamas, and Mark spun around, embarrassed.

Before closing the door behind him, he said, "When you're finished, Anna, I need to speak to you."

I was just putting away the last of Lily's clothes when my back pocket vibrated. Teela's phone was ringing. I rushed downstairs as I answered it, leaving Lily to finish her teeth.

"It wasn't London, Anna; it was Manchester, and I mean the whole of Manchester…is…is gone."

"What?"

"You felt it, right? I felt it; I'm not that far away."

"Yes, we felt it. That was a bomb?" I looked at Mark. "Manchester is gone."

"Who, the I.N. guy?"

"No, Mark. The city of Manchester."

The colour drained from his face.

"Chie," he whispered.

Oh, Lord!

8 It Was A Show, A Ballet

"Anna? Are you there?"

I lifted the phone back to my ear.

"Sorry, Teela, Mark's brother is in Manchester."

"There's nobody there anymore. It's literally just devastation now. I've been busy the last few days. I was on the phone with Karl when the line cut. The bomb didn't even make a sound, Anna. The rumbling came from the buildings collapsing, every single one for twenty miles. They tell me the vibrations started a tremor that took out more buildings right up to Liverpool."

I couldn't respond. Twenty miles, no, forty miles? Bolton, Wigan, Warrington? Gone. Greater Manchester was destroyed, not London. I sat down. I vaguely heard Jonah crying out, wanting to be told what was happening. Mark and I just sat, speechless, unable to deal with a situation that seemed so unreal.

"Are you still there?" she asked. Before I could respond, she added, "I'm sorry I took so long to call you; I'd just got into town ten minutes before the rumbling started, and I just couldn't stop watching it. I–"

"Watch it? Is it finally on the news?"

I jumped up to switch it on, stirring Mark into action. He stilled my hand, nodding towards Jonah at the same time that Teela responded.

"Not yet, reported, but no pictures or anything. I think people are too stunned. I was, and I knew what it was. I had discovered how soon it was too and found out some of the plans had changed, but I couldn't get in deep enough to see what they were. Guess, now I know."

"How were you watching it then? And who's Karl?"

"Karl is Manchester from the e-chat, and we..." She started to cry, then breathed slowly. "Sorry, we'd been working together these last few days. I've just come back from Manchester...urgh, I feel sick...we had a drone about a mile up that could peep right into your bathroom if we wanted it to. Man, this drone is awesome. I saw everything, clear as you like."

I thought I heard her vomit.

"T?"

"Is your house being watched?"

"Not that we've seen, but there's been a man following me, and your house had somebody on it. We managed to lose them. No one's been at our house as far as we can tell."

"I'm coming there then; don't be surprised to hear me coming in through the kitchen."

Our back gate led to fields, easy access for the athletic Teela to climb over it without trouble. I put the phone down with a trembling hand and faced an empty room. I hadn't noticed the boys leave. Hearing creaky floorboards, I went upstairs to investigate. Mark was on the bed with Lily and Jonah, scrolling through the listings on the telly. Lily was still making buzzing bee sounds, crawling around on the double bed the children would have to share for a while.

"Anna! We're going to watch a movie, aren't we, Jonah? We haven't seen a movie in ages. Our telly doesn't work." She bounced on the bed, and Jonah told her off.

I forced a smile. "What are you going to watch?"

She breathed in, ready to answer when Jonah chipped in.

"Please, no princesses. Or fairies."

"What about magic fishes?" she pondered.

Jonah shrugged, then smiled. "Fish are okay. Magic sounds better!"

Jonah wore the new black pyjamas Mark had bought. I picked up the few t-shirts to put away in the drawer and noticed the age on their labels.

"You're only ten?" I asked, surprised. I had thought he was older.

Offended, Jonah's chest puffed out. "Nearly eleven, next month."

Once the children were settled, Mark and I returned to our bottle of wine. Shock, grief, new responsibilities; things that had been waiting in the wings while we focussed on the children, fell at our feet like weights now that we were alone. Mark downed his glass and poured another.

I rushed forward and slipped my arms around his waist as tightly as I could until I couldn't breathe and had to slacken my grip. He sobbed into my hair while my own tears rolled, neither of us knowing what to say. I started to wonder why the target had changed. The I.N. had manufactured evidence tying Chie to a bomb threat in London, and I winced at my ease in accepting that they had framed Mark's brother. So, why change the target to Manchester? Chie had said on the phone he was there. Manchester guy, Karl, was there, along with the rest of his team. They were aware of the plot just as much as Teela, who was also there that day.

Grimacing, I assumed the I.N. had decided it was too good an opportunity to pass up. Oh, Lord, poor Chie, poor Mark. I silently prayed for them as I held Mark, not finding any words to use to comfort him. Not finding any thoughts to console myself.

I sensed the peace of God upon me. I felt the warmth rush through, instantly calming my fearful heart and stretched nerves—a sudden calm. Someone was praying. It was a knowing that God was sovereign and reigned always. Despite the political situation and fears, Jesus brought freedom. Jesus had taken the scales from my eyes, and I looked at the world with spiritual discernment.

Did Chie have faith? It wasn't something you asked or something on show. There were no such things as crucifix jewellery or hijabs anymore. There was no true diversity: society had been fully cultivated into Collective Thought. Inane. We all acted as though we did, said, and thought in the same way, but we were our old selves in private, the same as always.

Teela burst through the back door, startling us both. Before she spoke, she whipped the half-empty wine glass off the counter and finished it.

"I needed that," she said, holding the glass out towards me for a refill.

Mark saw to it. I gave her a long hug.

"I'm glad you're all right."

"Alive, but I don't know about all right." Her eyes darted about, making sure no one could see in.

She handed me a thin laptop case.

"Go ahead if you dare. Open it up and watch what those bas–"

I looked up from unzipping the case when she stopped. Mark squeezed past me to Jonah, who had appeared at the bottom of the stairs.

"Hey bud, is the film finished?"

"No, I, uh, heard voices..."

Surprised to see a child in my house, Teela gulped and forced a smile.

"Hi, sorry. I didn't realise you had company."

"This is Jonah. He and his sister are staying with us for a while–"

"A short while," Jonah butted in. He returned Teela's smile before speaking to Mark. "I'll go back up, sorry."

Making sure Jonah had retreated properly up the stairs, Teela said, "Maybe not watch that right now, eh? It's not for kids."

Outraged, she ushered us into the lounge.

"Flipping heck, I can't believe it. I knew it was coming, but still, I can't believe it. I've never seen an explosion like it. Ever."

She started pacing. "Tisak's got a lot to answer for 'cause if this were him, he had no problem with wiping out one of his own."

I frowned, confused.

"Braithwaites was in Bolton," explained Teela hopelessly.

Another check for the change of target. Lots of birds. One bomb.

"Who's Braithwaites?" Mark asked, not knowing the details of the Manchester case.

"They were one of the companies linked to the missing girls. Handy that one big part of the trail happens to be destroyed, leaving nobody to expose them."

"Not quite nobody." Teela was still pacing.

"Teela, come sit down. Tell me what you've been doing."

"What do you think I've been doing?" Teela hissed. Then remorseful, she sat down. "Sorry."

Nervous energy transferred to her hands which she steadied by grabbing a cushion and crushing it to her chest.

"I have to tell you something first before explaining everything." She paused to drink another mouthful of wine. "I have connections, well, *friends* outside the I.N. that I consult with sometimes."

"This wouldn't be Fred, would it?"

I reached for my phone while her head snapped up in surprise.

"How did you...?"

I played the message recorded at Teela's house.

"I didn't know if you'd heard it, but I deleted it from your machine, just in case."

"Yeah," she whispered, "good move. I don't know Fred. The meeting was set up through my friends, which didn't turn out the way I planned. The I.N. found out about it somehow. Like the message said, probably through the burner phone I'd used to contact Karl—once I discovered who he was."

Teela swigged more wine.

"My friends must have detected the trace and tried to let me know. I was already in Manchester by then, though. So I didn't know to ditch the phone and be more careful. Fred never showed up, a lorry load of I.N. soldiers did instead, and I was almost caught! I managed to slip past them and hopped on a tram. Funny though, when I got away, I realised I had dropped the phone. That stroke of luck saved my life."

"Thank you, Lord, for Your protection," I muttered under my breath.

"The I.N. obviously had tabs on Karl, which alerted them to me when I contacted him. Then they put tabs on me, and you," she looked at Mark and me, "probably the rest of the team too, and then my informer friends, but they'd be onto that." Teela chuckled. "They deflect everything to somewhere in the Oriental Emirates.

"When I got back to my…safehouse, my friends had left me one of these babies in the early hours of Friday morning." Teela pointed to our phones and smiled weakly. "I practically had to beg for yours; I knew you'd be fretting as usual!"

Mark snickered. He knew me as well as she did.

"That's why I couldn't call you before Saturday night. It isn't safe for you to use your phone, and I couldn't be sure how deeply they were watching you, so I left it in the night on Saturday and headed back to Manchester. Karl and I met at dawn this morning. Thanks to my friends, we had spent two days planning everything through secure chat, and when I got there, the drone was already in the air, whirring to go. We were tracking someone embedded into one of Stymer's companies. I have really extraordinary friends, and they know things. I don't ask how; I just take what they tell me, which is always true and follow the lead. They are why I'm so good at what I do."

"Are they NCs?"

"No, not exactly. They are 'Asiders'. Neither I.N. nor NC loyalists, but with connections to each and masters in both. These people have managed to keep their common sense and not be drawn into the collective, and they're not violent. Of course, the NC criminal policy includes everyone anti-Tisak and anti-Collective Thought, but that doesn't make them criminals. Well, it does technically, but it shouldn't. So yes, Asiders is a perfect description."

"Are you an Asider too, then?" I asked, intrigued.

Teela didn't answer; instead, she swallowed more wine and backtracked to her morning with Karl.

"When I got there, the drone was up, fully programmed with the details of the man we were looking for, and off it went. I told you on the phone if we wanted to watch you through a tiny crack in a window, we could, and you wouldn't even know about it. Scary thought, eh? It can detect voices, faces, cars, gases, and anything you ask it to detect. It eventually will. We found 'Mr Perkins,'" she acted out the rabbit ears, "carefully disguised in a local market through his conversation with the stallholder. Voice recognition. He's at my safehouse now with an associate, and luckily for them, they aren't in the city anymore. I just wish I'd persuaded Karl to come, but he thought it was best not to raise suspicion, so he went about his usual business. He didn't want to go on the run. Took his chances and lost, I guess."

"Associate, as in NC?" Mark asked.

"Yes. My friends, the Asiders, told Fred where I would be, and he sent Tom to babysit. I don't know why Fred didn't come. Anyway, we detained Javad Shirvani far too easily. He didn't bother to put up much of a fight. He was resigned to capture and execution, almost relieved for it to be over. I'll let him fill you in on the details of that another time. The reason the drone was still watching and the explosion recorded was because we were looking for your brother, Chie."

I took Mark's hand, empathising with the grief that lined his features.

"I asked Karl to find him for us. It was sweeping over Manchester city centre when the bomb went off. Karl was in the middle of saying the drone hadn't found anything in four hours. Highly unusual. I thought this group must be deep underground. Then, total silence. I didn't hear an explosion, which ordinarily you would before the lines go down, but nothing. Then we felt it."

I looked up when she fell quiet.

"I thought it was an earthquake at first. How stupid. But you don't expect to feel a bomb going off as far away as London. It's why Jonah and Lily are here. Oh, we should check on them," I said, getting out of my seat.

~

Both children were fast asleep as the title music played quietly on TV. Lily had Melanie tucked under her chin, her mouth slightly open and gently snoring. Strands of blonde hair framed her rosy cheeks. I turned to Jonah, clearly seeing his age now. Just a boy. In the ease of sleep, it was plain. He was clean, relaxed, and all tension and worry had left his features. With his eyes closed, you couldn't see the strain they held. Most surprising to me was that he slept sucking his thumb.

Fighting back the tears, I inhaled and pulled up the covers—neither stirred—then switched off the TV before heading out of the door with one last peek behind me. I was falling for those children. I shouldn't; I mustn't, but I feared it was already too late. I decided I would try to find out about their parents on Tuesday if I went back to work.

Mark and Teela were huddled together on the sofa, the laptop on Mark's knees. The look on his face was new to me, a mix of anger, disgust, and grief. It was too much. A hardening had shaped his countenance. Was this the moment people described as a life-changing event? One that never left them the same again?

I walked behind the sofa so I could see what they were watching. It was an aerial view of the centre of Manchester. I spotted the railway arches next to Manchester Piccadilly in the distance. The drone glided past the hospital, over the university complex, and turned towards Manchester's new I.N. sports complex that consisted of the Olympic village and Manchester City's football ground.

The athletic Olympic village came into view simultaneously as the centre of its grass started to open, and a cylindrical structure appeared in its place.

Teela paused the frame and looked over her shoulder at me.

"This drone is like nothing else. It's pansophic, so to speak. It has tiny cameras like a halo. It sees everything, hears everything, and records everything so perfectly that you can zoom in and out with no graining or blurring. Perfect. It might make you feel a bit sick, though, when the angles switch. Nothing compared to how sick you're going to feel."

"I can't watch it again. I need some air."

Mark got up and left when Teela unpaused the video.

The view rolled into the eye of the next camera, then the next, angling slightly differently every time. It was regular enough to bring about motion sickness, but I dared not look away as it zoomed in on a brilliant pillar of white light only three or four feet high, shooting up from the cylinder. It swelled at the top, middle, and bottom to become the pressure points for the rings that now burst out from them.

The release was like nothing I had known. It was a show, a ballet. Precise and in perfect unity. Those rings pulled the white light out like a blanket through the city. The brightest of white at its centre and its fringes darkening to a sky blue as it travelled. There was no bang, no fire, no smoke.

Then it was gone. The white light caught up with the blue, and nothing happened for a second or two. It seemed Manchester needed a moment to contemplate before it fell to the ground, buildings collapsing where they stood and trees in three pieces around its stump, its bark split along the lengths of the logs that remained.

That's when I heard it. The moment I knew a bomb had gone off. Seeing it was one thing, but hearing it? I understood now how the vibrations could travel almost 200 miles to my feet, taking out another twenty miles along the way.

The screen swooped over the landscape showing mile upon mile of almost neat piles of smoking rubble, many with their unbroken rooves sitting atop them like hats. Chie was in one of those heaps somewhere, and I looked away. I couldn't bear to watch anymore, not even tempted when it flicked back to the start. I closed the lid firmly. Those images would stay with me. I knew they would replay in my dreams every time I slept. I didn't need to watch the devastation again to ensure I had noted every significant detail. It was seared into my memory like a branding.

It was a breathtaking scene to behold—the beauty of its purity, elegance, and strength—and yet, the worst thing I had ever seen.

"You know the blast itself took less than a second. We slowed the footage down!" Teela murmured, still staring at the closed lid of the laptop. "Everything was so normal; I was watching the drone live, expecting to find your brother-in-law. The flash was so quick it didn't register at first. All I saw was everything crumbling..." She took a deep breath. "Minutes later, I felt the tremor."

I felt helpless. I sat feeling my way through numb and muddled thoughts, forcing pictures away before I started screaming. Time ran on as we sat, sighing through our tortured memories.

Teela stood up suddenly. "I should get back. I haven't slept since Friday. You have the secure number if you need me. I'll be in touch about a meeting with Shirvani, and we can get to the bottom of all this. At least, we can try to find some closure for the girls' parents. There's nothing we can do for Manchester now but execute whoever is responsible, and I will, Anna, make no mistake."

"You sure you're not one of these Asiders?" I half-smiled.

"I'm more NC, if I'm honest," she replied and slipped out of the door before I could react.

My mind reeled. I would never have guessed she sympathised with the NC in all the years I had known her. An Asider perhaps, but not a violent criminal. What was I to do with that revelation? Where did my loyalties lie? And what did she know that I didn't, capable of turning her away from Tisak, who she once loved and admired? I was a Christian. My loyalty would always be to the truth in my Father's Word. He was the one who had opened my eyes. Who had opened hers?

I went looking for Mark and found him sitting motionless on the landing carpet beside the children's door, depressed and withdrawn. As I watched him, he raised his swollen eyes to mine and pulled his lips into a tight smile.

"What are you doing sitting here in the dark?" I whispered, coming to sit beside him.

"Checking on the kids. I got overwhelmed with my own memories of when Chie and I were kids. The only time we slept together was on camping trips. We used to annoy the heck out of each other." He smiled. "This one trip, Chie stuck tape to my eyebrows while I slept because he fancied the same girl as me." He laughed gently. "I smacked him in the face. Neither of us got the girl; me with no eyebrows and him with a shiner."

"Well, I'm glad. You might have fallen for her, and then you wouldn't have me!" I sprawled across his lap with a childish smile.

He laughed and leaned down to kiss me. "When I was at the shop, everyone talked about the bombing. That's what I was coming to tell you. They said, 'up north,' and I thought it was a mistake; we expected it to be London."

I sighed heavily. "There were more targets in Manchester compared to London. Karl, Chie, Teela, and Braithwaites all knew about the plot. They're all witnesses, and as London was discovered as the target, it was changed to avoid anyone foiling the plan before they had a chance to set the bomb off."

Teela's phone buzzed with a message, telling us to switch on the news. We sat on the end of our bed and turned on the screen. We didn't need to select the news. The emergency report ran on every channel.

"Global reports claim that NC advocates and insurgents have destroyed five cities across the world," the host began. "Manchester in the north of Grand British Republic; Damascus in the northern Capital Province; Mexico City in the Midwest States; Canberra of the Austral Region; and Taipei, of the island Taiwan in the Oriental Emirates. All are confirmed as completely obliterated."

As the reporter spoke, satellite pictures of the ruined cities appeared. The destruction was so terrible that you couldn't tell city from city; with each picture identical to the last, each city looking exactly like Manchester.

Faces started to appear as words were spoken. I didn't hear them: Chie's profile, one of twelve, stared back at me. I couldn't move my eyes from the face that looked so much like Mark. The same dark hair, though Chie's was cropped very short, eyes more hazel than green, yet you could see those emerald specks if you got close enough. Or if he got mad enough like he had when he found out about his mum.

Blame was being apportioned to these people. The fault was officially assigned to the NCs by the I.N. and its media, assuring that they would be apprehended and executed.

"They may as well put a red cross over Chie's picture then," Mark croaked, "because he won't be giving the I.N. any more trouble." His face hardened. "It doesn't mean I can't, though."

"Mark."

"They've murdered millions, Anna, including my brother and then blamed him for it!"

"I know, but–"

"No buts. I disagreed with Chie before. I wanted this new regime—to bring something else, something new to the world. It needed a drastic change. I want peace, and if I'm honest, I want it at any cost, but the I.N. are just as transparent as the others, aren't they?"

"They get what they want, blame who they want, and always manage to keep their hands clean," I replied. "They push laws through to deepen the divide between them and the NCs, all in the spirit of unity. How is any of it different to the old ways? It's different because only one man benefits this time, and you can guarantee those benefits won't be in our best interest."

"Getting rid of him might be," Mark proposed viciously.

"There's no getting rid of him," I mumbled.

According to prophecy, the world leader would not be assassinated until the due time. Even then, he would return from the fatal wound alive, proclaiming he is the one true messiah worthy of the world's worship. He would actually be the indwelling of Satan. That was years away anyhow. First, the Israeli peace treaty would need to be signed before the eruption of biblical tribulation could begin.

"I don't know," Mark disagreed, "right place, right time, and all that."

"There's already a time and a place laid out for him, be assured of that, and our efforts will be better used helping Teela expose everything we can."

The report continued to show the cities and the damning mugshots of the twelve aggressors. Even with the sound low, it was uncomfortable to watch. They hadn't shown any images of the explosions yet, and I wondered why that was. They must have satellite footage. They must have more information than what they reported. We had a drone in the air, true, but they had a mightier one, and the I.N. loyal media were not giving the people the full satellite facts.

The camera shot of Baruun in the southern district of the Capital Province came onto the screen just as I was about to switch it off. I hesitated. Half of me wanted to hear what the image of the father of lies would say to a, yet again, crushed people. What deceit would ripple from his lips this time? The other half of me wanted to plunge the sword of God right through his heart, but I would have to make do with silencing him electronically instead.

Mark reached out and touched my elbow. "Don't. I want to hear it."

While we waited for Tisak to come on screen, the report showed photos of the palace complex inside the I.N.'s triangular-shaped headquarters that the 'all eyes on me' Collective Thought logo mirrored. Extensive grounds with an orchard and a fountain surrounded the four-towered palace which reminded me a little of the Taj Mahal. Wide steps led to the main entrance beneath a pointed arch of white and terracotta mosaic stones. The white marbled central dome sat atop, and on either side, white marble pillars stood grandly. It connected the front of the terracotta palace to tall pillars decorated with a V at the top for a window. Beautiful. Glorious. Subtle.

When Tisak approached the podium, Mark's eyes were glued to the screen with a hatred I hadn't seen in him before. All eyes were on the world leader mourning with his head bowed as if in prayer. There was no sound as he stood still and tense. No sound. No clearing of throats among his entourage; no wind to flap the flags, no crowd to clap and cheer. Eerily silent. He looked up into the camera with sorrowful eyes.

"Neighbours, I am lost. I am not afraid to admit this to you. I have vowed to be open and honest in all things. My emotional state is one of those things. Human, just like you, I am confounded by the evil acts of the Non Conformers, who continually fight against our quest for peace and unity, and above all, love for each other. Taipei, Canberra, Manchester, Mexico City, and in my very own province, Damascus."

I could almost feel him adding, 'the nerve of it' in his thoughts as images of the ruined cities appeared beside his head.

"Men of evil have come against us, Neighbours. We shall not let them triumph, and they shall not continue to assault what we have built."

Photographs appeared.

"These men are the pageantry of a former world. A culture ineffective for peace, owing to its division, pride, and competition. Neighbours, my heart is sickened. My soul is equally as heavy for those we have lost, as it is for those who remain, whose emptiness swathes and suffocates them. What I am about to show you pains me. It tears at the very fabric of love we have sown; it separates, destroys, and burns! It has roused such anger in me that it cannot be restrained!"

The scene moved to a satellite image of Damascus before the explosion. It showed the white light bursting into rings that travelled out into the city. It showed the ancient and unused spired churches, temples and domes of mosques crashing down, their rooves sliding off the heaps and rolling to the ground. One dome actually spun like a spinning top. The ancient archways and columns of the Old City were no longer a tourist attraction as they lay almost powder-like on what used to be a highly polished, tiled floor.

The camera returned to Tisak, who stared at the surface of his crystal lectern as he talked.

"These murderers will be held accountable and punished for this crime…No…" angry blue eyes snapped up, and a nastiness entered his tone, "an abomination is what it is! Forgive me, for I am not well-spoken at this time, as is customary, for I am aggrieved, and I have yet to dispel my emotion towards those responsible."

His piercing eyes stared directly into the camera lens. "Richard Cole, I believe you to be the leader of the Non Conformer insurgency. I hold you to account for these atrocities. There is nowhere you can go where we cannot unearth you. There is no one you can trust to conceal you. For the evil you have done, the reward for your capture has been increased to one million mouglar."

I caught my breath.

"I will no longer stand by and allow you to continue to invent such weapons with which to destroy us and what we, of the International Neighbourhood, hold dear. What class of inconceivable weaponry you have displayed. It leads me to believe that your terrorist group is much more accomplished and organised than I had thought. You shall get your reward, Mr Cole, when you hang."

9 LeyLucient

It was a slow morning. I awoke from a restless sleep with a headache and tense shoulders. Mark was not beside me, but I could hear Lily giggling downstairs with calls of "no!" and "stop!" and then more giggling.

I crept down the stairs.

Mark was holding Lily upside down by one of her ankles, and with his free hand, he was tickling her tummy.

"What should I do with this noisy little thing?" Mark asked, seeing me watching.

"I'm not sure," I said, coming into the kitchen to softly pinch her upside-down cheeks, "has it been fed?"

Mark turned Lily up the right way and set her down on her feet.

"Fed, watered, and now she's refusing to get dressed."

"Am not 'fusing," she snapped, "just want more tickles."

"You do, do you?" he asked with a mischievous look.

Lily didn't need more encouragement. One glance at the twinkle in his eye set her off screaming up the stairs. She flew past Jonah, who was coming down yawning and scratching his head.

"Morning, Jonah," I said as Mark raced past him to chase Lily.

Jonah smiled. "What's going on?"

"Lily isn't getting dressed, so Mark is persuading her with tickles."

"Oh," Jonah laughed. "That's never gonna happen now!"

"Mark can be very persuasive, trust me. Help yourself to breakfast."

It seemed Mark had the entire stock of food on the table, and Jonah was intently eyeing the choices. Finally opting for cereal, he sat down and started to eat.

"How is he today?" asked Jonah.

"Who, Mark?" I asked, unsure of why he was asking me.

Jonah nodded. "He didn't lie to me when I asked yesterday and told me about his brother."

I was surprised, not expecting Mark to have been honest about that.

"Did he tell you how?"

Jonah nodded again. "Dad used to lie to me all the time. They forgot we had ears when we couldn't be seen. I heard a lot they didn't know about while we stayed in our bedroom."

He ate another spoonful of cereal, and I smiled.

"I see; I will have to watch out for that!"

"I only spied because they kept things from me. I'm not stupid."

"They kept things from you because you're young and might not understand. Plus, they care about you. They would have wanted to protect you from what was going on and things that weren't safe." I swallowed a mouthful of coffee. "I know I'd want to protect my kids."

"You're the police, though, aren't you?"

"And?"

"You're one of them."

"Devil workers?" I asked, stealing Lily's spot-on term. "Yes, and no. I've been known to help causes I shouldn't."

"Would you have helped them?"

"Depends on what they did." I shrugged. "You said they were NCs. What were they arrested for?"

Jonah paused, thinking. "Susber… subserv…"

"Subversion?"

"Yeah! That's it! Illegal goods."

"Contraband. Like what?"

Jonah didn't answer.

"You can tell me. I'm going to try and help, maybe find out where they are for you, no matter what they did."

"Bibles, mainly." His admission was a whisper, so quiet I barely caught it.

"So, they were Christians. What's your surname?"

"Francis."

"Jonah! Jonah! Look!"

Lily raced down the stairs with Mark closely behind. She wore a new outfit.

"Pretty dress, look, red; my favourite colour."

Jonah grinned. "Very nice, Lily, girlie socks an' all!"

"Frilly, Mark said, didn't you, Mark? Frilly." She wrapped her arms around his leg.

Mark smiled. "I think I love her."

My phone trilled from upstairs. Not Teela's, which I carried in my pocket, but my normal phone. It was the station.

"Mrs Cole?" came the assertive male voice of the Commanding Chief.

"Yes."

"Simon Pothrall here. Excuse the hour, but as you can appreciate, time is short. Have you seen Teela Franklin since last week?"

"Um, Wednesday was the last time I think I saw her at work, sir. I met her at lunchtime, and I wasn't feeling well afterwards, so I left early."

"And you have not seen her since then? Have you had any contact with her?"

"She did not return my calls, but Greg said she needed some personal leave. I suspect trouble in the family."

'Family', meaning the Asiders.

"If you hear from her, demand she calls me immediately. It's imperative."

"Yes, sir."

Then, he breathed down the phone, "I trust you are aware of yesterday's bombings?"

"Of course." *We are on this planet.*

"Then you are also aware of the arrest warrant out for Richard Cole?"

"I am."

"Are we likely to find him at your premises?"

"Absolutely not!" I hissed, mortified at the thought of the dangers that would bring.

"When did you last have contact with your brother-in-law?"

I opted for the truth. "Actually, just last week. It was the first time we'd heard from him in a long time. We were surprised."

"What did he talk to you about?"

"Nothing which made any sense to me," I carefully replied, "and yet he was afraid."

"Of?"

"We couldn't really understand the words he was saying, sir, if I'm honest."

I hadn't lied.

"Can you contact him?"

"No. Not much point now. We know he must be dead. He was in Manchester."

Silence.

"Well. I, uh, I'd like to say I am sorry for your loss, but…have a nice day."

Nice day? Was he serious? I threw my phone on the bed and took out Teela's. I sent a message to let her know she was being summoned to call the Chief and returned to the kitchen.

~

The others were in the garden playing with Mark's football. I watched them awhile, impressed by how naturally Mark played with the children and how he teased them so easily, especially after the night we'd had. It was good his mind was not solely focussed on Chie, though, or the bombings and his vengeance against Tisak. I picked up the basket to put away but instead fiddled with the ribbons again.

Jonah burst through the door and grabbed his drink, swallowing it in three gulps. I looked up.

Breathing heavily and wiping his mouth with the back of his hand, he reflected, "Lily ties a good bow now."

I frowned, and seeing that, he explained.

"Dad used to get tired of trying to teach her. She struggled to get the hang of it, and he would get annoyed. Then, after they took them away, she was obsessed with it, night and day, until she could do it. After that, she wouldn't even let me help her. It took us ages to get out of the flat!"

Lily burst through the door, yelling.

"Is it true, Anna?" She turned to Jonah. "We hafta come in now."

Mark closed the back door and faced me.

"We have a job to do this morning, haven't we?"

"Have we?" Nothing came to mind.

Lily jumped up and down. "Can you have a red one? That's my favourite colour."

"I know that; you've already told me. A red what?" I looked at her and Mark.

"Car," they said together, then laughed.

"You up for some car buying, Jonah?" Mark asked.

Jonah was already fetching his shoes.

~

The car-buying experience did not enthral me. I was happy if I turned it on, and it got me to the place I needed to go. Vehicles these days needed drivers with tech degrees, and I just found it all too complicated. There was an advantage to having a Wi-Fi system linked to your personal cloud. It could play a song or video, read you a story, or tell one while it wrote it for you. You could enter the virtual reality threads and have the automated system drive you if you were inclined, but few people did. It seemed unnatural to most of us to relinquish such control to a machine, and it was not a popular choice. Colour ended up not being a factor at all, much to Lily's disappointment. She had fallen for a bright yellow one, far too conspicuous under the circumstances, but luckily it wasn't an option for us.

"Good morning, I'm Wesley. Can I help you with anything?" the showroom assistant asked while shaking our hands.

Mark mixed a 'Headsman in public hearing' tone to his voice. "That depends. What have you got that we can drive away now?"

I shot him a look, as did the salesman.

"Ah, that won't be possible, sir. With the updates on the rules, it's not procedure."

"I'm Headsman at Thurstworthy Manor Estate, so don't give me any blarney about procedures. So, I'll ask you again. What do you have that I can drive away now?"

When Mark took a deep breath, he grew. He widened his stance and clasped his hands tightly in front of him with a fierce expression. He looked so intimidating that Lily suddenly hid behind me and Jonah looked down at his feet.

Not receiving a quick enough response from Wesley, Mark took a step forward and spread his arms, saying,

"The cars are this way, are they?"

We walked further into the showroom, Lily still insisting the yellow one was her favourite while Mark and Jonah talked engines and speed and blah, blah. I stopped listening.

The assistant didn't come back again. Instead, the manager approached, and we left less than an hour later with a silver, five-door Toyota that Lily described as boring and wasn't even a real colour. It was an ex-display, nippy little thing, and the perfect blend-in car. At least Jonah enjoyed the trip home in it. Lily had refused to get in, opting to go with Mark instead.

"She'll get over it," Jonah said later when Lily was clearly still upset.

Everything was suddenly yellow.

"I had yellow shoes once; I did."

"Buttercups are my bestest flowers."

I laughed, exhausted because she was driving me mad.

Lily did eventually forgive me. I served us a yellow dinner of macaroni cheese and garlic bread. That seemed to placate her, and by the time I was tucking the two of them into bed, she was happy again.

"Been really glad of those kids today," Mark revealed as I sat down on our bed beside him. "It could have been really hard, but it wasn't with them here—I got through it. Didn't think I was going to last night, though. I'm envious you slept even the little amount you did."

"Sorry I napped. You're too comfy and warm; I can't help it." I snuggled into him again and smiled. "And you rewarded me with a car."

He kissed my head. "You, sweetheart, can have anything you want."

We both heard the noise. We stiffened and eyed each other, fear in my eyes, scheming in his as he climbed from the bed and tiptoed down the stairs. I had visions of the I.N. finally on the doorstep, ready to invade my privacy and storm our home. The secret watchman revealed, come to snatch me away for questioning, or worse, rehabilitation.

I heard a scuffle and mumbled voices and an "aargh!"

I ran down the rest of the stairs to find Mark in the corner of the kitchen, hand on his heart, saying 'Jesus' repeatedly. I reached for the light.

"No!" came the familiar voice that stopped me. "Don't switch on the light."

It couldn't be? I shook the impossible thought from my mind. No, it couldn't be true. He was dead; he was dead! He was…standing in my kitchen, holding a lighter near his face.

"Thank you, God!" I ran to him and threw my arms around his neck. "You were in Manchester, you were–"

"Already leaving when it went off. The vibes caught the backside of my car, and I skidded clean off the road. Half a farmhouse disappeared less than a mile behind me while I watched. Didn't know what it was at first."

Mark was still in a state of shock. I turned back to Chie.

"It isn't safe for you here; you can't stay. They've already contacted me about you today."

That got Mark's attention, and his head snapped up. The full day with the kids had been a busy one, and I hadn't mentioned it.

"I'm surprised they didn't see you."

"I always see them first, Anna. But just so you know, they're in a blue car, three houses down on the opposite side of the street."

Mark slipped into the lounge and peered discreetly out of the window.

"It's parked on the drive over there. Unbelievable!"

"They've only conned me once. Now, I con them." Chie shot me a grin. "I'm looking out for one of your locals. One of you has been looking for me. I assumed, hoped it was you."

It was Teela, but I didn't have the chance to say it. Instead, Mark crossed the kitchen and grabbed Chie by the scruff of his neck so quickly that I was startled.

Although he spoke quietly, his tone was hostile. "You let me think you were dead!"

Chie raised his hands in surrender. "I had no secure way of reaching you until I got here. First, I had to leave the phone with the team, and then I wasn't allowed to. We have strict protocols; it's how we don't get caught." He lowered his hands to Mark's cheeks. "I'm breaking one of them now just by being here, but I had to come. I had to make sure you knew I didn't do this; I didn't..."

Chie started to weep, and I sniffed myself when Mark pulled his brother in closer and hugged him tightly. There weren't many people as tall as Mark, and Chie wasn't that far off as he rested his head comfortably on his older brother's shoulder.

I could not imagine Chie setting those bombs. I could not imagine him being the leader of the NCs either, as Tisak had publicised, but I considered the possibility as I watched him sink to the floor. Chie was known to the Portsmouth task force, so fair to say, the I.N. gestapo too and even Tisak himself. Chie must be a leader for his name to be the only one of twelve mentioned by Tisak personally, and Chie was also capable. He was intelligent and skilled enough to run an operation of that scale.

I ensured the blinds and doors were closed before switching on the lowlights. I pulled two cans of cider out of the fridge and put one each in their hands. I felt uncomfortable and unsure of what to do with myself as they held onto each other. I sat on the worktop in my pyjamas, trying to be patient, but I had questions.

Mark slipped away and came back with an opened bottle of scotch.

"Large one?"

Chie nodded.

I opened one of the cans for myself and took a swig. It wasn't as though I had my task force head on, but my tone was firm.

"Chie, I love you, and I'm sorry about what you're going through, but I think you'd better start talking."

He frowned. "I don't know what else I can tell you. What did you find out?"

"Why you, Chie? Of all those other faces, why was it only you that riled Ciel Tisak so much? How does he even know you?"

His expression did not give anything away.

"Are you the NC leader, as he seems to think? What equipment did you buy from Braithwaites, and where on earth does Ian Stymer fit in?"

Mark was looking at me in astonishment, and the topics had sparked a reaction in Chie. He smiled.

"I see you found out a lot."

"Anna, you are not at work," reprimanded Mark.

I turned towards him. "I don't do this at work. This is wholly a family affair." Then to Chie, "I have, yes. Answer the questions."

"Well, first, I'm not the leader of the NCs, but I am head of the UK patronage. Second, Tisak and I have an understanding—he keeps trying to find and kill me, and I keep getting right up in the face of his devious schemes and habitually spoiling them. He's not been doing so well."

You reckon?

What luck! The antichrist's earthly arch enemy was my brother-in-law. And what double luck, he also happened to be the most wanted man in the GBR.

"Hey, I told my Commanding Chief this morning you were in Manchester at the time of the bombing. If you keep your head down, they'll carry on thinking you're dead."

Chie shook his head. "Tisak won't believe that unless he sees my head separated from my body. We exhausted the fake death one already."

"He might, you know," contributed Mark, "I called work and put in for compassionate leave. It's documented I've lost my brother, and I got four weeks off. Not being funny, though, Chie, Tisak isn't going to forage through what's left of Manchester for your remains."

"Maybe not, no, good point."

My eyes were boring into the side of Chie's head while they spoke. I wanted him to finish answering my questions.

"So, come on, Chie, what equipment did you buy? What can the I.N. prove?"

"They can prove we bought things from Braithwaites, the chemicals we use to create fake IDs, high-end printing, scanning and hacking equipment, satellite booster tech, stuff that helps us stay off the radar and stay alive! Braithwaites don't care who they sell to."

Sold to, I thought. Now, they have paid the price for dealing with the enemy to inoculate their own bank account. Bankruptcy was as good as any disease.

"One of the things they forged was the description on the invoices," Chie explained, "and I've bought LeyLucient apparently. Don't even know what that is."

LeyLucient? Ley as in ley-lines and lucient as in lucent, light, Lucifer? I described it as best as I could remember it.

"It's harvested ley-line energy merged with the new mass particle they finally discovered to create a new weapon. That's what it is."

"The bombings," Chie sighed.

"Can they even harvest ley-lines?" asked Mark. "I thought that was supposed to be a pagan ritual, spiritual stuff. And how do you know about it?"

"I don't know. How am I supposed to know if we can honestly harvest them? Why not? It's the info that came in the Manchester file, along with Ian Stymer's name."

"That guy is bad news. To the core, rotten," Chie revealed as he perched on the stool. "I don't have dealings with him directly. If I can avoid it, I will, but often one can't. Too many national doors only he can open, so we have to ask the I.N.

mole to get involved, which is something we're all loathed to do. She gives us information; we don't ask. It was never intended to be a two-way arrangement. Stymer is a dangerous snake and acts like he's Tisak's boyfriend or something, the way he sucks up. There won't be questions if the mole is discovered; there won't be a trial. There won't even be a record she ever existed. I could tell you stories about the I.N. that'll keep you up at night."

"I think we've had enough truths to keep us going awhile, don't you? I'm going to call Teela. She's the cop that's been looking for you."

I left Mark to explain while I called and updated Teela. She had news I immediately shared with the men.

"Tell them what you told me," I demanded, switching to speakerphone.

"Javad Shirvani is…was the Asider's informant inside Braithwaites. Tom and I nabbed him at the market on the afternoon of the bombing. I assume, Chie, that you are Fred?"

He swallowed. "I am, yes."

"I'll say nothing about it to you now. I'm going to wait 'til I see you in person so I can follow it through with a punch to your mouth for leaving me stranded in Manchester last Thursday."

She carried on when Chie didn't respond.

"Shirvani has some interesting information to share. Like, how Stymer brought the object to them and told them how to harvest the ley-line energy. When that was achieved, he gave them the method and formula to uncover the mass particle, which Braithwaites is most famous for. Shirvani also shared how the CEO supplied the NC organisations so that they could stay underground. When Stymer found out, things got tetchy. Everyone was nervy, too terrified and suspicious not to answer the questions. Shirvani reckoned they were digging a little too close to him. As innocent as it might have been, he bolted, even from the Asiders. Everything certainly came to light after that."

"Lots of birds!"

Manchester had become a very convenient target after all.

"What do you mean?" Teela asked.

"Who do we know was in Manchester or supposed to be in Manchester? Karl and the rest of his team. You were there, Chie was there, Braithwaites and Shirvani were there. How many other targets did the I.N. manage to take out or attempt to take out with one bomb?"

"So, you think London was only the original target because it's the former capital, and ending Manchester did Tisak a great service of some kind?"

"Perhaps, yes, but I also think there's a problem in London that Tisak needed to deal with. We should put our eyes on crime and missing people; it might lead to something. We can watch out for what's not reported on the news because guaranteed that will be the one we should probably be interested in."

Chie was impressed.

"Clever, your missus," he said to Mark before turning to me. "You want a job? Doesn't pay well but comes with various houses, company cars, and gadget toys to play with."

I laughed. "I might need a new job soon. I'll let you know when I get back to work whether I'm still employed or not."

"I want you to go back tomorrow," Teela piped in, "even if it's just for tomorrow. Find out and collect what you can and bring it to me. I'm going to send you three locations, and at half two, there will be people there to meet you. Separately, though, okay? If one gets caught, the other two can still make it. That's my plan. Once we're all together and we've gone through what we've learned, we can discuss what to do next."

I received the locations not long after the call finished. Chie confirmed one of the addresses was the safehouse he was staying in and concluded it sensible to return and be collected from there. Another was close to the high street where I could easily reach on foot. The last location was as far away as Chippenham, but Mark didn't mind travelling.

Mark took me into his arms. "You'll be careful, won't you?"

"I'll certainly try. Chie get off, all right?"

Mark nodded. "What are we going to do with Jonah and Lily, overnight if needs be?"

Melly was who I thought of.

"I'll sort it. Would you have time to bring them to me at two and still make your appointment?"

Mark inclined his head. "Uh, yeah. Do you know where Chippenham is? I'm not going on a tricycle."

"All right, sarky, I'm just making sure!"

~

At work the following day, I was hyperactive. Although there was excitement in carrying out my dangerous task, much of it was anxiety. Wearing a mask wasn't me; I didn't even get a part in school plays, but I had to make sure I was convincing enough to my colleagues now. So I tried to look like I had just lost my brother-in-law and showed a genuine disgust for the atrocity Richard had been accused of and the man he was said to have become.

I went through my messages before I started on everything else. Greg Prentice was chasing me for an update on his demands from last week. I could honestly admit I had nothing to tell him and put that in an intra-message as he wasn't at his desk.

The search I ran finally ended, and I gulped at the number of new results since Saturday. I copied the 69 links to the same encrypted drive I would use to save the details of the children's parents. There was a lot of evidence relating to Chie and the bombings. I set up the new search on London's recent crimes and hoped there was the capacity to store it all.

I ignored my colleagues' suspicious stares and halted whispers as I swept through the rooms to the Commanding Chief's office. I had been summoned to attend a meeting. My heart raced, but I tried not to let it show as I knocked briskly and entered the room.

"Hi, Anna," greeted an overweight Simon Pothrall. He lifted slightly from his chair and reached across the desk to indicate where I should sit. "Thank you for coming."

In the other chair sat the observer from the pub. He was a white man in his fifties, with peppered-silver hair and had a lean figure. I was sure my look of recognition gave me away before

I could hide it. His hands were together at his chest, fingers entwined, and he watched me with shifty, dark eyes as mine nervously darted around Pothrall's office.

"This is HS Paul Fraser from Baruun."

HS stood for House of Security. He was a spy. Baruun's House of Security combined the roles of protectors, investigators, and enforcers and had become notorious for how it policed its Neighbours. Stories to this effect were no longer reported, and most assumed Tisak had put a stop to it. The truth was that he owned all the media stations and controlled what was announced.

"Pleasure to meet you."

"Mrs Cole."

The observer studied me. He watched my eyes, expressions, and body language while Pothrall talked.

"HS Fraser has been given an assignment that will keep him around here for a while. So, I'll be allocating a workstation for him nearby yours, and I'd like you to work alongside him and be available to do everything he asks of you."

I had to decide quickly whether to agree or do as Teela suggested and ask for time off.

"I would, I mean, I'm honoured you would consider me for this, but–"

"Anna, you have displayed a talent indispensable to this station, and your skillset has ranked you in the top three on the researchers' list. Honour you have earned."

Prickles and warmth spread across my chest and neck.

"Actually, I was going to ask for some compassionate leave. My husband is mourning at home. So, I've cleared my workload, hoping to have the rest of this week off, with your agreement, of course, as Teela isn't back."

"HS Fraser, how does next Tuesday fit with your plans? Could we allow Anna this time with her husband?"

Fraser was suspicious as he stared at me. There was something about him that made me uncomfortable. I swallowed, finding myself shrinking under his scrutiny. I kept telling myself he couldn't pluck thoughts out of my head. He didn't know Chie wasn't dead; he didn't know Teela was underground investigating something she shouldn't, and he didn't know I wasn't loyal because I was a Christian. Safe.

Instead of looking guilty, I stared back with a frown. I was on the right side, and they were not. I walked with truth, and they with deception.

The I.N. did not know I was disloyal, I assured myself.

"I can keep myself busy until next week, Mrs Cole, be assured. However, I must be in contact with you by phone over this time. Will that be possible?"

"Yes, but I won't always be at home and available to talk privately. I'd appreciate the freedom to say that without repercussion."

My familiarity with the manipulation techniques of the I.N. and HS had been quick. I'd witnessed it many times and learned from them. At times, being 'unable to speak' equals 'up to no good', and I would not fall for that trap.

"Your assurances?" I asked, glancing at both in turn.

Pothrall nodded after Fraser agreed.

"Until next week then." Fraser rose and waved his arm towards the door, dismissing me.

I hurried back to my desk to collect my things before meeting Mark outside with the children. A ting on my computer alerted me to an email, and the whistle on my phone a message (I had left the other phone with Mark to avoid getting caught with it.) I read the message first. There was no ID and no number.

"Rude girl says, click it."

I frowned and turned to the email. No sender, no subject, just a hyperlink, four sentences long that gave no clue as to what it was. But rude girl, aka Teela, said click it, so I did. My screen whirred loudly, and I scanned the empty room—nothing like a guilty conscience to keep me on the edge of my nerves. Suddenly, a small black box popped up on my screen.

'Fred says hi,' came the green message.

"Shan?"

'Tom. Delete email, log out, leave the system running."

The box vanished.

Before doing as Tom said, I checked the data drive had saved the files I needed. Unfortunately, there wasn't much information on Jonah and Lily's parents, and I hadn't had time to fully go through all the details. Still, once I had explained to Melly that their parents were arrested last September for subversion, and their last known location was Sudeley Castle (the I.N.'s closest rehabilitation centre), she was persuaded to take the children overnight.

I packed up and met the Range Rover outside. After work, I hoped to make myself known to the children's landlord at the charity shop but decided not to. Who could understand how anyone would leave two children fending for themselves like he had? But at least, he had let them keep the flat. That was charitable because two-bedroomed flats above non-food shops in this town were highly sought after. He could have rented it ten times over at a handsome profit.

The children were subdued as they got out of the car. Mark's persuasion skills had only gotten them this far, in the flesh, but their hearts were at home with us.

"I know you don't like it, but it's just for tonight. We need to go; I have things to share, and some of that is about your mum and dad. I need their help to discover more for you, but at least we know where they are now." I gazed at Jonah. "There are also things about Mark's brother I've found that I need to share. Do you understand what I'm saying?"

Jonah slowly nodded, and then, following his example, Lily copied—probably not understanding why, and Mark took out their bags and flung them over his shoulder.

"I'll walk with you. The car will be all right a minute with the hazards on."

He bent to kiss me and then led the way to the public car park nearby, where I had arranged to meet Melly. After introductions and parting hugs, the children were gone, and Mark was racing away to make his meeting near Chippenham.

I turned and headed out of town into the industrial area of Little Hampton. We didn't have a vast amount of enterprise among the residents, but we had decent people with good, honest hearts who built up their reputations and grew successful businesses. One of these, to my amazement, was a popular logistics company. Their feelers spread across the world, and more so since they became the I.N.'s assigned logistics hauliers, so it took me by surprise when I realised it was where I was heading and twice checked it was the right numbered unit.

The man who met me flashed his headlights, and without concern, I got in. He was blond and bearded and wore glasses. He did not speak to me. In fact, he was a bit cold, nor was he introduced to me at the safehouse when we arrived.

Teela greeted me warmly as I stepped into the crowded room. Chie was already comfortable on the settee. I sat beside him and took his hand.

"You look well for a dead guy," I said with a grin.

"Until those words come out of Tisak's mouth, we'll take no chances," came a deep voice from within the room.

My driver, who I named 'Logistic Lionel', seemed to agree with him.

The sombre looks everybody wore made me feel like a child interfering in adult business: inadequate for the task.

"Heard from Mark yet?" I whispered to Chie.

"On route now. He ran into trouble getting from the funeral directors. He was late but made his meeting. He'll be along."

"What sort of trouble?"

Chie shrugged. "He was followed. I'm sure he'll tell you later."

He nodded towards Teela.

"The boss will start the meeting in a minute," he whispered with a smile.

Teela was getting her feet right under the table, and her eyes were wide with exhilaration, eager to get started as she curled her fingers around a mug of coffee. She checked her watch just as the door opened, and a woman stepped in, closely followed by Mark.

"Good, we're all here. Grab a drink; let's get going," Teela commanded.

Mark came to sit in the hardback chair next to the sofa where I perched. He took my hand and waited for Teela to begin.

"First, you need to know that in this room, there are Christians, NCs, Asiders, and civilians. If you don't like it, leave now. Everybody in this room has a reason to be here. Whether it's political, religious or personal, we all have a purpose. We all have a heart for what is right. I am here for Karl and the five missing girls, the embryo of a case that evolved into falsified evidence linking Chie and the NCs to a future bombing in London. I can tell you Tisak personally burned this case and denied the Manchester task force permission to investigate, so Karl sent it to me. You're all aware of what happened after that, as most of you were involved. So, I won't go over it again. Second, you need to know that the Asiders have asked me to share any evidence we find."

Teela turned to me. "Did you get anything today?"

I reached into my pocket and handed her the drive. "That's all the stuff relating to the bombings, the weapon, and Chie. There are also mass results on a search I ran about a hidden network running parallel to the main internet and any evidence which could help divert the heat from Chie, although I haven't been able to go through any of it yet."

Teela tossed the drive to a brown-haired man she called Tom.

"Data about Mr and Mrs Francis is on there too. I would like to be able to go through that. Jonah and Lily deserve to know about their parents, and I'd like to see if I can do something to help them."

Logistic Lionel shifted in the seat. "Julia and Daryl Francis?"

"Yes, if memory serves."

He sat back and closed his eyes, a pained expression on his face. "They were executed a month ago. God, I didn't know they had kids."

"You knew them?"

"Very well on the NC side of the table."

I glanced at Mark, knowing it was down to us to tell those poor kids that their parents were gone. But I didn't know how I was going to do that.

"Okay," Teela began, "not being insensitive but let's get back to what we're here for. In my experience, I've learned when things aren't going anywhere, or in the direction I want, I go back to the beginning and restart completely. That's what we're going to do now, starting with these–" she handed out copies of the missing girls' report, "–and Karl's recording."

She nodded to Tom.

Airy noises came through the sound system, and then a click or two before a robotic voice began talking. "You should have their names already; I sent them separately, and I shall refer to them as numbers one to five respectively. These ladies accessed and purchased contraband and occult items through a website called keepmyfaves. The profile login you need to open an account must come through an approved social media platform, complete with a photo ID and lifestyle preferences. It's quite an in-depth agreement the systems do together. It will either allow you or ban your IP address from joining. The accounts belonging to these…one to fivers had a common thread that eventually led me to the perverse 'Yes Please GBR', a site not for the faint-hearted, and I would recommend you don't look—you don't need to.

"I researched their banking transactions, and regular payments are going to three companies across the GBR, the main stockholder being Stymer Holdings. Having dug into the statements belonging to Braithwaites, being that they are the only Manchester based company, I discovered a trail leading me to NC purchases through the alias 'M Seymour', a man identified from the footage of the riots down your way–"

"At least we know that name's blown," Chie interrupted. "Better stop using it."

"–that was reason enough for me," the robotic voice went on, "you see, I know number four and their family, my motivation is a personal one, and I can't rest until I know. One way or the other. I had the required task force's NC motivation, but I didn't publicise it right away. I dug some more. I researched Braithwaites, a science-come-tech-come-astral-physics research lab, and dare I admit, I hacked into their encrypted files and found out some interesting new discoveries."

"Stop there," a small olive-skinned man said, standing up, "I'll jump in here, if I may, and make it plain for you. I'm Javad Shirvani. I've worked at Braithwaites for many years and watched the place grow with innovation, thanks to Ian Stymer. The year before the mock rapture, Stymer showed up, adamant he should have stock in the company in return for a conduit capable of containing spiritual energy never before harnessed by humans. I mean, he actually said that—humans. So, what does that tell you? Apes did it back in the day? No, I don't think so."

The comment had me wondering if Mr Shirvani was one of the Christians in the room. He had mocked the hint that other 'beings' had collected the ley-line energy in the past, and I reckoned Stymer's reference would lead anyone to think of aliens. But I knew of them, not as the world would because I knew 'extra-terrestrials' would embody the deceptive demonic practice—demons in fancy dress.

"I went to all the pagan and stone sites, including your local ones. It was my job to install the conduit and storage vessel. Piece of advice, though, don't try it on a windy day because every measurement had to be so exact, every mirror placed precisely. That was eerie, I can tell you. Their positions reflected half of its opposite mirror and half of one of the stones. It gave me the shivers, and a really weird feeling came over me."

He shuddered again with the memory.

"Mirrors?" Chie was not convinced.

"Well, it worked, as you can see! Then the Fritzman mass particle was discovered at CERN INc, for which, of course, Braithwaites was honoured. Although CERN had technically found it, it was through our research," he coughed, "I mean, Stymer's research, that we had the technology and method to uncover it in the first place. Combining the two of them is incredibly dangerous. Our science cannot reveal the origins of ley energy; it cannot understand its specific make-up. The closest we can get to describe it physically would be to say it's like breath. It carries things within its environment like breath does with gases and smells. The difference is we can't identify what it carries or adequately measure how much. We just know it's there by comparing the variances in its signature."

"Yet, since the bombings, I presume it magnetises energy sources to and from itself, and when that's combined with the Fritzman well, you get what you saw in Manchester. An energy that cuts, vibrates, and breaks down any mass, natural or synthetic."

"It can't be possible," stated the woman who had been Mark's driver.

"Naturally, I don't think it would have been. There's something very unnatural about the equation process. It's beyond understanding. Parts of it make sense, but much of it makes us look ignorant, so we stop trying. Stymer was beyond excited: I've never seen a grown man act so childishly. We were ordered to arrange a christening, would you believe it!? A naming ceremony for LeyLucient. Farce. If we had a party for everything, we wouldn't have the time to actually invent anything."

"LeyLucient!" I laughed. "Typical vanity of Apollyon, wouldn't you say, Javad?"

He chuckled gently. "Quite."

There were four of us who understood. These were the Christians, and Logistic Lionel was one of them. Everybody else looked bemused. I didn't clarify Apollyon meant 'the destroyer' in the Bible, the serpent of old—who is called the devil.

Javad continued as he perched back on his seat.

"The other reason I wanted to jump in at this point is because the information on the recording is extremely technical. The guy's well informed. It's so technical that I can't imagine anyone else in the room able to understand what he's talking about, and I've explained it as basically as I dare for you. What captured my attention was a difference in some of the details which, at first, I thought was a mistake he'd made, but I might have misunderstood. He speaks about fusion power and quantum physics, and exotic matter, which is basically negative energy, and it stirred something. He seemed to have more knowledge than me. LeyLucient had been tested with exotic mass. Now, I'm not going into the ins and outs; suffice to say that a positive and a negative produce a neutral reaction. So, the hint of teleportation exploration surprised me, considering the physics restrictions, but the clue is there in his detail."

"Are you saying what I think you are implying? Teleportation could now be an actual thing?" Mark was excited, although I hadn't been able to keep up.

"No. Not entirely. In my understanding, it isn't possible, but the details the guy had here indicates some experimenting with antimatter, but without the conclusions..." Javad returned to his seat and reached for his drink.

Teela stood up.

"I don't think there's any need to continue with Karl's recording. The six hours they had before Tisak shut it down procured evidence that implicated Chie in a bomb plot. There were equipment purchases, and false message chains between him and some unnamed characters assumed to be the other twelve alleged co-conspirators. None of the evidence exists anymore. Ha, well, it does. It's just for Manchester now and not London. Oh, and let's not forget the I.N. took out a witness and their family, too." Teela sighed crossly. "Chie, apparently, you bought everything you needed to build a weapon capable of destroying entire cities. They found coded messages in different languages they hadn't yet translated, but the London plot was clear enough. The next morning, their office was a hub of HS officers, and overnight, everything had disappeared. They'd picked it clean of the whole case and kept a watch on them all."

Her eyes wandered to Mark. "There is a reason for having you here at this meeting."

I frowned. What did he have to do with it?

"Okay," said Mark, intrigued.

"I looked into the staff at the posh house, surprised to see you down as the Headsman." She shot a look at me. "The posh house was where the girls were taken."

Thurstworthy Manor Estate! I paled. I wasn't sure if Mark had made the connection or if I'd even mentioned it, so I quickly told him.

"No, no way. Robert Forbes-Hamilton's a top bloke!"

"The old man, maybe. Junior, no. He's a masochistic chauvinist who's rich, spoilt, and a bit peculiar. He's too pervy for me."

The words came from the man in the corner with the deep voice. I couldn't see him clearly as he wore a hat and a thin scarf over his face. I named him 'Not-Pervy Pete' to keep track of who was who. They couldn't all be Fred. In the room were: Mark, Chie, Teela, me, the computer guy Tom (if that was even his real name), the Asider informant Javad Shirvani, Logistic Lionel—my driver and Christian, Mark's driver Chaperone Shelley, Not-Pervy Pete (another Christian), and a completely unknown man. He was a young with rust-coloured hair, and as he hadn't spoken yet, I named him Reticent Rusty.

"Well, he's rich and spoilt, that's true, but kidnapping girls into the house? I think senior Robert might have something to say about that," Mark argued.

"What you think isn't relevant!" Teela was good at bringing the topic back to the point. "I want, sorry, I need you to look at your data—entry books, camera footage, anything suspicious. I don't like it, but all of this is linked together somehow. We all want Chie exonerated, and we want those girls back home if they're still alive."

Not-Pervy Pete sat forward. "If they are, they'll be long gone. Lots of buyers out there; some prefer those 'broken in' and pay extra if it's done right. Junior likes the screamers, and when they run out of screams, they're moved on or buried."

I felt sick. Man was the worst of all species. At least, back when our legal system was just and fair, we'd had deterrents.

We'd had a repulsion as a society for what was unacceptable behaviour. But, legally speaking, now, there wasn't. Sex was a freedom no matter the choices. If a Neighbour's tendencies were violent, then that was okay if the partner was willing, and of course, most were too afraid to say they weren't.

Mark's snappy comment brought me back to the room.

"How do you know?"

I'd admit, Not-Pervy Pete's knowledge of Mark's employer had me curious.

"Best you don't know; I'm not who I was. I'll confirm I've known him now for fifteen years, since our late teens."

Impatient, Teela pushed Mark for a decision. "Will you do it?"

"Yes, but I'm off for a month; it might be a bit tricky getting in there officially." Mark held up his hand, halting the onslaught of comments about to erupt. "I'm not saying impossible. I'm sure Anna and I can develop a plausible ruse to have me summoned back there for a bit as the token authority figure."

"Right then, you and Anna do that. Then, Shirvani, let's see what we can retrieve from the Braithwaites archives." Teela turned to Tom. "Tell me you guys downloaded their servers to yours before Sunday?"

Tom shook his head, smiling. "We have access to the files through...what is it you call this lot?" He nodded towards Not-Pervy Pete.

"Oh, Asiders," said Teela with a chuckle.

"That's class," he said, grinning, "not one side, nor the other, yet fully integrated into both. Love it."

Teela raised her eyebrows in irritation.

Tom smirked. "I'll tap in, and Javad can go through it all he wants."

I stole a look at Chie, who appeared amused that Teela was ordering the group around. It should have been his department, considering he was the faction leader of the UK patronage, but Teela was on a roll organising who could deal with her list of to-dos.

Mark and I would concentrate on Thurstworthy Manor and the girls. We would enlist the help of Logistic Lionel if we needed any access to tech. Javad Shirvani was to research the files particularly relevant to LeyLucient, and he would work closely with Tom. Teela, Chie, and Chaperone Shelley would work on the leads I might have discovered on the data drive. I also managed to include some recent London crimes, and I would be interested to know if something came up.

~

The night had drawn in, and many of us were exhausted after hours of listening, studying material, finding leads, and debating their importance. Pizzas were delivered and demolished; my belly was so full that I yawned, yearning for bed as I sat on the floor surrounded by paper. We had gone old-school and left no online trail. As things were printed, it left no record of ever being on Tom's system. That meant a lot of paper.

Teela sat beside me, chin in her hands. "This is all mad, mate."

"Glad I got the three of you to myself," I whispered to her, Chie and Mark as we huddled together. "I had a summons at work this afternoon to see Simon Pothrall " I gestured to Chie "–my Commanding Chief. When I got to his office, an HS officer from Baruun sat with him."

I hadn't noticed the room go quiet.

"I saw him recently at the pub where Mark and I went for lunch. He kept staring at us. Pothrall wants me to work with him. He didn't say what, but I assume it's about Chie and the bombings. I'm rated top three on the researchers' list, Pothrall said." I squirmed, not wishing to boast. "We're to start next Tuesday."

"You were number two," Tom confirmed, looking up from his screen. "Karl is dead, and that makes you the new numero uno!"

Oh, Lord. Thanks, but no, I didn't want it. It just made me stand out and become top of the list for a Tisak assignment I didn't want.

Tom asked, "Which HS officer was it?"

"Paul Fraser."

Someone hissed, but nobody spoke. In fact, such a sinister atmosphere descended that we all started to pack away, taking our respective jobs home with us.

10 HS Paul Fraser

My hours of labouring over the Manor's blueprints and researching its history had brought up some planning application requests that prompted memories from Mark.

"I remember. Lorries in and out and always going around the back of the Manor. Didn't really affect us, though. If they had the paperwork and ID and were on our list, they gained entry, no questions. It went on the best part of the year with nothing to show for it."

"Nothing at all? No extension or outbuilding?" I asked.

"Nope."

"Maybe they were building somewhere to hide the girls."

Mark shook his head. "I'm still not entirely convinced about that."

"It is where the evidence leads. I just want to find my own way to the answers, and not Karl's and not the I.N.'s version of the truth either. I need to go into work, don't I?"

"Is that wise?" Mark questioned.

"I've got to on Tuesday anyway. I have an appointment with our stalker."

"You reckon he followed me then?"

"Yeah, I do."

The trill of the phone interrupted us, and Mark reached for it.

"Afternoon, sir. Right, okay…yes, I can come fetch it. No, no, we're still making the arrangements…of course, it's fine …we're doing all right, thanks for asking. What time is it due to arrive? I see; well, if I get there around six? Okay, see you then."

Mark smiled victoriously.

"We don't need a plan to get me into work anymore. Junior wants me to intercept a delivery."

"Delivery of what?"

"Didn't say, but he doesn't want it left at the Manor and asked me to keep hold of it." Mark shrugged. "Who cares? I can do what Teela wants now without raising suspicion."

Mark arranged for the night guard to start his shift later that evening, allowing Mark to privately search the gatehouse system for information which might help us. In the meantime, I researched the missing girls through their social media and internet history. Their ages ranged from sixteen to twenty, and each one was stunning. They had bought simple things from the keepmyfaves site, like banned films or classic boyband CDs. One girl had ordered a paperback book on Wiccan practices.

After saving their profile pictures to my laptop, I hacked into their private messages. Although the girls didn't intend to cause trouble, each was warned their accounts had been highlighted due to the items bought. Then it said this could be overlooked if they contacted the site staff on the following number. I traced it. It was registered to Ian Stymer.

One girl's private message to her mother was filled with excitement about being asked to attend a modelling audition. I couldn't trace whether her mother had received the message. Had it been intercepted? The missing reports only gave their descriptions; nothing had been mentioned about modelling appointments. Their families had not known.

The girls didn't have a modelling appointment. However, Karl had said he'd found money trails between the keepmyfaves and the YesPlease websites. So I delved further; Mr Robert Forbes-Hamilton Jnr. was one of its members.

Mark poked his head through the kitchen doorway.

"We're needed," he said sadly, "Jonah's asking about his mum and dad."

My heart sank. I hated the thought of them being hurt any more than they already had. I wanted to postpone it. Hesitantly, I sat beside them on the sofa and took Lily in my arms.

"I know we don't know each other very well, but I hope you can see I am not like the others that came for your parents. You've seen my Bible; you can trust who I am. You should know both Mark and I want you to stay with us."

I looked to Mark, who nodded.

"You aren't alone and never will be while we're here."

I brushed Lily's hair with my fingertips, and with a trembling voice, whispered, "Your parents didn't make it. I'm so sorry."

Jonah shot to his feet and ran out of the house. Mark went after him. Lily looked up with confused eyes, and I swallowed uncomfortably before plainly explaining that her parents weren't coming back. It was the hardest thing I had ever had to do, and my heart broke as she sobbed face down in my lap.

"I learned my laces. Daddy will never know I learned my laces."

I started to cry too.

"Jesus will tell him."

"Will He tell them I miss them?"

"He'll tell them anything you ask for in prayer, Lily."

The rest of the afternoon did not go well. Lily didn't want me one moment; then she did the next. Being the closest person she had to a mother, it confused her. I respected her wishes when she pushed me away and swooped her up into a cuddle when she asked for one. Mark had found Jonah at their flat flicking through home printed family photos, and they didn't return until five.

"You okay?" I asked, taking Jonah into my arms.

He froze but allowed it. The photo album he held stayed between us.

"Is Lily all right?" he asked.

"She's through there."

Watching the children grieve over their photos was agonising, and there was nothing I could say or do to ease their burden. Although attentive to them, I dug further into Ian Stymer, but having only public access on my laptop was restricting. I needed my software from work and decided to use Greg as my excuse to go in tomorrow. I wanted to see if there were any developments in his ongoing search anyway, and that would be what I would tell them.

~

Once Mark had arrived at the Manor gatehouse, he called me through e-chat. After confirming the dates the girls went missing, we watched the camera footage for the weeks directly following. I considered the reasons for the many vehicle entries. The night-time van visits were top of my agenda.

"Why would they have vans coming in the middle of the night? Don't that make you wonder? Can you ask, see what the night guard knows?"

"Don't read so much into it; it could be anything. Deliveries come at all times of the day. It doesn't necessarily mean anything."

"Will you ask?"

"Yes, okay, and I'll also see what paperwork I can find here in the office to tie up with the deliveries."

I didn't mention Robert Jnr. was a member of the deep-web site YesPlease. In fact, I wanted an unbiased element to my findings to remain objective, and Mark was the perfect instrument for that. So I paled when he walked through the door late that night, looking like he had discovered something he rather hadn't.

"I think you might be right. Same van, eight times over the last two years, always at night and according to the nightguard, always drove around to the back of the Manor."

"To where the building work was supposed to be?"

Mark nodded.

"Eight times?"

He nodded again.

"There were eight girls."

"Guess who the van is registered to? I got Tom to look it up. A Bristol based warehouse owned by–"

"Ooh, lemme guess, Ian Stymer?"

Mark handed me a picture. "It's always the same guy driving. This frame was the only clear image I could get."

"It's good enough. I'll get it over to Chie. He can get someone from Bristol to find him. You should know Robert Jnr. is a member of that porn site," I said, scanning the photo into my laptop. I sent it on to Tom with a note.

Mark sighed. "I'm struggling to get my head around this. If what that guy said about him yesterday is true…"

"That Robert likes screaming girls, you mean? Not-Pervy Pete said he'd known him since they were teenagers. I expect it's completely true."

After he frowned, confused, I explained the names I'd given to the strangers in the room.

"At least I can keep track of who's who and who said what."

I nestled into his arms, with the quilt tight under my chin, and as the conversation finished, I drifted into a troubled sleep.

~

HS Fraser was accessing my system when I arrived at work the next morning.

"Ah, you're not supposed to be here," he mumbled.

"Clearly!" I dumped my bag on the desk. "Is there anything I can find for you? I'm sure I'd be much faster at locating it than you."

"I noticed an ongoing search in the logs and came to check for myself."

"Then you should speak to Greg; he asked for the search to be raised. Has it discovered anything yet?"

"Uh, I haven't got that far. Apologies, Mrs Cole. Please, take your seat, and I'll leave you to it."

Flaming cheek! Though I was more concerned with how he had broken through my password when I'd had to write it down. I logged out. The username was his. Did HS officers have administrative access to override such passwords? Lord, what hope was there of keeping anything private anymore? I logged in under my own username and got to work.

A box flashed up on the screen. The green typed message read, 'what are you doing at work?' and I replied I was accessing a new search. 'Stop, it's being watched. GO HOME.'

I closed all the searches down: Greg's, Chie's, and London's, and went to find Greg.

"Hey, Anna, condolences from all of us."

"Thanks. Mark's doing okay, considering. He's arranging a memorial; you know, as there isn't a body to bury."

"What are you doing here?" Greg asked.

"I just wanted to make sure nothing else had come up on the search you asked me to do. But unfortunately, there's nothing there, so I've just closed it down. I'm back in on Tuesday, but I have an assignment with the HS officer, so I don't think I will have time to pursue it."

"Yeah, we heard about that. He wants you to investigate the bombings. I heard them talking in Pothrall's office yesterday." Greg leaned toward me and spoke quietly. "Is Richard Cole really your brother-in-law?"

"Yes."

"Wow, you think you know someone."

"What are you saying, Greg? Are you inferring–"

"No, sorry, I never intended…it just surprised me, you know, one of our own is related to THE top guy of the NCs."

"Not that I need to explain myself, but I can assure you, Mark and I were not aware of what Richard was doing. We hardly spoke to him. You can't choose family, though, can you? Let's hope I'm not assumed guilty by association."

"Point taken. Sorry."

I sighed. "It's not you, no, I'm sorry. I'm a bit insecure about it, as you can appreciate."

"Yeah, I do. No worries on that search; they've quit bugging me since there are more pressing things to deal with like finding those twelve disciples."

I snorted, "What?"

"'The disciples of terror', the media is calling them."

I shook my head in disbelief. What else would the world take from God's precious book and use it to label evil? Yes, to quote scripture, "they call evil good and good evil."

"Mrs Cole, I was not expecting you until Tuesday."

It was the first time Simon Pothrall had ever come to our offices, preferring we went to him.

"Sir, I know. I just wanted to clear the results from a search I was doing for Greg. It was important, and I had to come to the high street anyway."

"How are things at home?"

"Okay, Mark is better than I expected, but we weren't as close to Richard recently, and now we know why."

I hated insinuating that Chie was guilty, but until I could prove otherwise, I had to go along with Tisak's report the same as everyone else.

"Maybe I should have you stop by again tomorrow. I am baffled why HS are happy to wait until Tuesday before investigating these twelve disciples who murder so callously. I want them found and held to account now!"

I longed to tell him it was because they already knew what evidence I'd find. It would be there, ready on a platter, all neatly tied up and incriminating, waiting to be uncovered by the sister-in-law. Therefore, it must be true. The I.N. would blame Richard, and it would be me that discovered and proved it.

"Sir, you call me back in if that's what you need–"

"No, no," he interrupted, "apparently, it isn't necessary. Have you seen Teela? I'm considering putting out a mis-per on her."

"I spoke with her this morning," Greg confirmed. "She's not missing; she isn't in the country. Sir, she apologised but was adamant family come first."

Pothrall grunted and left.

I gathered my things and made my way home, straight to my laptop, where Tom had left me instructions on accessing my work system away from my desk. That was a blessing, and I began my search on Thurstworthy Manor Estate. I found a lot of entries mostly connected to Braithwaites during the year of the 'building renovations', with orders and deliveries of equipment by the thousands. There were hints of crimes involving Robert Jnr. That, no doubt, Snr. had bribed local police to cover up. No sooner had an allegation been made than the police or the victim dropped it. I noted the names down along with their addresses.

I then came across something interesting. A booking reference for a limousine to collect Ciel Tisak from Bristol the week before the mock rapture. I smiled to myself and printed it off. This was a find. Tisak had visited the Island of the GBR lots of times. There would be hundreds of car hire orders and invoices and plenty of travel information available if I wanted to find it. It was strange then to only find a booking reference: no invoice, no hire agreement, and no return journey planned for the world leader. The I.N. had wanted to hide evidence that Tisak had been there and attempted to clean behind them.

~

Before the sun rose on Saturday morning, the secure phone rang.

"Anna, we got the driver. He'll be here in half an hour. Get your backside down to the haulage if you want in."

HS Paul Fraser wasn't watching the house this early in the morning. I checked twice for tails before I turned into the industrial estate. Logistic Lionel waited in his car for me again. I yawned as I got in.

"Morning."

He nodded a greeting. "How did the Francis' kids take the news?"

"Not well. They don't want to talk much about their parents with us. They'll get there, though. We'll make sure of it."

"It was a big loss to us. Them too, I know, but to us, a massive, massive loss."

"Their son said they were arrested for contraband."

"Yes, it was all they could prove, but the I.N. knew more than that. They had watched them for months. They knew Daryl and Julia had NC connections and would have gone through a horrible time. The I.N.'s extraction methods are particularly rough. Old China's got nothing on them."

"Couldn't you have broken them out or something?"

He snickered darkly. "In your line of work, you ask me a question like that? Tell me how, if you know. I'll make sure I do it for my next many arrested friends before they're shot dead."

"Sorry, I didn't mean to be insensitive."

He looked across briefly with raised eyebrows. "Is there a way to break people out?"

"I don't know, but I did discover something this morning."

I explained finding HS Fraser at my desk and how he had passwords that allowed him to access and search my system.

"If we could get something similar set up, maybe we could have access to more things than we do now. I'm going to speak to Tom this morning."

"No offence to Tom, but I think it will need someone a little closer to home to pull that off. Like someone inside the headquarters in Baruun."

"Do we have someone?"

Logistic Lionel shrugged as we pulled up to a different safe-house. It contained the same people, and I updated them about the Manor's invisible renovations backed up with orders and delivery notes from Braithwaites.

Teela came up from the basement laughing.

"Sorry, Anna, your guy's cracked already! I couldn't wait, and as you know, I can be a little scary when I get going. As much as I hate Tisak, I do love to use the power he has over people. I got what we needed, but I'll let you ask him yourself."

In the cellar, a man in his mid-twenties sat chained to the pipes. Other than Chie, I had not interrogated anyone before. I'd watched Teela lots of times and reflected her ways as much as possible.

"Can I go now? I told you what I know."

"You haven't told me. I want you to tell me now."

"I pick up the girls, and I drop them off. Simple."

I stared and slowly raised my eyebrows. No, he was going to do better than that.

He sighed. "Okay, I usually receive an encrypted message telling me where to go, so I go. The girls are sleeping when they're put in the back of the van, and they don't wake up. I came from Scotland all the way to Wiltshire once, and she slept the whole way. Weird, right? But hell, I got paid well, none of my business."

"Where did you take them?"

Frustrated, the prisoner replied, "You already know that! Thurstworthy Manor."

"How many times?"

"Twelve…maybe more. I don't know." He shrugged.

"Then what?"

"Then what, what? I drive home again."

I leaned against the wall and folded my arms. "When you get there, what happens to the girls?"

"Someone comes, picks her up and disappears through the door with her, and I get my mouglar."

"They get taken into the Manor through the back door?"

Confused, he replied, "No, they never go into the Manor."

I needed Mark. I knew the land around the Manor a little but could not recall an outbuilding there.

"Where then?"

"The garages. Although they don't keep any cars in them. They look separate on the outside, but it's one huge room. I saw it once."

I started to leave.

"Can I go now?" he asked.

"I don't know. I think I have what I need."

"Why's the I.N. investigating anyway. Not exactly up your street, is it?"

"That isn't your business."

"That's what she said," he whined, "I haven't broken any laws!"

"Did we say you had? One of the girls did, and it's why we're looking."

I left him mumbling something about not wanting to hang around in the cellar all day as I climbed the stairs to the room where Teela sat with Tom.

"Have you got a satellite view of the Manor?" I asked Tom. "Where's this garage he's on about? I don't remember seeing it there before."

The image showed the far right of the estate, surrounded by lofty trees. If I were on the ground looking, only the thin mud road would indicate anything being there. It led to a massive, run-down garage space.

"This is where he reckons he took them. Looks a little too shabby to hold prisoners to me."

"Does a bit," agreed Tom, "it probably isn't on the inside. Will Mark check it out?"

"We can ask. What have you found from the data drive? Anything on London?"

Teela jumped in. "We have a few leads. We've got a Shan on it."

"A Shan?" I thought that was Teela's codename.

"Shan is a female NC, and Fred is a male."

I laughed. "So, how do you know which Shan and Fred?"

"We don't need to know if we haven't sent them. That's the point."

"As long as you haven't got more than one running at once."

"It only matters if we don't know them, and there are things in place for that. Don't worry about it. By the way, your search on Chie brought up all the new information you'll find next week with Fraser."

"Anything that can actually help us defend him?"

Chie laughed from the kitchen. "Are you on this planet with us, Anna, or just visiting?"

"Is that a no then, Chie?"

"It's a flaming 'of course not', of course!" Chie came into the room. "They would've made sure of it. There's no way Tisak would make a mistake like that after he burnt the original like he did. There will be nothing to help now; no offence, but it's thanks to your Manchester lot."

"Well, they would've preferred not to have investigated as well, wouldn't you agree? Now, they are dead because of it."

"I know, sorry. It's just there isn't a defence for me now. I will always be labelled as the terrorist who blew up Manchester."

"You need a new face and some ID."

Chie laughed. "I know that. Fred's onto it. I've been at this a while now, you know. I've hidden before."

"But it's the first time your face and name's been plastered on world TV as the most hated man on the planet."

"Don't worry. It's being sorted."

"Anna," Tom called. "What system does Mark have access to? Does it connect into the Manor?"

"I don't think so. It's just security information. Check with him, though. Why are you asking?"

"Gonna try and get in. I might send the drone up too."

"Karl's drone?"

Teela smiled. "Ours now! Tom hacked in, and I flew it home."

"See, something else that bothers me. How easy it was for you to find Javad in the market using voice rec. Why can't Tisak find Chie the same way?"

"They wish this was their tech! This is Karl's, and he never shared it with anyone except me. Plus, we had the area where Javad was hiding. Tisak can't drone the entire world looking for one man. Well, he could, but it would take too long."

"What will the drone do at the Manor that we can't see now?"

"It's not just to see," said Tom with a laugh. "It's to listen!"

Teela went to the top of the cellar steps.

"Chie, get Fred. Let's get this guy dropped off somewhere."

Everyone but Teela and I disappeared into the kitchen while Not-Pervy Pete brought the van driver up from the cellar. On their way to the door, I stopped them.

"Before you go, were you ever asked to collect any girls from Thurstworthy and deliver them somewhere else?"

The van driver shook his head, and just before Not-Pervy Pete pushed him through the door, Teela stuck her arm out to stop him.

"Don't forget, sonny, you tell, and I'll have you thrown into the rehabilitation centre in Baruun. No one comes out of there. Get me?"

He nodded, and they were gone.

I called Tom back from the kitchen and mentioned how Fraser had accessed my system at work using his own login.

"I know; I was watching. Your IP flashed up as actively logged in but not under your username."

"How long was he on it for? Because when I got there and asked if any searches had come through, he told me he hadn't got that far."

"Let me check. I'm in your system. It tells me what you're doing all the time."

I groaned. "I'm not sure I wanna know that!"

"He logged in at 08.53."

"Okay, he lied then."

HS Fraser had access to my computer for over an hour.

"What was he looking at?"

"Everything. All your files, old cases, calendar appointments, and emails. He scanned it all. He has also added some spyware. The I.N. views everything through its own system, but things you do privately weren't monitored. They are now. Watch out for Fraser. Seriously, he's clever and vile and has no conscience about what he does."

"Great! That's just great. Thanks for telling me, I suppose. Has Javad uncovered anything yet?"

"Not really. He just keeps going on about how fascinated he is. He reckons this LeyLucient undoes the layers that hold things together. Like if you ripped open a bag full of sweets, they'd fall out. This is similar. It takes the packet away, and the insides just spill out. That's what LeyLucient does to stuff. It breaks down what holds it together."

"Couldn't science do that already?" I asked.

"Not like this. I see a grown man almost wetting himself over it. He wouldn't be like that if it were something they could already do."

I pulled my phone out and saw home was calling.

"Hi, Anna, how long will you be? An HS officer, sorry, what was your name again?"

"HS Paul Fraser," I heard him say.

"Yes, HS Paul Fraser is here to see you. Can you make your way back?"

~

The commanding HS Paul Fraser looked very comfortable on my sofa with an empty cup of coffee in his hands. He hadn't removed his shoes, which instantly annoyed me, and he was in my home on a Saturday, uninvited. He looked satisfied I felt awkward about his visit.

I smiled brightly. "Sorry to keep you. I wasn't expecting visitors. How can I help?"

Fraser stood and handed me a copy of my previous searches. "I was hoping you might explain this."

I scanned it as I sat down, then looked quizzically at him.

"I wonder what some of those keywords had to do with the task you were set. You looked specifically at Portsmouth, and you incorporated bombing into that search. I'd like to know why."

Busted.

"I wanted to look at different angles as suggested," I replied. "Greg hadn't got anywhere, and he asked me to look under every stone. So, I tried different ways, different words."

"It appears a coincidence then you should add Manchester and bombing into the same search just days before the destruction of said city, doesn't it?"

"I…uh. Yes. I hadn't considered it."

Fraser was not persuaded. "Personally, I don't acknowledge such things as coincidences. In our line of work, they ordinarily mean something quite different. Don't they?"

I rolled my shoulders. "Sometimes, yes. Not always. What are you accusing me of here?"

He leaned forward and rested his elbows on his knees. "I'm not sure yet because being the sister-in-law of Richard Cole, this does not appear to be merely a coincidence."

"Sir, it is what makes me so good at my job. I improvise with my searches, go places others don't, and I'll follow seemingly unimportant tangents if I find them because you never know where they lead."

He gave me a knowing look and smiled a loathsome grin. "Quite. It is also what makes me so good at my job. I do the same thing."

I had to step carefully. "Then you understand. Sometimes, you throw in a bait line and see what bites."

"Did anything bite?"

I laughed. "To be honest, I think you would know more than me. I hadn't the time to go through many results, especially with not being at work this week."

"And the results you did access were only ones with Portsmouth references. Why was that?"

"I can't remember; maybe Greg mentioned it. I'd have to ask him to confirm. None were relevant, so what difference does it make?"

He pursed his lips. "None to concern you."

"Are we not on the same side?" I asked, shocked he felt the need to keep secrets from colleagues.

It was his turn to laugh. "Indeed. That is the question. Are we?"

"Excuse me, but I think you should leave now. How dare you come in here and accuse me when you have nothing to corroborate it!"

"I have your relationship with your brother-in-law."

"Who is under a pile of rubble somewhere in Manchester along with his NC friends! He was the leader, wasn't he? As Tisak pointed out. Stands to reason they'd be together."

"That's Imperial Kiengir Tisak, if you please, and you still maintain Richard Cole is dead?"

I sighed, annoyed. "That's where he said he was. I've already told you this."

"He has not called you since."

It was a statement, not a question, but I answered anyway. "No, he has not called us since. You can check if you like."

Fraser smirked. "Thank you for your permission."

He rose from the sofa and retrieved the search list before turning back to me with hooded eyes.

"If you don't mind, I'd like to get started on Monday and not Tuesday if you are amenable? I have a pressing matter looming, and I need to return to Baruun by the end of the week. I would like to allow plenty of time for us to work through the evidence I have uncovered in your absence, on top of what you find through your very curious search patterns."

"A week? We can't sufficiently investigate one bombing, let alone five in a week. It's not enough time."

"It's ample time. I think you will reach the same conclusions when looking at the evidence I have revealed. I will leave the file on your desk, ready for you to peruse when you arrive. 9 am?"

"Fine. I'll see you on Monday."

I sighed in relief when I closed the door on his retreating back. Mark appeared at the top of the stairs with eyes full of concern. He put his fingers to his lips to indicate a possible listening device. I nodded and used the possibility to our advantage.

"What have I done wrong?" I asked, faking a trembling voice. "Have I ever given my employers reason to doubt me before?"

"They'll see that. Let them investigate you if they want to; you have nothing to hide, do you? You have to expect it. Richard was my brother."

Mark checked the places Fraser had been while he spoke, but we both knew if he'd left something in our house, he would not have left it somewhere easy for us to find.

"Anna, can we go to the park?" Lily climbed onto my lap.

"Yes, come on then, fetch your shoes. At least, you take them off when you come into the house." I hoped Fraser heard that.

We left through the back gate, and once we were far into the fields, I called through the secure phone to update Teela.

"Give it an hour or so before you make your way back," she advised, "Tom is dying to try out the drone; we'll send it over and see if it picks up any activity from your house. Then, we'll call you back."

Wow, the drone was good. Was there anything it couldn't do?

~

Teela called back within half an hour. "You were right to be worried. There are two bugs. I can't tell where they are, though, but you should leave them there. It will look suspicious if you go searching for them."

My voice raised an octave. "I have two children at home! I can't expect them to be careful with their words."

Teela fell quiet, then, "You could all come and hide with me?"

"That's an option we're most likely going to need soon. I'm working with Fraser next week, though. So, let's see where that leads first."

In simple terms, we explained the situation to the children. They too easily understood the limitations of talking at home.

"It's not the first time we've had to," Jonah said, "and we know what to do."

"Ooh, Jonah. We get to do hand signs again!" Lily beamed. "That's fun, 'cause only you'll know what I'm saying."

"You'll have to teach me some," I interrupted, "else I won't know what you're saying."

"Do you know any sign language? My aunt was deaf, so we learnt it while we learnt to talk," Jonah explained, signing the words as he said them.

I shook my head and laughed. "That's about as much sign language as I know."

"Shaking your head's not it!" Lily laughed. "This is no."

She put her middle and index finger together and hit them against her palm, and then she touched her right index finger to her left ring finger.

"Oh, okay, I'll remember that," I replied as I pulled my ringing phone from my pocket. It was Dan.

"Hi Anna, thought I'd bell you. You haven't been over in a week. Claire's getting worried about the bomb–"

"Hi Dan, yes, sorry, things have been hectic here," I interrupted, as he had called my traceable phone, and I was afraid he might say something he shouldn't. "Mark's brother was in Manchester, so we're a little preoccupied right now, and it's not a good time to speak. Can I call you back when I'm free?"

"Er, yeah. Of course. Catch you later."

I returned his call within seconds from my secure phone.

"Dan, we're in a dangerous mess, and for your protection, you mustn't call me again. I don't want House of Security coming anywhere near you. I won't be joining you for ministry either. HS are following us; they're bugging our house. They're looking for Richard, and because they won't find him. I imagine Fraser taking us all down: he'll find some Collective Thought we've broken, and threads will lead to you. I can't have that."

He chuckled calmly. "We are not afraid. We're not given a spirit of fear but of power and of love and of a sound mind. So, those who hope in the Lord will renew their strength. They will walk and not grow faint."

"Amen, thanks. I needed to hear that."

"What happened to London then? We got friends out of the wrong city."

"They changed the target and cleaned the trace. Then they took out the team that discovered the plot. If Manchester hadn't sent the case to us, we wouldn't even know."

"Have to say; it was a mighty bomb to crumble entire cities into rubble like that."

"You have no idea." I described LeyLucient as best I could.

"The essence of the Breath of God!"

Perplexed, I asked, "What do you mean?"

"I have studied a little about ley-line energy. It is, I understand, a spiritual force, an energy that comes from the earth—much too mystical for modern science. I perceive it to be the breath of God. He is before all things, and by Him all things hold together. Job 34 says: If he set his heart upon man, *if* he gathers unto himself his spirit and his breath, all flesh shall perish together, and man shall turn again unto dust. How did God create the earth, Anna?"

"With words."

"Psalm 33, 'By the word of the Lord the heavens were made, their starry host by the breath of his mouth, for he spoke, and it came to be: he commanded, and it stood firm'. The one thing scientists are continuously discovering is what they call a strange force that holds matter together. They don't know what to call it, and they don't know how to identify it, so they call it cosmic glue. I call it the Word and the breath of God."

"Amen. So, what are you thinking?"

"That this Lucient stuff undermines that. It counters the command."

"No one or nothing can undo God's command but God Himself!" Even I knew that.

"Exactly. He's allowing it! Anna, God's protective hand is lifting from the earth, and His wrath is coming soon."

It wasn't the type of comment I wanted lingering in my thoughts as we said goodbye. I went in through the kitchen door, unable to express my worries to Mark. He wouldn't appreciate what Dan had explained, but more importantly, I had unwanted spying ears in the house. Javad would surely be interested if he hadn't already concluded himself. He did, after all, describe it like breath.

~

I didn't attend the ministry prayer meeting that night, but I had one of my own in the field behind our garden. Jonah came too, and we sat together to pray.

11 NCs New Recruit

On Monday, I entered the station apprehensively, returning the greetings of the desk sergeant politely on the way. HS Paul Fraser had done as promised and left the file on my desk. Inside were twelve photographs of the Non Conformers accused of the bombings: Chie's at the very top. Under those were phone transcripts and intercepted mail instructions from Chie, well from Richard, to the other eleven. I read the lies—the targets, the transport, the best place to position the bomb to ensure maximum effect, and who placed it in which city were recorded. The entire plan could be pieced together from it.

Underneath those were details of the purchases made through Braithwaites, and just as Teela had described, they were labelled as codes rather than items. These were ordered, purchased, and delivered under two aliases. I recognised M Seymour as the name Chie used during the Swindon riots, according to Karl, and a C Shepard.

I began my search on the system, and to avoid speculation from Fraser, I added curious keywords like Mercedes—to represent Chie's favourite car, a certain brand of tea because he liked a particular foreign one and had it imported, and investments—just for the sake of something else. Insurgent money was often tied up in assets. I prayed before I hit enter that whatever I discovered would not make anything worse.

Portsmouth results pinged off the chart. I had sixty-five within a few minutes, and I got to work. C Shepard was the name mostly being hunted by Portsmouth, and this C Shepard had committed many acts against Collective Thought. The task force really got serious when Mr Shepard attacked a transport van and freed prisoners on their way to rehabilitation. The excitement in my spirit heightened. I found myself internally celebrating that he had got away hurting no one, and the escaped prisoners were never recovered.

Good on you, Chie!

I felt a renewed respect for him. I hadn't understood why he battled against the new regime until recently. More so since Tisak burned a serious case that could have saved lives.

I found the same evidence Fraser had kindly left for me, which I organised in my own way on the system. The same way I would for any other case. I made sure everything I did followed procedure or my usual pattern. I could not hide anything, ignore anything, nor escape updating the system with my findings. Something I had done before to protect the Christians' hidden websites.

"I don't trust you, Anna."

Paul Fraser was leaning on my desk, looking over my shoulder. I jumped and felt like a coward.

"There's this niggling feeling I just can't shift. I don't like it."

I rolled my chair back angrily as I stood up.

"Then what's the point? What advantage is there to me doing this for you? I want the person responsible held accountable too. Do you think I would hide evidence, doctor evidence, or burn cases just to keep Richard out of trouble?"

"Burn cases? Why do you say that?"

"Shall I leave? Let you just get on with this on your own? I'll even keep my search running for you. That'll save you some time."

The other members of the team had stopped and were watching us. Fraser continued to stare at me as I glared back. I was told to be careful of him, but I was too angry at the I.N. to care, and despairing of the systematically planned lies that had Chie tied up so well he had no escape.

"Has your search discovered anything yet?"

"It showed me why you were so interested in my Portsmouth searches and came to accuse me at my home about it on Saturday," I replied, loudly enough for the other team members to hear. "That is not acceptable work practice."

He grinned that sinister smile again. "Anything else?"

"Nothing more than you, yet. If you trust me enough to allow me to continue…"

"All right. Continue. I'll sit right here while you do."

"Please, must you?"

"Yes," he replied, bringing a chair from another desk and sitting on the other side of mine.

I stared at him indignantly. "If you'd like to check the files, I have set you up as a collaborator. You have access to it and everything I put in. Then, you will have no reason to doubt my loyalty."

For once, I could speak without lying. God forgive me. I maintained that Chie was dead when I knew it not to be true, and I was keeping many secrets. But I wanted to find the true culprit, and I would try to find ways of proving Tisak was responsible.

Fraser brought his foot to rest on his knee and sighed in thought. His eyes didn't leave my face.

"It is difficult. Your repertoire of skills is phenomenal, and each member of this team speaks so highly of you. I am conflicted between that and the qualms I have about you. But I will entrust this to you, for now."

"Why, thank you for the compliment threaded in there somewhere, HS Fraser."

I turned back to my search results, and while I worked, Fraser sat mostly staring at me. Until he noticed something in my expression that caused him to stand behind me to see what it was.

My keyword for Chie's foreign tea brought up five GBR Island residents who had regular deliveries, and I knew one of them was Chie. One of the addresses, perhaps more, were safehouses belonging to the NCs. I had to share it.

"You searched for foreign tea? Why would you do that?"

"Because I know he likes it, and I want to prove I'm a loyal Neighbour who wants justice. No matter who the guilty party is. There are five addresses on here. One of them will be Richard."

It was hard to keep the name Richard at the forefront and not say Chie. It was how I knew the file was full of lies. It did not contain, anywhere on the I.N. interface, the name he would be known as among the NCs. If Chie were guilty and there were real transcripts and mails to find, it would be that, or the name Fred brought to my attention, not Richard.

"Update the system with the details, please. Right now."

With a heavy heart, I did as he asked, sincerely hoping Tom was watching and already warning the safehouses.

Please, God, let Tom see.

Fraser walked away from my desk, pulling his phone out of his pocket (filling Tisak in on the new information, no doubt). Praise God's timing that he did because Tom's message box popped up on my screen.

It said, 'What are you doing? You're killing me!'

I replied, 'You're killing me; get off and keep watch. Fraser is here!'

The box disappeared, and I resumed with the results. I smiled inside. I found proof that Chie had been in Manchester on the day of the bombings: a car hire agreement under a C B Shepard registered to an address in the centre. I added it to the files.

I uncovered many things about my brother-in-law that put me in awe of him. His skills, bravery, and genetic pig-headedness, a trait I was already familiar with in my husband, were unrivalled. Chie risked his life daily, saved others, and intruded on many I.N. secret plans which, dubiously, weren't hidden from me. Had they upped my security for this case? I couldn't remember having this level of access before.

The most surprising discovery was Chie could pilot a plane. When had he learnt to fly? It wasn't noted in his file, and I didn't add it. I could pretend it hadn't jumped out at me as relevant to even check.

What it had presented was the opportunity to get in and out of the country easily.

"The Kiengir is pleased and asked me to thank you personally for your service to the Neighbourhood," HS Fraser said with an insincere smile. "To be asked to investigate one of your family under these circumstances must be difficult for you. However, he wants you to know he understands."

I tried not to sound sarcastic. "Thank you. It's nice to be appreciated in the workplace. Then he'll also be pleased to hear I have found confirmation that Chie…eery Richard is dead."

Fraser sniggered. "Cheery Richard?"

I smiled and produced a grainy shot of him in Manchester town centre, talking to a girl with her back to the camera.

"Well, he looks happy here, doesn't he? Anyway, he hired a Merc that day, so we know he was there, just as he told Mark and me."

Fraser took the photo and sat down to study it, and I turned back to the search results which brought more problems than results for the NCs. I discovered an investment company in addition to five houses and had to log the details. I hated myself for giving Tisak so much. I had hidden my treachery to the I.N. by becoming a traitor to the NC.

By the end of Wednesday, I had exhausted the search results, fully documented my files and presented the lying evidence to Fraser and the I.N. network with a live reference number. House of Security in Baruun would manage it now and instruct the nearest task force to find and apprehend the other slandered men.

Now I hoped my part of the investigation was done, Fraser would leave Little Hampton, stop following us, and return to the rock he'd emerged from. Instead, he chose to remain at the station. I recalled an important matter he had to attend to. Why wasn't he leaving to go do that rather than following me and watching me at work?

He came to ask me about the children before I left that day.

"Mrs Cole, with respect, there is no record of you having a family of your own. I wonder, who are the children living with you?"

An unknown parental protection came over me.

"That's none of your business," I replied, but he gave me a menacing look, so I quickly added, "some friends passed away, and Mark and I took them in."

"Is it a standard procedure you follow here? Isn't it customary for Wiltshire County to respect the guidelines written for orphaned children?"

Stubbornly, I replied, "It is, I'm sure. Are you aware of what happens to kids in these homes?"

"I'm aware they learn Collective Thought and come of age as loyal citizens. What is so wrong with that?"

"And the other things? Would you want your children sent there when there are willing people to look after them?"

"If it is procedure. Given your ministry preferences, I do not foresee it being accepted. I will put forward a proposal to the International Small Neighbours Association. They will be in touch."

~

On Friday morning, as I left for work, I saw Fraser sitting in his car watching the house. I looked straight at him, and he returned the favour before starting the engine and driving away. Had he sat outside all night hoping we would do a midnight flit and give him reason to arrest me? Our last conversation stuck in my thoughts while I walked to my desk. Fraser would have to literally go through me to take those children away.

Greg pulled me to one side before I managed to put my bag down.

"Have you heard anything from Teela?"

I shook my head, lying again. "Why?"

"Pothrall's just promoted me. She's out. Did she resign? I wondered if you knew anything."

"No, first I've heard of it." I laughed. "Congrats, I guess. What's on the agenda then, boss?"

He chuckled and said, "Work, work, work 'til you sweat!"

I smiled. "Just like any other day, then?"

~

It was towards the afternoon that Tom's message box flashed up for the last time:

'GET OUT, GET OUT, THEY ARE COMING FOR YOU! AND DON'T GO HOME; THEY'RE STORMING IT.'

Hiding my panic, I snatched my handbag and keys and peered through the Perspex doors. The corridor was clear, so I ventured out and ran to the stairs. I heard boots coming up, so I went up one floor instead of down and raced through the corridors towards another stairwell. I made my way to the ground floor and peered out through the fire-door window. The reception was filled with soldiers. I was not getting out through there, and I was certain the back exit would be covered too. I wasn't sure where to go. I headed to the rear entrance to spy Logistic Lionel, chatting casually to a soldier there.

"What's this, then?"

"Move away, please, sir. I.N. business."

"Ooh, who you got in there, then? Love a good drama me! Is it one of the bombers?" he asked.

"We haven't been that lucky, unfortunately. Move away, please; it's just another NC reprobate."

That met with a fist to the guard's face and he went down with his nose bloodied. Logistic Lionel planted another before tossing me a bag.

"Put it on and hurry."

Inside was a blonde wig and a light purple coat which I put on, then strode through the rear car park arm in arm, me watching my feet as we walked. We passed masses of soldiers looking out for a dark-haired woman wearing red. That was what Fraser had seen me wearing when I left the house this morning. They didn't look twice at us as we got into Logistic Lionel's car and drove away.

Logistic Lionel sighed in relief and laughed.

"Respect. I wasn't sure you'd make it. I thought the back was the best place to go; hoped you thought the same."

"Thank you, Lord! What about Mark and the kids? Tom said the I.N. are at the house."

"I haven't heard anything. Teela called to say they were coming for you, so I grabbed this from my stash and met you at the back door. Totally broke the rules. I've shown my face now, but when someone takes in a couple of strangers' kids then they are probably worth the risk. Try Mark on this."

He tossed me his phone, and I called Mark.

"Anna, why aren't you answering your phone?"

"I don't have it. It's in the car, and I can't get to my car right now. I'm using Logistic Lionel's phone."

I mouthed I would explain when he looked over, puzzled.

"Where's your normal phone?"

"In my handbag."

"Take the battery and ID card out until Tom can sort it."

"Where are you?" I asked, fishing out my phone.

"Sitting in a café in Chippenham. Glad I took the kids out now. I'm thinking of booking into a B & B for the night and heading back early tomorrow. I don't know where else we can go."

In the background, Jonah eagerly said, "I have somewhere we can go."

"I don't think the flat is the right choice here, mate, sorry," advised Mark.

"Not the flat, I'm not silly. I had somewhere planned for us to go once the flat was rented out again. It's out in the sticks."

"Jonah, you're a star. Man, I love this kid!" I yelled in excitement. "Where do we go?"

Three miles out of town, we waited at the side of the road for Mark.

"Logistic Lionel? Is that what you call me?" he asked cheerfully.

"I can't call you all Fred; it's too confusing!"

"What have you named the others?"

He chuckled when I told him about Not-Pervy Pete.

"Oh, he'll like that! Betcha he keeps it. I've known him a while, and even I don't know his real name!"

Mark pulled up behind us and got out, leaving the children in the car. He came to the driver's window and all but kissed Logistic Lionel for what he had done for me, which he humbly waved off as all part of what family did. Logistic Lionel didn't want to know about the new place, so he left us, and we moved on.

"Did you walk all this way, Jonah?" I asked, surprised.

"Nearly every day. I was doing the best I could with what my dad taught me. The roof doesn't leak anymore, but it's cold in there during winter."

The cottage was derelict. Windows were broken, and the garden was overgrown, but all the better it didn't look lived-in. We could be safe here for a while. Mark pulled open the half hanging door of the garage and tucked the car in.

"Lead on then, Jonah, seeing as you're the man of the house now," said Mark, grinning.

Jonah led us in through the repaired and re-hinged back door. In the modest kitchen, tools lay across the surfaces, and the work dust covering the tiled floor contained Jonah-sized footprints.

"I haven't been here for a few weeks. We didn't think we'd need it anymore."

"I'm sorry, Jonah."

Lily folded her arms stubbornly and cried, "Not your fault. It's always the devil workers. They ruin everything, and now, we don't have a nice bed or TV, and I don't have Melanie."

I kneeled and hugged her. Lily's doll was the most important thing in the world to her, next to her brother.

"I'll get Melanie. I promise I will, somehow."

"No," she sighed, "they will catch you. I love Melanie, but I'd rather keep you."

~

Chie called an emergency meeting the next morning, and the four of us piled into the same safehouse used to hold Robert Jnr's van driver. No one was rested. Sleeping on the floor of a chilly cottage had not been the most comfortable, and I considered whether staying here was more appropriate—at least there were beds. Chie was livid. He paced the room angrily, cursing Tisak and Fraser, and he would not be pacified.

"Do they really look for absolutely anything they can arrest a person for? What's next? Excuse me, sir, but you're wearing white socks; that's ten years for you! Anna, what you wanna believe in is up to you, but they were going to take these lovely kids away from you because you are a Christian. Now that ain't right. We sent the drone over to your house, and much of your stuff is a charred pile in your garden. I can't imagine what the inside looks like, but trashed is guaranteed. It's guarded at the back and front, so we couldn't keep the drone up for long, and we couldn't send the Manticore in to explore without raising suspicion. Sorry, we'll try again in a day or two."

The Manticore was an inconspicuous bug inside the drone that acted independently from its mother. It emitted a trackable frequency and had a less powerful camera, but it could scan for other bugs.

Chie was agitated and would not sit still.

"This is all my fault. I never meant for you to be involved. I made sure I stayed out of contact with you, years without you, Mark. I hated it, and for what, for them to find a way to get at me by getting at you, anyway? He's gonna pay. I'm gonna make sure of it! If Tisak wants me guilty of a bombing, then I'll give him a real explosion to blame me for, even if I have to suicide bomb the palace myself. He cannot be left to continue this madness. Enough is enough. He's got to go. I am no murderer, Anna can vouch, she's seen my 'crimes'. Damn, she's burned five safehouses this week!"

I started to cry. It was embarrassing. The I.N. had invaded my home, burnt my things—my Bible—that was all that mattered to me, and I felt violated. The guilt I endured for giving away the safehouses was second to that, but added to the misery, regardless.

"You won't be bombing anywhere, Chie," Teela smarted.

Angrily, Chie replied, "He needs to go!"

"Yes, but that isn't the way. Aren't there innocents in Baruun? Aren't there babies and children just like Manchester? Friends of yours are there, too, aren't they? Do they deserve it? Bombing just the palace is wrong. His servants aren't to blame, flip, not even the soldiers are really. Most of them are just like I was, believing they are doing the right thing."

"He's hurting my family because of me."

Chie flopped onto the sofa exasperated, and Mark sat to comfort him.

"He's trying to catch us because he knows we know things."

Logistic Lionel leaned forward in his chair, clasping his hands together.

"And Fraser expected an easy target with Anna; there was only one guard at the back. I reckon he was there to keep someone like me out rather than stopping Anna. They wouldn't have expected her to be alerted."

Logistic Lionel looked weird. I couldn't get used to it. When I saw him yesterday, he had blond hair, a beard, and wore glasses. Today, his hair was shorter and brown, he'd shaved, and I assumed he wore contacts because his eyes were blue now and not brown.

He laughed as I stared. "Stop looking at me, will you. This is the real me without my disguise. I am King Fred when it comes to incognito, and now I need a new disguise. Tough luck that I will have to advertise for a new maintenance guy at the haulage firm."

He rubbed his smooth cheeks, and I noticed the bruises on his knuckles. He had hit that guard hard.

"Mark's looking for a new job." I flashed Mark a teasing smile.

"Hey, Anna–" Teela handed me papers "–got a result of the London search you did. The I.N. took out the last Saudi prince. Oddly enough, the files don't tell us why, even though it should."

"There isn't access if the case belongs to HS. That's probably why. While searching for the bombing evidence, my security level was increased. I saw files with unfamiliar pathways to our usual. Perhaps even secret files. Nothing came up relevant to Chie, but we're at least aware that there's another system within the I.N. framework we don't have access to. Tom, did you get anywhere with the admin login?"

"I can't get in deep enough."

"We can." Not-Pervy Pete leaned forward in his chair. "I've appealed to the HQ spy. He wasn't happy about it but is investigating for us."

The NC and Asiders working together were proving to be a good union. The two groups had used each other in the past, but they had never joined forces in this manner before. The bombing had Teela physically bring the two groups together for the first time.

"I have some info for you, Not-P…" I paused when Logistic Lionel chuckled, "um, I uncovered a few complaints against Robert Jnr. that I thought might interest you, only my laptop is at the house with the addresses on. I'll have to search again, but it could be worth looking into. They were all swiftly closed: pay-offs, probably."

"I want to do that with you," Mark suggested to him.

Not-Pervy Pete shrugged. "It's okay with me," he agreed, looking at Teela and Chie for confirmation.

Neither had an issue with it.

"Got them," declared Tom. The monitor fired into action and printed the addresses he'd accessed from the laptop I no longer had. "I've downloaded your hard drive, then crashed it so the I.N. won't have anything. The addresses are fairly near, but it would be easier if we got compatriots on board."

"No." Mark's facc was rigid. "I want to know directly from them. I will hear it for myself."

"You're still not convinced, are you?" I asked.

"I don't want to be convinced it goes on at all, let alone by my employer, who I have shaken hands with, drank scotch and laughed with. Makes me sick to think he's…like that."

Javad burst into the room, frightening Lily and made her colour outside of the lines. She sighed and started a new picture.

"I have news! Great but terrible news!" Javad clapped his hands excitedly. "I have revealed something in the Braithwaites files. We all remember that flesh-eating pandemic, right, and how we all went for the vaccine? Braithwaites had nothing to do with creating that. Bizarre then we should have the vaccine details and medical files at all, let alone on millions of people worldwide, but not everyone. Even more bizarre to find a form of teleportation has been discovered. Experimentally, according to the records, there were promising results showing six live subjects survived."

"Bizarre; why?"

Teela asked the question, but Javad looked straight at me.

"It explains the mock rapture."

I was horrified; Dan had been right. Tisak *had* performed it to undermine the word of God.

"How?"

"Can't tell you how yet; I can just see they did."

Silence fell. The science of tomorrow had been here yesterday, and no one knew what to make of it. If Tisak could snatch away six bodies and teleport them safely, could he do it for millions? At once? And taking only their flesh?

Mark was quiet. The severe expression he wore trespassed into his beautiful eyes, and I looked away. Even when he had hated my choice to serve God, he hadn't looked as hostile as he did now, and remembering his mother's death was never a good thing. Then, finally, he lifted his eyes to Not-Pervy Pete.

"Where's the nearest girl? I'd like to get started before I agree with Chie and do something stupid like blow up Tisak's palace myself."

"Just outside Oxford."

Mark turned to me. "You'll stay here, won't you, with Teela?"

"I'm coming too!" she declared, collecting her things together. "Forbes-Hamilton is my case; they're my missing girls, and I want in."

I shrugged. "I guess we'll stay with Tom then."

Chaperone Shelley walked in, smiling and lobbing a secure phone at Tom.

"Easy pickings that was! In and out in four seconds. I'm getting better, eh?"

Tom looked at me. "The showroom hasn't registered your car on the I.N. server yet, so they don't know it's yours. We've brought it home. This is the phone out of it. We couldn't let it fall into the wrong hands."

Chaperone Shelley held up a bag. "They'll be looking for Mark's Range Rover too, so I got some of these for you."

Inside the bag were new registration plates.

"If you want it sprayed another colour, let me know. I have a contact in Bath, they'll do it cheap. Though, not being funny, you're a pretty distinctive guy. You don't blend in, so there's not much point if you ask me."

"He won't be when I'm finished." Logistic Lionel jumped up, smiling. "C'mon, I'm gonna make you black!"

I laughed; I couldn't help myself. I looked forward to seeing that. They disappeared upstairs with Chaperone Shelley, and Teela and Not-Pervy Pete went into the kitchen to plan their interviews with Robert Jnr's alleged victims. When Chie left with Javad, Tom glanced at me.

He nodded towards the children and opened his hands with a shrug—he couldn't speak freely. There was nowhere left in the safehouse to go where we could talk privately, so I suggested the kids might want to watch Mark's transformation. They were curious and ran up the stairs.

"I have a mission for you," Tom said, leaning forward and taking my hand. "You're the only one here who can do it and get away with it if they catch you. First, I need someone to get inside the Manor."

He brought the drone's thermal imaging records up on the screen.

"These are the thermal frames of the Manor. These are people, you see, mostly over this part of the house. Here, this big block of colour, that's their servers and man, it's some equipment they got going on there. Serious gear."

He pursed his lips.

"I'm curious to find out what it's running. It might just be a generator, I don't think so, but if it is, then it's on all the time and powering something other than the Manor. They get utility bills, so it can't be that."

I was having a mini panic attack, and my throat dried up.

"I can't do that! I'm not equipped or trained to do anything like that."

"I'll deal with the cameras through the security computer. All you need to do is get into the server room and put this near the hard drive. That's it, stick it on, twist the top and wait 'til the light stays fixed, then get out. If they find you, you're looking for Mark."

"Tom, come on. I'm wanted by the I.N. I think they'll be onto that."

"No, that's just it. They haven't made your warrant public. No one else knows they're looking for you or Mark. If one of the Roberts sees you, just say you're worried about Mark. I dunno, maybe he didn't come home last night."

"I don't know, Tom. I'm not exactly the right person for this."

"You have a better chance of making it look innocent than the rest of us could."

I laughed nervously. "You haven't seen my acting skills."

"You'll be okay. Ten minutes, that's it. In and out. I'll look after you, I promise."

Movement on the stairs quietened us, and I looked up to see Mark coming down, dark-skinned and with dreadlocks down to his shoulders. Lily and Jonah were in stitches on the landing while I pulled my lips together to stop myself from laughing.

"Don't…even…say it!"

"Wasn't gonna," I said, then bit my cheeks to stop any laughter. I looked away to gain back control. "You look dashing."

He gave me an indignant look, not amused by my teasing, before rounding up Not-Pervy Pete and Teela, then swept me up in his arms.

"You'll stay here? I need to know you'll stay here. Don't go back to the cottage on your own. Promise me."

"I won't; I'll wait. How long will you be?"

"A couple of days. They're all within fifty miles of here."

Not-Pervy Pete slipped the addresses into his pocket.

"C'mon then, sooner we go and all."

Mark leaned in to kiss me. I backed away, and Logistic Lionel snorted.

"It won't smudge; it's dye. It'll take a week to wash out."

Mark was horrified, and I couldn't hold it in anymore; from the pit of my belly, I laughed as tears ran down my face. I did let him kiss me, even though he smelled of paraffin. I wrapped my arms around him and held on until Teela removed me so they could leave.

I hated to be apart from Mark, with the danger surrounding us. What if he didn't make it back? What if this was the last time I would ever kiss and hold him? I shoved the thoughts away before I decided to chase after him and demand he come back.

~

That night, while the other members of the safehouse slept, Tom and I got started on our own strategy. He gave explicit instructions I was to follow without fail if I expected to get in and out of the Manor cleanly, and I would go the day after tomorrow.

12 The Manor

I pulled into the narrow lane running along the back of the Manor estate gardens and followed it until it started to bend away. I remembered from our walk that Mark had parked up before he had driven this far. I pulled in, leaving my keys and secure phone hidden, and searched for the gate covered in moss.

I was dressed in a flat cap, jeans and a green t-shirt and looked like a boy. It was necessary in case the I.N. were watching the Manor via satellite. I carried the hack disk in my pocket and my new phone, which Tom had kindly set up for me. I was ready for the scariest moment of my life.

I found the gate locked, and it was impossible to climb, as was the wall behind the hedges. There was no point in me trying. I looked around, hoping to see something that might help. I hunted for tall and thick fallen branches and rocks, things that I could use to create a platform or a makeshift ladder to try to close the gap. Nothing. Then, further along the stream, I saw something promising and smiled. The tree was perfect. One of its majestic branches reached out and held hands with another on the other side of the wall.

I praised God. He had built a bridge for me.

I took a deep breath, found my footing and shinnied up the fat trunk, breaking into a sweat by the time I reached the branch. I sat to catch my breath, wishing I'd worn something with longer sleeves. I could see into the grounds. It was not six yet, and there wasn't a soul in sight. I tottered across with the branch between my legs and carefully found my footing down to the ground.

I had memorised the blueprints; I knew exactly where to go. I checked my watch. In two minutes, the camera at the rear would loop the image of the last ten minutes, allowing me time to gain entry through the back door. I hoped, by this hour, the staff would have unlocked it. Harvard would be after his bacon butty as he walked the grounds, and I would have to be inside before that happened.

I counted down the seconds and then set off at a fast run.

The door was ajar when I reached it, and the kitchen was quiet. I dipped my head in to assess before I entered and crept around the side to a doorway and set of creaky stairs leading down to a long corridor. Panic rose when I heard the staff coming back, laughing upstairs, and Harvard was among them. Although I saw no reason he would feel the need to come down here, I slipped into the nearest doorway to hide.

I was in a plush office, and the walls were adorned with pictures of Robert Jnr. with lots of influential people and celebrities. The one with Tisak was featured the most prominently. They stood together, as close as brothers. It hung behind the tidy desk polished to a sheen, and all the drawers were locked. There was also a filing cabinet in the corner. I suspected it was locked, and one hard tug on the top handle pulled the entire cabinet towards me. It squeaked against the floor. I braced, but the kitchen had fallen quiet again. I slipped out and headed further along the lengthy corridor towards the server room.

I couldn't resist peeking into the other doors along the way. One was a bathroom, a full-on wet room with all manner of beauty products for both sexes. The door next to it led to a bedroom. Just a single bed. Nothing else. I sighed heavily and closed the door. Robert Jnr. was definitely guilty, and I bet he had proof in those grubby drawers of his.

The air in the server room was uncomfortably hot, and it was hard to breathe. I could hear the buzz of electricity running behind the silver panelled walls to my right. My nerves were jangling, and my hands shook as I looked at panel after panel covering the equipment. I wasn't even sure where to begin. I took out my phone. Maybe if I sent Tom a photo, he could tell me where he wanted the hack disk. I returned it to my jeans; there wasn't a signal here.

There was a touchscreen with code running. I minimised the box because the researcher in me couldn't help but have a nose.

I don't know how long I stood there reading and uncovering information. Although disappointed not to find out anything about the girls, the stats I read were pretty damning. I seethed, scanning name after name after name: 3,756,524 entries, with their blood type and genetics. The same number of tailored travel jabs had been allocated to these unfortunate souls through Braithwaites, as Javad had found. I dug deeper. I uncovered records about tribes in the Austral Region who had fought the consensus of the rapture. They considered themselves prophets of God, filled with the Holy Spirit, and had argued that if they hadn't gone, then God hadn't called. Their protests had caused much unrest after one member strongly believed they had been left behind, and she committed suicide.

Reading further into the files revealed a communication from Tisak. He'd noted the tribes had not registered for testing, and blood samples weren't received during the first pandemic; and therefore, were not checked for antibodies. He also confirmed limited internet access in that region.

I didn't fully understand the relevance of either comment, but there was no doubt Tisak had performed the mock rapture and thus deceived an entire world away from their only Saviour, Christ Jesus. I had discovered a ploy of the enemy, and nothing could deter me, and nothing would stop me from exposing what he had done. A name change for it was most definitely in order. Then again, it should remain the mockery it was! Perhaps the name was apt after all. I was sure it would be how God would describe it—with derision and contempt rather than the charade that Tisak had performed and later named it.

I maximised the original box, leaving it running, and tried to locate the hard drive. I looked beneath the touchscreen and felt around the panel at the bottom, hooking my nails in and giving it a slight tug. It shifted enough to slide my fingertips in and yank it away. I pulled on the shelf, slid it forward, and pressed the tiny device Tom had given me to the base. I twisted the top, as he had shown me, and watched the tiny light blink incessantly while it hacked into the Manor's network. Tom assured me it would be quick, but it felt like an age.

I was aware time escaped me. I had already been in too long. I was annoyed at myself for not thinking ahead and getting the device activated sooner; instead, I crouched and waited for the light to stay orange. An unsettling came to my spirit, and my ears were on alert. I heard shuffling outside the door: the only door in and out of the server room. I carefully replaced the cover with a small click and backed away. I was still stepping backward towards the far wall when the door started to open. There was nowhere to go, and I prepared myself for what was coming next.

I heard voices in the room. I expected to feel the coldness of the wall on my back. Instead, I experienced a cold ripple through my skin, and I was in a corridor, staring too closely at a portrait of Tisak.

There was no time to consider the walking through walls theory as I heard male voices drift through the painting.

"I 'eard summat, I'm tellin' yer."

"Yuh 'eard the fans is all. There's no one in here, is there? Paranoid or what!?"

Assuming they could hear me if I could hear them, I held my breath and tried not to think about where I was and panic or how I'd travelled through a wall. I was grateful to be hidden.

Thank you, Lord.

"Summat don't feel right."

I heard a sigh.

"Look, there!" –squeaky footsteps– "Not shut properly."

I heard the click of the server cover.

"Don't mean nothin'."

"I 'eard it, I told yer."

"Yeah, you said. Ever fought it just unhooked from cooling off? People don't just evaporate, you know."

The other man laughed. "'Less it's the Kiengir's doin'!"

"Don't let 'im 'ear you say that. It's Imperial Kiengir to the likes of us. C'mon, it's all good in 'ere; we've got stuff to do."

I heard the door close and the room go quiet, but I could hear air rushing and a loud thrumming in my ears. I realised it was me. I breathed in slowly through my nose and stepped back. I stared blankly at the painted face of an evil man. Even with smiling, handsome eyes, as it depicted, there was an aura about him, an unease. Tisak was nearly fifty, yet he looked younger in the painting, and the artist had portrayed him perfectly. He was a beautiful man with thick caramel coloured hair, flawlessly smooth olive skin and the whitest teeth I'd ever seen. He didn't look a day over thirty.

He never looked a day over thirty.

I hated the thought of having to touch Tisak—even being in the same room with his face on TV was about as much as I could handle. I felt treacherous as I lifted my fingertips towards him and watched them sink into his nose. I pushed my hand in and back out, then stepped through. I rushed back to the server, took off the cover and pulled out the shelf to check the mini device. The light was fixed and orange, and I sighed, relieved it was connected, running, and completely undetectable. Unless it was physically found, it would run forever. I replaced the cover properly this time and stepped towards the door. I heard the same two voices getting nearer.

"Summat's rung them alarms, Baz."

"Yeah, yer right. Sorry."

I ran back through the wall, forward this time, and looked for another way out. They knew someone was in the Manor. I didn't know what alarms I'd set off, but I wasn't going to hang around to find out. I had to get out; now. I had done what I was sent to do, and we would find the proof we needed for Tisak's arrest. Oops, apologies, I meant The Imperial Kiengir, Ciel Tisak.

I followed the thin hallway. The air was unusual; it felt old and forgotten. At the end was an archway leading to darkened steps going down. My curiosity piqued. Was this where they had kept the girls? They were not here now. Their heat signatures would've shown up on the drone's thermal sensors, and Tom had only informed me of extra guards arriving yesterday afternoon. We assumed it was to cover Mark's leave. The other bodies belonged to the residents and staff.

I followed the steps down, cringing against the occasional string of cobwebs that brushed against my hair. The air was staler as I descended, and putrid at the bottom. It smelled of urine, vomit, and old blood. A light glowed at the far end of a bricked corridor with prison bars on either side, and I was grieved. I hadn't expected to find jails, maybe lockable rooms like the other one, with at least some comforts, but inside each cell was only a thin mattress and a bucket. Nothing else. I involuntarily shivered.

I moved on. At the bottom was a silver door with a scan keypad beside the frame. Useless to me. The prick test alone would give away that I was not an authorised staff member. This entry pad scanned the retina, a fingerprint, recognised a voice, or tested your blood. It would choose for you if you wanted to gain entry. I preferred the keypad. Good old-fashioned codes that could get you in. If only I had another mini hacking tool because without one, I was going back the way I came, and I would be caught.

"Water," someone whispered.

I spun round.

Each cell had been the same, except the one behind me; the only one I hadn't looked in, assuming it was unoccupied as well as all the others. According to the thermal images, it should have been, but we had not considered areas too deep for imaging to pick up a reading.

There sat a straggly figure wrapped in a tatty blanket. The woman looked rough. Her bobbed black hair was nest-like and matted, neglected for some time, and her lips were dry and cracked.

"Water, please," she croaked.

I showed her my empty hands and went to the cage door. I pushed, pulled and tried to slide it, but it would not budge, not even a rattle against its frame. She flopped against the wall and wailed. It was a haunting moan that lacked strength and volume but held so much pain; I dropped my woeful gaze.

"How do I get you out?"

I looked, but there wasn't a keyhole, grip hold, or an electronic switch on the walls.

She glanced at me with strange eyes and shook her head, lying down underneath her blanket. I couldn't just leave her, but I had no idea how to get her out.

"How do I unlock it?"

Her dry lips peeled apart when she replied, "It opens when he comes."

God, what was I to do?

Voices in the distance caused us both to look up. I explored around me. There was nowhere I could hide. I felt along the back wall, hoping for another portal, but I met with hard, cold brick.

"Quickly," she hissed at me, "the code! Do exactly what I say. I'll give you the number, but keep the number pressed for as long as I count, okay. Do you understand?"

I didn't but turned to face the keypad opposite her cell.

"8, 4, (1-2-3-) 7 (1-2-3-4-) 2, 5 (1-2-) release."

Nothing happened, and the voices got closer.

"It's not working!"

"Because you aren't doing it right. It's not just a code; it's also got timed pressure. Do it again, 8, 4 (1-2-3-) 7, (1-2-3-4-) 2, 5 (1-2-)."

Tssss.

An airlock released, and the door slid aside.

"Go!" she cried, flicking her wrist.

~

A small light turned on above my head and the door slid shut behind me. My heart was thumping in my chest. As I stood motionless, the light dimmed to off, so I made every effort to remain still, trying not to draw attention to the fact there was an occupant in the room. However, I could not be sure that a slither of light wouldn't find its way through a crack in the doorway.

I heard a faint hum in the room but nothing beyond the door. Maybe it was secure and soundproof. I allowed a few minutes before I stepped forward. The air was different in this space—fresh, cool, and with no odour. An overhead light came on and then another as I walked…and walked, illuminating the steel gangplank I followed alongside the wall. I went down metal steps and around to a lower level and stepped off into an aisle rather than descend any deeper. More lights lit as I moved forward to reveal curved, coffin-shaped objects stacked in blocks of four on columns that extended from beneath me. They lay half a metre apart. As far as the lights would allow, I could see them above, below, and on both sides of me.

What were they? Pods?

They were metal based with a translucent cover, so I peeked in. Empty. Though shaped like a human, I saw dented contours in the white bottoms. I continued along the gangway to row after row of these strange pods, peering in periodically to see no faces. I was glad about that. Were they stasis pods, or was that entering too far into the realms of fantasy?

Fantasy. It was simply the reality of today.

Tisak had the best and brightest working together for him, and not competing with each other as they would have been before. Now, they combined their ideas and knowledge to such degrees it was almost impossible to combat the evolving science and digital tech that these people produced. Our guys were good, yes, but they weren't a patch on who Tisak employed.

Thank God for our informers.

I reached the end of the aisle with no idea which direction to take as darkness descended where I'd stood still. I couldn't see far enough ahead to get any bearings. I chose left and walked, pressing down my rising panic.

I needed to get out, and I couldn't see where I was going, but what I really wanted was to leave with that woman. I would come back for her. I would have to. I would not just leave her there to rot the way her captors had.

A fresh set of lights lit, and against the wall, there was a switch handle. I pulled on it.

Tclunk, Tclunk, Tclunk.

The immense space lit up in sections, and I gasped. Hundreds of rows of pods rolled into view, going left and right and down into a lighted blur…bottomless. There were none on the top level above me. I saw no other gangplanks coming across the width, only the one I had left behind that joined the stairs and then swept the outskirts of the whole area. I'd assumed anyway, I couldn't see either end. I scanned as far as my eyes would allow for another exit, failing miserably. I would just have to keep going, but not before taking a few pictures on my phone.

I found another set of stairs and climbed up. I was as high as the space allowed now, and I convinced myself that there had to be another way out somewhere. And if it were anywhere, it would be on this floor…level; there were no 'floors!' I kept going, less concerned with the sounds of my footsteps against the grated metal walkway echoing back to my ears. Another exit became visible, and I started to run, realising I needed a code as soon as I reached it. It didn't matter whether it was the same one; I couldn't remember it, and my heart sank. I wasn't getting out. There was no way I could get out.

The door slid open suddenly, and before I could react, hands grabbed me, and the lights went out.

13 Oops, Was Not Expecting That

I woke to stiff shoulders and an aching head. It was lolled forward, and my vision cleared so that I could see my bare, goose-bumped thighs. They had removed my jeans but thankfully left my t-shirt alone, and it clung to my clammy chest and back. My arms had been pulled back. I barely noticed the scratches from my tree climbing; the corners of the chair were digging into my armpits, and my arms were twisted and anchored together with something heavy and slightly warm against my wrists.

I wriggled them, trying to uncoil my frozen arms, which sent a shockwave up into my shoulders. The scream made my head hurt, and pain pulsed into my right ear. I smelled blood. My naked, numb feet were tucked around the backs of the front legs, secured with the same gadgets that I guessed held my wrists. I felt the same weight and warm sensation; they zapped me too when I tried to re-adjust my ankles and bring feeling back into my toes.

The large space I was in had huge arched windows, high up near the roof, and they were the same style as the Manor garage. Pale light filtered through them. Was the sun going up or down? How long had I been here, bound and left unconscious? My shoulders burned.

I was not getting out.

No one was coming to rescue me. No one other than Tom even knew I was here. Though not sure, I suspected my captors knew who they had caught because I had woken up. They hadn't killed me yet. Therefore, I was valuable; I had the information they could obtain from me.

Yes, they must have known exactly who they had caught. And Mark would be next.

I realised I was slipping in and out of consciousness every time I came around, and my anger flared because I hadn't managed to stay alert. I lifted my head with resolve, determined not to pass out again.

It was completely dark outside now. Dim light came from behind me, but I couldn't turn. The restraints holding my arms twisted against the back of the chair made sure of that, and it was painful enough to adjust my shoulders without being electrocuted when I tried.

My laboured breathing was the only noise for a long time. Then, I heard a thwop-thwop-thwop nearing and becoming louder as it circled the roof. The vibrations intensified, pressing in on me as the helicopters landed, first one, then the other. Thumping footsteps marched outside the windows in front of me.

Time was up.

Whoever had arrived had probably come to deal with me.

I heard them before I saw them. They came from behind me on a fast march. Booted feet swept either side of me in unison. Thump-thump-thump-thump, stopping only when the head linesmen met to create a shape around me. The scene was eerie; rehearsed. Each soldier knew exactly where to stand, how to stand, and where to look.

The three men at the corners I could see faced away from me, weapons bared, as did a few others in their lines. The ones in between them had designated areas of their own to scrutinise. One looked up, one looked out, and the other glared directly at me. The pattern repeated all the way around to cover every inch of the place. Even in the areas you might consider good hiding spots, they would have seen you, eventually. No one else could possibly be as still as these guys had become.

"Mrs Cole."

It was not a voice I expected. It was a voice familiar to me. I gulped.

"Rebellion may well run in the family. Would you agree…Anna? Do you mind if I call you Anna?"

My blood ran cold. He was behind me, and just hearing him say my name felt like a knife stabbing a voodoo doll.

"I asked you a question."

I flinched. He had come right up close and bent low. His earthy breath swept the side of my neck, and I could smell his aftershave, scents of pine and patchouli. His hair tickled me, and my stomach lurched. I turned and tilted my head automatically in revulsion.

"Actually, I'd rather you didn't refer to me at all." Every part of me trembled as I answered, but I had God's strength, and this man could not take away my faith.

Amused, he huffed and retreated.

"Spunky, that one," he said to his comrades, who laughed.

I lifted my eyes to meet another soldier's dead ones glowering down on me. It was unnerving the way he watched without blinking, so I shut my eyes; it was too much.

Have mercy on me, Father. I pray it's quick. Give me the strength to endure and the words I need to do your will; I pray, in Jesus' name. Thank you, God, my King, my Jesus–

"I wonder, Anna, did you honestly believe you could enter an establishment such as this and not be noticed?" His tone was playful and full of scorn. "Did you truly?"

I remained quiet; my eyes firmly shut. He was not far behind me. I could hear his pacing footsteps, and I felt the tension rise in the room like a poisonous gas.

Was he annoyed I refused to answer? Part of me was ecstatic at the thought.

"Oh dear, I think maybe she did, after all," he said with a chuckle.

I would not bite. As much as he sought to insult me and desired for me to feel every inch of my failings, I preferred to let him think I had trespassed without considering the consequences. Let him also think that my reason for being here hadn't successfully been carried out.

He continued in his slow but perfect way.

"I must apologise for my lateness, Anna. I did not intend to keep you waiting for so long. You see, I had hoped to be among those that apprehended you, but alas…the world's needs beckoned, and I was delayed."

He'd hoped to be among them? What did that mean? I frowned, vaguely recalling it was being studiously watched by at least four soldiers in the room. I felt the unnerving bubble again. It was a five-hour flight from Tisak's base of operations in Baruun. For him to hope he was among them…that meant…he knew I was coming!

Only Tom and I had made the arrangements. Nobody else in the group knew anything about it. How did Tisak know? I swallowed, the muscles in my neck tightening.

"I see that provoked a reaction," he breathed into my cheek and chortled, "I would like to determine why you are here if you would be so kind as to explain yourself."

My skin pricked while he spoke to me. It was disconcerting to feel him so close behind me, conveying the strong and powerful persona of a world leader in total control of a weak and vulnerable me. I may have been rendered almost paralysed by the restraints, but the use of my voice was my choice. I stayed quiet, and the unanswered explanation grew heavy in the air.

Tisak might have discovered I was coming, but he hadn't known why.

He inhaled deeply and sighed. "Is it to be like that, then? Are we going to become unfriendly with you?"

I almost laughed, but then fear overtook me. How much more unfriendly could a person become? I was bound, half-naked; I'd been hit and electrocuted and scared. I shuddered as a trickle of sweat rolled down the side of my face.

Tisak gripped my shoulders so suddenly, so tightly, that I was startled first before I felt the sharp pain rip through me. My twisted muscles tensed further under his extraordinarily hot hands, and I cried out while struggling against his dominant grip. The restraints burned electricity up into my shoulders and legs, and I screamed out again.

Tisak snatched his hands away and hissed, "What is this?"

Was he talking to me?

I fought through the lingering agony of my arms while another bead of sweat ran down my temple.

"Are we barbarians?"

Did he want me to answer that?

"Is there any need? What can she do? Switch it off." I heard the scuff of shoes. "Now."

Though no one came near and touched me, somebody had obeyed. My wrists and ankles cooled; the warmth of the restraints faded and was no longer active. There was compassion in him, after all, and it took me by surprise. I lifted my shoulders gently, then regretted it.

"I would much rather handle a person without being electrocuted," Tisak went on.

So much for compassion, then.

He was right behind me again. Couldn't he face me, or was it a tactic to sneak around behind me where I could not see his approach? Did I want him to face me? I truly didn't think I could hold his gaze for very long. He returned his hands to my shoulders, less severely this time, pushed his thumbs into the base of my neck and pulled me tight against the back of the chair.

"I have my own informers, Anna. As do you, I am sure. And as you have uncovered all of this, it can only lead me to conclude that you do, but not for long. They will be discovered and dealt with."

As will yours, I thought, knowing someone had told him I was coming.

He released me, and I heard a shuffle. I opened my eyes and stared ahead, but noted he was studying me from the side a few metres away. I found it hard to believe he was here, with me at his mercy. Of all the places in the world he ruled, he appeared in the same one as me. Seeing him there out of the corner of my eye was about as close to reality as I wanted to get. I breathed deeply and shut my eyes again.

"Are you afraid to look at me?"

Yes, I was. I was afraid that I might burn up from a fireball rising from the ground the moment I made eye contact with him.

Greater is He who lives in me than he who lives in the world; I heard the Spirit gently remind me. My eyes flew open, and I stuck out my chin but failed to turn my head and look directly at him. He would have to come to meet my eyes.

"Forgive me, but I am going to say something illegal to our beloved Collective Thought." He must have noticed a surprising expression because he stopped and inserted, "Ha, does that shock you? Need I say it shocks me too. I find you quite mysterious, Anna. I have yet to meet another woman as quiet as you. Resilient too." He entwined and stretched his fingers.

Yes, utterly illegal; to make comparisons, especially those gender targeted, was an offence to Collective Thought, but then he was probably used to pliable women. He expected responses to his questions. He expected gushing apologies, admissions of mistakes and begging. He would get none of that from me.

He could send himself to rehabilitation if he wished, I supposed.

"Have you nothing to say for yourself?" I felt his stare as he finished with, "other than what is apparent on your face, of course."

I was not a good actress and even worse at hiding my emotions. Chie's teasing voice flickered in my memory, prompting me to focus on something fixed, so I stared at the backs of the soldiers in the corner—not one of them had moved since they assumed their positions. I was positive, in fact, as I thought about it, that none of the other soldiers facing me had even blinked.

They were machines. Humans walking in waking comas.

Tisak was undeterred.

"As you wish. I will continue then to read you instead. You speak loudly in your body language. It is not just your face that reveals you," he jeered. "I see your thigh muscles tense. I watch your abdomen quiver. I can even time the pound of your heartbeat as I observe it moving the fabric you wear. I see your fear, Anna." He laughed again. "I can feel it."

I was helpless to control my instinctive reactions; I was not even aware of having them. It was hard enough to keep my breath flowing evenly. It was hard enough to accept this would be the last day I would spend on this earth. Monitoring the fear was impossible.

Strength, Lord.

"Allow me then to tell you a few things." He paused for effect. "It appears you have found the rapture beds, most unfortunately for you."

Rapture beds! I shifted minutely in my seat. It was making sense now.

"Hmmm. Did I just give something away? Ah…you did not know what they were. No matter." His voice circled behind me as he walked to my other side. "You would have worked it out for yourself because I know you have made other discoveries that are not of your concern."

My lips pressed into a hard line, and it did not go unnoticed.

"Tsk. My knowing things makes you feel uncomfortable, does it not?"

It was as if he had dug into my skull and plucked out my thought when he added,

"Or is it more how I know that worries you? How could I know you are aware of LeyLucient and what it does? How could I know you are fully aware that it was I who orchestrated those city attacks?"

He did not appear troubled in admitting these things in front of his guards.

My words came without conscious thought.

"I know something else, too. I also know who you really are, *Imperial Kiengir Tisak*." I hadn't known I could be so sarcastic.

"I know you do."

I was tempted to peek a look at his expression. He was admitting that in front of people!

I narrowed my eyes. "Then you know God wins."

He sighed and spread his arms. "We know. You win. You might even get to have your fluffy little life with your fluffy little God, or you might not. Either way, know something else…. victory is ours, too."

He came closer, but my eyes stayed glued to the backs of the soldiers at what had been the farthest corner from him.

"How many do you think my god takes from yours?"

Oh Jesus, help me, please.

"Not this one," came my curt reply.

Tisak shifted irritably, took another step forward, and angled towards my eye line. He looked beyond me, lifted his hand, and circled his pointed finger. He turned to a soldier to my left.

"Not you."

I guessed the gesture was meant to relieve the room when they started to file out, staring at the backs of one another's heads. In moments, I was alone with him and the empty shell of a soldier-man that served only the commands he was given. I had nowhere left to look.

And there was no way out. Lord, into your hands I commit my spirit.

"Are you ready?" Tisak asked, calmly, smoothly.

Oh, God, ready for what?

He stood in front of me.

"Look at me!" he demanded, gripping my chin and pulling it side to side, but my eyes were set—he would have to meet mine. I couldn't make them slide to his gaze even if I wanted to.

Tisak stepped back. "Look at me or never look again."

The guard approached, holding out a dagger. Tisak took it and turned it over in his hands.

I cringed and closed my eyes. I breathed against the fear that should have been powerless. I breathed against the racing of my heart and the tension my body held and ached with. I breathed to combat the nausea at even the thought of obeying, and I slowly peered at him, starting at his feet, while silent tears ran down my cheeks. I was humiliated, and my defiance had fled.

Tisak was always the same—immaculate and perfectly groomed. He had just spent hours travelling, yet he looked pristine. He wore genuine Brogues, tailored, black trousers with no jacket over his electric blue shirt, and as usual, no tie. My eyes stopped at his smooth chin. He had beautifully soft and supple skin, sun-kissed coloured and closely shaven with no wrinkle.

I halted there, unable to slide my eyes up the last few inches to his icy eyes, but he fingered the sharp end of the dagger, flicking his fingernail against the tip to make a menacing, tinging sound.

I sighed and met his stare.

I didn't burn, melt, or explode against the walls. Instead, it felt like I was floating. I caught my breath, not knowing what to expect next.

He swooped closer to me until he was only a pace away, and I had to raise my chin to keep eye contact.

"That was not so bad now, was it?"

I wasn't so sure about that.

Tisak held up the dagger, balanced at its point on his fingertip, and the guard came and took it from him. Wasn't it strange that this soldier knew exactly what he wanted?

Tisak was close enough to smell again. The aroma of his aftershave tingled my nose, and my laboured breath audibly dragged it against the flesh of my throat. It made it itch. At the same time, there was confusion, a conflict inside. I liked his smell.

Lurching a final step forward, Tisak closed the space between us, and I whimpered, expecting him to strike me. When I cringed and stared into my lap, he crouched down, resting his hot hands on my naked thighs and squeezing hard with long bony fingers.

"Now, now, let's not squander the progress we have made. You were doing so well."

I squirmed under the excruciating contact he forced upon me. Did I prefer the queasiness I felt when I viewed him or the repulsion and pain while he was gripping me? I looked back to his face, panic pushing at the thin elastic of my control.

His gaze pierced my soul, and his words tingled on my skin. "Are you ready?"

I blinked pathetically. Was I ready to do what? Die, cave in, be tortured? It took a moment to organise my one worded answer.

"For?"

"To learn…and then to tell."

I narrowed my eyes, struggling to understand what he meant.

"I tell you things; you tell me things. It is how conversations progress; yes?" he asked, gripping my thighs even tighter, and I winced again.

Tisak stood up, leaning in, planting his weight on his grip and brought his face closer to mine, rapidly gaining on the distance I generated between us by stretching my neck as far from him as it would go. He breathed his heady scent over me as he laughed, his nose almost touching mine.

"You have no need to fear me," he said gently. "I have no intention of hurting you."

He was hurting me now, and my countenance must have reflected the doubt that raged inside because he laughed again and lifted his eyebrows. My glance flicked to the soldier.

"Eyes on me, please."

Tisak wouldn't give me a moment to relax. He enjoyed observing my struggles between obedience and stubbornness too much.

"I wish not to be obliged to remove such…exquisiteness." He examined each of my eyes, and they rolled under his glare.

What was it that wanted to lure me in against my will? Everything about him was attractive. The way he looked and smelled, the confidence he oozed, his intelligence, and the overall manner that he held. I knew, if not for my God, I would have been swept in, into the illusion that he had created to hypnotise an entire world. The illusion that made you want to do whatever he asked.

His uncompromising stare continued to bear down on me, growing more staggered when, I presumed, I hadn't reacted in what was the usual way. I wanted to like him. I wanted to do what he said. But there was something stronger in me that wouldn't allow it.

Tisak was irritated but grinned. "How interesting!"

Without looking away or moving position, he lifted a hand from my thigh and gestured to the guard. "Bring my jacket." Then he leered at me with a crooked smile. "Let's get started."

Tisak stood up straight and backed away, taking the jacket and drawing my phone out of the pocket before handing it back. He scrolled, tapping, studying and reading, accessing my data on it. That was new. How could he infiltrate my security defences?

I looked down at my lap while he was distracted. His red hand marks were stark against my pale skin, and I was reminded again of the reality: I would not make it out.

"Anna, please, must we blind you?"

Tisak had turned my phone to face me, displaying one of the pictures I had taken of the pods. The rapture beds.

"I cannot allow you to keep them, you understand. I have attached a multifaceted virus to these, now blank images on your cloud, Anna, and it will ferret out any device that has or tries to access them. They will be entirely immobilised."

He paced a short distance in front of me.

"Tell me, Anna, where are the locations of those devices likely to be?"

Long gone, hopefully. The instant I was caught and the security of the safehouse affected, the NCs would have cleared out.

"I don't know," I replied honestly.

"Come now," sneered Tisak, "I trust you do not expect me to have any conviction in your statement, do you?"

"It's the truth."

He raised an eyebrow. "If you insist." He bent low to my face, and his glare was ablaze. "I may not be effective in halting the rebellion of the people, but I can certainly set them back a few decades."

My shoulders slumped painfully, causing my forearms to burn more than they already did, but that agony was nothing compared to my distressing thoughts. Both the Asiders and the NC networks would be obliterated. Tom had access to all, including my online storage.

Tisak seemed pleased with my response and backed away, showing me the rapture bed photo before handing the phone back to the guard.

"That is one of my greater achievements!" he boasted with a smile. "Are you of the same opinion, now you know all the facts?"

Was he looking for congratulations? Good wishes and praise?

"I couldn't possibly be intelligent enough to fully appreciate it, I'm sure."

"Shall I explain then? Would you indulge me?"

I looked away, blinking, but he did not pull me to obey this time. Instead, he appeared not to notice as he began animatedly.

"How have I managed to select mostly Christian subjects? Would you like to know about that?"

No, I had guessed the answer to that one.

"The virus of the 20s gave me access to blood. Everyone was tested for antibodies, if you remember, even you. Cross-reference them against public censuses, church memberships and government petitions, and I found an ample number of Christians for such an impressive undertaking. Then the second pandemic had to come so that a vaccine could be given out. Millions of Neighbours were told their antibodies needed an added push if they intended to travel to certain countries. Those inoculations had an extra something in it just for those selected Christians, an ingredient for my LeyLucient to find, already programmed with the genetic structures of each person's DNA. Then, it was able to collect and displace, pick them up and put them down somewhere else! How marvellous! It can very much pull apart and reattach every cell within you. Did you know?"

I remembered queuing for the vaccine. I also remembered the discharge contraption having to read a prick test of my blood before it gave the nurse my tailored syringe. I hadn't needed the health check-up or a travel jab. I wasn't a Christian at the time.

"What a stroke of luck, most of those who had survived the returnings turned away from your God to serve mine!" he chortled derisively and said again, "victory is ours, too."

This time, my eyes moved to glare at him voluntarily and with tenacity.

"It is what you people call the great falling away, so I believe," he explained as he neared me again. "Is it not?"

He had learnt the dance. The closer he came to me, the more nervous I became, and he played very much up to that as he circled behind me, like he had in the beginning, and placed his hands heavily on my shoulders. Despite the burning pain it caused, I didn't tense against his heat.

He brought his lips close to my ear. "Now your turn."

I was getting used to this line of questioning and had better control of myself. I did not recoil. That was until he grabbed hold of my cheeks and whipped my neck back to view his upside-down face, and I released a rasped scream as I tried to breathe through the thinned channel of my throat.

I heard a click; it echoed quietly in the room, yet it hadn't captured the attention of my tormentor.

"I must ask you again, and I insist this time that you answer me in detail. Give me the locations of your friends. Your brother-in-law, Richard Cole, particularly."

"I told you, I don't know. I really don't know," my croaky voice mumbled, "and Richard is dead."

His deep laughter boomed. It still echoed when he released me, and I brought my head forward, circling my shoulders, which again I regretted.

"How much more deception can possibly fall from your lips?"

"You would know," I muttered, much too quiet for him to have heard.

Tisak brought a chair and placed it butt up to my knees. He sat on it with his legs astride, leaning in.

"Really? I would? How so?" He entwined his fingers as if in prayer, then rested his arms flat against the crease of my thighs, his balled hands resting at my groin.

My heart lurched.

"Look at me, please."

I thought I'd gotten away with that. I wasn't sure I could mentally deal with it, as well as his hands. I glanced up submissively.

"I don't know where they are; I've told you."

He smiled. "You said," he replied while slightly wriggling his fingers, pushing his knobbly knuckles into the insides of my thighs. It wasn't a sexual act. It was a tactic to demoralise me, and it worked. It took my thoughts to places I didn't want to see.

"What about your husband? You must know where he is?" He tilted his head, noting how I had curled my toes against the shock of the topic change. He noticed every move my body made and responded with an unsettling expression; he enjoyed it. "Now, I perceive how to influence you."

Just by watching me, Tisak knew. It was often his words and facial movements that told me I'd expressed anything at all.

"Mark Cole is Headsman here at the Manor, is he not? Though not for much longer, credit to you."

"Mark is loyal to his job and knows nothing about this." I hadn't lied; he didn't know.

"I would rather he reveals that to me himself. Perhaps score a hat trick and detain Richard Cole while I am at it. What do you think?"

I sighed. "My husband is innocent of this. And Richard is dead."

"So you keep stressing. Only I know it, as a fact, not to be true. How can you keep lying right to my face like this?" he spat, scowling at me, and he released his balled hands to grip angrily at my thighs before sliding them up harshly to my hips and back again into another tight grip.

I shrieked in pain.

"I know he is not dead. You are a Christian, yes? Does not your law state not to lie?"

Tisak did not take his eyes off me, and I was powerless to remove mine if I wanted to keep them, so I found a way to bear it by concentrating mostly on the bridge of his nose. It freed my mind to think clearer.

He couldn't have known Chie wasn't dead, not for sure. But then he should not have known I was coming to the Manor today or was that yesterday? If he had an informant, then it was one tightly in with us or high up the Asider chain. It was pointless knowledge to me now; I would not survive to share it with anyone.

"Lie, lie, lie. That is all you have done for many weeks. HS Fraser was particularly concerned about you having such access to our databases. How many other Non Conformers have you protected, thereby undermining your position with us? You are deceitful and underhanded. I wonder if I was mistaken in allowing you to investigate Richard Cole. Perhaps I should have permitted HS Fraser to arrest you the moment he became suspicious. But I am a fair man. I prefer to be certain."

I scoffed, "You were not mistaken! It was deliberate. I could see that. The case was too clean, too perfect, and what better way to cement the lie than to have me, his sister-in-law, confirm his guilt!"

Tisak's backhand came fast and hard and struck me on my left cheek. The chair wobbled. Little lights freckled my vision, and a new ripple of nausea rose as I groaned woozily.

"Do not be INSOLENT with me again, Anna Cole. I have had people bleed for less." He returned to my thighs, squeezing and pressing down his weight again. "You are not looking at me. Why are you not looking at me?"

The soldier withdrew the dagger when Tisak saw me lift my head and obey.

"There's nothing I can tell you about them," I whimpered, "but I will tell you I only came here looking for the girls. It's always been about the girls."

It was the first time I had seen Tisak genuinely astonished. He sat right back in his chair with a blank expression and took his nasty hands with him. He had no idea what I was talking about.

"The evidence brought us here. That isn't going away. And until those girls are returned to their families, along with perhaps the hundreds of others sold by Ian Stymer and Forbes-Hamilton Jnr, this case won't rest, whether you get rid of me or not," *or Mark for that matter*, I finished in my thoughts. I didn't want that topic brought up again.

His eyes narrowed as he recovered. "What girls?"

Other than the one in the cell inside the Manor, should I mention her, or would that hang a death sentence over her head? Maybe that would be preferable to her because I was going to die and not be able to get a message out to say she was even there.

"There are several I could mention who were kidnapped and sold through this Manor." I reeled off the names of the girls as the old, excited researcher rippled out of me.

"What interests me, Anna, is not where you came from but what you found along the way and for that, I am afraid I cannot let you go."

He brought his knees in further, crushing mine, and leaned forward to rest his elbows.

"Unless you have anything valuable to share, I will leave you in the hands of my men."

Shocked, I hissed, "What, are the lives of hundreds of girls not precious enough for you?"

"Not particularly," he admitted, then smiled, "not unless they are Non Conformers. I would offer them freedom in exchange for their loyalty."

Tisak reached out for his suit jacket, and the soldier approached with it.

"I do so like a nice suit," he said, standing as he slipped on his jacket. He rubbed the cuff deep in thought. "Clothes maketh the man, would you not agree?" He performed a flawless spin.

The man's ego repulsed me. For someone who claimed to hold no airs and graces, Tisak was unbelievably vain. Christ maketh the man, my friend. Had he not heard?

"What a shame you shall not see the day that my god will come," he murmured, proudly beaming while doing up his buttons. "The day he shall don his suit!"

As if that was Tisak's only purpose—to become the skin of Antichrist—to offer his body to his god so willingly. The worshipful way he had spoken made me suddenly throw up. Tisak took a few steps back and whistled loudly. I heard a scurrying behind me and an approaching set of footsteps. The new guy sniffled at the vomit on me and the floor.

Tisak turned aside to speak to him. "You know what to do, then you know what to do after that. Do wait until I am out of the room. I do not want blood on my shoes."

The man nodded sharply. Tisak grabbed the man's hand and placed my phone in it.

"Dispose of this properly before returning to your duties."

The man nodded one last time and turned to rest his focus on me. He did not move until Tisak and his soldier had left the building, then he circled behind me.

Okay, it was time now.

Lord, I'm coming home. Receive my spirit into your arms, merciful Father.

The cold barrel of the gun nuzzled at the base of my neck. I held my breath.

14 A Hazmat, Really?

"WAIT!" the voice hollered from somewhere behind me.

The gun dropped from my neck.

One of the guards came beside me, holding something blue. He signalled at my restraints, and they unlocked.

"Put this on," he said, throwing the blue item at me, "and get rid of the t-shirt. You stink."

I sat for a moment nursing my shoulders, still reeling from my near-death experience when the butt of a rifle struck in-between my shoulder blades.

"Do what ye told." The second guard's Glaswegian accent was heavy. He held up a restraint to me. "Ye've endured level two on these beauties. Canna imagine what level three does? Wanna find oot?"

I opened the folded item. The material was smooth and crinkly, and it rustled as I pushed my legs through and slowly pulled it up. It was an all-in-one. I turned my back to the men in the room and removed my t-shirt, then slipped the blue suit gingerly over my shoulders.

"The Imperial Kiengir thought that a hazmat was appropriate for you." He grabbed hold of my wrists, and the restraints were put back on. He looked at me strangely, then bent to my feet and slipped the gadgets on my ankles. "You must be summat pretty special. The Kiengir never changes his mind. Never. Ever."

Praise God.

He led me barefoot out of the door. I started to struggle when I guessed where they were taking me. The helicopter rotors were in full swing, loud and windy, and one still had the door open—waiting for me.

The guard who had been ordered to shoot me held up the remote.

"Level three then, uh? Ye wanna see what it's like first?"

Shaking my head, I stepped forward and was placed in the only empty seat, in the centre of a row opposite another line of soldiers' blank faces. Tisak wasn't on this post-army transport helicopter, but I was sure his absence would be short-lived. We would soon arrive wherever he was taking me, and the questions would begin again. I breathed nervously. I preferred the bullet.

The journey didn't take long. Why was that? Whenever I wanted to go anywhere, hours seemed like days. Now, transport was putting down at an old RAF landing strip next to Tisak's opulent plane in what seemed like minutes. My wrists were held together in front of me, and the ankle restraints were only wide enough for me to take small steps. I was pulled off the helicopter and then dragged up the flight stairs to the rear plane door, where they shoved me forward and into a seat. Once in the air, I was taken to small sleeping quarters. I wasn't sure why it surprised me. Of course, Tisak had bedrooms. The door slid closed behind me, and I was alone.

The room was basic. A single bed covered with a navy duvet, a bedside cabinet and a wardrobe. I sat on the bed, then pulled the duvet around me and cried. It felt good to release it, and it was some time before I wondered whether my sobs could be heard elsewhere. They subsided, and I slept.

~

I was shaken roughly awake, and the duvet was pulled from me.

"Up!"

This was a new face. A scary face. He was a Capital Provincial with tawny skin, black hair and eyes like a starless night: dark and empty.

"The Imperial Kiengir apologises. He would invite you to come and sit with him, but as you aren't appropriately dressed…he hopes you appreciated his joke. Toxic was how he described you."

The man pulled me up by my arms and pushed me out of the bedroom. He took me to a bathroom further down the aisle, the shower already running. He took off my restraints and indicated I should undress. I hesitated until I saw the look in his cold, black eyes.

I complied and stepped under the water.

The guard watched me through the glass partition. I had never felt such shame, and I prayed he wasn't getting some kind of kick out of it. I nursed my thighs more than my shoulders and arms. The bruises were already showing, and dark red dots had come up from the burn Tisak's hands had given me. I stepped out and dried myself, and then my watchman handed over a white shirt and a navy skirt. It looked like a flight attendant's uniform. He did not give me anything else, and I was taken back to the bedroom. Someone had left a prepacked sandwich and a bottle of water, and although it had been at least a day since I last had anything, I wasn't hungry. I settled down to eat the sandwich anyway; starving myself would not help. It was only fear impeding my appetite.

I wondered how far into the journey we were, assuming we were heading to the world's capital. There wasn't a window to look through or a clock, and it was disorientating enough without being uncertain of the day. Worse, was the insecurity I had about why Tisak had changed his mind. Oh, God, what did he have in store for me? If he had changed his mind—something, apparently, he had never done, then it had to be for something important.

~

I awoke to a chill in the air. I sat up. Tisak was leaning against the door frame, watching me with penetrating eyes.

"What a difference a shower makes," he said, smiling and admiring the view. "Now that you are not bleeding and covered in toxic substances, I can see what your husband finds attractive in you."

I gripped the duvet tighter around myself.

Tisak laughed and pointed to a small camera in the corner.

"No need, I have been watching you," he confessed and laughed at my horror. "I came to inform you, we will land shortly and as you look and smell more appropriate, I would like to invite you to come and sit with me."

I wanted to ask if the invitation was one I could decline but thought better of it. Instead, I was compliant and followed him until he pointed to where I should sit. He pulled the belt across my lap, tighter than necessary, and it stung. He sat beside me with a satisfied grin.

"Have you been to my city before, Anna?"

I shook my head.

"Shame. It is a beautiful place. It would have impressed you. I apologise then, in advance, that you will not receive the same hospitality provided for my usual guests, but I shall assure you it will be nicer than the place from which I have just plucked you."

So more than a chair then? Thanks. But I did not agree. Neither this, nor the room he would later keep me, was better than the place I would've been in had the bullet been discharged. I would be with Jesus now, and nothing or no one was more pleasant than that. My primary concern was why I was even on Tisak's plane. What game was he playing? Or worse, what did he have in mind to do to me? I couldn't give him information; I didn't know any. All safehouses were renewed so regularly, I had hardly visited the same place twice. On top of that, I was missing, which would automatically reset all NC (and Asider) security defences. They would not return to any of the houses I had known.

It wasn't the sort of thing you asked the world leader, though, was it? Excuse me, but why am I here? Why did you change your mind and not kill me? And what value do I have if I have nothing to tell you? Did one even ask Tisak questions? Not even his journalists did that anymore.

"Hmmm, interesting. What are you thinking about?"

Tisak had been reading me again.

"What I'm doing here with you," I answered churlishly. So much for worrying about asking him a question when it was my tone that prompted trouble.

With a wry smile and a sarcastic tone, he said, "Ah. It speaks. Albeit so rudely. Are we becoming a little too comfortable?"

I automatically apologised, then shook my head at myself. Why was I apologising to him?

"There is plenty of time to discuss that later, Anna. We are about to land."

~

The weather was stifling, and the helicopter journey over to the palatial home of our beloved world leader left me weary and irritable. It wasn't the best of moods to be in when sitting next to someone who desired nothing more than for a person to be submissive and suppliant. Under different circumstances, I might have been in awe of the view below me. It was a breathtaking sight. The world government building was shown often on TV, but seeing it in real life was astounding. The lavish palace had been built from the ruins of Persepolis and built triangularly around it was the I.N. headquarters (built like the old pentagon had been). At the three points of the I.N. headquarters were tall, glass skyscrapers that housed and employed the capital staff. We descended towards the towers, into the palace grounds, and I jumped down onto concrete that burnt my bare feet. I was pulled along quickly, though, so I didn't have to endure it for long, then taken through the elaborate arch made of terracotta and white stones and onto the cool Persian mosaic tiles of the grand hallway.

Tisak stopped abruptly and turned to me, spreading his arms proudly.

"Welcome to my home. I would like your stay here to be as comfortable as possible. So, I am presenting you with a choice. I can either offer you accommodation at the very top of my residence or at the very bottom."

Tower or dungeon? That was not a fair choice.

"It will depend on if you behave. Are you willing to be good?"

I nodded because what else could I say? I would rather the comforts and take my chances.

A reserved older woman took me. She didn't speak as we climbed the majestic staircase that had me breathless when we reached the top. We walked the length of the palace, it seemed, before she stopped and pushed me up some tight, winding stairs to magnificent servants' quarters.

She pointed as she spoke, "Bath; bed; sit," then spun around and left me. There was a curt click on the door lock at the base of the steps.

The space was in three sections, but only the bathroom was partitioned off with a tall, gold folding screen in the right corner. There was a queen-size bed with ample storage along the left side, two armchairs and a small table in the centre. Not bad lodgings for a captive.

What was I to do with my time now that I was here for the foreseeable? It was hot, and difficult to concentrate. I thought a lot about Mark and the children, hoping and praying they were safe and hadn't come to any harm because of what I had done. Did the gang know Tisak had taken me hostage? The anxiety resurfaced when I thought about Tisak's informant walking freely among my family and friends. I had to find a way to let them know, including where I was. And I hoped the cell woman was where I had left her. If I could get to a phone, then I could tell them about her too.

Thinking about her worried me. Tisak hadn't asked how I got inside to take photos of the rapture beds. Maybe it was obvious who had helped me, and if so, the woman would most likely be dead already.

At dusk, a young local girl wearing a long white dress came carrying a food tray. She placed it on the table and scarpered down the stairs without a word. I lifted the silver lids to see rice, chicken and vegetables, and noticed something written on a napkin tucked under the glass of juice.

'I tell them you here. They do something.'

Thank you, God!

It was comforting to discover one of our own in the palace, and I would try to talk to her when she returned. I ate the delicious food, not stopping to think if it was safe to eat. It smelled too good, then I resumed my sitting and staring at the wall. There wasn't much else to do other than look out through the V-shaped, glassless window, and to do that, I had to stand on a set of drawers.

The girl returned and collected the tray. I went to speak, but she shook her head, and without a word, nor another note, she retreated down the stairs and locked up. My bubble of hope burst, and I sat back despondently in the chair. Tisak would come for me eventually, and I had to decide how to proceed. Continuing to claim that Chie had died in Manchester seemed futile when Tisak categorically knew it wasn't true, so I would have to admit I'd lied to him and face the consequences. I hoped my admission would pacify him, and maybe he would believe me when I tell him again: I honestly didn't know of Chie's whereabouts. Recalling the obsessive look in Tisak's eyes while he demanded information from me was unnerving. He wanted Chie. It was almost an aching need to be rid of the annoying human rebel nobody could catch. I could relate to the feeling in my line of work. No one liked an elusive renegade, which was exactly what Chie was. Me, not so much. I was stupid enough to get caught.

I prayed through the evening and into the black of the night until my emotions were spent, and peace descended. The air was cooler, and I climbed into bed, still wearing my clothes. The ache in my arms and shoulders had worsened, as over-stretched muscles often do, and my attempts at easing it hadn't helped. The restraints on my wrists held tight, so I couldn't bathe and get some heat into my muscles. I wished I had thought to ask the girl for medicine.

~

The following morning, I woke up startled by the girl coming in with breakfast. Stiff and hardly able to move, I sat up like a plank, groaning in agony.

"You in pain?"

I nodded.

"I ask." She was gone again.

I pulled a piece of toast from the plate and nibbled on it. I couldn't face more than that. From my chest up was agony; even breathing strained the sore muscles around my breasts. I held my head in my hands, but it did not help the stabbing headache. The girl did not come back. There was my answer. Tisak had wanted my stay here to be as comfortable as possible.

~

Hours later, I was summoned to an ornately painted, air-conditioned room at the foot of the grand stairs and placed on a white two-seater near the window by the same man that had watched me shower. I was not feeling well. This was not the best of positions to be in, and I was right at the bottom of my game.

Lord, over to you; I have nothing left to give.

Tisak strode energetically into the room, followed by the older woman carrying an extravagant tray. She placed it on the table by the window and served local tea and a light lunch. I couldn't even reach for my cup and just sat there staring at my fingers.

Unimpressed, Tisak snapped, "I serve you refreshments, and you refuse?"

I did not want to—it went against every stubborn, prideful and obstinate characteristic in me, but I started to cry. I managed to at least hold it back to a chin trembling, teary waterfall rather than the wail I wanted to scream out and rock the palace with.

"Ah, yes, that escaped me!"

Tisak slipped his hand into the pocket of his beige linen trousers and popped the lid of a bottle. He handed over two tablets, along with the tea, then sat down opposite me, almost gushing.

"I have received the information I have been waiting for. I prefer to have my facts before I interrogate. Although I am a proficient lie detector, I have deemed it necessary and more intelligent to have the counter-details prepared in advance."

"Okay," I replied, resigned to answer anything he asked because I couldn't find the strength to resist.

"We *are* making progress! Shall I ask you about Richard Cole now or later? Are you going to tell me he is dead again? There is plenty on our agenda that requires discussion. You may choose."

"Will you consider taking these off?" I lifted my hands from my lap.

"I might."

Dejectedly, I looked down at my lap and sighed. Okay, I would jump the hoop.

"I lied."

"About Richard Cole? I know."

Silence hung in the air.

"I don't know where they are now, though. I promise you."

The restraints around my wrists unlocked, falling loose in my lap and I instinctively lifted my hands to hug my shoulders. I winced; the painkiller had not yet kicked in. Tisak reached forward and took them from my lap, and I flinched, then cringed when he snapped,

"Please, do not do that! Are we no longer of the same accord? Why would you give me any reason to hurt you today?"

I tried to relax. Or should I say, I tried to fake that I had relaxed?

Tisak handed me a list. "Whether you know the locations of these people is inconsequential now."

The list said: Richard Cole, Mark Cole, Teela Franklin, Thomas Strauss, Javad Shirvani and seven other names I probably knew, but as the names I'd invented, or Fred. So many of the NCs called themselves Fred or Shan; real names were rarely used.

"How much does your husband love you, do you think?" he asked, watching me. "Why are you confused? It was a simple question, was it not? Do you think he would do anything for your safe return?"

I couldn't decide how best to answer. Yes, I hoped he loved me enough to storm the palace Rambo-style, but Mark was not that witless.

"I'd like to think so," I answered honestly.

"Would you say he loves you more than his brother?"

So, an exchange was his plan.

"Well?" he asked impatiently.

"You can't seriously think they would believe that? They would never agree to an exchange or trust you enough to follow it through."

"Why would they choose not to believe it? Are my promises not fulfilled? Is my word no longer respected among the Neighbourhood?"

"I..."

"Eyes on me, please, Anna."

I looked up.

"What if I promised? Do you think he will comply, then?"

He paused to study me.

"I have a series of delights I thought I might share with him about what will happen to you should he refuse. Do you think he will comply then?" he asked, still watching me.

"After that, I was considering a few other possibilities. I would be surprised if he allowed you to enter that kind of service...Do-you-think-he-will-comply-then?"

I opened my mouth to speak, but nothing came out. I was too busy organising the words. Chie would turn himself over in exchange for me, no doubt, if I would go free. But Tisak confirmed only yesterday, I would never go free.

"All right. Let me try an easier question. What were you doing with the servers at the Manor?"

My heart sank. Lying was not an option. "I looked at the files."

Tisak sighed loudly. "That is not an answer. I am astute enough to already know that." He leaned toward me. "What were you looking at in particular?"

I thought it best to keep the missing girls at the forefront, so I looked away and replied, "I explained all of this yesterday. I am looking for five girls."

"Ah, yes. The unpleasant Mr Stymer. He is not a nice man but a capable one. Did you find anything?"

I shook my head.

He sighed irritably. "What did you find instead?"

"A list of names, medical records…it didn't mean anything to me." I omitted to add the other items I had read and the hack disk I'd hidden.

"How sure are you that the girls were held at the Manor?"

"Unequivocally."

"Would you like me to have them returned?"

"Yes."

"Will you at least look at me while you supplicate?"

I met his eyes and repeated myself while a slow-burning resentment flowed into my veins. How submissive did a person need to be for him to be satisfied? I felt the anger blush on my chest, and he smiled. I'd forgotten the blouse I wore had no buttons above the cleavage.

"Next question. Hmmm. Maybe I should point out first that I have intelligence on this. Then you will not choose to deceive me…How did you obtain my key code?"

Argh. I knew it was coming. Oh, God, I was going to get that lady killed. I could not give her away.

"It's a code known by few. So now, tell me, how did you come by it?"

I couldn't lie, and I couldn't tell the truth. It was an impossible situation.

"Would it make any difference if I said it wasn't compromised?"

Tisak looked stunned.

"Certainly not, but you evade my question at your peril."

"I…I can't tell you," I said finally.

"Then you leave me NO choice." Tisak stood swiftly and went to the door. "BRING THEM IN."

Six frightened men were shoved into the room and forced to their knees by the butts of the weapons that the soldiers held. Tisak paced in between them and me, and whether he listened to the sob of the innocent man saying over and over that he hadn't done it, I couldn't tell, but Tisak didn't speak for some time. Why had he brought them? They had nothing to do with me not willing to answer his question. I baulked, starting to slowly get the message.

It was not what I expected.

"One of these men gave you the code, Anna. One of them is a snitch. Point him out and let the innocent ones return to their families."

The sobber went quiet, mollified by knowing he wasn't the guilty party.

"It wasn't any of them, I–"

"It is one of them. We are the only eight people alive who know it, and you, Mrs Cole, are the second person to use it. Can you guess who the first person is?"

My expression must have answered because he continued.

"Correct, me. I am very keen to squeeze out those disloyal to me, and I am shrewd enough to know you have an informant right here in my headquarters, so, again, I ask you. Which one of them is aiding your cause?"

I shook my head.

"You would like me to murder the other five, is that it?"

One of the guards brought him a handgun which Tisak cocked and aimed ready at the bowed heads of the men.

"No!" I screamed, jumping from my seat. "It wasn't any of them!"

15 From Height to Depth

Leaping from my seat was not a clever move, especially when the room was filled with men employed to protect the Kiengir. The initial surprise of waking in the quarters wore off, and I recalled the scary faced man diving onto me and smashing my face down onto the table.

I climbed from the bed, stiff from my other injuries, and went to the mirror. I felt the swelling around my cheekbone, and some bruising had started to show. I turned away, not recognising the stranger staring back. The sun lit the bathing area as it had a little before dusk yesterday, so it appeared I had been out for the entire afternoon.

The door opened, and the young girl came up. She gawked at my face but didn't comment. She handed me some wash items and underwear, then slipped my hand inside the folds of the towel, pulling me behind the screen. She signed not to speak and pointed at the ceiling, then her eyes and ears. She opened the fold of the towel to show me paper and a pencil and expressed that I was to only read and write behind the screen. She put the towel in the cupboard and left.

To learn another camera watched me was mortifying, but at least I could bathe in private. As Tisak had freed me of all restraints, I ran the water and enjoyed the heat soaking into my aching body.

I found the typed message with the paper when I towelled dry.

> *Anna, I had to watch them take you. Sorry! I couldn't stop it. We'd both be dead. He wouldn't have shot you, though; I was on that. Heard about the rat and virus, too. Fred's sorting it. I know where you are; we're working on a plan. Love you; don't forget. Stay strong.*

Alarmed didn't cover it. Mark had been watching that night! How was he not captured? There must have been around fifty people in the Manor garage, each highly trained to seek out uninvited guests. I was appeased Mark knew about the informant, and things were being done to seek them out. I wrote a reply and tore it from the page while the water ran to rinse the bath. I couldn't stop thinking about Mark after that, and while I dressed, my thoughts drifted back to the day we first met…

It was mid-September and unusually warm for the UK. It was great to be able to wear my favourite white summer dress again, even if it would be for the last time that year. I carried a handful of books, as well as a heavy bag thrown over my shoulder, along a path at Bath University.

"Hey, pretty lady!"

The smooth voice came from an ice cream van parked alongside the kerb. It was sheltered beneath one side of an avenue of trees that bordered the gravelled path. I looked up with a shy smile to greet a black-haired, tanned man leaning through and filling the side hatch.

Wow. My lips parted, and my pulse rose, growing louder in my ears. It took a second to pull my scrambled thoughts together. He was older than me and very striking. I couldn't yank my eyes away from the stubbled face beneath his floppy, black hair.

"Can I tempt you?" he smiled widely, pointing to the menu.

His smile was all I saw. There was nothing but his grin for a thousand miles until I felt the heat spread across my chest. I politely informed him it was not hot enough for ice cream while subconsciously placing a clammy hand beneath my throat. The red blotches had surely broken out.

"Not too cold for it either," he countered lightly, while tilting his head and raising his dark eyebrows.

I didn't accept it at first. I stepped closer, and his gaze gripped me. While my heart erratically thrummed, his emerald-green eyes raked over every detail of my face. He took in my light complexion, deep brown eyes, my thin nose, and full pink lips.

"It will have to be a proper whippy," I said.

His face lit up with another broad smile, and his eyes danced with glee.

"All the trimmings?" he asked as he pulled his broad shoulders back through the hatch, the sound of cloth scraping against the plastic edging, and grabbed a cone.

"No thanks, just plain."

I expected the usual foray of comments like, 'that's a bit boring,' or 'what, not even a flake?' but he said nothing. The gorgeous man pulled down the corners of his mouth and complied with my wish with a shrug. I watched him while he worked. He had manly hands: strong and capable. I wondered what his talents were. His outdoorsy stance was too broad for the inside of that van. I remembered the seams of his coat resisting as he moved.

When I glanced back at his face he was holding the finished cone halfway to me, as though he'd been briefly stunned. I was mesmerised too, and my heartbeat cranked up another level as I sucked in a quick breath, holding it, knowing that if I let it go, it would betray me by trembling. Something had just ignited in me. I tucked my books under my left arm and took the cone with my quivering right hand, passing it into my left so I could hunt out some cash. Honestly, the scene that followed hadn't seemed real. It replayed more like a social media video looping the same ten seconds. Slow-mo: hardback books careering to the ground, my ice-cream cone crushed in my fist, and then landing with a splat all over the covers. That hadn't happened to me; it was someone else's blunder I repeatedly saw.

He was out of the van and down the tiny steps in an instant and was bending to collect the three books from the ground before I had even registered the mess. My eyes followed him to a nearby picnic table, where he pulled out a pack of wet wipes from under his arm and began to clean the books. I joined him gingerly, unable to wipe the incredulous expression off my face.

"Ah, you read," he said, turning one of them over and scanning the back.

"Yes, handy when you're doing a master's degree."

He laughed.

"English," I explained with a grin.

There was something about the charged atmosphere which had thrilled me, and the stirring I'd felt when his elbow brushed against my arm as he cleaned another book was like static electricity.

He pointed toward the mess on the pavement. "That's…unfortunate."

He turned to face me, and his gaze held mine for so long it almost set up camp.

"I was really looking forward to watching you take your first bite."

The air between us became a vacuum. It sucked away; gravity causing our faces to lean in close. He kissed me gently with warm, soft lips.

"I'm Mark," he murmured between breaths, still close enough to feel the brush of his lips on mine. It was the only part of us touching.

"Anna," I whispered in reply.

~

Tears rolled down my face, and I sighed heavily. It was not the best time to be thinking about Mark and the family, but I missed them desperately. I wiped away the tears and sat sideways on the bed, leaning against the wall. I focussed on surreptitiously seeking out the hidden camera; looking briefly here, then there, whether I'd spotted something or not. Mark and Chie would have been proud of my undercover skills. I saw it above the bath. Casually, I drifted my eyes away. Now I knew where the camera was, and I could make every effort to keep my back to it.

During the evening, I moved the furniture. Before, the chairs had stood behind the small table facing the stairwell, and the camera had full coverage of anyone sitting there. I moved the chairs to the other side of the table, which allowed the camera only a small sideways view. A small victory, but the only thing I could control, even if it was just where I sat. I paced the room, blowing out my cheeks and groaning from intense boredom. I didn't mind being alone, but I hated a restless mind.

Huffing, I approached the tall drawers and bent to rest my forehead on it. Give me at least a book to read.

The girl did not come with food that night, and the water from the bath tap was not safe to drink. Tisak had chosen to starve me, which I took as an injustice. When I had jumped from my seat, I had no intention of harming him. My focus was on saving six innocent men who I thought he intended to kill one by one until I caved in and told him the truth, but he had not given the impression he was willing to consider other possibilities. I was more surprised when Tisak suggested one of them had revealed his personal code to me. He was adamant about it, and from his reaction, it was some sort of personal override key. The same one which had likely got him through the security on my phone. Pretty nifty code to have if I could remember it.

My note to Mark had included a list of instructions: 'Manor, server room, back wall, hallway, stairs, cells, RESCUE THE WOMAN!' The woman knew Tisak's override code. I couldn't remember the numbers, but she knew them, and I believed she knew even more than that. I prayed she was still there and safe, and our people would get her out cleanly.

Pacing and groaning didn't get me anywhere, and I flopped irritably into the chair.

I missed my Bible. I missed my ministry group—Melly, Dan, Claire, and the others. I thought about the last time I had met up with Melly at the café and her revelation about the violent last few months of her marriage. Fresh visions of her with bruises popped defiantly into my mind. I pushed them aside and pondered whether she was right about Pastor Dan Hawkins. Had he confronted Arla's father?

Dan was a scary-looking dude. He would be perfect in a gangster role from downtown New York if he were an actor. He was of average height but enormously thick in body with skin like black coffee, short, tight curly hair and a round face. He was welcoming when he smiled. Not so very welcoming if he wanted to make someone feel uncomfortable, especially with the scar that ran from hard, narrow eyes to the bottom of his left cheek, all puckered and jagged. It had not been treated by a professional, so it took the centre stage until he smiled; then his brilliant white teeth dazzled.

Yes, I could see him doing just as Melly had surmised. Maybe not in sending the aggressive husband away but by challenging his behaviour at the very least. I suspected one warning would have been enough for Arla's father to run without regret and with a quickie divorce in mind.

I shut my eyes and began to hum a tune I loved. I dared not sing the words out loud, but I sang them in my heart, slightly hidden under a bushel perhaps, but not out of shame, but out of self-preservation.

The crack of a gunshot outside interrupted my humming. I stepped from the bed and climbed the drawers, gasping. It felt like I had been hit by a bus. I couldn't see down into the grounds, only the lower part of the I.N. headquarters, and one of the skyscrapers was visible through the tiny V.

I looked around the room again. I was familiar with every crack in the wall, every scuff, every cobweb. I had even named the odd-looking spiders and prayed none of them was venomous and bit me. Then, sometimes, I prayed they would. I was getting antsy—stir-crazy—and I needed to get out of this room. I sat sideways in the chair, making sure my back was to the camera and rocked my feet over the arm. I desperately needed to get out of this room.

I was almost catatonic when the girl brought some food. She smiled at me for the first time, but I could see she had been crying—her eyes were red and swollen. She swept from the room, leaving me alone again, bored, lonely, and growing more irritable with each passing minute. I noticed the painkillers she had left and assumed Tisak had allowed it.

Tisak was a confusing man. He had no compassion yet did compassionate things, like giving me nice quarters rather than throwing me into a damp cell and allowing me medicine when he probably didn't care if I was in pain. What was it to him? It puzzled me why he would treat a prisoner, the NC prisoner at that, so…courteously, chivalrously even.

The older woman came to fetch me this time. She tossed the ankle restraints on the bed and waved her hand. I put them on and followed her to a less grand set of stairs at the rear of the palace. I still wore no shoes, and sharp grit and stones often caught me. She led me to an orangery which was cool from air conditioning and sat me down on a distressed metal chair next to Tisak. A much older man was standing beside him.

The stranger approached me and tilted my face. He poked and gently fingered the cut at my hairline from the Manor incident. Then he examined both cheekbones and confirmed neither was broken but couldn't rule out a fracture on the one that had met the table. He took many pictures and then asked me to remove my shirt. I refused; I wasn't wearing a bra.

"Shirt, please," he said again, his eyes quickly flicking to Tisak, who was staring at me.

I stood and turned my back to them and removed the shirt, holding it over my chest to cover my breasts. Ten minutes later, after having to also remove the skirt, I was dressed again and seated back at the table. I was not critically injured but was prescribed antibiotics to prevent infection and more painkillers.

Tisak was getting doctors to see me now? I knew he planned on a person swap, but he needn't go along with the pretence. He wasn't going to let me go, and he wouldn't keep me as a prisoner forever, so my long-term health wasn't relevant to his plans. He saw the doctor out and invited someone else into the room. It was the guard who had smashed me into the table, the scary man who had watched me shower. He kneeled at my feet, face to the ground, and begged my forgiveness. It was heartfelt and believable, and I was utterly baffled. Why was he doing that?

"Thank you, Sul. That will be all. Come, Anna, walk with me in the garden."

I followed, still confused. What was that about?

We left through elegant metal doors. I began to wonder when Tisak went to work, or was it just part of the plan that he fitted visits with me into his busy schedule? It was a different kind of captivity, a polite version of incarceration.

"I thought you might appreciate the fresh air and benefit from some sunlight. Perhaps a new view to look at? New pictures in your mind for you to stare at when you are alone in your room?"

Did he watch me all the time?

"Thank you," I responded politely as we walked. The lawn was soft underneath my feet.

"Your actions were not from the roots of intelligence, were they? I have severely reprimanded my guard for acting so rashly, yet he seeks to protect me; that is his duty. Although I cannot comprehend why he thought I had anything to fear from an unarmed, skinny little wretch who cannot sufficiently lift her arms to even strike me."

Gee, thanks.

"Are you recovering now? How is your discomfort today? I do not believe you were wholly honest with the doctor."

Why did he care? I hadn't been completely honest, I admitted to myself.

I shrugged, finding it less painful to do so and replied, "I'd prefer it if I had something to do."

"Such as?"

"I would like a Bible."

Tisak clenched his fist and released it, exaggeratedly slow, before he crossly asked, "You would have me break the laws of Collective Thought twice in one week?"

One week? How long had I been here? It had been only three days. Hadn't it?

"It isn't illegal to own a Bible."

"True, not yet. But it is illegal for me to provide one that is not your own." He paused in thought. "If you would like, I can send someone to your home and arrange to have it couriered here for you? Shall I do that?"

I hoped the question was rhetorical because part of me wanted to say, yes, please, go fetch it. I needed the word of God, and I wasn't a mature-enough Christian to know verses by heart. The other part of me remembered I.N. soldiers had already been through my things and had most likely destroyed the only copy I owned.

"A book then? Paper to draw, write? Music? Something. Anything!"

"Hmph."

Tisak said nothing more about it. Instead, he led the topic back to where we had left it the day before—if indeed it was the day before.

"You'll be glad to know, five of those men were released this morning on account of the guilty party confessing his disloyalty. He was executed immediately, as I am sure you heard. I will not hear any more about how 'it wasn't any of them', and neither will I accept any more deception from you. This is the last time. Do you understand?"

He stopped and turned to face me, lifting my chin with hot fingers to ensure I looked at him.

"Do you understand? The very last time."

Tisak meant every word. I nodded, then swallowed awkwardly and pushed away the memories of my Manor experience. Instead, I focussed on why an innocent man would take responsibility for handing out a secret code to the NCs when he hadn't. It didn't make sense. I hoped he knew at the end that he might have saved a woman's life, mine if I didn't tell, or hers if I did.

"You asked if it would make a difference to me if my code had not been compromised. Do you remember?"

"Yes."

"Explain what you meant, please."

"Merely that I was the only one given it."

"You had direct contact with the headquarters here? Just you?" Tisak was not convinced, and his glare darkened. "I smell deception again, Anna. We have just spoken about this."

"No lies. It was just me. I forgot it straight away. As you can see, I couldn't get back through the door, or else I wouldn't be here. I can't pass it on even if I had got away. I don't remember it."

We approached the rear of the grounds, where fountains of water gushed from a statue of Tisak, spilling down from his mouth and raised hands. He sat me down on the wall with my back to the basin. He sat sideways on, swept his fingers through the water, and flicked them at me with an amused expression.

"Are you willing to continue with that claim?"

He swished through the water vigorously, and I was unsure of his intent.

"How long do you think you can hold your breath?"

"I stand by what I said, and I stand by my agreement. I won't lie to you again."

I might not tell you everything, I thought, but I would word everything so carefully in the future.

"So you say, but I have experience in your word not being your bond. Tell me, what is my deterrent to ensure truth abounds?"

I looked from my lap to the hedges, turning the back of my head to him, and replied, "I think you are deterrent enough."

"Good. Let us move on then, and in anticipation of my code getting into the wrong hands, I have ordered a trace on it. Time will soon tell."

We walked by the orchard facing the right side of the palace and swept along the entire grounds up to one of the HQ towers. We headed towards a set of red-cushioned chairs and a table where refreshments had been left. I drank thirstily.

"Your medical photos shall have a nice effect. I intend to release them to your group of friends. I hope you do not mind. I appreciate they contain your…personal areas, but I am hopeful it will enhance the reaction."

The bruising to my upper arms and shoulders had begun to fade, as was the one received from the butt of the rifle, but the newer grip marks to my forearms had developed. I also had a cut on my head and swollen cheekbones. I still had the bruise and burn to my thighs and marks around my wrists and ankles. There was plenty to produce an abundant reaction, and I had to admit, I was not ecstatic about the photos being available for anyone to see.

The girl in the white dress appeared from the corner of the palace and headed tentatively towards us. She carried a phone.

"Excuse me, Imperial Kiengir Tisak. Telecall for you."

She passed him the phone and waited beside me. He stepped away to take it but kept his eyes on me throughout, not giving us a moment to communicate.

"Excellent," he said, handing the phone back and dismissing her. "Transmission received, but I must be patient a little longer. I am sure they will want to devise a plan to undermine me. In fact, I shall expect nothing less! I often wish we were under different circumstances and Richard Cole worked for me. What a true Neighbourhood we could be then if we all stood in unity."

He smiled.

It was these types of conversations I detested most when I was with Tisak. He talked as if he sat with a loyalist. Of course, I wasn't, and my facial expressions gave away my feelings. Tisak never missed them, and somehow, he always read them accurately.

"Why the scepticism? Do you not agree?"

He always asked the right questions (the wrong questions for me) in such a way that responding with absolute truth would cause me trouble. He knew I would not agree. I was part of the NC group and a Christian. There wasn't an answer I could give that skirted around the truth of my thoughts.

"You know I don't," I replied simply.

There wasn't a need to add that the lack of God's law in the world destroyed any chance of harmonious unity. Tisak would have known I believed that. His face dropped, but any admission I could've given him would have infuriated him much the same way. Wise people didn't provoke a quiet-angry type of person, a seether, which Tisak was. I had found them to be the most dangerous of all. These people bit you quickly, sharp and deadly, like a serpent.

"I think you should go now," he said abruptly and pulled me up by my arm.

He pushed me to walk ahead until we reached a small rear door, where he shoved me through while barking orders at the older woman to have me escorted back to my room.

I stood, wondering what else I was supposed to do to keep the man happy. He wanted truth but didn't want that truth to be what it actually was. He wanted loyalty and punished the honesty of those that didn't give it. Much worse than that, he murdered the pretender trying to walk both sides.

The older woman shot me an intolerable look. "You annoy him again!"

Defensively, I retorted, "He expects the truth, so I'm giving it."

"No!" she cried, shaking her head, "you say yes and no and lots of 'I'm sorry.'"

"I won't."

"Then you will die."

I huffed. "That's already a foregone conclusion."

She frowned.

"I'm going to die anyway, Ma'am, whether I am loyal or not," I explained.

The woman relaxed and pointed to a chair. "Sit."

She pulled a cake from a larder shelf and handed me some. "Eat," she commanded and poured me something alcoholic, then called out, "Esta!"

The girl in the white dress skipped into the kitchen.

"The Imperial Kiengir returned to work. Take her to her room and bring back to me these."

She placed the key and the remote for my ankle restraints into her hand and left the kitchen. Esta kept watch at the door, and then came to the table beside me.

She whispered, "You know Minu?"

I shook my head. What was it, a language or something?

"She cousin's wife. Minu Darab. He shoot cousin today."

In broken English, Esta told me that the man who had stepped forward and confessed to treachery was her cousin. His wife, Minu, had been taken from him over a year ago and was presumed dead. When he discovered Tisak's code had been given out and it wasn't by him, it left only her. The other men in the room were not traitors. Discovering his wife had been alive all this time, Esta's cousin came forward, filled with guilt. He lied, hoping to finally be able to protect her.

"She know it. She sister to Imperial Kiengir."

I finished the last mouthful of wine with a splutter. Tisak had a sister? Tisak had a disloyal sister! The news could not have been more welcome.

"Yes, I know the woman you mean."

"Is she safe?"

"Soon, hopefully."

Esta quietened as she took me back to the room. She removed the shackles, picked up my breakfast tray and left apologetically, pocketing my note at the foot of the stairs. If the message was delivered to Mark, I had every hope that Minu Darab would be liberated after her year of imprisonment, and I smiled at the thought of what help she could be to the resistance. Tisak's sister was someone worth having onside, and I prayed fervently for her, as obsessively as Tisak did for Chie's capture. Knowing about his sister and having that over him somehow made up for my bruises being on display for all my 'friends' to see.

As much as I loved being rescued and going home, I was confident Mark would not agree to any proposals, and although Tisak didn't go into detail, I had a fair idea of what kind of torture he would implement. I feared him. I had the burns on my thighs and the vivid memory of his eyes from that first night. They were kinder in Baruun until this morning when I saw another glimpse of the evil man that he was. If Chie and Mark did not agree to his demands, more photos, or maybe footage of me receiving fresh injuries, would begin. Once those promises were fulfilled, I would then be sold along with the other girls, as Tisak had threatened. Didn't take a genius to work out into what trade.

The NCs would come up with a plan to get me out and get me home. I had to believe it, and it would be without involving Chie. I was not worth risking him for. Mark would have a different opinion, Chie too probably, but when it came to the resistance, we needed him more than we needed me.

I was prepared. I would handle the pain of whatever Tisak did to me, but I would make them kill me after that. I would enforce suicide-by-soldier rather than endure the next phase he had planned for me.

~

It was, I believed, three days later that they summoned me to another meeting with Tisak, and I had absolutely no patience. I had spoken to no one, not even Esta, when she came with food, and I had even taken to answering my own thoughts. I prayed mostly and had started to pray out loud because I couldn't stand the silence anymore, nor my memories—the good and the bad, simultaneously making me lament in different ways. When I'd arrived in Baruun, I had been determined not to lower myself and beg for anything, but for the sake of my mental health, I had to do something and soon, before I started to bang my head against a wall just for something novel to do. Then again, I suspected that was exactly the kind of thing Tisak would want me to do.

He wanted to own all control.

The scary man stood in the room; he didn't look at me, more through me as I passed him in the doorway. It was the same room at the foot of the stairs with a large window. I sat in the same seat on the sofa, facing the same small table, undamaged, unlike my face.

There were no refreshments for us; the niceties had played out, and now, we were on to a new approach. What was coming next?

Tisak was already seated and was scrolling and reading, rudely ignoring me. I supposed it was preferable to a question I would have to answer truthfully, and with a truth he would not like. Eventually, he stared icily at me, and I sat back, surprised, flicking my eyes away. It was the look I expected him to wear the first night we met when I was afraid to make eye contact with him in case I burned. This was that look.

"Every time I speak to you, I feel like I am teaching a child. Three things I have demanded of you. One is that you look at me. Two that you are honest, and three, you are not rude. Each time you push the limits of my patience."

I flashed him a brazen look, then considered his words. I dropped my eyes. Keeping two out of the three wasn't bad, considering the extreme depressive level of my patience. I had looked at him…and it was honest.

"And there you are, breaking numbers one and three immediately."

Tisak stood up and left the room, leaving the soldier on guard.

"You should not provoke the Kiengir."

Indifferently, I shrugged. "Why not? What difference is a death sentence in ten seconds, ten hours, or ten weeks? I would rather it was over with now. Just put me out of my misery before you put me back in that room!"

The guard, Sul, didn't reply. Instead, he continued to stare ahead, looking through whatever he was looking at, and only moved to reposition himself less at ease when Tisak returned carrying a steel briefcase. He also held his phone.

Tisak asked me to sit on my hands, then plopped the case on my lap and opened it away from me. I didn't peer over to see what was inside. Instead, I kept my eyes obediently on him as he had asked; again. He took the pictures he wanted and took the case away. He placed it on the table, turning it to show the contents of neatly arranged tools pressed inside a foam backing. I gathered they were on the list to become my new friends.

Fear lined my face. As much as I wanted to be, I was not a machine, and this last week or more had ground me down into stress levels I hadn't experienced before. Tools like those were designed to hurt people like me, so I concluded the outcome of Tisak's transmission of my injury pictures did not meet his expectations, and it was round two on the table, literally.

Lord, I think I would rather have the bullet now. Can we go back, please? Can we go back?

Tisak pointed to a blade that curved. "This one is better for the eye socket, in case you were wondering which of these I will select if you continue to disobey me. This one will be for your tongue if I catch you in a lie again. I will not hesitate, for it supplies me footage to show your friends, and I have reached the end of my patience."

I knew the feeling. I was there too, and I tried not to think about it. I fought to keep my face neutral as I stared endlessly at the bridge of his nose, but the pucker in my forehead happened before I knew it. It was a 'your patience? Join the club' expression, and it caused Tisak to narrow his eyes. I was startled when he snapped the case shut and moved it from my reach.

Wow, did he suspect I was going to go for him? What happened to the unarmed, skinny little wretch who couldn't sufficiently lift her arms to even strike him? Hmmm, she might just be nuts enough to do it these days.

"I am afraid you are in the hands of your husband, Mrs Cole, and regrettably, they are not safe ones. I have given another day. That is all. This is not a process I would like to resort to, and I shall give them every opportunity, despite your impertinence, to comply."

They would not comply to an exchange. I knew it, and Tisak knew it. I'd already admitted neither Cole would believe he would honour it. But an exchange wasn't his true plan. What he truly expected more than compliance was my rescue.

"Sul, ensure she is secured in the cells."

Sul, the scary guard, nodded.

I should be careful what I wish for. That kind of change in scenery wasn't quite what I had in mind.

No no no no no. I didn't want to go. I wanted my little cosy room back with the bath and nice bed, yet I stood up and waited to be led to my designated punishment like a robotic child on a timeout. Inside, I protested, and my spirit raged; it cut right through the back of Tisak's head as he rounded the door, his prized silver briefcase in his clutch. Sul held his arm out to the door. After me then, was it? I took small, hesitant steps while he kept a hand on my shoulder, guiding me through the door under the grand staircase and down—not up, into somewhere dark, damp, and cold. Old. Ancient. Forgotten.

"You should not provoke the Kiengir."

He lit a torch, placed it on the sconce, and steered me into a cell.

Minu Darab had more than I. I didn't even have a bucket. Sul remained outside the gates of my cell, standing sideways to me and staring down the corridor. Was that what Tisak meant by *secure in the cells*, my own personal guardsman? One who liked to watch women in the shower and bash their faces with tables.

I sat down with my back to him and sang to my God.

Cannot let my heart be troubled. You've already won,
Will not let my faith subside, I come close and seek the One,
Shall not fear for what lies ahead. We're numbered in Your hand,
Like the jewels in a crown, we will sparkle over Your land.

Nestled into Your bosom and into Your perfect rest,
I climb onto eagle's wings and fly in Your strength,
No other keeper of my soul but You, no other Ruler, no other God.
I lean upon the Rock whose shield becomes eternal peace,
encircled by Your angels with commands to guide my feet,
The authority is Yours, oh sovereign Lord. The keeper of my soul.

~

"They come at dark. You no sleep." Esta was handing a dress through the bars with a pair of used plimsolls.

I jumped up from the hard ground and took them from her, asking, "Who's coming?" Then I noticed Sul standing behind her, staring out just like before.

"Coles come."

I looked over at Sul and back at Esta, confused that she would talk about my escape in front of this particular guard, and hoped that 'Coles' wasn't a deliberate plural.

"My brother," she explained, "he won't tell."

Brother? No! How different they were from each other in personality and age. Esta looked in her early twenties, Sul at least mid-forties.

"NC?"

Sul scowled at me behind Esta's back.

"No, he loyal and angry at Kiengir. He love me, and he love Minu. You help her?"

"I told them where to find her."

Explicitly. Even down to the wall.

I was pleased I remembered the wall. It would give me something to waste my time with, considering I didn't know when 'at dark' was. When I had left it, the sun was bright, but down here, it was nothing but flame.

Esta and Sul were not speaking English, so I didn't know what they were arguing about, but she finished with, "say it!"

Sul turned to me. "She wants to say sorry you're in the cells, but God has blessed you. It is easier to free you from here than upstairs; it was where the plan ran into problems and why there has been a delay."

I was shocked. "Are you Christian?"

Sul remained stony-faced while Esta nodded excitedly.

"I go now. May God shine His face on you."

We were both sobbing when she tore herself away and was gone for good from my life. She had done everything to help me and stayed inconspicuous in the process. Her brother returned to his position and resumed staring at nothing. I thought about the wall in the server room at the Manor.

It was too quick for my brain to fully register a scale, but I recalled it feeling almost painfully cold. It had sucked me through and out again, like drawing and repelling a magnet simultaneously. I suspected it had LeyLucient properties. It was the only thing able to transport bodily cells safely, and thanks to Dan's theory about Ley being the very essence of the breath of God (His word that holds the command of creation together), transporters would collect and displace the spirit and consciousness of the person as well. Science could move the mass, the vessel, but not displace the life. The wall had picked up my body, and my spirit, and put me down on the other side just in time not to be discovered. The Lord had used Tisak's creation to protect me!

The victory was short-lived. I shuddered at the feelings I was reminded of when faced with Tisak's portrait, then laughed aloud as I realised it was nothing compared to the real thing. The way his eyes bore into me, scanning me and reducing my ability to resist obedience. The smell of his breath, which had hypnotically encouraged me to like him.

Crikey, so much of me wanted to go back into the server room and leave the way I was supposed to. I could've been home, safe, and not in the hands of someone intent on stealing away my allegiances: to the NCs, my family, and my God. But I wouldn't swap the incredible and positive possibilities that had arisen from it. Minu Darab and the beds—if I hadn't seen them, I wouldn't have believed it. I had also learned plenty about Tisak. He commanded respect with fear, and if it wasn't given willingly, he would hurt you civilly. He wanted to appear gracious, allowing me to choose my room and herding me into behaving. He held me suspended between wanting to obey and wanting to defy. Or was it God holding me there? He was my defiance, after all.

"Why are you angry at Tisak?"

Sul was shocked I had spoken to him. Had it been that long?

"My anger at *the Kiengir* is not your business."

I shrugged; *suit yourself*. I was sure it had something to do with the show he put on in the orangery. Tisak controlled everyone, and if he told you to be contrite, then you were contrite. I continued to hum a tune.

After some time tracing pictures from the cracks in the stones, I had another visitor. I expected it at some stage before I was taken from the palace. Tisak would rarely miss an opportunity to boast or shame or scare me. I felt consoled, knowing this would be the last time I would have to face him. Well, I hoped so.

"I have arranged for an escort familiar to you, Anna. He will take you to the rehabilitation centre at first light. Please make sure you have everything ready."

I half-smiled. I had best make sure I left time to pack my suitcase then!

I wanted to remain there, lying with my back to him, but Mark was coming, and I didn't want him to find a cold, dead wife waiting. So, I got up, turned, and looked at the bridge of Tisak's nose.

"You remember HS Paul Fraser?"

My heart fell. I remembered him all too well. I nodded and said yes.

"Wonderful. I want you to feel secure by having an acquaintance escort you. You will go via the tunnel into the capital's rehabilitation centre. I do not have sentenced prisoners marshalled through the palace grounds. Now, I come with other delightful news. You can depart from here knowing I have located your missing girls. In the spirit of being true to my word, unlike you, I have had them taken home, or should I say, some of them. Two, unfortunately, had no homes to return to in Greater Manchester, but they have been well compensated."

Disgusted with the satisfaction he oozed, I curled my lip, remembering how he was the one responsible for obliterating their homes and families in the first place. Despite that, I was relieved the girls were safe. Taking another escape route at the Manor had generated another good result.

"Thank you."

"Thank you, 'Imperial Kiengir.'"

I kept my tone calm. "Thank you, Imperial Kiengir Tisak." The words were bitter. Besides sarcastically, I had never referred to him by his title before. I almost added a curtsy for effect.

"I am thoroughly disappointed to see your family has not attempted to rescue you. I have increased my security unnecessarily, it appears. I apologise it has come to this. I trust you understand. Like any parent, I must follow through with my promises and not create delinquents."

I chose to be nice. Understanding.

"I appreciate the compassion you have shown me." I noted the frowning eyes of Sul. "You offered me a nice room. You removed the restraints when I asked. You gave me some food, water, and medicine. You brought me a doctor, even. You weren't obliged to provide any of that for a prisoner."

Tisak frowned infinitesimally. "No. I was not."

I enjoyed the moment of confusion on his face. I moved my eyes to look directly into his.

"I appreciated the compassion." So much more since I had only damp concrete to sit on.

"Good. I am not a monster." He paused, then added, "yet." The creepy side smile he stretched before turning to Sul dissolved my confidence.

"I shall have someone come and relieve you."

Sul nodded blankly.

"Good night, Anna. Do try to have a good one, won't you? I do not envisage the nights ahead being better than this one."

Somehow, it was okay. Six girls were safe because I went to the Manor. Nothing else was relevant. I would go knowing they were free from whatever torment they had suffered. I was going to escape, and if we didn't succeed, I would make sure I was killed before they took me again. And frankly, Mr Imperial Kiengir Ciel Tisak, every night after this one would be fantastic, whether I was free or dead.

16 Cell to Shell

I changed into the dress and plimsolls before the changing of the guard. Sul had seen it all before, and I was less ashamed than I would have been if I'd waited because the new guard was young and often leered at me.

Thwoop.

I glanced up to see the dark-haired guard sink to his knees and fall forwards. He lay in a heap with a tranq dart poking out of his neck, and suddenly Mark was there, fishing through his pockets for the cell buttons. I cried with relief to feel his arms around me again, so gentle, afraid to hurt the bruises that were barely there anymore. He murmured encouraging words about how much he loved me, how I was safe now, and how I still looked as beautiful as ever.

Mark took me by the hand and marched us further down the stone corridor, past the door into the palace and to a gated tunnel at the bottom. He closed and locked it behind us, picked up the torch he had left and followed the tunnel silently, still gripping tightly to my hand. I was grateful for the shoes. I could hear a crunch beneath my feet and thrust away the vision of Fraser pushing me through the tunnel without them. I tightened my grip on Mark's hand.

Up ahead was a hard hat and a florescent bib lying on the ground, and Mark slipped them on.

"We need to be really quiet," he whispered, "and we need to hide the way out before we leave, so be patient."

He quickly kissed me, then picked up a telescopic grabber and pulled on some rope hanging from a hole high up in the tunnel wall. He caught it, hoisted himself up and squeezed feet first into a hole just big enough for his scrunched shoulders.

I had to climb that, and my body wasn't up to it, but with Mark drawing on the rope from above, I only had to withstand two pull-ups of my own. We snaked face to face until he was helping me out into a large square hole, showing an uncovered water pipe.

"I have to hide it all now," he said quietly and handed me a torch. "The van over there is unlocked. Get in the back; there's somewhere for you to hide inside."

In the van, I found a compartment with the entrance ajar and climbed in. I closed it behind me and breathed. It wasn't over, but I was out. It was quiet except for occasional footsteps. Maybe they were Mark's, but I swore I could hear a Midwest Statesman singing.

"Emergency repairs, is it?" somebody asked. "Bit late to be working. ID, please."

Mark yawned into his sarcastic Texan accent.

"Sure is, an' ima rootin' tootin' from being dragged from ma zees."

"Shite, that's ripe!"

"You're damn straight, ma friend. It's leakin' sewage out yonder. Gedding' in the dirt. You wanna check it out?"

"Rather not. The stink's up my nose already. How long is it gonna take?"

"Have the re-placement pipe in transport, so uh, maybe 'nother day or two. Just golla make it good here, an ima gonner."

"I won't keep you then, Mr Sanders."

It went quiet, and a few minutes later, Mark climbed in and started the van. He turned on the radio and tapped the panel that separated us.

"Knock twice if you're hidden."

I tapped twice, and the van began to move.

We arrived on the outskirts of an airport surrounded by a chain-linked fence. A gentleman was waiting there. Mark handed him the keys.

"Everything is ready. Get there early tomorrow, five am. You'll need that time to finish up before they discover she's gone. No matter what, when you hear the alarm, get out, finished or not."

The man nodded and pulled open the cut in the fence, secured it when we were through and took off in the van. Mark took my arm, and we jogged towards a small plane, the engine already running and the door open. As we climbed in, airport control confirmed clearance for take-off, and the small plane taxied, sped, and took off into the night.

~

I slept for most of the flight. It was the first time I had fallen securely asleep since before the Manor, and that had everything to do with being cradled like a baby in Mark's arms. When I woke, though, I was startled to find myself on another plane, and it took me a moment to remember I was not at the palace anymore, nor back on Tisak's plane.

Mark wasn't beside me. Instead, I found him in the cockpit sitting in the first officer's chair next to the pilot, who turned to greet me.

"Here she is!" Chie grinned widely. "Glad to see you alive and kicking."

"Thanks for coming for me."

Mark got up and drew me to him. "We would've died trying, Anna."

Chie murmured in agreement and lifted his hands to my shoulders. I zoned out as pictures of the Manor ordeal crammed into my mind, and pricks of fear covered my skin. Tisak's hands were on me again, heavy on my shoulders and shocking me. They were on my face, pulling my head back and making it hard to breathe…

"Clear this up for us, would you?" Chie asked, breaking me from the horrible vision. "How much did Mark have to squeeze himself into that tunnel? 'Cause, man, I still can't imagine how he fits."

Mark landed a punch on Chie's shoulder, and they laughed.

I smiled weakly. "It was a tight fit."

"Was it like being born?"

"Breech? Yeah, a bit." I smiled at the image, placating Chie, who was just trying to keep my spirits up. My mood was obviously low.

Mark handed me water, but my stomach didn't want it, and even though I was thirsty, just the thought of it heightened the nausea I felt. Although the fear had lessened, and I was safe, something else lingered. A lost sense of self-security that *he* had enjoyed taking from me. I returned to the seats I had slept in. I tried to pray. I tried to remember scripture or worship songs, but nothing was in my empty head. Words would not come, and my passion for the Lord hid somewhere in a cell of its own.

~

The journey to the safehouse was just as intolerable. I sat in the back, gripping onto Mark, and had to repeatedly tell myself that I was safe. Each time I napped and opened my eyes, I expected to see the tower or the cell. Instead, I was faced with the immediate proximity of another person, and I panicked. Had I become one of those sleeping girls and been swept into the underground of sexual slavery? The first time it happened, I hit out, and Mark had to restrain me before I realised and rested again in his lap while he gently brushed the bruises on my cheekbones. He forced me to drink by tipping water carefully between my dry lips. I refused any food. I just didn't feel like it, still too sick from the ordeal for my stomach to hold anything down. In the absence of adrenaline and fear, I had nothing.

I napped, woke afraid and had to be calmed. The pattern repeated throughout the drive. It would take some time to recover. I understood. I would never forget, but I hoped I could move on, eventually.

Chie didn't take us to the safehouse, where my lovely children would be waiting. We arrived at the cottage in slightly better repair than the first time I had seen it. We had windows, now at least. I climbed from the car with aching legs and followed them in. There were kitchen items and clothes from our old house, and the cottage had been cleaned. It looked much more like a home now than it did before.

Surprised they took the risk, I asked, "You went back to the house?"

"Chie couldn't bear for Lily not to have Melanie," explained Mark, "she cried for three days straight. At least Melanie helped a bit while you were…gone."

Lily had already lost so much. Though thankful she had her precious dolls back, I felt nothing else.

"How did you manage it?"

"Chaperone Shelley went in and fetched it. We sent the Manticore to check first. It was set up to interfere with the bugs while she was in there getting our stuff."

Chie added, "It was that or keep on rescuing Jonah from the street 'cause he kept sneaking out to go there. He wanted to fetch your Bible as well."

My lack of emotion did not go unnoticed. Jonah was lovely and brave to want to do that for me, but I suspected my precious Bible had been burned to cinders. Oh, how much I wanted to hold it in my hands again and renew my passion and strength with His word.

"I expect it's gone for good," I sighed heavily.

Chie disappeared up the creaky stairs and returned, holding out a new Bible to me.

"We got this for you. I know it isn't yours, but all the same, it's a Bible."

"Thank you, Chie."

Ordinarily, I would have given him a massive hug. A gift like this should have me jumping with excitement and joy, but I just took it from him and sat in an old chair to read.

Psalm 147 opened in my lap. 'The Lord builds up Jerusalem; He gathers together the outcasts of Israel. He heals the broken-hearted and binds up their wounds. He counts the number of the stars; He calls them by name. Great is our Lord and mighty in power; His understanding is infinite. The Lord lifts up the humble; He casts the wicked down to the ground.'

~

Numbness was the best way I could describe it. I had an unbreakable shell, protecting me, defending me, and only certain things like questions penetrated. Questions I could not answer, like how I was and what had happened to me. My conscious brain refused to remember, but my subconsciousness reacted independently, especially to statements that ended with a question. Those typical of the way *he* would ask them.

The first day after my escape, I mainly sat reading in the old chair. I was given things to eat and drink, which sat beside me, unwanted and untouched.

Another thing to penetrate through to me was a bath. I stepped in and felt a little joy staring at the bubbles and popping them absentmindedly like I had done in the tower. It killed time. Then Mark had washed me because after an hour, when the water had turned cold, I hadn't done it.

On the second day, Mark handed me a glass of water and gently demanded I drink it. I took the glass, swallowed it in a few mouthfuls, and handed it back without a word. I might have been away from Baruun physically, but I was still compliant psychologically. When Mark told me to eat, I ate, a little. When he told me it was time for bed, I went and slept.

I dreamt.

His eyes were always there, burning through my skin and into my very soul. Just those cobalt-blue eyes, no bridge of a nose to focus on as they zoomed towards me and pierced the safety of my sleep. Sometimes, they evaporated or fell like raindrops before they reached me. Other times, it felt like they ripped right through my eyes and into my head. The worst one of all was when his pupils stretched into a black smile, and I would hear his dark laugh. That was the one from which I woke screaming.

After the first night, Mark had not slept in the bed with me. Too many times, I had woken and scrambled out, petrified because someone was beside me. It should have been comforting to know Mark was there, but it wasn't, and I hated that I'd overreacted. I was hurting the man I loved. I couldn't bear it. The hard shell protecting me prevented me from crying. Fear had been the only thing that kept me alert in Baruun. It was the only thing that kept me attentive to the whim of the enemy. Now it was gone and in its place was…what? Shock? Shame? Emptiness?

There was nothing. Even as I read scripture on the third day, I felt no relief. There was nothing. I sat, re-reading the same verses; the letters drifted into my brain and disintegrated before they meant anything. I wasn't ready to come out. I wasn't sure I would ever want to.

Chie and Mark stayed with me. Sometimes, I answered when they spoke. Sometimes, I stared blankly through them. I nibbled on the toast I was brought because I was told to, unable to break the submissive spell *he* had placed me under.

'We are hard pressed on every side, yet not crushed; we are perplexed, but not in despair; persecuted, but not forsaken, struck down but not destroyed.'

The apostle Paul spoke directly to me as I read second Corinthians. I felt a reaction, a stirring in my spirit, and I realised it hadn't been fear that brought me through the ordeal in Baruun. It had been the grace of my God. A mist shifted. I thought about the children, my husband, and my friends. I remembered about the informant, the rapture beds, and Minu Darab. I could also hear Mark and Chie whispering in the kitchen.

"She is not okay, Chie. Look at her; he's taken the life out of her. I can't watch it."

"She will be. We'll make sure of it."

"I shouldn't have let them take her; I should've–"

"Should've what? Had a crack at Tisak with fifty armed soldiers just outside? How was that gonna help? You made the right decision. As hard as it was, it was the right decision. Neither of you would be here now, you know it. C'mon bruv, let's not do this again. I don't think I could go through a repeat of that night."

"It was pretty much the worst night of my life, Chie. I'd take her leaving me ten times over than see her looking like she did in those pictures again." Mark sighed regretfully. "She looks better now, at least."

"And she's home. It'll take time, but she's home with you."

"She shouldn't have been anywhere else, though, should she?"

I rose from my seat and moved to the kitchen. They were surprised to see me there.

"Chie's right," I said quietly, looking at the floor, "you did what you should have done; what you were supposed to do. Please, don't do this. Don't hate yourself. I know you made the right choice because you heard about the virus in the pictures and about…his informer." I would struggle to say his name for a while. "Do you know who it is?"

"Not yet," Mark replied, gently pulling me into his arms. "We haven't mentioned it to anyone either, not 'til we're positive."

"Did you find Minu?"

"Um, yeah. That's a story for another time. She's at the safehouse now."

What had happened to me? I should have been ecstatic Minu was out of the Manor, but I felt almost nothing.

I carried on looking at the floor as I talked.

"If that day had gone differently, she would still be there, locked up. The missing girls wouldn't be home, and we wouldn't know there's a spy in our midst. So please, don't. Just don't."

I pulled away and returned to my Bible. I had spent so long alone in silence, it was what comforted me now, this quietness and God's word. If only I'd had my Bible while sitting alone in the palace tower. Maybe I would not feel like I wanted to hide from what had happened to me.

"Anna?" It was Chie coming into the room. "Did you say the girls are home?"

"Yes. He told me the day I…you came." I shrugged, not knowing when it was.

"How did you manage that? Did Tisak sort it?"

I cringed at his name and nodded.

"Why?"

"Because I was obedient."

My voice broke. I shrank away once more and back into my Bible, sitting on the very edge of the seat.

Chie stepped closer. "Anna, please don't withdraw again. Please. Mark is checking with Teela about the girls."

I said nothing. I was nothing. I stared at the words in my lap.

"Where has the stubborn, bold Anna gone? If I asked you right now to go to the Manor, would you?"

More questions. It was one I could answer honestly, though, and not cause further repercussions. I shook my head. He placed his hands on my knees, and I blanched, unseen by Chie. He bent his head and rested it on the back of his hands.

"Listen to me, please listen. Get better, get strong," he looked up and growled, "hell, get angry, but do something!"

I did nothing.

"Look at me, Anna."

Panic swept over me.

"Look at me, Anna; you haven't looked one of us in the eye since, not once."

It wasn't Chie's voice I heard anymore. It was *his*.

'Look at me, or never look again.'

It vibrated through to the core of my being. My Bible slid from my lap as I started to hyperventilate, and I covered my ears.

Chie took hold of my shoulders and brought his face closer to mine. "Look at me, Anna."

Mark shouted as he rushed from the doorway. "Don't say that to her!"

I heard the smooth voice saying, 'look at me, be honest, do not be rude. Look at me, be honest, do not be rude'. I began to wail. I slipped to the floor with a heart-wrenching cry as despair threatened to suck me further into the pit. Chie took me into his arms and curled around me as I kneeled face down on the floor. He held me tightly, securely, his cries together with my own.

"I'm so sorry, Anna. This is because of me; I did this to you. It's all my fault…it's my fault..."

~

"How are you feeling?" Mark asked, pulling me into his arms gently by my shoulders. He bent and kissed them.

I tried not to stiffen, but it happened before I could stop it.

"Better," I answered, rubbing my sleepy eyes and taking the fresh coffee he handed me. "Thanks."

It was day five, and I had improved. I was talking and more at peace in my surroundings, but in my mind, I was still trapped in Baruun. Mark had tried to coax me into talking about things, but I brushed him aside. I hadn't been ready; I still wasn't. I didn't want to talk about what had happened, and I couldn't decide whether it was selfish of him to talk about his experience or if he was trying to encourage me to open up.

"I won't ever forget Tom's face when I was summoned back to the safehouse, and you weren't there. You'd been gone all day. He literally crumbled, telling me what he'd made you do. Teela and I found your car, and I sent her back with it. I hid in the garage block when the helicopters circled; I saw how they'd trussed you up," Mark growled angrily. "It's meant to be a last resort, to hold dangerous criminals capable of absconding, not for someone like you. It was mean and unnecessary; I know; we experienced it in training. I stood it for a couple of hours! You were like it for almost a day. Then the Manor was crawling with guards, and I couldn't do anything."

I said nothing. I stared into my cup, praying he would stop.

"I can't believe I just stood there and watched while he hurt you. Coward that I am. I almost killed him so many times, but I don't know; something stopped me."

I recalled the click echoing that night and cringed. My neck had been forced back by his uncomfortably hot hands.

"Please. Stop."

"I want to kill him." He laughed darkly. "Teela's already planned it, and she's looking forward to doing it after seeing the photos of what he did to you."

"It wasn't all him."

Here I was now, defending the man who had arranged to send me off to be tortured and sold. What was the matter with me? Why didn't I hate him?

"Responsible all the same. I blamed myself. Tom and Chie have blamed themselves. But there is only one person guilty of it all…and he will pay."

Mark had not grasped it; the violence had not affected me—pain and bruises fade away—it was the psychological power he held me with that had done the damage. The threats, control, and the calmness in how he executed them were the most intimidating, fraught with dominance and terror. His patience and mercy had allowed me to keep my sight and tongue, and I was forced to feel grateful. No, not forced. I had wanted to feel grateful; I had wanted to please him, and at the same time, I felt sick about feeling that way. Always the conflict.

The compassion of an uncompassionate man still puzzled me when I allowed myself to remember. I trusted Jesus had my back and my front. I trusted His Word, so I let it help me. In those moments, I began to heal and was finally ready to have the children visit the cottage. I knew I would not frighten them by being devoid of all feeling and was confident I could fake a smile. I felt optimistic that there would be nothing physical for them to see other than the scar on my hairline.

I hadn't considered the weight I had lost and the pallor of my skin. I didn't know the light had gone out of my eyes. Neither had I counted on Teela walking through the door and gasping in shock before she looked away. Did I look that bad? Whether the children noticed or not, they didn't show it.

Lily came straight to me and wrapped her arms around my neck so tightly I could hardly breathe.

"I love you, Anna," she whispered into my ear.

She refused to let go for an hour until Mark bribed her with chocolate. She took the bar and sat beside me, snapping it in two and plonking half in my lap with a sweet smile. It was then I was truly reawakened, and my anger started to grow. I looked at the beautiful girl who had suffered the loss of her parents so young, and something switched on in me. *He* had almost taken away another mother from her. Instinct sparked, and the familiar urge to protect Lily and Jonah swelled. I could not let Baruun depress me anymore. I would not let that man succeed in taking my sanity.

"The Kiengir thinks he's untouchable," I murmured quietly. "His ego and pride are so beyond reality that this is where we're going to hurt him. I want to see his sister."

"Sister?" Teela repeated, surprised. "What sister?"

For the first time, I looked someone directly in the eye. Though a much lighter blue than *his,* hers made me falter briefly before I replied, "I want to see Minu Darab."

17 The Traitor

I knew the moment I walked into the safehouse who the traitor was. It was written all over his guilty face as soon as he saw me. Mostly, people looked shocked, pitiful and full of sorrow, not fearful. I debated whether to turn back and say something or continue going to meet Minu properly for the first time. I was still deciding when I knocked and entered her bedroom. She was looking out of the window at the late evening sky. I smiled when her face lit up. She rushed forward to hug me and kiss my cheek repeatedly, tears flowing while she mixed English with French words I didn't understand. She was healthier than when I had first met her. Colour splashed her cheeks. She was washed and fed.

Minu pulled me onto the bed to sit beside her. "Tu m'as sauvé! You saved me! You sent someone for me."

"You tried to save me, Minu Darab."

She looked surprised I knew her name, then afraid.

"Esta helped me."

"You were at the palace?" More French escaped her lips with a torrent of angry spit, and she started to tremble. "You escaped the palace?"

There was only one part of my palace experience I was willing to share, and it was hard to find words to explain what her husband had done, then how her brother had murdered him. I decided not to keep it from her. I needed her as determined as I so that she would help us undermine him as much as possible. As much as I needed to in order to shake it from my system. As much as God would permit.

"Your brother found out about the code you gave me. I didn't want to give you away and refused to tell him. He threatened to kill these men he'd brought in, adamant one of them was guilty. Your husband was among them."

By the look on her face, I could tell she had some expectation of what was coming next.

"Esta told me he confessed when he realised you hadn't been killed. You were the only other person besides those in the room who knew it, and your husband knew you must have given it to me. He confessed to protect you. Then–"

"Ciel killed him." Tears were falling. "Mon frère, c'est le Diable. Jésus aie pitié de nous! Have mercy, Seigneur."

Horror suddenly lined her features. "My son?"

I had no knowledge of a son.

"Esta would know."

Eventually, she turned to me. "Merci, thank you."

"Will you give us the override code? Will you help us?"

"Mon frère mérite ce qui lui arrive!" She saw my blank face. "Désolée, sorry. I will do it. My brother deserves what is coming."

Minu followed me down the stairs that led into the back room. Everyone was there. Reticent Rusty, whom I hadn't seen since that first meeting, smiled and nodded in greeting. Not-Pervy Pete sat in the corner cleaning his fingernails with the tip of a flick knife. I closed my eyes, quickly pushing away the memory of the last time I had encountered that.

Tom couldn't look at me and continued to stare at his screen while Chaperone Shelley held his hand. Teela, Chie, and Mark huddled together, whispering over a stack of papers, and Logistic Lionel paled when I dropped my eyes to look at him square in the face.

"Why?" I asked, calmly considering how angry I felt. "Why did you do it?"

He opened his mouth to speak, but only breath came out. Everyone in the room looked over.

"I want to know why you betrayed us! Tell me, after everything you know, all the lies he's told!" I turned to Chaperone Shelley. "Please, will you take the children out for a minute?"

"No!" Jonah was adamantly going nowhere.

"Lily then," I asked her, "please?"

When the two left, I turned back to Logistic Lionel, who remained in his seat with Mark on one side and Chie on the other. Not-Pervy Pete had come to stand right beside me.

Javad appeared from another room.

"What's going on?"

I snarled at Logistic Lionel, "You gave them up too, didn't you? Mr and Mrs Francis? You informed on their parents!"

Jonah turned red and soared across the room like a torpedo, landing on top of Logistic Lionel with his fists pummelling. Besides protecting his face, Logistic Lionel did nothing to stop him. None of us did for a few moments while our brains caught up. Teela pulled him off and held him tightly while he screamed and shouted abuse at the man responsible for handing his parents over to the I.N. and to their deaths.

"See what you have done!"

"I didn't know!" he cried out, shamed. "I didn't know." He sobbed into his hands.

Not-Pervy Pete stepped forward.

"What traitor does not know?"

"Before I met you all, I trusted I was doing the right thing. I believed in my job, in my operation. They lied to me. They told me the bombing plot was yours, and I was to get information from you. Teela just assumed I'd been sent by the Asiders when I approached her."

"Don't put this on me!" she cried.

Lionel grew angry. "Then, after the bombings, I was livid with all of you. You were the ones responsible, or so I thought, and one of ours had turned to support it."

He looked at me.

"The day you met me at my car, I almost drove you directly to Sudeley Castle myself instead of the safehouse."

He cringed when Mark lifted his fist.

"Don't," I begged, "no more violence, please."

Mark froze, deciding whether to ignore my plea and then dropped his arm. He leaned forward, stabbing his finger towards Lionel.

"You told them about Chie!"

"No, I told them about Richard. Luckily, I didn't know his nickname then, and I haven't revealed it to the I.N. since. Teela told me on the phone, Richard hadn't died in Manchester like you thought. I passed that on, yes, but then I met you, Chie. I heard and saw for myself what the I.N. had done, and I believed you. I'm sorry, I didn't know."

Not-Pervy Pete was shaking with anger. "You knew when you gave them Anna. Tisak knew she would be at the Manor—you must have told them."

I shivered at the mention of his name.

"Yes."

"Why?" he asked.

"How?" Tom asked at the same time.

Mark's jaw tightened.

"I heard you planning it," confessed Lionel, "and Alex wanted answers, information on the place where Richard was, and I couldn't do it. I couldn't give him up because I knew he wasn't the one responsible for those attacks. So, I lied. I told them he wasn't with you."

"And you offered me up instead?" I asked.

He looked guiltily into his lap. "It was the lesser of the two evils."

"But you helped me escape Fraser's clutches. Why? I should have known there was not a chance you could have reached the station in time to help me out."

He looked at me with teary eyes. "They hadn't asked me for you yet. One of the reasons I didn't want to know the cottage's location was in case they asked…and because of them." He nodded towards Jonah. "I never knew they had kids."

He began to sob again.

"Should that have made a difference?" Teela shouted while hugging a quietly crying Jonah. "Maybe it was just as well, considering where they would have ended up if you had grabbed them. Instead, they were left alone for months because you took their parents!"

Tom threw photos that scattered across Lionel's lap.

"You haven't seen these, have you? Go on! Take a good look!"

One photo slipped to the floor. It was of me. A battered and bruised me with hopelessness in my eyes. I assumed it was the first time Logistic Lionel had seen them because he slid out of his seat and vomited into the bin.

"I didn't know," he whispered over and over.

Tom lunged forward and grabbed the back of Logistic Lionel's shirt.

"What did you think they would do to her? How far do you reckon they would've gone if we hadn't gotten her out, eh?"

Tom went through the photos and held up the one with the 'tool' case openly displayed on my lap. He pushed it right in front of his nose.

"This is what! Come on, tell the truth. You didn't even care! You don't even care what he planned to do with her after that."

Lionel was about to object when Tom threw him against the wall.

"Twelve days they had her for. Twelve! I blame myself for that! I sent her in. I promised I would protect her, and all the time, she was walking into a trap because of you."

How many days?

Lionel sank to the floor. "No, it's because of Alex Saunders and Paul Fraser! They saw I'd helped her when they viewed the security cameras. I lied. I told them it was only to gain your trust. It was the lesser of the two evils; I had to give her up, or Alex was gonna partner with me, which would've led to you all being caught. I didn't tell them why she was at the Manor, though. I didn't tell them why!"

"Somebody, please get rid of him." Tom bit his lip.

Mark and Chie lifted him and plonked him in the armchair, each resting a heavy hand on his shoulders. Reticent Rusty pulled a handgun from the back of his trousers and cocked it.

"No!" I cried, "for goodness' sake, stop!" I reached out and put my hand over his gun. "This isn't the way. I don't want to become just like *him*, like...Tisak." His name was a whisper. "Let him go."

Logistic Lionel's horrified gaze rested on me, and he replied quickly, "I don't want to go. I want to get even with them. I want justice for those people and for the scapegoats they've already caught." He inhaled deeply. "I want to bring Alex Saunders down more than anything else. The man is bad. I'm asking for you to forgive me." He looked straight at me.

Mark leaned in near to his face. "You have got a fat chance of that ever happening."

Everybody started talking at once, then Shelley and Lily arrived back with a bagful of goodies. Jonah recovered rapidly when he heard them, as did we, leaving the weighted silence hanging as Reticent Rusty returned his weapon to the back of his trousers.

"I got sweeties!" Lily smiled, digging into the bag and handing out packets to everyone, then she reached for Mark to pick her up.

The murderous atmosphere abruptly ended as Lily persuaded everyone to eat what she had chosen for them. Even Logistic Lionel, with shaking hands, nibbled at his, feigning enjoyment. But there was something about the way he did it. He cared; it showed on his face now as he looked at her, and when she gave him a huge smile, I saw his heart break. Then when he hid the photos by his feet under the armchair he sat in, grace for him enveloped me.

"Lily," said Javad, "I need help with something. I just can't seem to get a good enough drawing of DNA. Do you think you might be able to help me?"

"What's BMA?"

"D-N-A. Let me show you on my computer. I'll teach you all about it. Would you like to?"

Lily nodded and took his hand. Javad winked at me as he led her into the room next door.

Minu, who sat on the bottom stair, spoke without looking up from the floor.

"It is dangerous for me to admit, under the circumstances, but sir, you saw me when I arrived here, didn't you?"

Logistic Lionel looked up when he realised Minu was speaking to him.

"Yes."

"You know where I came from?"

"You were held in the Manor."

"Can you guess who sent me there?"

Logistic Lionel did not respond.

Minu rose and stepped nearer to him. "Do you understand now?" She produced an exact match of the notorious 'no messing' facial expression that only family could replicate. "You perceive it now, do you not?" she asked in *his* way.

Lionel was horrified, and Minu seemed satisfied he understood.

"My brother snatched me away from my life because he could. I didn't approve of his ways and was not afraid to tell him. He's my younger brother." She shrugged, then returned to the step. "I became a threat, and I was supposed to be killed, of course. Ciel ordered that in front of me, but the man did not do it. He used me at first…and when he tired, he kept me around in case I became useful as Ciel's relative. Is this a man you would like to be loyal to? One who would have his sister executed because she did not agree?"

"I didn't know!"

"Yeah, so you keep saying." Tom sighed, bored with the same excuse.

I didn't think even *he* could sink as low as to have his older sister murdered. Weren't we supposed to look up to our elders? I didn't have any. I had only Mark.

"I never thought Tisak would do that to you, Anna. I never knew he was that kind of man."

Images formed in my head. I didn't want to go back to when he was right in my face and breathing on me, but I couldn't stop it. I remembered the pull and the desire to want to like him, to please him. I realised God had protected me from being drawn under his spell.

"I told you about the tunnels and the pipes at the headquarters. I was key in your escape plan. That's got to count for something?"

"You can't hand a glass back good as new after you've smashed it, though, can you?" I asked. "But I do understand you're not knowing. I trusted him, too, when the world needed a whole new strategy. Then I met God, and now I know who the man is. Now, you have some idea too. What are you going to do about it?"

Determination burned in his eyes. "I want to stay and fight right alongside you. If you'll let me?"

Jonah burst from Teela's arms. "No way!"

I had forgotten he was in the room.

"I won't go back to them," Logistic Lionel said, rising from his chair, "unless you want me to be a double agent. Let me know by the morning." He hovered by the front door and turned back to me. "If I was forced to live on the outside of this and not fight with you, I don't think I want to live at all. And I have no time for those who beat their wives, so my resignation will be the bullet between my boss's eyes, which will be in the morning."

~

We argued once he had left. I started to feel distant from it all, and instead, remembered my simple life and chats with Melly before all of this began.

"We cannot trust him." Not-Pervy Pete had a deep, commanding voice, and there was a hush. "We cannot!"

"Here, here," Tom called out, along with murmurs of agreement from others in the room.

"We need to leave. Get packed up people; we're moving on," said Chie.

"Wait," I said, reaching out for Chie's arm, "we can't all fit in Jonah's cottage. I don't think Lionel will say anything. I believe him. My gut is saying to wait."

No one looked impressed.

Chie frowned. "Are you saying you want to take him up on his offer?"

"Yes," I admitted, fearing an honest answer would lead to more trouble.

"No!" Jonah cried maliciously, "you can't!"

It was not the best idea for him to be involved in this difficult situation. How was I to persuade an almost eleven-year-old boy that the man who had handed in his parents was not the man responsible?

"He didn't know what he was doing, Jonah. He followed orders. He isn't to blame here. Most soldiers aren't. They do as they're told because they don't know any better. A few of us in the room are just as accountable for what happened to me as Lionel is for your parents. Chie for constantly getting into I.N. business and bringing them to our door; Tom for sending me to the Manor; Teela, because, no offence, if not for you, then Logistic Lionel couldn't have used your Asider link to gain a foothold into the NC group; and me too: I didn't leave the Manor when I should have. But as Mark rightly pointed out, there is only one person truly to blame, and Logistic Lionel knows the truth about him now."

"He doesn't know *the* truth!" replied Jonah.

I felt a surge in my spirit. "Not yet, but he will."

Not-Pervy Pete sighed.

"We need to evangelise," he groaned, obviously feeling the leading of the Spirit, too. "I don't think I can love him enough to do that."

"Then let Jesus. He loved me enough; He loved you enough, and neither of us deserved it. Is Lionel any less deserving than us? We have all fallen short of the glory of God, yet Jesus came and died for us while we still drowned in our sin. If I can have forgiveness, if you can have forgiveness, why can't we extend it to the one who asks? Even to the one who doesn't..."

Teela sighed in amusement. "Well, I dunno about him, but your evangelising is working on me."

"Jonah? Shouldn't we forgive 70 times 7? Isn't that what the Bible says? Do you think it's our job to judge this man or God's? Hate only hurts you. If Lionel had died today, he would have died a sinner, but tomorrow he might die a brother. I don't want his blood on my conscience like he will always have your mum and dad's on his. What if it's God's will to use him to further His plan?"

"Anna, seriously." Mark tried to look kindly at me, but I could see his patience was strained. "You can't judge this whole situation on God, not after everything that's happened. Not all of us believe."

"You still say that after everything you heard? He all but confessed he was ready for the devil, you heard him. He also admitted to orchestrating the mock rapture. You heard that too, right?"

"It doesn't make the Bible true."

"No? Shame I couldn't record it. Then all of us would hear, for not so much what he said, but how. It made me throw up."

"Ciel believes it," Minu confirmed, "he knows it. He stands against the Almighty and does not fear. He stands before the destroyer and offers himself. I do not understand it. His god takes life, my God gives." She paused. "I vote we forgive the man and use his resources."

Not-Pervy Pete leaned forward, interested.

"Anna. What did Tisak say exactly?"

I winced at his name again. "He confessed to using the viruses as his route to select the Christians he needed. He admitted using LeyLucient to literally pick them up and put them down inside the rapture beds he'd created, then gushed about how proud he was that most of them who returned fell away from the Lord." I swallowed bile. "Then he referred to his skin as a suit for the Antichrist devil."

Teela pulled a face as she headed for the kitchen. "That is sick."

Accentuating each word, Mark added, "If it is true."

"This is the man who claims there is no God. He wipes out the Holy days; he undermines God's word and fakes miracles in front of the people! When their backs are turned, and they can't hear him, he admits God wins. A God he says doesn't exist. Say, why would he do that if none of it is true?"

Silence fell.

"How involved was Logistic Lionel in getting me out of Baruun?"

Chie growled, "He practically planned it."

"Then he tells the truth. You flew a plane into the world's capital and got me out. If Lionel didn't believe us, Chie, you wouldn't be standing here now. And he'd be a million mouglar richer." I smiled at Minu. "I vote yes too, and before you all kick off, let me tell you why. I want Stymer, I want Junior, and I want to *END* those websites. That's just the beginning."

Teela looked horrified as she came through the kitchen door. "Anna, you did just refer to Tisak's skin as a suit for the antichrist, didn't you? Sorry, it's just registered."

"Not the antichrist, that's Tisak; Antichrist: Lucifer. An antichrist is anyone anti-Christ. The antichrist (little a) is Tisak today. The Antichrist (big A) is the Tisak to come."

"Satan is not referred to as Antichrist in the scriptures." Not-Pervy Pete drew a small Bible from his jacket pocket and put on a pair of glasses.

"Oh. Well, it's another name I call him. He's the ultimate of all antichrists.

He opened the Bible near the back.

"Let me tell you what the apostle Paul had to say on it, if I may, from 2nd Thessalonians 2: 'Now concerning the coming of our Lord Jesus Christ and our being gathered (raptured) together to him, we ask you, brothers, not to be quickly shaken in mind or alarmed, either by a spirit or a spoken word, or a letter seeming to be from us, to the effect that the day of the Lord has come. Let no one deceive you in any way. For that day will not come, unless the rebellion comes first, and the man of lawlessness is revealed,'—that's Tisak by the way—'the son of destruction, who opposes and exalts himself against every so-called god or object of worship, so that he takes his seat in the temple of God, proclaiming himself to be God. Do you not remember that when I was still with you, I told you these things? And you know what is restraining him now'—personally, I believe the restrainer is the Holy Spirit under God's command but there are other theories out there—'so that he (Satan) may be revealed in his time. For the mystery of lawlessness is already at work.'"

He looked up at everyone in the room. "The 'lawlessness' has been manipulating the entertainment and media industry for decades, and more recently, the virtual world."

He returned to the scripture, "'Only he who now restrains it will do so until he is out of the way and then the lawless one will be revealed,'—that is commonly believed to mean the death of the man, Tisak, and his resurrection through the possession of Satan—'whom the Lord Jesus will kill with the breath of his mouth and bring to nothing by the appearance of his coming. The coming of the lawless one is by the activity of Satan with all power and false signs and wonders, and with all wicked deception for those who are perishing, because they refused to love the truth and so be saved. Therefore, God sends them a strong delusion, so they may believe what is false, in order that all may be condemned who did not believe the truth but had pleasure in unrighteousness.'—this is, dare I admit, Logistic Lionel—'but we ought always to give thanks to God for you, brothers, beloved by the Lord, because God chose you as the firstfruits to be saved, through sanctification by the Spirit and belief in the truth. To this, he called you through our gospel, so that you may obtain the glory of our Lord Jesus Christ. So then, brothers, stand firm and hold to the traditions that you were taught by us, either by our spoken word or by our letter. Now may our Lord Jesus Christ himself, and God our Father, who loved us and gave us eternal comfort and good hope through grace, comfort your hearts and establish them in every good work and word.'"

Minu smiled. "Amen. No one can convince me God's word is not true. For it is the world we see today. I vote yes, still."

I did not look at anyone else but Jonah for consent. He was young and perhaps too young to understand, maybe too personally involved to make an objective decision, but I could not, would not proceed without his blessing. I trusted in God and what He said.

"I want to do all I can to reveal the truth and use any method the Lord provides. I know you don't like it. I know you must hate him, but do you trust me?"

He stared at me a while before he came towards me, nodding gently, and sobbed again as I held him.

"Teela's been fired, and I'm a wanted NC. If we use Lionel's sources, we can get the evidence we need to bring them all down—evidence we don't have access to anymore. We cannot let these men carry on harming people like this. And Mark's boss is one of them."

"Is he the one who blew the car up?" asked Jonah, looking at Mark.

"What car?"

"Cheers, Jonah!" Mark tutted and took my hand. "Don't have a hissy–"

Hissy?

"–but I called Harvard the day your note came from the palace. He was the only person I felt was safe enough to get Minu out without raising suspicion. I've never seen Harvard look so serious before the night he brought Minu here. I told him everything, and he wasn't too impressed to find out you were the prisoner held that night, either. Anyway, Harvard called me…Friday, wasn't it, Chie? We'd been back what, two days, I think. He said Robert Jnr. wanted to talk to me, and I wasn't answering my phone. So, I called him. Robert said to me, 'have you still got that package?' and I thought, crap, yeah, still sitting in the boot of the Range Rover. I'd forgotten all about it. I said, yes, of course, I've kept it secure just as he wanted. Then he asked, 'Is it with you now?' Yes, I lied, and lucky I did because the bomb he'd put in the box took out the front of the Melksham safehouse where I'd left the car parked. Anna, it would've taken our house and most of the neighbour's clean out if I'd brought it indoors that night. If we had been in there..."

Flaming heck. I lifted my curled fist to my mouth.

"Forbes-Hamilton tried to blow us up?"

Mark snorted, "He tried to blow us all up. Tisak can't be happy you escaped."

I shook my head slowly as things settled in my mind.

"It makes me nervous knowing just how long they've known we've been on to them. The girls were what started the case off. We got it late Tuesday, and by Saturday at the latest, Fraser was watching Teela's house. HS knew Karl had passed the case on through her phone calls, as we thought. The I.N. must have known since then. Robert Jnr. would have as well." I shuddered. "I sat and lied to Fraser's face. They all knew Chie wasn't killed, and he knew we'd uncovered the bomb plot the whole time!"

"And I picked up a parcel, not thinking twice about what was in it because I needed to get access to work's security cameras," Mark reminded us.

Casting her vote, Teela said, "Maybe that could be our new spy's first job. He can find out who ordered the hit. And then he can find out the word on the palace tiles—from those who walk the floors to those who do the chores."

"Good plan," I agreed, "and as we know a certain girl who does both things, we can check we're being given the right information."

"Esta!" Minu's face was so delighted, I couldn't help but smile.

"Esta," I agreed.

18 Which East Port?

The following morning, the door of the bedroom the four of us shared burst open, and Reticent Rusty's fury was ablaze as his eyes scanned the room.

"Where's your boy?" he demanded to know, pulling the covers away from an empty bed.

I yawned and sat up. Mark too.

"Is he up already? I didn't hear him go out."

"He isn't downstairs, and neither is my SWG!" Reticent Rusty's INc Smith and Wesson handgun, the Graphite, was always kept with him.

Mark sprang out of bed in his shorts and ran through the house, shouting Jonah's name.

"He's not here!" he cried, frantic with worry.

"He wouldn't take it. He wouldn't," I argued, defending the lovely boy who had learned that Lionel had a hand in his parents' execution. "Would he?"

"The boy is resourceful, I'm telling you," Chie said grimly. "Five times he absconded trying to get to your house. We all but tied him down in the end."

"He's learnt our patterns," Teela said, deep in thought. "I didn't go to bed until four. What about you, Tom?"

"Fell asleep here not much after you."

Teela sighed heavily. "We were the last standing. I reckon he crept out maybe half four, five this morning."

"And took my gun!"

Not-Pervy Pete groaned, "Stupid boy, why?"

"He wouldn't go after Lionel, would he?" Mark asked.

Chie's head snapped up. "Get him on the phone."

A barrage of swearing came out of the speakers. Lionel was not a happy man. Jonah had not gone to find him or gone to his logistics company, nor was he at the flat. Any of those reasons would have been preferable to the scenario that I made out from in-between Lionel's profanities.

"He went for Alex Saunders this morning. Stuck a gun right in his face and blamed him for murdering his parents. He's currently sitting in your station in a load of trouble waiting on the ISNA!"

"Oh, God, no!" Not the Small Neighbours Association. Anything but that.

"That's not all. Guess who has pictures of him on the I.N. register? HS Paul Fraser. They've linked him to you, and he's already on a flight."

Great. I hated that guy. He would use Jonah to draw us out, and he wouldn't care if the boy was hurt in the process. Fraser admitted even his own kids would go to the ISNA if needed. Who was some other kid to him?

"Fraser's flying? Now?" I asked.

"Yep...with a plus one."

No no no. Tisak couldn't come. Tisak can't be here. Again. Coming for me. Again. I froze.

Jonah. Remember Jonah.

Chie fired into action. "Lionel, get over here! We've a plan to make."

There was something going on around me, a rush of activity and voices which I ignored.

They had Jonah.

Tisak was coming.

They had Jonah.

Tisak was coming.

Tisak was coming...

Jonah's name pierced through and pulled the uncontrolled rollercoaster of my memories to a halt. They had Jonah.

I got on the phone to Melly.

"What's the name of Arla's father?"

"Alex. Why?"

Alex and Melly Saunders.

"He's got Jonah. The I.N. have him at the station."

Her breaths quickened. "He works for the I.N.?"

"Yes. He's been handling an informer of theirs here at our safehouse. He's upper level at Sudeley Castle Rehabilitation

Centre. According to the records, he isn't usually in town, but he's been at the I.N. post for a couple of weeks now."

Thank you, Lionel.

Melly groaned deeply. "Perfect job for him, then. He would've been too afraid of Dan to carry on taking his anger and hatred of God out on me, so he made himself all-powerful against anyone else by working in a rehab centre. Probably hoping I would turn up. Oh, God, he would just love that." She fell quiet, then, "do you need me to do anything?"

I could tell she hoped the answer was no. I would never ask her to face her abuser like that. I said no, of course. We would handle it. Though I asked her to pray.

~

"They would take him to Sudeley surely. We should head there," Rusty said.

"Or the homes," Teela suggested.

Chie shook his head. "The homes are for the good kids; the turned kids. Jonah won't be there." Certain of the choices, he added, "It's Sudeley Castle or the Manor. We'll know in a minute."

We waited for Lionel, and he was taking an age to arrive. I wanted my new son. I wanted to go, be proactive and not sit about waiting for other people to feed me information, especially not from one who was yet to prove his loyalty. He had sent a message, but there still wasn't news of Jonah since he had been collected from the station, and Lionel should have been on his way an hour ago. I hoped he came alone and not with a band of soldiers because I had all sorts of misgivings landing like heavy rocks.

The video call came from his phone at midnight. I stared at Lionel's upturned wrists on the screen with my mouth open. They were strapped to the arms of a chair with the same gadgets that had held mine. I guessed he was set to level three because his body kept jolting every thirty seconds. He wasn't conscious, and his face was a mess. I gasped and closed my eyes.

"Greetings, Neighbours."

My eyes snapped open. Chie and Mark stood on either side of me, and the face I dreaded most in the world was peering into our safehouse from a monitor. It looked straight at me.

"Good to see you again, Anna. Although it is a shame you look so well. I shall enjoy rectifying that."

"You can try!" Mark put his arm out protectively over me.

"I will. Thank you, Mr Cole, and I foresee a victory."

Tisak smiled the knowing look he once had used on me. He had something on us. His pleasant tone was diminished by the vengeful look he gave Chie.

"We meet, finally, Richard Cole."

"Can't say it's a pleasure," Chie replied indignantly.

I struggled to keep a straight face—until *he* looked at me, and I found myself pulling my expression to obedience, once again staring at the bridge of his nose. Tisak couldn't even hurt me here, but it was like a switch he'd flicked, and I was there in the Manor all over again.

"You did not learn the manners I taught you, Anna."

"Stop talking to her!" hissed Mark, standing in front of me and blocking his view. "I'm coming for you."

Tisak laughed. "Is that so!?"

I stepped around Mark to watch Tisak gesture to someone offscreen.

"I am actually counting on that." His face grew serious. "Come, fetch your friend, or you can claim your new son. We are ready. Though I recommend you do not take too long to decide. As Anna will tell you, I am a fair man, and I always offer a choice." Tisak leaned nearer to the screen. "So, make one quickly. This one is dying, and the boy is being prepared to leave for somewhere, far, far away from here."

I swallowed, desperate not to show anything on my face.

"You will return the boy Jonah," Minu said, coming down the stairs. She stopped in front of Mark and bent her face into the camera lens. "You will return the boy Jonah, mon frère."

Tisak's voice lost all confidence and came as a breath. "Minu!"

"Return him, Ciel."

Whatever ran through Tisak's mind was hidden behind a stony expression, and then his eyes grew treacherous. Was he remembering her misdeeds or the ones of Robert Forbes-Hamilton Junior?

"Make your choice!" he said finally. "He and I are here at the Manor—" he briefly showed Lionel "—your son sleeps in a lorry on its way to an eastern port. Make your choice and make it soon. You do not have long."

Minu spat the words as if they had left a bad taste in her mouth. "I will tell them. And then I will tell them all."

Tisak shrugged nonchalantly, and the screen went dark.

Tell us what?

"We have his code, oui? It can help us." Minu reached for the old-fashioned remote for the TV. "Come, I will show you. Dépêcher-vous!" *Hurry!*

We huddled in.

"T is 8 at the count of one. See, first letter. I is 4 at the count of 3. S is 7 at 4 counts, A is 2 for 1 and K 5 at 2 counts. That's his fancy code. TISAK. You hold the numbers down for the correct number of counts, and it gets you into everything, everywhere."

"But only if Tom can get around the trace put on it. He'll be watching for us to use it." I sighed heavily. "Which port? East, he said?"

"Whichever one is assigned as Tisak's go to," Chie replied, holding a phone to his ear. "Shan, red alert. Tisak is in the country. He's got one of ours at Thurstworthy Manor... Wiltshire, yeah. He's also grabbed one of our kids and stuck him on a lorry heading to an eastern port. Need to know which...Who does the I.N. use? Who's in Tisak's deep pockets? Find that out first...You've got fifteen minutes."

He dialled a Fred and explained all the details.

"Gather everyone to Wiltshire. Anyone who can get here in what, less than twelve hours? Drop whatever you're assigned to and come now."

There were three more calls the same.

"We're going to war," he said, smiling at us.

I laughed. "Don't be so ridiculous."

Chie laughed then. "I'm not! We won't get Jonah out of the hands of the I.N. with fluffy words, Anna. They'll be expecting us, and they will shoot to kill."

Lord, what do we do?

"Count me in," said Mark, giving Chie a brotherly hug.

Did I just hear right? Did Mark just enlist in a war against Ciel Tisak? I was all set to voice my indignation about that when Chie's phone rang.

"Shan…" Chie's face paled, and he replied, "better get your team up here."

He turned to Mark. "Lowestoft, probably going on to the Netherlands."

I flew up the stairs, hurriedly packed, and got Lily from her bed.

"You're going to see Melly. You remember her and Arla?"

She nodded sleepily and asked, "Why?"

"We're going to get Jonah now."

"Okay. You tell him he'zo naughty," she yawned.

Melly's was the safest place for Lily to be since the safehouse was possibly compromised and at risk. Melly didn't mind. She was happy to see me and pleased to help. She smiled nervously and promised to pray along with the rest of the ministry group.

Our next stop was the cottage where the rest of the team had been setting it up as the new safehouse. Chie picked up the drone and placed it into the car's boot, and Javad and Minu settled into yet another new home.

"You should stay here too, Anna," Mark instructed.

I raised my eyebrows. "Nope, I won't."

I was going to get my new son.

Mark looked at Chie, who smiled and shrugged. He turned away from me, picked up the heavy bag that Chie had pointed out, and stuffed it into the car.

Teela hugged me. "You be careful! And come back with that boy."

I nodded, and Pete entered the kitchen.

"NC HQ, the base of operations, is officially open. The first people should be along in the next hour or two, and Shelley's gone for supplies."

"Anna," called Chie, "let's go."

I was ignorant of where the journey would take us. I knew our destination was farther than Cambridge, which was over 3 hours away, so I asked which road we were taking. Mark laughed when Chie glanced at him, tutting and shaking his head.

"Anna, we are not going on any road."

~

We pulled into the private airstrip twenty minutes later. Chie's small plane was parked and ready. A group of men milled around it, and Chie was happy to see them. I would have preferred not to be reminded of the last time I was on his plane, but Chie's exhilaration lifted my spirit.

"This is it, friends. The big man himself is at Thurstworthy Manor Estate. But he's number two on my list. Who wants in on a ten-year-old's rescue first?"

When they all pulled their weapons out ready, Chie smiled.

"Hop in."

Was killing the answer? Surely not. Weren't we supposed to be better than that? Wasn't I? What would Jesus do? Well, He had destroyed a seller's market in a Jewish temple. Weren't we doing the same thing by stripping a sinful seller's market?

Jesus hadn't hurt anyone, though. He had never killed.

If Jonah reached the Netherlands, we would not trace him. That was what they did so well for the I.N. and the NC. They made you disappear. I had encountered the issue once before when I looked for a Non Conformer, and we had never found him. He was probably one of Chie's!

INc Seething Airfield lived up to its name, and the owner was livid we were there at such a late, or early, hour. He was lax in his duties, too sleepy to notice Mark swipe his keys from the coat hanging on the chair and slip them into his own.

Chie laid the drone down on the grass bank and called Tom.

"Switch it on where? No need to be rude; the hole under its tail is all you needed to say." He fumbled around the rear end for the switch.

Eight of us squeezed into Seething's hatchback. Lucky for me, I sat on Chie's lap in the front while the four men squeezed in the back seat. They did not look comfortable, and neither did the smallest man half scrunched up in the boot.

The drone lifted and flew off east with commands in its thermal detector to seek out warm, unmoving bodies like the ones that slept inside lorries. We took the A143 towards Gillingham. The view on Chie's device suddenly zoomed in. The drone had picked up a lorry that carried seven immobile bodies. Not one of them was a small boy, according to the data.

"We can't just leave them! What if it's another batch of girls?"

Chie glanced up. "It's them or Jonah, Anna."

My heart sank as the drone flew on. I said a prayer for them and then prayed for our success and Jonah's safety. I prayed for the end of Stymer and Forbes-Hamilton and for the end of the nightmare unfolding on the planet. The drone zoomed in again. This time, the data matched what it was programmed to estimate as Jonah, and it hovered while the Manticore was dispatched. Finally, it flew down to attach itself to the roof as the drone rose and glided away.

"This road is no good," moaned Chie, "we can't overtake these other lorries fast enough. Pull off just up here, Mark; this one is coming up."

We took the A146 up through Toft Monks and joined the B road. The dot on the tracking map blinked.

"We've got to stop that lorry before it reaches Lowestoft. There's a golf course up ahead. Get off here, Mark; we're ahead of them. We'll cut them off there."

We watched the dot get closer to our location, and Mark drove the car onto the road, headlights forward, and stood at the door waiting. As soon as the lorry came into view, he flashed the lights, and the driver started to slow.

It was too easy. Why wasn't he swerving? Why didn't he carry on and smash into the car? The lorry pulled in. Where were the I.N.? I stood at the side of the road with Chie's team beside me, pointing weapons at the lorry and its driver, who was now climbing out.

"What's all this? I've a ferry to catch!"

Chie stepped forward.

"You're that Richard Cole!" the driver cried with panic on his face. He fumbled through his pockets for his phone.

Chie raised his hands as he closed the gap between them. "I am, but I'm not who you think I am. I'm not a bomber. I'm not a murderer, and I DO NOT kidnap little boys."

"Not heard anything about you doing that. Hey, that's my phone!"

Chie threw the phone inside the cab and asked the driver to open his trailer. Mark pulled him backwards and guided our protestor to the rear, where he was made to unlock the doors.

He gasped to find a sleeping boy amongst his cargo. "Where'd he come from?"

"He's coming home with us, if you don't mind," I said, climbing in and kneeling beside the son God had lent to me. I tried to wake him, but he was out cold.

Mark carried Jonah to the car, and Chie drove this time as I squeezed down into the footwell with every bit of me digging into either plastic or Mark's knees. I was more comfortable than the men in the backseat, though. Mark had Jonah across his lap, his heavy legs dangling over Chie's shoulder, and his feet hung near the face of one of Chie's friends as we drove back to the airfield.

It went freezing cold for a millisecond.

Suddenly, there was more room for me between the dashboard and the people on the seat.

Mark held a boy-like shape of empty clothes, vacant trouser legs draping over Chie and his seat. Jonah was gone. Vanished. In the blink of an eye.

Just like the mock rapture.

I started screaming. Chie skidded to a stop and jumped out of the car, swearing, as did the men in the back. Jonah's trainers falling in their laps had incited terror. Mark stared blankly at the empty clothes, then drew them into a ball at his chest. He looked at me as I took ragged breaths, my fingertips gripping onto his knees.

His voice came slow and deep. It scared me.

"I'm going to kill him."

Tisak had sent us on a futile chase that he knew would be fruitless, and we had fallen for it. It had been too easy. He should have secured the lorry with guards or had at least some defences—we'd expected a fight. But instead, the driver had let us rescue Jonah and drive away.

~

The flight back was subdued. Mark was too quiet. He clenched and unclenched his fists while staring through the porthole at the breaking dawn. Jonah was gone, and we returned to Wiltshire with his empty clothes. We debated his 'displacement' to the Manor, but realistically, he could be anywhere Tisak chose to send him. It was just a matter of navigation. He could wake up in the palace cells of Baruun and to the dead eyes of Sul, but that didn't seem likely if Tisak was in the GBR. Jonah had also been injected with whatever ingredient LeyLucient needed to connect with. I shivered at the thought.

We pulled up to the cottage and hid the car beneath the trees. The garden was full of people, and Chie smiled with a dark satisfaction as he mentally counted the heads of his allies.

"We're on!" he said as we stepped into the cottage.

Teela and Pete were organising teams into position over the plans of the Manor's grounds, and we expected the last of the arrivals within the next two hours.

As we walked in, Tom looked up and spoke to Chie.

"We'll have enough men by 8."

Shelley coughed, as did four other Shans in the room.

"Apologies, ladies." Tom nodded contritely and handed Chie a slip of paper. "Harvard called about fifteen minutes ago. Activity going on at the Manor and two Ridgbacks just left."

"What's a Ridgback?" I asked.

"It's a twelve-troop army combat transport vehicle. It's armoured and has two machine guns and a grenade launcher. You name it. I expect it's been fitted with it."

"Where are they going? Why are they going? They're expecting us over there, right?" I asked.

Tisak had something on us, I remembered.

"Incoming!" Tom whipped the screen around to face away from the room and stepped away. "Lionel's phone again."

Chie and I moved forward to answer it while the room fell silent. I wasn't afraid to look him straight in the eye this time, and yes, I forgot my manners. It was rude.

"I want my boy."

Tisak grinned. "Wonderful. Then you must come and fetch him, Anna. I enjoyed the little ruse in snatching him from you. I knew you would seek him first, of course. Our other friend here is still resistant to death: he lingers on painfully." His expression became frosty. "My amusement has now expired; it is time for the climax."

"Oh, it is time, all right," I replied, mimicking his perfect pronunciation with every letter. "Your plans shall shatter at the feet of the Rock."

Tisak paled a little but continued to glare at me.

Chie side-eyed me with a frown, then peered at Tisak, aggravated. "Hate to break up whatever this is," he pointed from me to the screen, "but Anna won't be going anywhere."

It was my turn to side-eye him. Yeah, like heck I was staying here.

"No. Please, do not disappoint me!" Tisak pleaded, but it had a sarcastic feel to it. "I now have her down as number two on my list. I would appreciate all of my eggs together in one nest so that I can sit on them," he growled, "and crush you all at once."

Someone hissed, and Tisak gestured with his hand to someone off the screen again.

"You have company. How thrilling! This is going to be fun!"

Tisak stepped aside in time for Robert Forbes-Hamilton Jnr. to be yanked forward by a soldier. Apart from his ruffled hair and collar, he looked unscathed.

"Delighted you could join us, Robert. Please, allow me to introduce you to Anna, who you know is your Headsman's wife, and his brother, Richard Cole. Where is Mark? I would ask that he join us."

Without thinking, I looked up and scanned the room. Chie nudged me and shook his head, but it was too late. I had already given away that Mark was on the premises somewhere.

"I have time. I will wait."

Tisak sat and relaxed in an armchair while inspecting and picking under his fingernails. Tea was poured for him, and unconcerned, he sipped it.

"We could discuss how you arrived at the lorry so quickly?"

Mark stepped into view.

"Ah, that can wait. There he is, Robert!" Tisak said, bringing his hands together in excited thankfulness. "Say hello to Mark."

The greeting was awkward. "Hello, Mark."

Sorry, I tried to blow you all up.

"Now we are all acquainted, where is Minu Darab?"

Tisak couldn't watch us all, so he chose to watch Robert paling and nervously fumbling with the flaps of his jacket pockets.

"Not here," lied Mark sternly. "What's your point?"

Ignoring him, Tisak started on Robert. "Sit, my friend. Tell me, where is Minu Darab?"

"I…uh… She went missing, Imperial Kiengir."

"And how, may I ask, did she achieve that while deep in her grave? You confirmed it to me yourself, did you not?"

Robert trembled. "Yes, Imperial Kiengir."

"Magnificent!" Tisak clasped his hands together in mock fascination. "Tell me then, when did this miracle occur that saw a corpse resurrect into a fully breathing body? Please, enlighten me."

Robert exhaled with a hesitant smile.

Don't lie, whatever you do.

"Are you aware I know of your preferences with the young ladies?" Tisak asked him.

Robert did not respond, and despite myself, I enjoyed his discomfort.

"No? Well, I have met a few of them. Five of them, in fact. I unanchored them from the dark hole you subjected them to. Much to their gratification, I can assure you all." Tisak smiled, remembering. Then his expression turned chilly. "Did you send Minu Darab to one of those dark holes?"

"No! Never," Robert Jnr. panicked, "no, I did not. She was here the whole time, undamaged."

"Undamaged?"

"Only me. Only I..."

Tisak stood briskly and went off-screen. I spied Harvard hovering on the grounds in the window behind Robert's chair.

"Something's coming!" a Fred shouted from the garden.

Chie shut the laptop, and Tom rushed forward to grab it as Teela cleared the table of the papers. People filed in from the garden, and Shelley was pointing them to under the stairs.

Gunshots fired from outside, and glass and plaster rained down while bullets flew around the room. Something sharp caught my cheek, and a warm sensation trickled down my face as I dived to the floor.

"This way!"

I heard Shelley, but I couldn't see her anymore, and Mark was pulling at my arm.

"Stay low, on your front, and follow me."

Using my elbows and keeping my head low, I inched towards the stairs as fragments of the cottage showered over me. The noise was deafening, but the cry of someone shot in the kitchen still reached my ears. I turned my face to the ground, not wanting to see him lying in the doorway.

We went down some steps and into an old cellar. NCs were filing out through a gap in the wall. Minu and Javad went through next, and Mark and I followed them into a sloping, unlit, bricked tunnel. Our pace picked up when there was a large explosion, and we assumed it was the cottage being destroyed;

another Bible lost. We rushed through the endless straight tunnel using the torches on our phones—without any signal, they weren't useful for anything else.

Everyone stopped to regroup in a large space where the air was cold and stale. Within a few minutes, it was confirmed we had lost four of our friends. Sad as it was, I was grateful it hadn't been anyone I knew.

"I think I know where we are," Shelley said, coming out of the tunnel neck behind me. "Jonah pointed out the tunnels once after we'd raided the Coles' last residence. He didn't take me in, but he showed me where they were in the cottage. He said they led to an old RAF base. He also said he found other tunnels leading off which he hadn't explored."

"Teela, did you bring the map?" I asked.

"Yeah."

Teela spread it out on the ground. The Manor's plans were folded up beside her.

Shelley pointed. "The cottage is here, the base is there, we are somewhere under here."

I stuck my finger in. "Thurstworthy is there. West of us. Mark said there were building works at the Manor for almost a year with nothing to show for it," I explained. "Maybe they excavated and extended the tunnels while they built the valley of the rapture beds? If we find one leading west, we might find a way into the Manor. Something about the smell here reminds me of where I found Minu."

It was the smell that had lingered in the corridor where Tisak's portrait hung.

"Drag something along the left side of the tunnel wall as we walk. Just in case there's another secret portal."

The valley of the rapture beds raised questions, which Javad and I answered between us while the many NCs unpacked their weapons. Then came the portal questions to which our group already knew the answers. Everyone else was stunned.

Teela outlined the plan, and what those plans meant sank in: firstly, for lives on both sides and secondly, we had to make sure we got out before phase three. Basically, we 'civilians' would do little. The original plan was for us to stay at the cottage. I was not happy about that either, but I was the only one. Everybody who knew me was satisfied it had been the right choice, and once the others knew of my Tisak involvement, they agreed. As we moved deeper, expecting the exit tunnel I believed would lead west and to the Manor, I asked Javad about the bombings.

"Did you discover exactly how LeyLucient worked as a bomb? I know you said it acts as a solvent to the cosmic glue of mass, but I still can't quite work it out."

"I did, Anna dear. You must wonder how it managed to do it with only a pillar of light three feet high."

Just generally, Javad. Don't get into semantics.

"I'll explain. When LeyLucient encounters mass, cells, it breaks them down; if that is what's required, depending on what you add. In the case of the bombings, it was. The rings you saw, the blankets, carried LeyLucient right into every structure at three different points: from the bottom foot on the ground up to the third. Those rings travelled through whatever stood in its way and took the outermost shell right off every atom it touched for a twenty-mile radius. It did it so fast, if you remember, that it took a moment for the mass to react. How could anything remain standing if you remove sliced chunks of anything in three different places?

"No man, woman, child. No pet, wild or farm animal, no tree. Every car and building…no bomb, no sound, no fire." Javad sighed. "The vibrations of the falling buildings added to the effect, of course."

He scratched his chin. "Does that answer your question?"

Yes, I thought, and wished I hadn't asked.

"Mon frère est un homme méchant! Evil!"

Minu raged with more French I didn't understand. I understood those words, though. Her brother was an evil man.

19 The Valley of the Rapture Beds

There was a big debate on what the NCs would do with Minu, Javad, and me while they waged war outside. We stood facing a familiar looking silver door. I couldn't tell whether it was the same door I had met with the last time I was here, where my escape had abruptly ended. If it was that door, then the rapture beds were on the other side, and it would mean there was another way from here into the Manor; because whoever had caught me that day had come from this side of the door.

The team didn't plan on using Tisak's code to open doors until the fighting started. He would have the code tracked. That wasn't an option now: we were stuck behind a door I knew led into the Manor, until we decided to open it…

I voiced the portal theory while they argued over who was staying behind to protect us. They could do what they wanted. I was going for Jonah, end of. I expected him to be in one of the pods, sleeping and unaware. Please God, let him not be electrocuted in a chair, which is what the rest of them thought. I had to consider there were over 3.7 million pods underneath the Manor grounds. I couldn't imagine how deep it went, but I recalled not being able to see from one end of the space to the other once I'd finally got the lights on. I mentioned that too.

"How would we get him out of one of those beds, Javad? How would we even know which one? We don't have hours to look."

"Assuming he is in one," he argued.

"We need to find the lab then. There will be something running. We have three options. He's either in a rapture bed, in the cells, or sitting in a chair with Lionel. You lot are going to him, and I am heading in there." I pointed at the silver door awaiting Tisak's code. "The other side of the valley has another exit leading to the cells, so we'll check there first."

"You'll need me then if you're gonna be in the computers," offered Tom.

"And me to know what the science is saying," Javad added.

The NC group returned from exploring tunnel tangents for an alternate route. They had found stairs leading out.

Mark hugged me tightly. "Love you. Be careful. You know where to meet me?"

I nodded.

"Get out as soon as you have Jonah and wait there for me."

"You just make sure you meet me there, you understand?" I kissed him.

I broke away to see Chie sweeping Teela into his arms and drawing her in for a passionate kiss.

Oh, how long had that been going on?

I looked away, wishing I could feel happy for them. I was, in a way, but he took the joy out of everything.

Once they had left, Teela, Tom, Javad, Minu, and I unlocked the silver door. We stepped in and closed it against the sound of sporadic gunfire. The metal in the beds and columns gleamed under the bright lights.

"Oh my..." Teela gasped.

I ran directly for the cells first to make sure Jonah wasn't locked in. Empty. I was frustrated and worried. I looked across the array of pods and wondered which of them Jonah slept.

We took the metal stairwell down. Each column and row of beds was in perfect symmetry—up, across, and down. Then something changed. There was a long window stretched across the grey wall, and someone inside with their back to us, working. There was also a lift at the rear. One by one, we sidled along the gangway to the door and entered using Tisak's code. The lab technician was surprised to see us with weapons bared. He raised his hands.

"Where's my boy?" I asked, stepping ahead of Tom, who grabbed my arm.

Teela shot at one of their systems.

"She asked you a question."

He pointed out of the window at...which bed exactly?

Javad pushed him out of the way and sat down at the workstation. Tom secured the prisoner, and I shuffled forward.

"Which one?"

The lad shrugged. "I just feed him. Body and mind. He went to the fair. He had fun."

"Bring him here to this room now." Teela pressed her gun to his temple.

"I…don't know how."

"Then I suggest you scramble up off the floor and sit over there next to my good friend and help him work out how you're going to do it."

"No, I won't. Not while the Kiengir is here!"

"The Kiengir has problems of his own. There's a war going on up top. So I'd advise you to get Jonah out fast if you want to get out in time."

He did as Teela asked, with Tom following behind.

She reached into her bag, pulled out Jonah's clothes and shoes, and then handed Minu and me some metal cubes. We stuffed them into our pockets.

"On the gangplanks, place one of these on each of the end columns: that's where the supporting weight beams are, and…" she paused, calculating, "one somewhere in the middle. Press the centre as you place it: you should hear a crack. Minu, you do this area. Anna and I will go down. Hopefully, these guys will have the answers by the time we're done. We have about an hour."

Teela and I descended deeper into the valley, where the air stayed fresh. We started to place the cubes. I was worried about Jonah, and our friends above ground who were fighting and dying to help rescue a child they had never met and liberate a reformed traitor. If they found out about him, they would probably kill Lionel themselves.

I remembered Teela's kiss. It was happier than anything else on my mind.

"So, you and Chie, since when?" I asked, genuinely excited for her.

Teela smiled hesitantly and went quiet for a time.

"Since the night Tisak sent those photos and everybody went to pieces. Mark was angry, guilt-ridden, and sick. Tom was the same. Me, I planned a murder!"

She laughed, then her expression saddened. "Chie went someplace else. Somewhere deep inside. I forced it out of him in the end. He blamed himself. Still does. He's the NC they want, after all. You see, your escape was planned by then. We could get to and from the palace undetected, but we couldn't get in and out of the palace. It's too secure, and the HQ is impossible. Chie decided to exchange himself for you, and I talked him out of it. I shared my murder plot and it just sort of happened between us."

Many good things were coming out of the worst ordeal of my life.

"I'm happy for you. There'll be no getting rid of you now that you're my sister!"

She smiled sadly. "At least for a while. It could've been our last kiss."

She had a point. Death lurked at every corner these days.

We placed the cubes and headed back to the lab. Tom was clutching his head in frustration as he sat in front of a screen, and the lab tech was arguing over dosage maths with Javad.

Minu came and stood beside me. "They found the numbered bed. Tom's figuring out how to bring it here."

"How do we remove the stuff he's been injected with?" I shouted to the lab technician.

"You mean the Honer? It's used now," he replied, chuffed he knew the answer. "One dose, one trip."

"Honer? What is that?" I asked impatiently.

"It's what LeyLucient looks for to bring them here. If you have it, you will come here. One dose, one trip."

He smiled when one of the bed columns started to move pods. It was coming up on one side and down the other with a zippy buzz.

Javad whooped in joy. "Tom has just programmed it to do that!"

I kissed Tom before hanging over the railings, watching impatiently for Jonah to appear.

The technician in the lab instructed the exit process for Jonah now that the three of them were working together. The pod came to rest beside me, and I bashed on the lid.

"Get him out!" I cried.

Finally, the lid slid from beneath my palms, and Jonah opened his eyes, sucking in a breath. He looked at me, confused. Teela threw his clothes over while I took out his cannula and helped him down to the aisle where he got dressed.

I hugged him tightly. "What were you thinking?"

Baffled, Jonah replied, "I don't know what happened. Where are we?"

"On l'a eu. We got him!" Minu smiled widely.

"Minu, when Harvard came, did he take you out through the painting?" I asked.

She nodded.

"You remember the way—how easy it is?"

She nodded again.

"When you get to the kitchen door, look left and run straight across the grounds all the way to the back. There's a gate there. That's where Mark will meet us. I need you to take them all there. Find the stream and wait there."

"And you?"

"I will follow you. There's something I need to do first," and it involved Robert Jnr's desk and filing cabinet for his contacts.

Teela had overheard. "I don't think so, missy."

"Please, get Jonah out. I have to get into that office."

"Then so do I!"

"And leave Tom to protect three people on his own? No, I don't think so."

"Who's gonna protect you?"

"Jesus," I smiled.

Teela pulled a face and spun around to face the lab tech. She pointed to the door at the rear of the lab.

"You. Where does that go?"

"Lift to upstairs. Won't come until the other guy comes to take over, though."

"Right then, up the stairs we go," she said, before warning the lab technician he might want to follow us.

Breathlessly, we climbed, stopping some distance from the top. The cut on my cheek was sore and bleeding. It had dried, but it cracked again every time my face moved. Teela was about to add more cubes when I stopped her.

"I'll do this, you go."

"I don't want to leave you," she argued.

"Go, please go."

It took a lot of persuasions, but they finally left, and I placed the explosives before racing to the silver door and peering into the cell hallway. I met the same familiar scene of empty cells and then stepped up into the tunnel. Soundlessly, I crept along the wall, almost reaching the painting, when I saw shadows approaching and voices nearby. I tucked into the storage recess inside the wall, pressing my back up tight against its side, against the direction they were coming from. Hopefully, they would walk right by and not even notice me.

"The code's been used, sir, a few times, but I was fighting the resistance and have only just seen it."

I froze, not breathing, and trying not to imagine the handsome face of the man who wanted to harm my friends and me.

I saw his head turn as he was still walking past me. It was almost as if someone whispered in his ear I was standing there, lurking in the shadows. Either that or he could see through bricks now. His eyes met mine. He stopped, turned the rest of his body, and reached out with his fingers to my throat. I was lifted from my feet, struggling for breath, and I kicked out, attacking his sleeved arm fruitlessly with my fingernails.

HS Paul Fraser was ecstatic to see me, but with a grin that faded as I was passed into the crook of someone else's strong arm. The guard dragged me along the corridor and up another set of stairs that took me into the Manor. I was taken into the room and thrown into the same chair *he* had sat in during our last video call. Next to me was a dead Robert Jnr. I turned away.

Although it saved us the trouble of putting a stop to him and his crimes, and despite the things he had done, I felt shame to have enjoyed his humiliation. He had died a sinner, and there was no joy in that, no matter who he was. Repenting, I felt the Lord's presence, and I was strengthened in Him. I didn't feel any fear. I felt power. Peace and joy flowed inside me with a passion for righteousness.

HS Paul Fraser had Robert Jnr's body taken away. Only one guard remained in the room. He looked like Melly's daughter, Arla, so I guessed he was Alex Saunders. I saw what Melly had found attractive: tall, dark, with a hint of Spanish in his features. His grin when he saw me watching chilled me.

Fraser checked the seat that had been Robert Jnr's before he sat down, pulling up the fabric of his I.N. navy-coloured trousers as he did so.

"Liars are cowards. They either lie because they cannot or will not face the truth, or they lie because they cannot or will not face the consequences. I've been dying to answer a question you asked me once. You asked, 'Are we not on the same side?' Indeed, I can say that, no, we are not. I don't like traitors of any kind, but at least those like Richard Cole are upfront about their views."

"Would you like me to be upfront now?" I asked sharply, thinking of a few choice words I could say.

Alex clenched his fists, and Fraser laughed.

"That'll be a first! When we worked together, Mrs Cole, you lied for both reasons. I knew all along what you were doing. I directed the case in Manchester. I had closed it, and your searches told me exactly what you were doing and how much you knew. But the Kiengir was insistent you investigated Richard Cole."

"I know. He wasn't happy I'd figured out why that was and was honest about it."

Fraser frowned. He hadn't overheard the conversation at the Manor when I was caught the first time around, and *he* had hit me.

"You were harbouring a highly sought Non Conformer while claiming he was dead. I am not as forgiving as our glorious leader, and your next trip to the capital will be with me."

I would not be returning to Baruun. I would rather die. Protect me, Lord.

Alex stepped forward. "The Kiengir is ready."

Since when? How did he know that? He had been standing here with us the whole time.

HS Fraser nodded and turned to me, smiling. "Showtime!"

Alex grabbed my forearms and tore me from the chair, shoving me forward and into the tunnels. I prayed while we walked through walls, then penetrated the familiar garage space I had tried so hard to forget. Clusters of soldiers dotted the room. Lionel sat, head hanging forward and covered in blood. The restraints weren't jolting him anymore. If he was still alive, he was not well.

On the ground lay bodies, some of theirs and some of ours. Soldiers surrounded prisoners. Freds, Shans, Shelley, Rusty, Mark.

Mark!

He was being held on his knees by three soldiers and groaned when he saw me. While he struggled under their grip, one poked him hard in the chest with the butt of a rifle.

Fraser took me nearer to Lionel. There was an empty chair beside him; he plonked me in it. I stared at Mark across the garage as he stared at me, trying not to show his struggle to breathe.

"All eyes on me, please." Tisak's voice floated through the air as he said the familiar phrase of the Collective Thought mantra.

I dragged my eyes from Mark and swept them across the other faces on the way to the man I detested. The man who is due for destruction. I thought I saw Greg's stunned face and had to look back to check.

"Anna Cole!"

Tisak's shout made me jump, and I turned to glare at him.

Oh, I despised the man. Tension rolled from everyone while he stood, demanding respect and commanding control. Things he neither deserved nor had earned. I seethed, gripping onto the chair arms.

"What?" I snapped. "You want me to obey you after you kidnapped my boy, beaten people–" I glanced at Lionel, he was awake, "–tricked us and now going to murder us?"

Tisak was not amused. The frightening look he showed no longer influenced me.

"If Richard Cole would reveal himself, then we will all go home!"

I laughed shamelessly. "No one here believes that, especially us. It's kill or be killed; we all know it. It's not over until we're dead. There's time yet, and please, do not insult us by lying."

A man I recognised as Ian Stymer stepped forward.

"Allow me."

"No need," said Tisak, "let her get it out of her system. It might save her life later if she wears herself out now."

Mark yelled and struggled under the soldiers' grip. Tisak turned.

"Ah, that one you may kill. I do not need him. Now, Anna, why do you insist I am a liar?"

Stymer prepared his weapon while he walked towards my lovely Mark, and my pulse raced. Anger flushed my chest. It seemed like God had been holding me back until that moment, the elastic stretching and stretching. I flew off my chair screaming and threw myself at Tisak as the gunshot rang out and echoed around the room.

Then it was pandemonium.

I crashed into Tisak, and we both went down. I landed on top of him as his head hit the ground. Stunned, he flung me off and recovered unnaturally quickly. He plucked me up and threw me at the wall. My breath escaped with a sigh as I sank to the ground.

People were engaged in hand-to-hand combat all around me. There were too many fighters to see clearly who battled who as I caught my breath during these few precious seconds, looking for Mark. Somewhere, a sniper lurked in the shadows. It was one of ours; only *his* soldiers were going down.

Chie. I was certain of it.

Tisak's advance towards me suddenly halted when a crack appeared in the ground between us. The hour was up, and the valley explosives were going off, but the garage shouldn't be tilting. The intention was for the cubes to bring down the columns, not the Manor.

I scrambled to my feet and spotted a weapon. I scooped it up. I hadn't held a gun before and was surprised by how heavy it was. I pointed it at Tisak, not knowing if there were any bullets in it. If only for a second, it felt good to see him look fearful. Soldiers gathered around to protect him, and Sul was in front, staring at me. He was Esta's brother and had allowed my rescue. I could not pull the trigger. If I was honest with myself, I wasn't firmly set on pulling it for Tisak.

Firing their weapons, they ushered Tisak away with Sul as his rear guard while the ground rumbled on and the crack opened further. I looked along the ground for Mark, fighting back the anguish that threatened me. I'd heard the shot. I breathed against the tears.

Lionel staggered up from the broken chair as parts of its frame stayed squeezed between his arms and the restraints. I ran and swung his arm over my shoulder, and we headed towards the door.

HS Paul Fraser hadn't left yet. He appeared behind us, and Alex Saunders blocked the doorway.

"Not this time, you don't," Fraser said, making a grab for me, then teetered and fell when Greg hit him on the head from behind with his gun.

Alex launched an attack just as Greg pinpointed his target and pulled the trigger. Alex sank to the ground, holding his chest.

I worked hard not to panic.

Greg helped me support Lionel through the door and across the grounds to the mossy gate with no interference from living soldiers. Many dead ones scattered on the grass, but the dipping of the 17 acres of estate grounds was more daunting. A section of Thurstworthy Manor had broken off and sunk to the cracked sloping ground, bowed and now looked like a shallow bowl. I considered its stability as we skirted along the rim and through the hole in the smashed gate. Lionel was breathing heavily. We sat him down against a tree to rest, and I turned to Greg, shocked.

"What did you do?"

He shrugged his shoulders. "Sorry, but you don't kill a bloke for no reason, and Mark hadn't done anything to warrant it! I figured after I shot that Stymer guy, well, I think I was already fired."

I kissed Greg on the mouth, and then hugged him. "Thank you!"

Embarrassed, he added, "I also got the message you embedded into Richard Cole's file. Clever you."

I didn't know what he was talking about, but I guessed Tom had something to do with it.

"I never fully believed your message or what HS said about you. Crap, you weren't wrong, though! There's no way you turned traitor, and I started to doubt which side was good. I knew you weren't a bad sort; you know what I mean? A traitor just ain't you, and it ain't Teela either."

I thanked Greg for his allegiance and listened to him tell me what I hadn't seen.

While I had flown across the room towards Tisak, aiming to destroy him, Greg fired his bullet and Ian Stymer hit the ground. Mark had dropped too and rolled away from the soldiers holding him. I hadn't seen the other prisoners react in the moment, either. They wrestled with the soldiers that held them, and one by one, they broke free to continue the fight. Chie, I guessed, sank into the shadows to seek out targets.

There was still a chance. Mark, Chie, Pete, Shelley, Rusty…

Lionel groaned, and I crouched down.

"Thanks again," he said appreciatively. "I would've understood if you didn't come for me. You've all risked everything."

I smoothed his damp hair. "Jesus loves you, Lionel, and He says you're worth the risk. Even to His death, you're worth it."

He smiled. "What about yours?"

If that is what God needs.

"I'm Chris. Nice to meet you." He still had on the restraints, and the piece of broken chair stuck out as he offered his hand to shake.

I shook it, then turned to Greg. "Can you get him to Teela and Tom down there? They'll sort these out. I'll wait here for the others."

I lingered just inside the gate and looked across the land. The Manor looked like a doll's house with the side panel removed. I could see into the individual rooms. The missing chunk had fractured and slid down the dipping ground.

People were running across the bottom of the shallow bowl and coming faster than the runners were two chasing Ridgbacks. I ran forward and screamed. Then, on instinct, I looked up into one of the trees. Someone was pointing a rifle at me. He fired a second after I felt a hand on the back of my shirt and was yanked back through the gap in the gate. Teela stepped through and shot the guard. He fell from the tree.

"I wasn't gonna leave you unprotected again, missy," she said.

The Ridgbacks were gaining on the seven runners, and raining bullets hit the ground, sending chunks of soil into the air. Beneath my feet, I felt the vibration of every one as the NCs ran towards us from the dip. A crack came that echoed louder than the bullets. The base of the shallow bowl caved under the weight. The land disappeared, and the combat vehicles were swallowed down into whatever was left of the valley of the rapture beds.

Thank you, Lord.

Simple words. True words. His faithfulness knew no limits because Mark was coming. He was running with other people I didn't know. Chie was not among them. None of our group was among them. A brief stabbing pain went through my heart. Brief. It was selfish; I admitted to myself, but Mark was okay, and it was all that mattered to me in that second. Mark was okay. Jonah was out, I was out, and we were alive. Mark swept me up when he reached me. He hugged and kissed me, and we escaped through the gap in the gate to join the others.

Tom and Teela had been proactive, too. They had arranged for vans to collect us. One of them was already disappearing down the track. The other engine was revving, waiting for us. We jumped in and skidded away.

20 Arla Stevens

Bewildered, I sat in the safehouse near Chippenham. It was the one Mark had gone to the first time we met up with the NCs, where he had met Chaperone Shelley. It wasn't a house; it was a warehouse large enough to drive the vans inside and be completely hidden. Friends of Chie had left us with new equipment and vehicles the day before, then drove the vans away. Tom had spent most of his time getting our IT set up and secure while Mark, Jonah, and I went to fetch Lily from Melly's house.

Melly was pleased to see us. Touching the cut to my cheek, she offered to tend to it. I waved her off: it was too late to do anything that would reduce the scar. I told her about Alex. She flopped into the chair, relieved he would never harass her again, and she now had freedom from the man who had hurt her. Her mood lifted.

Alex Saunders was dead. Ian Stymer and Robert Jnr. were dead. The case was solved, the mystery of the mock rapture revealed, but we had heard nothing from our friends. Javad never made it to the gate. He lay somewhere under the grounds of the Manor. Two guards had spotted them running and given chase. He was shot in the back before Teela managed to shoot the second guard. My heart ached for the beautiful man who helped to rescue my new son. The one who had explained the secrets of LeyLucient that the rest of us didn't understand. Now he was dead and unable to explain it to anyone else.

Javad had been willing to risk his life. Ever since Teela had picked him up at the market on the day of the Manchester bombing, he was resigned to death. He wasn't afraid—he knew where he was going. I thanked God for his life and the help he had been for us.

~

At the table with Teela, we waited for news. We hadn't heard from Chie, Rusty, Shelley, or Pete. There were other names filtering through the NC chat, confirmed as either dead or in hiding. None I recognised. None that Tom recognised. It didn't mean those names hadn't belonged to any of the people we knew.

I looked around for Minu. She had walked the length of the warehouse in tears. The bond she had built with Javad had been abruptly severed, and she was heartbroken. She grieved his loss with angry growls. She was Tisak's sister, all right, but she was good. Righteous.

I rose to pace beside her. I didn't speak; I just walked with her while she mumbled mostly in French.

"He is a menace! I have known it for many years. He hated mama et papa and their faith."

Minu stopped pacing and stared into the distance.

"You must know our parents died when we were teenagers. Ciel was sixteen. I was just eighteen. Did you know?"

I shook my head. I hadn't researched Tisak's family history.

"The report said Islamic terrorists murdered them, but they didn't. I caught Ciel one day in some sort of dark worship. I don't know; it sounded a bit weird in a strange language. It was dark and oppressive. I was afraid of it. I backed out when he saw me: his eyes were far away, yet they felt like they were inside me."

Remembering, Minu shivered. I understood exactly what she meant.

"There isn't an occult record of its exact style of ritual sacrifice, but it was what actually killed our parents, and I knew Ciel had done it. I knew."

"Minu, no! You know this for sure?"

She nodded and looked at me. "No proof, of course, but I knew before he stood over me one day and took pleasure in telling me. He thought I would stop trying to prove it if he told me. That was right before he ordered Robert to ensure I was buried nice and deep."

Tisak had lied at the palace cells. He was a monster now and before.

"Chie's okay!" Teela squealed to anyone who could hear. "Hurt, but he's okay. He's coming here." She smiled at me excitedly. "Anna, he's okay!"

I smiled back, feeling confused after my other conversation. Mark bent to kiss me and then swept Lily into the air. I thanked God and praised Him out loud. I didn't care who heard me. Chie was okay, and I smiled again.

"Any news on the others?" I asked.

Teela shook her head. "Nothing yet."

Minu had gone back to her pacing. I left her to her thoughts and sat beside Mark. He had cuts on his face and an impressive bruise on his chest from the gun he was hit with. They didn't bother him much as he leaned over and kissed me again. It still made me tingle all these years later.

Waiting to know if any of our other friends had made it out was unbearable, so when the car carrying Chie arrived, we excitedly rushed to meet it. Teela, ahead of us all, opened one of the rear doors and climbed in, throwing herself onto Chie, who groaned in pain. She slid back out apologetically and helped him out.

I watched the face of the driver. He smiled, big white teeth flashing against his West Indies skin, his South States skin. Harvard Jones. Mark got there before me, pulled Harvard from the car and hugged him, smacking him on the back in delight.

"Thank you, my man!"

"Anytime, brother!"

Mark helped Teela with Chie as I walked beside them. His arm was held with a sling across his chest, and beneath that, dried blood coated the clothes on his left shoulder.

"Bastards got me," he groaned again as he lay on the makeshift sofa of crates covered with a blanket.

Harvard brought a bag of medical supplies and placed it beside him. "He needs a doctor and surgery, I reckon."

Tom got straight on the phone. The NC's nearest doctor was in Bath, but she arrived and set up the heart monitor within fifteen minutes, then laid out equipment and gave orders. First, I had to rub down the table with an alcohol solution before I helped Chie to lie down on it. Then she handed me an apron because I would be assisting her…what could I do that would help?

I could look away as she dug with tweezers into the bullet hole. Yes, I could do that, and I peered at Teela, who had kneeled beside Chie's face and encouraged him to look at her. Even then, as Chie screamed and Teela cried, I was reminded of the Kiengir. Again, I was suffocated with the words, 'look at me, be honest, do not be rude,' ringing in my memory.

Chie screamed again, with fingers gripping the edge of the table. As he stared into Teela's eyes, his breathing steadied, and he grew calmer. There was such love between them, whether they knew it yet or not: I could see it flooding from them. Chie growled deeply and tensed up, and then the doctor pushed wet, soiled linen into my gloved hands. The bullet sat on top.

"Can't you give him something for the pain?" Mark cried, finding it hard to watch his brother suffer. He held a frightened Lily in his arms, who had hidden her face in Mark's neck.

"No drugs!" Chie was adamant. Between puffs, he added, "Can't run if I'm asleep."

"Can't run if you pass out, either!" the doctor tried to persuade him.

"No drugs."

"Well, I've given you a local, anyway. I'll do the stitches in a minute."

Chie pushed his chin to one side and reluctantly tore his eyes from Teela to glare at the doctor's face. "I said no drugs!"

"Sorry," she wasn't sorry at all; she was amused, "but I made a solemn promise when I became a doctor not to allow unnecessary suffering during a procedure. As this is surgery, I did what I thought I needed to do. It won't stop you from running. The injury, on the other hand..."

Chie was about to argue.

"Shush! See, it's working already; you're all bolshy now and getting in my business." She smiled gently. "Resume your staring; I'm going to stitch you up now."

"He's on!" Tom called from the corner and turned up the volume.

At his crystal lectern facing a cheering crowd, Tisak didn't look as perfect as usual. He seemed tired, a little pale, and nursed his ribs under a navy suit. I hoped that was my fault. I had hit him like a missile, and he had been my soft landing.

"Greetings, Neighbours! It gives me immense pleasure to announce the mystery of the mock rapture has been solved."

I should have known he would tell more lies. It was the deception of Robert Forbes-Hamilton Jnr. that had changed the world, and pictures of what remained of the valley of the rapture beds were shown on the report. Footage showed some of the pods had been excavated and laid out on the grass. They didn't look as shiny now: all dented, scratched and dirty.

Tisak shared the involvement of Ian Stymer and the recently destroyed Manchester company, Braithwaites, in the plot. He confirmed both men had been killed trying to destroy the evidence. Although NCs hadn't been blamed this time, I wondered whether we were originally meant to be the scapegoats. Tisak went on to boast about how 'he himself' was injured during the battle when bringing the men to justice, always trying to prove he was in on the fight with the lowly soldiers. Yet, he did not condone war. Hypocrite.

I yawned and shook my head. "Unbelievable."

I turned my back on him and tuned him out. My gaze rested on Jonah. He stood at a window, staring out at the landscape beyond. I stood beside him and took his hand in mine.

"Are you all right?" I asked, kissing his head.

"No." He sniffed. "I've done this!"

I turned him to face me, and he looked up with tearful eyes.

"No, you did not. The battle was coming at some point, Jonah. What you did ignited this one, but the spark was always going to come. It would have happened anyway. Do you see?"

"But Lionel, I mean, Chris..."

I hugged him tightly. "He got caught trying to help you, yes, but none of this is down to you, none of it, you hear?"

Jonah nodded.

The doctor tapped me on the shoulder, stitched up my cheek, and dressed it despite my protests. Then she saw to Chris before she left with explicit post-check instructions. Chie was having none of the 'fussy' aftercare. He spent most of his time in contact with NCs across the globe, making each leader aware of the real story in Wiltshire.

Tom set up NC News and worked for hours on a full briefing, a start to finish written diary of what we had uncovered, including the kidnap ring. He published the registration number of the lorry that carried, I believed, girls sleeping on their way to hell. The report exploded everywhere. Then it went mainstream. The people were finding out and seeing another side to the I.N. and Tisak's regime, though, mostly the new findings were spun as conspiracy and resistance propaganda.

News filtered through during the following week that neither Shelley nor Rusty had turned up at any NC locations and were presumed dead. Tom already knew. Days ago, he knew. He told me she would have called. She hadn't been captured, and she hadn't come home. His girl was gone, and although he didn't need to hear it through the NC chat, it cemented it.

Teela couldn't find Pete. She tried her original contacts, but we never knew his real name, and they didn't know who had come. The problem was that Pete wouldn't know where to find us. This was NC safehouse level twenty up the command chain. Only people like Chie and the few that had needed it would know. Without direct contact with senior NCs who trusted him, Pete hadn't a chance, and we were all here, uncontactable to anyone outside the NC framework. I prayed he had made it and was lying low somewhere.

Mark and I managed to have some well overdue alone time. We felt like teenagers sneaking outdoors, looking for a private spot to kiss and cuddle. We hadn't had an intimate moment since before Manchester. That was too long ago.

Jonah had stopped blaming himself and spent a lot of time with Chris, aka Lionel. I didn't interfere; this was Jonah's thing to work out with him, and we were there if he needed Mark and me. Chris' side of the story started with the message he had sent to say there was no update. Then, he had gone to the station to find out where they had taken Jonah and asked a few too many questions. Alex became suspicious, and when Chris growled about Forbes-Hamilton, he had accompanied Chris to the Manor, where he was arrested.

I hoped Chris hadn't shared the rest of the story with Jonah, but he must have. Jonah overcame his fury against him and came to tell me that Chris now knew the truth. I understood, remembering the night we had found out about 'Lionel', and Jonah had yelled that knowing the truth about Tisak was different from knowing the truth about Jesus. Chris knew now.

Lily was feeling much better since the yucky blood stuff was gone. She sat on my knee to speak to Chie.

"How's your bandage?" she asked, pulling his shirt and peering underneath it.

Chie laughed. "The bandage is great!" He reached for his button. "Wanna see?"

"No!" she cried, eyes widening in horror.

Chie pulled her onto his lap. "Lily, nothing can get me down! Then who will sneak you sweets when Mark and Anna aren't looking?"

He winked, and she laughed.

"So, you're invisible then?" she asked earnestly.

Chie looked at me and frowned. I whispered, 'invincible', and he was off with funny stories and crazy antics. He's a meta-hero now. One that can't even die from guns.

Nobody at the station or in the I.N. knew what Greg Prentice had done. Alex Saunders was confirmed dead, and Greg had been the only agent he'd asked to accompany him to the Manor with Chris. How had nobody seen him shoot Ian Stymer? Nobody! I was reminded of similar patterns in scripture. Besides the obvious spiritual blindness reference, I also remembered King Saul not finding David in the cave, the lions not eating three faithful servants, and enemy armies attacking themselves because of the protection from God. God had been faithful. Throughout it all, He had come through, and I had matured in Him. I had leant on Him while I was in the palace. Though I had missed the scriptures, what I had instead was His presence, power, and peace. I knew I must have had it because I had endured it all.

~

Chie turned up one morning in a nice car. It was blue. From the back, he lifted out a bag and held a large envelope in his hand. He handed it to Mark and gave me the bag. I peered in. Hair dye. Extremely vivid yellow hair dye. I thought about the time Mark was disguised with dreadlocks and giggled, voicing my disappointment that I wouldn't see it again. Mark scowled as he strode over. Tom sent me a file. He had taken a photo that day, and I laughed out loud as I looked. Then my face dropped a little when I remembered why I didn't get to see it again.

"This is the new you," Chie said, watching as Mark dipped into the envelope and pulled out new passports and papers. "One for each of you. Nice to meet you Marcus Stevens, Arla Stevens. This is our tenancy agreement for your new house in Cambridge. Rent free, of course, as long as I can come and stay sometimes."

Marcus, Arla, Lillia, and Jon Stevens. We were a family, and my heart swelled.

"Seriously, Chie! How have you done this?"

"Not me. The North States NCs bought it. The Coles are a household name, thanks to Tom's NC News briefing. He has a website up and running now. Did he tell you? Got 65,000 members in two days. North States says thank you to the Coles."

Right. We were as famous as Chie now.

~

Lily, we hoped, had remembered the correct date of Jonah's birthday, and we decided to combine a leaving party with a surprise birthday party. It was almost impossible with only one room between eight adults and an overexcited girl of six, but we managed it. It had been both a happy and a sad event because we left the next day for Cambridge.

And I was blonde! I hated it.

Our new house was stunning. It was a three-bed detached property on a new housing estate with a school nearby. Jon and Lillia Stevens would not be enrolled in an I.N. school. Thanks to Dan, they were off to a clandestine ministry school, and they were due to start on Monday.

We had tried to convince Minu to come with us, but she declined, preferring to stay with Teela and Chie and help head up the UK patronage. There was still no news of Not-Pervy Pete, and I prayed God would reveal something.

"Are they settled now?" I asked as Mark entered our new, fully furnished bedroom and sat on the bed.

He laughed. "Oh yes! They're very excited about starting a new school and making some friends. It's been a long time since they've had that experience."

I bounced gently on the bed, and my feet were twitching. Excitement built, and I wanted to blurt out the words, but I managed to get a grip and stay calm.

Mark narrowed his eyes and smiled. He was probably wondering what trick I had planned to surprise him with.

"What is it? What are you all fidgety about?"

"I have a bit of news of my own," I said, passing him a small white stick.

Mark's mouth fell open when he took it and looked. "Is this…are you?"

I nodded, and he swept me off my feet and kissed me passionately.

"We're having a baby?"

He kissed me again.

In the background, on the muted TV, the camera zoomed in on a pair of hands signing the treaty that promised a seven-year peace for Israel.

***

History Now

From the beginning of civilisation, mankind has harboured a deep-seated desire to know the future. This desire has manifested itself in many cultures, from reading animal entrails, tarot cards, palms, witchcraft, and astrology. Unfortunately, none of these methods has provided the insight or outcomes their practitioners or adherents have wanted.

Innate within humanity is the need for peace, security, stability, certainty, and justice. History is peppered with examples of leaders of every secular and religious sort imaginable. Governments of every political hue promised to meet such deep-seated cravings. All have come; the majority are gone: in some cases, leaving only dust as the only evidence of their existence.

The second world war peace settlement reshaped and reset the geopolitical framework. The United Nations was created to replace the failed and discredited Versailles treaty League of Nations. To the majority, the UN was a harbinger of peace and unity, a place for discussion instead of war. To the very few, it was a baby step to the formation of a world government.

Peace, order and justice did not prevail. Man's nature and historical enmities, petty jealousies, injustices (real and perceived), land disputes, and the need for material resources and political power were the driving forces for increasingly frequent conflicts.

When the UN was founded, less than 3 billion souls inhabited our divinely created home, planet earth. With ever more people came the immediate need for food, medicine, resources, travel, and industry. Such relentless pressure on earth's finite resources created inevitable animosity between religions and people groups.

The world rocked on its social and economic foundations. Beset with this onslaught, the planet seemed to be retaliating with volcanic eruptions, earthquakes, and landslides. Moreover, the weather on the planet, which held sway over their lives by providing light, heat, wind and water, and in turn, food, began to alter.

Imperceptibly at first. Later, with a venom of its own. It wreaked physical and economic damage across the globe. The need for food increased apace. Wealthy nations called for more, new, better foodstuffs. Poorer states cried out for enough to survive.

Similar pressures were evident in the field of medicine. Ground-breaking new substances for the first world were developed. The cry from the third world was simply for enough vaccinations to keep well. These demands led to myriads of experiments in animal, plant, and human health. New medicines were forthcoming. Previously unknown viral and bacterial life forms were an inadvertent by-product of research.

A new cure—a new pestilence. Who knew? A crisis was brewing. Where lay its roots? What would the outcome be?

Return

The Ten Territories

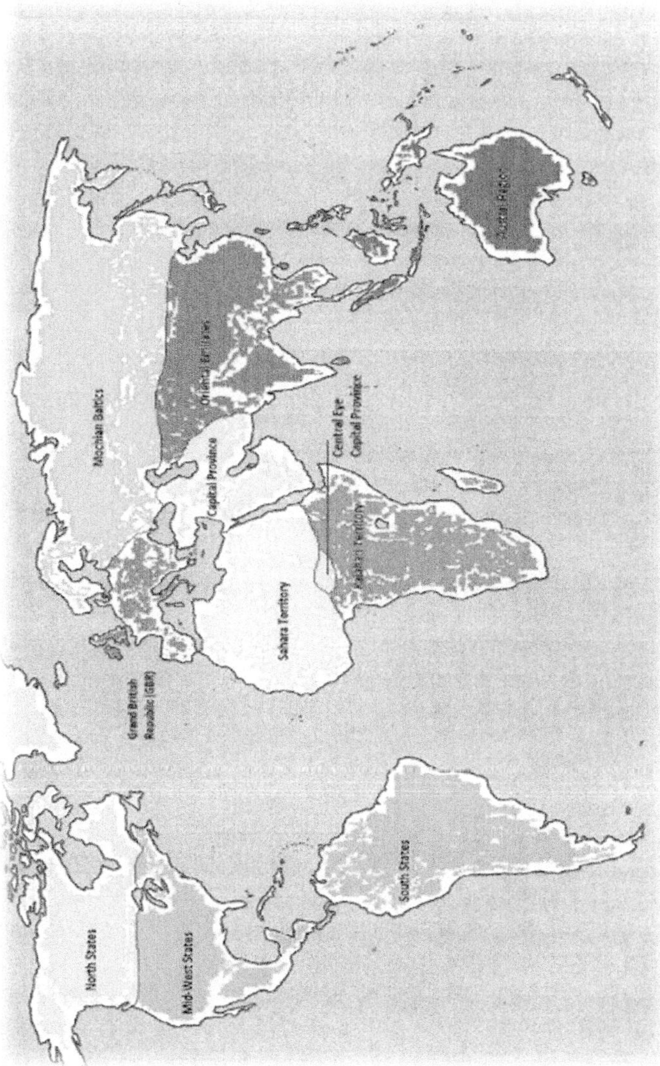

Cambridge, England

I was isolating, and I was not allowed out. Apparently, although my husband Mark didn't say it as I bluntly will, being this heavily pregnant meant I couldn't waddle fast enough if I needed to get away. I was nearing the end of my seventh month, and movement was restricted, so I did not take Jonah and Lily to school, go shopping, or go to work. I stood no chance of evading capture by the forces of the International Neighbourhood if we were recognised.

Living conditions had declined for the Non Conformers since the Manor battle. The world leader, the Imperial Kiengir Ciel Tisak, had tightened security around the mainstream internet. Our access had been cut off completely. The I.N.'s technology truly was impressive, even by Tom's standards, and they had done the same to block us from their network as the NCs had done to block them from ours. But they had added traps that triggered viruses inside unusually coded firewalls.

It would have led them right to our door.

That said, we did still have our own NC Network, and it was useful. Not as valuable as the I.N.'s, but it served us well, most of the time, and it was all we had since our informers had been silent for months. As a result, we remained as inconspicuous and as underground as possible. We stayed away from public places and gatherings that might bring us unwanted attention.

I was still blonde and hated it. My skin was too pale for light hair, and I looked unwell. Add to that the huge dark eyes, and I was just weird. Lily loved it, though, because I had hair like hers, and we had the same bogus surname. In Lily's eyes, I was now a 'proper mummy' in a proper family.

Mark and I had become mum and dad full time since Lily made the mistake of calling me Anna in front of her 7th birthday party guests. Not mum, as she was supposed to have said, and not even Arla at that! Most of our neighbours and acquaintances in Cambridge knew us as the Steven's family, even those in my church ministry group. Lily had come up with the solution on her own and never called us by our names again.

Jonah hadn't known what to make of all the changes in our lives, nor how to feel about Lily calling us mum and dad, but he was mature enough to deal with it and understood. He preferred to keep things the way they were, Anna and Mark on the inside, parents on the outside. He never forgot, so he didn't need the permanence, and his decision was fine with us.

The saga of the 'Sleeping Girls' continued despite the deaths of Ian Stymer and Robert Forbes-Hamilton Junior. I was fruitlessly searching for new evidence with my laptop when Teela came through the door. She grinned at me, already stuck into a screen.

"What's on the agenda today, then?" she asked, nosing over my shoulder.

I looked at her with playful suspicion, unsure I should voice my thoughts. "Do you want to know so you can support me, or are you going to be my mummy about it?"

She narrowed her eyes. "Well, now, I'm definitely asking!"

"Am I telling, though?" I asked, adding a teasing laugh.

She sat beside me at the kitchen table and rested her chin on her hands. "Try me. Come on."

I pursed my lips. "Okay, but don't throw a fit because I've thought about nothing else for ages. First, I'd like to contact Greg, and I have my reasons. Second, I need to go back to the Manor."

Teela was not impressed.

I silenced her profanities with, "I need some leads, T. We can't just keep going around rescuing the spills and not the whole cup. We need to stop this at the top, starting with Robert Jnr's files. There's nothing more to find on the NC Network. I need the I.N.'s, and that's why I need Greg."

Teela pointed at my swollen belly. "Aren't you forgetting something?"

That again.

"I'm pregnant, not unable! And I understand I have to hide, but there isn't anyone at the Manor now since part of it slipped into a massive hole, and Robert Senior had a stroke. I need those files, T."

"There's no way Mark will allow it."

Teela was spot on. Mark was my only deterrent, the sole reason I hadn't bothered to express my feelings months ago. I knew it would be useless and didn't fancy a battle with my husband over something I hadn't yet decided to do. Now though, all my leads were exhausted, and I refused to stand by and watch those men get away with what they did to women.

"Well, we'll see when he gets back, won't we?"

Mark and Chie would soon be home from the best job ever—mine—until I wasn't allowed out. I used to help Mark run the network's underground trading centre known as The Market. It catered for all NC needs—whatever it was, and fellow NCs worked together to supply us, now that we couldn't go to the supermarket or anywhere else and pay like ordinary people. That was thanks to the scanners the I.N. had installed over the summer. Border crossings, shops, public buildings, and transport vehicles now had scanning facilities merged into door frames. They read faces and alerted local I.N. soldiers. It was designed for someone like Greg to find a fugitive like me. We generally didn't take the risk. If a face had a record, it would get them caught.

The scanners weren't always monitored manually. If it spotted a face that matched with one on file, the system would automatically ping an alert to the I.N. The NC wouldn't even know. Once a scanner had us flagged, the streets' surveillance cameras picked us out and never lost sight of us. Then the fancy new communication towers were erected—all tall and sleek—the enemy could follow our thermal heat signature wherever we went. There was rarely an escape from the eyes of the towers, so the Market stepped up as our demand for supplies grew.

NCs like us couldn't be officially employed. Even though I was paid through the NC launderers for a job I didn't have by a firm that didn't exist, we still couldn't buy from a standard shop. Marcus and Arla Stevens' crypto account fluctuated mouglar balances to show income and expenditure on a regular basis, but none of it was real. There wasn't any crypto cash to actually exchange for physical items, and it was tantamount to stealing, anyway. Instead, our Cole crypto account in the NC network brimmed. We traded in dollars, and all our purchases were made through the Market. Mark supervised the Cambridge branch, and his younger brother Richard "Chie" Cole was his boss.

I stood at the living room window, waiting for them to come home. I wasn't looking forward to voicing my request, but I hated the anxiety of waiting to do it. I didn't need the added fear when I heard the world leader's voice on the radio. It heightened my nerves to beyond stretched, and I switched it off within seconds. Since the spring, I hadn't seen or heard any of Tisak's broadcasts or written announcements. I couldn't bring myself to look at him, and whenever I heard his voice, it took me straight back to his control and threats. His electronic presence flicked a switch in my brain, and I would see the Manor again, mostly, but sometimes, the palace tower in Baruun.

When I found myself alone and in the quiet for too long, I drifted back to palace times. So I was glad when Chie and Teela came to stay on a semi-permanent basis last week. I was a whale. I needed the help, and keeping mentally active eased my lapses in reality. I was grateful for Teela's company; it made staying home easier, and I had stopped the need to change rooms just for a different view, assuring myself I wasn't back in Baruun, and this wasn't captivity.

It did not stop the reminders, though. Little snapshots of memory still registered, which I converted to power my campaign for other missing and sleeping girls. The removal of Ian Stymer and Robert Jnr. had not slowed the number of missing person reports. NCs across the world worked hard to intercept deliveries of the girls I managed to track. Still, those already 'homed' were untraceable, and the police did not have the capacity to solve the hundreds of cases every quarter.

If only I had succeeded in accessing Robert Jnr's files, which I hoped remained under the Manor. Files that, I prayed, had not sunk irretrievably into the abyss I had dubbed the valley of the rupture beds. I would have leads, names, and details. I would have something other than a scar on my cheek to remind me of the day when we had lost friends. Pete had not been in touch, and we assumed he never made it out of the Manor. It was difficult to confirm because we never knew his real name, and Teela's Asider contact wasn't sure who was missing. I sighed and prayed, as I did every time Pete came to mind.

Mark's car pulled up, and I swallowed in apprehension. I watched him and Chie come through the door, both smiling but with peculiar expressions on their faces—those that said, 'nur-nur-nur-nur-nur, I-know-something-you-don't-know'. I didn't fancy dropping the 'I need to go back to the Manor' statement because they seemed so annoyingly happy.

In the end, I spat it out. "What!?"

Mark kissed me on the forehead, fit to burst. "Don't ask because I'm dying to tell you, and it'll ruin everything, and then I'll be in massive trouble."

Ooh, surprises.

Teela didn't pay any notice as she played with Lily on the living room carpet while the dinner cooked.

"Stop smiling at me all funny then," I said, "it isn't going to help your cause."

There was a hum of restlessness over dinner, and Chie kept checking his watch. It had me wondering what on earth was going on. Impatient excitement swelled in them as intrigue grew in me and the knock at the door had them both behaving younger than Lily. They leapt up from their seats but made no move to answer it.

"What is the matter with you two?" I asked. "Oh, I'll go, shall I? It isn't like I'm hugely pregnant or anything!"

I reached for the front door and pulled it open in shock. The kind, dark-haired, deep voice of one of my favourite Christians wasn't what I expected. It took me a second to breathe, compute, and reach out to draw him in for the hug I thought I would never have. In this lifetime, anyway.

"Praise God, Pete, I can't believe it's you!"

"Well, this is a nice surprise!" he said, smiling and unable to resist putting his hand on my bump. "Congratulations! When are you due?"

"1st February, and it can't come soon enough!"

I pulled him into the living room. Lily squealed with delight and Jonah flew down the stairs when he recognised the voice that belonged to the friend we thought was lost.

"You lot aren't easy people to track down," Pete moaned, after he had hugged everyone and settled in a chair. "The NC contacts of my Asider friends either didn't know or wouldn't say where you were—which is good, don't get me wrong—but it delayed me."

Teela huffed and flicked her eyes. "We've been asking after you for months. My guy didn't know you."

Pete laughed. "That's good then. Obscurity is what I plan for. Not so good when trying to find all of you. My NC News membership was three months old before someone believed I was genuinely trying to reach Tom. Eventually, I got a message through, and he responded."

"How long have you known?" I asked, looking suspiciously at Mark and Chie.

Mark grinned and replied, "Since this morning. He contacted the Market to wind me up with a ridiculous order. I mean, who needs 500,000 buttons, anyway? I can't believe you almost persuaded me as well!"

"Why did you call the Market to do that?" I giggled.

Pete laughed. "It was the first weird thing I thought of. I wanted to surprise you, but Tom said Chie might shoot me by mistake if I didn't make my presence known, and if I had to call first, I was doing it in style!" He turned to Mark. "So, when are they coming?"

Mark grinned with the laughs in the room. "Funny!"

"Other than stalking us, Pete, what else have you been up to?" Teela asked.

He grinned widely. "Well, first, let me formally introduce myself and tell you that my name *is* actually Pete."

Ha! Who'd have thought?

"That's handy," sighed Jonah. "It's hard to remember to call people by different names. Chris started that trend off."

"Good that you don't have to for me then, Jonah!" Pete said, and then answered Teela. "My face got uncovered while I fought with a guard at the Manor. He got away, so I had to stay off the streets for months. I holed up with some friends and tried to find out who made it and how I could reach you." He coughed. "I gather the traitor got away. I didn't see him strapped to the chair before I bolted from the garage."

Chris Ames, aka Logistic Lionel, aka the traitor, was discovered to be the I.N.'s informant inside our safehouse. When he realised the truth and believed us, Chris turned to our side. He chose not to turn Chie in and got caught trying to rescue Jonah. He worked with NCs now and managed their local ID and disguise needs. Praise God, for He is always faithful.

The I.N. lost other skilled employees. I was ranked #1 on the I.N.'s researchers list back in the day. I used to track Non Conformers who would not adhere to Collective Thought—renegades like me. Back then, Teela was my boss and had been an effective and successful team leader. Greg, who now ran that team, became one of our associates. I won't say informer because he hadn't informed, but he protected us and our hidden network from discovery. Since my unofficial resignation, my work system was thoroughly wiped along with Tom's spyware and the NCs' access to the I.N. database, which we desperately needed to protect NC identities. Fake documentation was all well and good as long as the data was the same as the I.N.'s. To even get back in there would be a start.

I hoped Greg would help with that. When we had asked, he replaced the photograph of Jonah that the House of Security agent, HS Paul Fraser, had stored on the I.N. database with another boy of the same age. Now I.N. scans of Jonah's face would reveal him only as Jon Stevens and not the elusive Coles' new son. His real identity would definitely trigger a search and bring soldiers to our door. We adults had to be more careful. Any scan would recognise our true identities. It would be impossible to find and remove—or switch—every record of our picture that appeared on the world stage, especially Chie's. Changing any of those photos would expose Greg as a sympathiser.

Word on the palace tiles was that Tisak still accessed our personal files. He looked and yearned for our arrest, mostly for Chie's, but Esta had confirmed Minu and mine too. Chie enjoyed plucking at the strings of Tisak's annoyance. The beloved scanners and towers were designed to squeeze out rebels, and freeing captured NCs became the top priority. Chie's team in Gloucester arranged the rescues and the easiest way to achieve them was en route to the impenetrable rehabilitation centres. It had been a full-time job in the first few months, but now, most NCs were clued up and avoided detection and capture. That gave Chie and Teela free time to spend with us while Minu investigated her brother.

Minu Darab incessantly sought ways to undermine her brother. Most times, she couldn't sabotage the inevitable success of his plans, but she always managed to cost her brother time and money—both of which were important to him. That made her popular among the NCs and Asiders, and she was often passed leads on what was coming next.

"Ciel has been a bad boy," she told me on the phone during the summer, then went on to tell us about the scanner installations weeks before they were mandatory on the streets. She even knew why.

"He'll spy at every public door and will not rest," she had revealed. "He looks for me, his unruly, defiant sister, and pretends that it is for his nephew's lost mother. He searches for Chie, the bomber still hunted by the world, and he seeks you because you got away and have no manners."

A familiar knot appeared in my stomach. *His* voice echoed in my head, repeating the same chorus of 'look at me, be honest, do not be rude'...until I remembered flooring him, and I laughed instead. I had taken a little joy in remembering his speech after the Manor battle; he stood tending to sore ribs, and it had felt like a little victory. Tisak was almost successful in breaking my spirit during my time at the palace. I hadn't realised just how much until I was rescued. To recover, I had disappeared inside an unbreakable shell that, for a few days, even kept out the God who had saved me. Twice. Probably saved me more times than that.

Now it was early December, and we prepared for a Christmas which wouldn't be celebrated as it was last year. No baby was born, the world said. There would be no Santa for Lily to see, not that she minded. She was too old for fairy stories now, according to her school friends. There were no more carols or a lighted tree decorated with tinsel and baubles in the town centre—not in December anyway. Lily had asked why the Christmas tree was going up at the beginning of August, and I had explained it was a decorated holiday tree for the Tisak celebrations. She understood that with a whisper of "devil workers" and did not ask to go. We would not have gone even if she had. It wasn't worth the risk and certainly not a place for children, especially after day two when clothes appeared optional, and parties stretched on to fill the four days.

The rules of this specific annual holiday meant nobody stayed indoors. We were to be close neighbours with street parties, everyone accounted for and having fun, so we couldn't even hide out at home. Instead, we went underground and fobbed it off as the annual family get together to people who had asked, then driven to the safehouse in Gloucester—to a house where thermal imaging couldn't see you hiding from the rest of the world.

Virtual Reality booths popped up everywhere like old cash machines. They were made available to revellers at special prices during the festivities. New VR experimenters were less inhibited and more inclined to try them out with alcohol and drugs inside them. Popularity and usage soared after that. Dual Verismo VR saw people with awareness in both realms through tech in their eyes. From their point of view, they were linked to virtual surroundings with either other virtual people or software added characters and saw reality simultaneously. From my point of view, they were mad, gripped in action and speech dislocated from reality, doing pretend things like making a cuppa in the middle of the park.

The booth's VR software really took you in, according to reports. To the point that sometimes, people forgot it wasn't real. Some of them didn't want to come out at all. There were recommendations and limits to usage with timer prompts, but it was not always adhered to. Once, a person died of starvation. It was said the person ate online when they were hungry and hadn't fed the physical body. That was not 'public news', but it had happened. Minu regularly found out little secrets about her brother, and she would get excited at the prospect of making any part of his life difficult.

Her video face did not look excited tonight.

"Ciel is to speak again. On Saturday. I wonder what it is this time that I shall have to investigate and try to stop." Minu sighed. "It is tiring to always fail."

"Stop that!" I fired out. "It annoys him; that's good enough for me. Let it be for you too. You know you won't stop it; if that is God's will, it doesn't mean we fail."

"Oui. I suppose you are right. But still, it would be nice, Lord. Just once." She smiled. "How are you feeling?"

"Fat."

Minu laughed. "Tu es belle, ma chérie. Beautiful. You should come and visit. The school holidays. Oui?"

"If I can get through the door!" I grinned.

"I remember it," she said, her smile fading as she did.

Poor Minu. After Tisak murdered her husband Maral and found Minu to be alive after all, he suddenly became very interested in finding her son. Samuel 'Sam' Darab was seventeen and susceptible to Tisak's charms. Minu constantly worried about him. He was a kind, loving and impressionable young man, raised to know the instruction of the Qur'an since Maral and Minu's fathers were both Iranian, and Islam had been the religion of the family. She told me once how her parents coming together had caused all sorts of trouble.

"The people of a quiet village in southwest France did not welcome it," Minu had explained, "where a young, pretty

Catholic girl was forced to denounce Jesus in order to marry a foreigner and a Muslim. My mother's ancestors were Italian, but we had lived in France for four generations—same village, same house." She laughed. "When she fell in love with my father, it was like magic; she used to tell me. My parents moved away and did not return. So Ciel and I grew up in another town that did not always accept us. Half Iranian, half Italian—not even the least bit French!

"It explains many things about my brother and his desire for unity. Explain, not excuse! How is it, you say? My poke of the nose into my parents' deaths disturbed him, and he was not pleased I had become a Christian. He sent soldiers for me, and that was the day I did not go home."

Minu met Jesus during the mock rapture, and her faith remained just as strong after Tisak returned all 3,756,524 of them. She could not persuade Sam to faith, though. By fourteen, his inherited god was the one he served. He was not interested in another. Impressionable, yes, but when it came to Islam, it had stayed Islam.

Esta never brought news about Sam, and I often wondered why. It didn't help Minu at all. Had Tisak found him and Esta couldn't say? Was it that bad? Or was he safe and there was just no news? Minu had complained that Esta called less and less over these past few months, so instead, she worked on a palace plan just in case Tisak had taken him there. She planned to use the tunnel system Mark had trespassed in the spring to fetch me. Getting into the palace was a different story, with guards, cameras, and thermal detectors making it far too secure.

But that was Minu's mission; mine was to persuade the room that a heavily pregnant and wanted fugitive ached to go back to the fiasco scene and speak with a man who would probably hate me because of it.

Chie laughed until he realised I was serious and looked at Teela, who nodded.

Mark was horrified. "Nope. Forget it. No!"

I was offended and resented being treated like a baby.

"It has been months since anyone's been there. There isn't any danger at the Manor anymore. I don't get why this is such a problem. I'll be under the Manor, anyway."

"Anna, it's too risky," said Chie, "and not worth it."

"It is to hundreds of girls, Chie, and they're who I'm doing it for. We have to stop this from the top."

Silence.

"We could ask Greg to go," suggested Teela.

And here I thought she was my friend!

"No," my tone was adamant, "I want to go. It's unfinished business to me because of Fraser and his weird telepathy, or whatever it was."

I shivered, remembering how his head had turned, looking at me as he walked by. It was like Fraser had already spied me through the wall I'd hidden behind. He should not have known I was there—I was adequately hidden—it was almost as if someone had told him.

"Anna, you're nearly eight months pregnant, and you want to go climbing? How do you think you're going to do that?"

"Who said anything about climbing, Mark? The part of the Manor I want hasn't collapsed. I'm positive." I wasn't entirely, but I remembered the blueprints and what I thought was left of the Manor. I also trusted in God's peace as the answer to my question in prayer.

"No." Mark was also adamant.

My resolve didn't budge. "I am asking because I love you and I respect you. I am asking because I want to know who sells and who buys sleeping girls. I am asking."

I meant, and he knew I meant. I was on the verge of going anyway, but I'm seeking your approval.

Pete took my hand.

"May I help in any way? I hadn't planned to go back, but this case was my reason for joining your investigation. I'd be glad to go for you, Anna."

"With me!" I corrected, though Pete had given me an idea, and I turned to Mark. "Come with me then?"

He frowned, but it was a decent compromise.

"If you go, Anna, we all go," Chie piped up.

I laughed. "We can't all go. There's the Market and the kids."

"And you're taking one of them with you," argued Mark, pointing at my bump. He was not impressed I was pushing it.

It stabbed in my heart. He wasn't wrong, I supposed.

"A couple of days. We could. A day even is enough. In and out and home here with Robert Jnr's files."

That was what mattered.

"If you go, we all go." Chie was resolved on that.

My heart sank. We couldn't all go.

"Don't do this. You're manipulating me because you know I'd want to protect everyone, and that isn't fair. Don't force me to give up on those girls."

"And you?" Mark said irritably. "It's okay for you to protect everyone else but yourself, and we're supposed to just let you, else we're the bad guys?"

"I don't see me running into trouble. Come with me. Pete too."

"And me," said Teela.

"And me," added Chie.

If I was going, they were all going.

My raised eyebrows turned to Chie. "The Market?"

"Can be sorted."

A bubble of excitement rose. Christmas was coming early, and Minu was about to have a couple of children on her hands. I smiled. Leads were coming.

~

Pete and I were the only ones left on the sofa later that night. I munched crisps again. I hungered for all things unhealthy these days. Pete looked at me intently while I sucked the salt from my fingers.

I stopped and frowned. "What?"

He smiled and replied, "You're so…carefree. I haven't seen you this way before."

I huffed. "I don't know about that! Carefree was before Karl's case landed on Teela's desk, and even then…" I trailed off as I recalled Mark and I had almost split up because I had found Jesus.

"It's nice to see you this way. Less tense, less hurt."

"It's nice to see you at all, Pete. Thank you, Lord! I missed you."

"Me too." He smiled half-heartedly. "So, it irritates me to have to warn you not to be too carefree in these times. Do you know what I'm talking about?"

I shook my head.

"Another shaking is coming, Anna. The sifting of the wheat and tares. There's an open war going on underground. The news won't tell you, but it's carnage worldwide, soldiers and resistors alike. The mock rapture report from Tom woke up many civilians, and they began to see the threads of Tisak's end game. To conquer. To have full control over everything."

"He already does."

"He led the world, Anna. He hadn't yet 'conquered'. His eyes and ears are everywhere now— you know yourself that if he wanted to listen to our conversation, he could, if he knew where to find us. He used Collective Thought to manipulate and desensitise. Now you will see that enforced to severe degrees. He will conquer their minds, and his success is already assured."

I had no reply. There wasn't space left in the world for more of Tisak's swelling dominance. We barely had any room for our own.

"The shaking is just a matter of time. Part of it has happened already, the mock rapture saw to the great apostasy, but those who remain faithful will endure another shaking, now the Israeli peace treaty has been signed."

My face dropped. The first place my head revisited was the ruined special memory between Mark and me. We were excited to discover I was expecting our first child…third child, but one I never thought we were able to have. It was typical of Tisak to get in on my delight. Now when I thought of that day, and how happy Mark had been, I would see those hands signing the treaty and kickstarting the tribulations in God's Holy Book. Both things weaved through my thoughts.

Most of the world was annoyed at Israel's refusal to join the Collective Thought alliance. They were the only country to decline the opportunity to become one with Ciel Tisak and his government. Israel was split between those who loved their Torah and those who loved their sin. The Prime Minister, Elon Kohen, had just come into power when the treaty was agreed after a final plea—threat—was given publicly by Tisak for them to conform. A swift referendum was implemented, and just over half of the citizens wanted to unite. Democracy, because we knew best.

"The global earthquake is coming, Anna. The sixth seal. The fifth we live in today. Collective Thought and the rehabilitation centres take our martyrs…or turncoats if they renounce the Lord Jesus. Persecution is at its worst in history, and it will only increase. I hope ministry pastors are preparing the flock to stand in their faith."

That was a scary enough revelation, but an earthquake, too? I wanted to go to the Manor more than ever now before the files were lost forever in the heart of God's creation. It was more mature than praying for God to have the men swallowed up in a biblical seal judgment.

"Is that the one that says all mountains and islands will be out of place?"

"That's the one. Revelations 6." Pete sighed. "I wish Javad were here so I could ask him what he thinks, but I've concluded two possibilities: either the South American anomaly shifts poles and moves the pieces on the face of the planet, I mean, that is well overdue now, or just maybe, the harvesting of LeyLucient could be responsible."

"How?"

"If what your old pastor said about ley energy is true and it is the breath of God, then only He himself has allowed it to be withdrawn. If you weaken a command, holes appear, and it must, logically and biblically speaking, eventually lead to the destabilisation of the earth from within. Science always claimed that earthquakes couldn't happen across the world at once, but the Bible says it does. I think LeyLucient causes it to happen."

We were living in insecure times, both physically and spiritually. God, please, help us.

"Javad would've loved to study that, but what you say makes sense to me."

"The more Tisak takes, the sooner it will come, I reckon. Have any of you tried the VR booths?" Pete asked.

I shook my head at the conversation change and frowned. Where had that come from?

"I haven't, and I suspect the rest of them haven't; they wouldn't have had the time."

Pete sat forward and pointed at me. "Don't. It's a case of mine that I'm working on, and these booths will be how he conquers minds."

Arla Stevens: https://amzn.to/3185UP2

Printed in Great Britain
by Amazon

82512192R00173